Contents

CURSES THAT BIND

ELL STEPHENS

Prologue

At the dawn of creation, several races of mythical creatures were created alongside humans. One race in particular was known as the Fae. Fae were legendary supernatural creatures that possessed many unique characteristics and abilities. The most notorious characteristic was the ability to shape shift between their small, fairy-like form into human form. Fae are known by many names throughout time across the various lands, from "Tuatha De Danann" in ancient Gaelic Ireland to "Fairies" in present-day America.

Over the years, there have been several different myths and legends, both good and bad, surrounding the Fae. Some people believed the Fae possessed an innate ability to heal and were thought to be friendly healers. Others thought they were demonic evil beings that thrived on chaos and mayhem. Seeking them out when they didn't want to be found could be deadly. People have speculated the phrase "don't go looking for trouble" originated from dealing with Fae. One legend even described the Fae as fallen angels not good enough to enter heaven, nor evil enough to join hell.

In truth, Fae were a supernatural race with many gifts, one of which was an innate knowledge to heal and cure the sick. They had extensive experience in using plants and herbs for healing, and many people sought them out hoping for a cure for either themselves or a loved one. Being masters of communication was another gift they possessed. Fae could understand any language spoken to them, allowing creatures from all walks of life and different lands to communicate with them beseeching help from their gifts.

The greatest gift they possessed was the gift of magic. The knowledge of magic was passed down from one generation to the next since time began. Use of their magic always came at a cost. Fae Magic could affect the Law of Karma, the universal law by which all creation must abide. Karma has existed since creation and is described in many ways. In the oldest book ever written, the Bible, the phrases "An eye for an eye," and "Do unto others as you would have them do unto you," are descriptions of Karma.

Karma is the universal principle of cause and effect. Basically, a person's intentions and actions determine the path of the future outcome, whether in this life or another; thus, good intentions and actions bring good fortune whereas bad intentions and actions bring bad fortune. There are always consequences with altering fate, regardless of whether the magic used was for good or evil intentions. Nature maintains a harmonious balance and changing one thing can affect many others.

Being shapeshifters, Fae could shift into a human form which allowed them to move around freely among humans undetected, thus affording them protection. In their pure form, the Fae were tiny beings no taller than a wildflower that grows in an open field. They had small wings that allowed them to fly, float, and glide through the air like butterflies. Fae preferred their solitude while in the fairy-like form because humans were fascinated by their small stature and wings, especially the human children, who would chase after them or worse try to capture them. They despised being hunted or chased for others' amusement.

Fae were unpredictable as well as mischievous. Not everyone appreciated their mischievous nature. The Fae found humor in doing pranks on others for entertainment or when an individual annoyed them. They would pull stunts on people who irritated them as a way of getting others to stay away.

Victims of their mischief learned to fear the Fae and would share the details of their misfortune of crossing a Fae as a warning to others. Many people wore medallions made of cold-iron to keep the Fae away. Cold-iron is iron ore that has never been exposed to flames or heat and is poisonous to Fae. People hammered ore into different shapes to make decorative medallions to wear.

Unlike most non-human races, the females of this race were the stronger of the two sexes in the strength of gifts. Fae women had an uncanny almost unnatural beauty. They were unlike any other creatures. They had translucent butterfly-like wings that glistened when the rays of the sun or moon shown upon them. Their tiny bodies were curvy and voluptuous with most of their features being human-like, but on a smaller scale. Most Fae women had long, flowing hair, with the look and feel of silk.

The male Fae had shorter wings draped with a leathery membrane and curved upward with a claw shape tip at the top which were used as weapons in combat. The males were natural born warriors. They were muscular in stature and when in human form were taller than most human males. They were described as ruggedly handsome and resembled Viking warriors in their human forms.

Fae lived in family groups referred to as clans which resemble a small community. The elders, male and female, were the leaders of each clan. Each member of the clan had specific tasks assigned to them. The women handled the job of making lotions, potions, and the mixing of herbs. Their ability to cast magic was superb compared to males. The men dealt with the labor and protection of their clans. Fae lived in peace among themselves for many centuries.

Although many cultures have legends and myths about the Fae, the area known as Ireland was the birthplace of their ancestors. One clan of the Fae, known as the Fae of the Willows or Willow Clan for short made their home among a crop of willow trees deep in the woods of an area known today as Glenariff. The Willow Clan had a peaceful and prosperous existence for years.

In time, another supernatural race called the Fomorians invaded Ireland. The Fomorians were a hostile, monstrous race of supernatural creatures that did not get along with other races. Fomorians claimed Ireland as theirs and did not want outsiders on their land. They considered outsiders any race that were not Fomorians, including races that already called the land their home before their arrival. Outsiders either had to serve under the Fomorians or be wealthy enough to bribe them to live in peace, which did not sit well with the Fae Clans.

A war broke out between the Fae and the Fomorians that lasted for years, which took a toll on the Fae. After years of battle, only one Fae clan was known to still exist, the Willow clan. The elders of the Willow Clan came together and decided to flee by ship in hope of finding a peaceful existence again.

After a long difficult voyage, their ship found its way to a seaport in the New World called La Nouvelle-Orleans, present-day New Orleans. They took notice that the humans who inhabited New Orleans had no knowledge of any non-human race existence. The Willow Clan longed to have a peaceful existence once more. They decided to stay in the New Orleans area, but needed to govern themselves with stricter laws to live by to achieve the peace they desire. Their most important laws were to keep to themselves, never shape-shift in public, and remain in human form always while around humans.

The Willow Clan settled on the outskirts of the city of New Orleans. This area afforded them the seclusion and privacy they desired. They placed a cloaking spell around the perimeter of the area for added protection. After settling down, they discovered other races besides humans in the surrounding area. The Fae noticed the other races kept to themselves too, never showing their true form around humans either. Even though each species was cloaked with secrecy, everyone seemed at peace with existing together, at least for a time.

The slave trade in the South brought a religion called Voodoo over from Africa and Haiti through the Caribbean. Many people around the New Orleans area became intrigued with magic along with using magical potions and lotions. Voodoo allowed the Willow Clan to practice their magic for profit without being noticed. They were able to sale their own goods at the French Market in town while keeping their homes hidden. Their lives were once again peaceful for many years until a tribe of Native American shapeshifters noticed them. Then, they became the hunted once more.

A Native American tribe, called the Rougarou, lived in the swamps near New Orleans. The members of the tribe could shape-shift from a human form into wolves and were called Werewolves. The males of their tribe were more significant in stature when compared to the human and Fae races in both height and build. Unlike the Fae, male Rougarou had greater abilities than females.

There was a hierarchy that existed among the tribe. The leader was known as the Alpha, and second in command was called the Beta. Rarely a female Alpha, or She Wolf, was born into a tribe. When it happened, the males didn't tolerate it. Once the female infant or child showed traits of being an Alpha, the males would eliminate the female by death.

All the males in the Rougarou tribe were at least six-foot-tall or taller and were very muscular in stature. They possessed a real masculine attractiveness that many women found irresistible, even women from different races. The males had chiseled, sharp jawlines framed with dark brown to black hair. They had a robust and rugged disposition about them with a deep, gravelly voice that could frightened most people. Being a wolf shapeshifter, they had heightened senses always, regardless of their form. They could shift into wolf form at will. The males were normally possessive and protected what they considered "theirs" at all cost.

The females were much like the human females in size. They were attractive in ways that drew your attention. Their hair was usually long, thick, brown to auburn in color with a wavy texture. They too had an athletic build.

The Rougarou could see, hear, taste, and smell things that

humans couldn't. Because of this ability, they could detect that the Willow Clan were not human as they pretended to be. The Willow Clan were drawing unsafe attention by being more open with their magic once the humans began dabbling in voodoo which increased the chances of their true identity being discovered. This, in turn, would put other non-human races endanger of being discovered by humans.

The Rougarou heard the negative myths and legends surrounding the Fae races that existed in Ireland and would not wait to see if the stories were true. They wanted the Willow Clan gone from their territory before any trouble started, but the Willow Clan were tired of running. They were ready to make a stand. Thus, another war began.

Legend states a member of the Rougarou tribe seduced a female Fae through trickery and lies. Over time, he romanced her and lured her away with a promise of true love and marriage. After he isolated her from her clan, he demanded that she lead his tribal members to the secret location where the Willow Clan were living or face death. She chose death over the betrayal of her clan.

The girl's grandmother was one of the influential elders in the Willow Clan. She had knowledge of the darkest of magic, which she was forbidden to practice by the laws which every member of the clan followed. When the elderly woman learnt of the fate of her granddaughter, she was beyond furious. The thought of them using her granddaughter's love as a weapon to destroy her was more than the old woman could bear. She allowed the tremendous pain she felt to control her actions, and in a state of emotional distress she spun a curse wrapped in dark magic against the Rougarou tribe to avenge her granddaughter's death.

It was a dual curse that contained an element of love combined with the elimination of the one trait the Rougarou tribe valued the most, the ability to shape shift. She froze the shapeshifters in the human form, never to shift into the wolf form again.

The second part of the curse cost the shapeshifters their true love. Their souls forever entwined with the Fae. To kill a Fae for the Rougarou tribe would kill their soul mate, leaving them with an overwhelming feeling of empty and loneliness. She wanted them to feel the overwhelming pain she felt after losing her granddaughter if they ever killed another Willow Clan member.

When the curse began, the Law of Karma intervened, and the consequences of her actions took form. Fate dealt the old woman an eye for an eye. The price of the curse was for the Willow Clan to pay the same consequences. The Rougarou became their soul mates as well. Also, the Fae would stay in human form for eternity, alongside the Rougarou tribe. Their beautiful wings forever lost to a balance maintained by Nature.

As a reminder for future generations to never use magic for revenge or use love as a weapon, future tribe and clan members were forever marked by a birthmark as a constant reminder of what hate and misuse of power had cost them. The Willow Clan's birthmark was in the shape of a butterfly, while the Rougarou's birthmark was in the form of the paw print of a wolf.

The members of the Willow Clan desperately tried to undo the curse to no avail. Through desperation, they devised a plan. The Willow Clan hoped that ending the lives of the entire Rougarou tribe would break the curse. Too afraid of Karma's wrath, they decided not to try to destroy the Rougarou themselves. They decided to let others do their dirty work. They created horror stories about the Rougarou tribe, spreading the stories among the humans. This plan began the Rougarou werewolf legend of the Louisiana swamps.

They also discovered a hidden secret of the Rougarou- silver affected them just as cold iron affected the Fae. This knowledge combined with the horror stories they spread put fear into humans. Out of fear, the humans hunted the Rougarou to what they thought was extinction. Without knowledge to anyone, a small number of Rougarou managed to escape. Unfortunately, the curse did not end.

As time passed, the New Orleans' local non-human community discovered the trickery that the Willow Clan used to rid themselves of their soul mates hoping to lift the curse. Instead of being known as the Willow Clan, they became called The Black Widow Clan around the New Orleans area. They were treated with cruelty and banished.

Humiliated, the Willow Clan wanted to abandon their history and culture in hope that future generations would never make the same mistake. This included never teaching them how to use their magical gifts. The risk of one clan member using the dark side of magic causing the whole clan to suffer the consequences was not a risk any clan member was willing to take.

The elders of the clan had meetings where they wrote the complete history of the clan in journals, along with their knowledge of magic and herbs. They assigned one family member each generation to be the guardian of the journals, so if the need ever arose, future clan members could have access to the knowledge kept hidden.

From that moment forward their true identities, abilities, and gifts were never spoken of nor practiced again. As generation after generation passed, the history of the Willow Clan became a myth, even unto the family lines themselves.

In time, the tragedy of the curse caused fear to develop among the other non-human races. The heads of each race met and decided this could never happen again. They formed a council. The council had the task of developing a plan of how to maintain peace among non-human races. The council was comprised of two members from each non-human race. Since the Willow Clan disappeared, and seemed to no longer exist, they were excluded from the council.

The council drafted laws to keep peace along with balance in Nature. One of the strictest laws was to never exhibit behavior that would draw the attention of humans, which outnumbered the non- human races. Everyone agreed that human knowledge of their existence usually ended in chaos and death for the non-human races.

The council needed someone to police the different races, ensuring individuals abide by the new laws. This policing gave birth to an elite group known today as the Guardians. The Guardians are a group of the fastest and most robust members among the non-human races, tasked with the sole purpose to keep and maintain peace among non-humans. They monitor any suspicious activity and will do whatever necessary to keep peace and order.

Over the years, the Guardians developed into a tight brotherhood among their members. Like a military unit, the organization has commanders with teams in which they lead. Each team member is willing to sacrifice their own life to save another member of their team if need be. They adhere to a "No One Left Behind" mentality.

Each member of the team receives regular pay and bonuses based on assignments. One can become quite wealthy working as a Guardian, but the rush of adrenaline they get is what keeps them working.

Chapter 1

Willow
"Shit in a handbag"

I never understood urban phrases such as "You're shitting me" or "Shit in a Handbag" until my life went to "Shit in a Handbag," then I knew. My name is Willow Black. I am a twenty-eight-year-old competent, reliable, and well-respected emergency department physician. I am a realist. People have used words such as logical, organized, and an all-around well put together person to describe me. I used to agree with them. Now this is the story all about how my life got flipped-turned upside-down; yes, I am a Will Smith fan.

My story begins on the day I am in my bathroom staring at my reflection in the antique oval mirror hanging on the wall. The image staring back at me is startling. I clench my fists around the edge of my white pedestal sink in shock. Gone is the competent, reliable, and well-respected doctor I'm used to seeing. In her place, is a crazy-looking mad woman I don't recognize. My honey-kissed blonde hair is now a jumbled mess. Strands of hair have escaped from my hair clip and are sticking out encompassing my head.

I glance beyond my wild hair to my face. Shit, I can't recall ever seeing my complexion so pale. I wasn't this pale even when I had the flu last year. My eyes shock me the most. On any other given day, I classified them as one of my better features. Today, my mascara is the only makeup remaining; but, it's no longer on my long thick eyelashes. Instead, my eyes resemble racoon eyes, with my mascara smudged under and around them both. Gone are the crystal blue eyes that usually stare back at me. In their spot, are stormy blue eyes which appear as though they belong to a crazed demented person.

Next, I focus on the rest of my body visible in the mirror. My wrinkled seal blue scrub top was clean and pressed when I put it on for work this morning. The front of my scrub top where the V-neck begins right above my breasts is soaked from the dribbles of water that escaped my mouth when I guzzled it earlier. I continue to take an inventory of the rest of my appearance but realize I can't see the rest of my body in the mirror. Without delay, I step back from the sink as I look down at the rest of my body to my feet. My scrub pants are a wrinkled mess and resemble my scrub top minus the water. At least my feet still look normal. My well-manicured coral polished toenails are shining up at me.

After the inventory of my body, I focus my attention back on the pedestal sink. With trembling hands, I pick up the last pregnancy test I took. I need to verify I read it correct the first time. I can feel my heart beat start to race again as I see the test results. Yep, same as the other tests- positive. I need to calm down, so I can think rationally. After dropping the test stick back down on the counter, I clench my fist back around the edge of the sink like it is some kind of life line. After a minute, I release my grasp on the sink and turn on the cool water to douse my face with it. The cool water does nothing to calm my current state of panic. I turn the water back off and glare back into the mirror to appraise the crazed woman again.

"You appear as stressed as a whore in church!" I shout at my reflection. "You had a plan! Unwed motherhood was not a goal on the plan! Great! Perfect! Now, I sound as crazy as I appear standing here yelling at myself!"

I draw in a deep, long, soothing breath to locate my inner Zen. I need my peaceful, happy place they refer to in my yoga class, so my spiritual Zen can get control of my emotions. After a few minutes of deep breathing, I'm dizzy and lightheaded with no Zen.

"Perfect! Just perfect!" I decide it's in my best interest to go to a peaceful place other than my bathroom to rest before I hyperventilate and injure myself.

It appears, Lady Luck took a vacation and didn't send me an email much less a text message or tweet to announce her absence from my life. The last thing I need is to pass out from hyperventilation in the bathroom and smack my head on the antique claw-foot tub. Better yet, strike my head on the toilet and end up with a head injury to compliment my new crazy-looking image! Then, I would end up in the emergency room where I work for my colleagues to bear witness to my mental meltdown.

I step into the hallway and head toward the parlor of my four-bedroom antebellum-style home. As I walk, my mind drifts back to a point in my life when Lady Luck had smiled upon me. Her smile felt comparable to a warm ray of sunshine caressing my skin. It was the first day I viewed my house and knew I was home.

I had found my perfect home, or my perfect fixer-upper home in the Garden District of New Orleans, the city where I was born, raised, and the city I love. The house is two-story with four bedrooms along with three and a half baths. It has a parlor room, wrap-around front porch, and a carriage house in the back- built in the late 1800s. The prior owners neglected the house over the years as evidenced by the peeling paint and rotten wood. But I saw past that to the potential it held.

According to my real estate agent, many people turned and fled after stepping through the front door, but not me. Against the advice of family and friends, I placed a bid the first day I saw the house. I became a first-time homeowner one month later. Renovations began as soon as I moved into the house. To the best of my ability, I restored my house to its original grand-eur. The updates of adding modern plumbing and electricity were the finishing touches.

As I enter the parlor room, I take solace in how captivating the place is with the meticulous details of its nineteenth-century décor. A warm sense of pride fills me as I admire the work and effort I poured into my home. Much of the painting and refinishing I completed myself. I ease back onto an antique leather lounge chair next to one of the front windows overlooking the St. Charles streetcar line. As I take a deep, soothing breath in and out, I notice my inner Zen seeping back into me.

As the initial panic subsides, I struggle to figure out how my 20-year plan, once on track, became derailed. The 20-year plan is a life plan I've been pursuing through the years. As I reflect on the circumstances causing the derailment, I realize the 20-year plan no longer exists and has now turned into "Shit in a Handbag". I've been following this plan for half of my twenty-eight years of life. In one afternoon, a pregnancy annihilated the whole plan.

I've always been a planner and liked everything organized. My 20-year plan emerged from my parents drilling the desire of being self-sufficient into my brain. When I was seven years old, we witnessed my aunt, which is my mother's sister, and her daughter move back in with my grandmother after my uncle died in an automobile collision. My aunt could not support them after my uncle's death.

She asked my grandmother to help her get back on her feet, which my grandmother did with open arms. My aunt's self-esteem shattered with the humiliation she felt when she had to reach out for hand-outs (her words not mine) from family. I never wanted to experience that type of hardship.

The determination to succeed drove me to develop a plan for my life. I refused to depend on anyone other than myself, so I came up with the 20-year plan.

The 20-year plan started with graduating high school early, which I did at sixteen years old as the Valedictorian of my class. I accomplished this by becoming a bookworm and sacrificing my social life. While everyone hung out with friends at parties, I hung out with books in the library. The next step of the plan was college. I enrolled in college after graduation, then medical school, graduating at the top of my class in both. I achieved my goals with constant studying, which continued to impede my social life. My achievements and vigorous work paid tenfold. They gave me the opportunity to secure my dream job as an emergency room doctor here in New Orleans.

I accomplished the next phase of my 20-year plan by finding what I thought was my perfect guy, known as Bill Mathis. Bill is now known as Bill the cheating selfish prick, or rat-bastard for short by my family and friends. Bill was not my first boyfriend. He was my third.

I only had one boyfriend in high school to whom I lost my virginity, Jason Landry. That experience was ok. It wasn't the mind-blowing sexual experience you read about in a romance novel, but I guess not the worst sexual experience in history either. Jason and I ended our relationship as friends when he moved several states away to attend college. I attended LSU, so I could stay near friends and family.

I met my second boyfriend while attending college. His name was Shawn Broussard. When our relationship progressed into a sexual relationship, it was more pleasurable than I had ever had with Jason. Still, I didn't see fireworks or have an out of body experience during climax as I have heard other women describe. Sadly, most of my orgasms were still self-induced.

Shawn attended medical school and had to devote as much time to studying as I did. We were perfect for each other. We both understood the amount of time and dedication that medical school required. After graduation, Shawn received a job offer in California that was too good to pass up. Again, I chose to stay in New Orleans to be near my friends and family. We ended the relationship as friends. We still send birthday and Christmas cards to one another each year.

Now, looking back, I think my lack of experience in relationships was my downfall with Bill the rat-bastard. I fell hard and fast for Bill's boyish charms. Bill was tall and lean. Not a muscular lean, but not scrawny either. He was handsome but knew it, causing his arrogance to grow.

I put time and effort into our relationship. I worked hard

to balance time between my work and spending quality time with Bill. Keeping organized and dedicated to both was more manageable once Bill moved in with me.

Two years into our relationship, I was ready and eager for the next step in the 20-year plan. The next phase of my plan comprised marrying a great guy and having 2.5 kids with a dog in my four-bedroom home.

I strived to create the life young girls dream of, so I thought. My life was proceeding as planned until the day Bill came home from work and gave me the "it's not you but me" speech ending with the "need to find myself" speech.

After the initial shock of his rejection, I did what every sound- minded woman insists on doing. I helped him pack for his journey to find himself by throwing every bit of his shit out the front door into the yard while he dashed around screeching at me to stop. The police showed up after I had doused everything in lighter fluid and found me with a lighter in my hand.

Since I had spent my whole life in this town, I knew the cops that arrived on the scene. I attended high school with one, and I treated the other one in the emergency room for a bullet wound a year ago.

They gave me a shoulder to cry on once I could no longer hold back my unshed tears. They stayed perched with me on my front porch and drank coffee while I drank margaritas. We watched Bill the rat-bastard gather his shit out of the yard and leave.

It didn't take long for Bill to find himself. I learned a week after the breakup, my former perfect guy had hooked up with his perfect new girlfriend three months before I helped him in moving out. This is where the cheating part of his new name evolved.

Bill's departure caused a sting to my pride, self-esteem, and my confidence with the male gender. I am not a beauty queen, but I know from the attention I get from men I'm not an ugly duckling either. I lack the experience on how to keep their attention while appearing as a confident woman instead of an awkward nerd.

My hair is long and wavy with honey-kissed blonde highlights that are natural and not out of a bottle. It always garners compliments on the occasions I wear it down cascading around my body, but long hair impedes caring for the sick. By the end of my shifts my hair usually ends up pinned on top of my head or pulled into a ponytail, so why not start out in a ponytail each day? Now, I usually sport a ponytail or some other simple form of an updo on days I work.

My vision isn't the greatest in the world. I like to blame it on my many hours of studying. I choose to wear glasses over contact lenses, but I have contacts to wear when I need them.

My glasses aren't geeky thick, and besides contacts dry out my eyes when I'm stuck working long shifts. Even with my glasses on, I still receive compliments on my eyes. My eyes are a brilliant blue surrounded by long thick lashes, which as I've mentioned before, are one of my best features.

At five-foot-seven-inches and 135 pounds, I am at my ideal weight. The many unintentional skipped meals while I'm busy saving lives ensures this. It's impossible to sit still for a decent meal when working in such a fast-paced, demanding job. Thanks to good genetics, women in my family have voluptuous, curvy bodies with full breasts that draw a man's attention, whether wanted or not.

Chapter 2

Willow
"Hell in a Handbasket"

Somewhere along the way of dealing with the heartache of betrayal and rejection while tasting the bitterness of defeat, I came up with a new plan for my life, Plan B. Plan B consisted of focusing my attention on my career.

If other people can say screw it to a home life and make a career their priority, why can't I? After all, work allowed me to buy and restore my dream home which gave me happiness. So, why can't work help me forget the misery that Bill the rat-bastard had caused along with helping me reclaim my happiness again?

From that time on, I poured my heart and soul into my career, focusing on helping people in need. Plan B gave me gratification along with purpose. There was one problem with Plan B - it ended with me spending lonely nights in an empty bed.

The yearning for the perfect husband to have the 2.5 kids and a dog with lingered in the back of my mind. I longed for someone to come home to after a hard day's work. Someone I could cherish, and who would cherish me back. I ached for a lover to share my life with. Someone to make those lonely nights warmer and cozier. Then, I thought of the heartache that another relationship may bring and concluded I should just buy a dog.

My Plan B went to "Hell in a Handbasket" six weeks after I came up with it. The downward spiral began when a 17-year-old boy with chest trauma from a car accident rolled into the ER. "Dr. Black! They need you in the trauma bay STAT!" Sharon, the shift charge nurse, yells from across the ER.

Sharon is a damn good nurse and is always calm. She's been working here in the ER since before I started. She is an older woman with short brown hair whose looks remind me of the actress Linda Hut. "STAT" is the term we use for EMERGENTLY.

As I make my way to the Trauma bay, I realize the condition of the patient must be dreadful for Sharon's calm personae to slip. As I enter the room, I can sense the uneasiness in the air. "Damn, he's a teenager," I mumble to myself as I examine my patient.

The boy has a panicked look in his eyes while grasping his chest. "Mi pecho me mata!" he screamed. He seems to realize by the expression on everyone's face that no one in the room can understand him, and in return, he cannot understand anyone. His face is etched in fear as evidenced by his wide brown eyes.

"So, this is what all the hysteria is about," I whisper under my breath, "language barrier." Generally, assessing a patient goes so much faster when the patient can communicate with you, inform you of what hurts, and tell you how they're feeling. Everyone knows I'm fluent in many languages. Most of the time, I'm called to aid with cases that need an emergency interpreter. I say a thankful prayer that Spanish is one of those, then reassure the boy in Spanish using what I hope is a soothing voice, trying to calm him.

As I assess him, I realize that he's dying in front of my eyes. The tests and exam show he has internal bleeding which requires emergent surgery. I know that based on the rate of his decline, the boy will never make it to the operating room. I have no choice but to perform the surgery here.

"Damn, if we don't open his chest now, he will die," I say to Sharon in English, knowing the boy will not understand me.

I give Sharon the order for sedation and to get the anesthesia team in here STAT. I ready the boy to open his chest. Once he's sedated and on a breathing machine, I begin the operation in the Emergency Department room. It's effortless, as if a higher power has taken over me while I perform the procedure. A surgery that is flawless and successful.

Afterward, I feel drained from the adrenaline high that's been flowing through my veins. Before I head home, I speak with the boy's family giving them the news their son is in critical condition but expected to make a full recovery.

On my way home, I call one of my BFFs, my cousin Nicolette Young. Nicolette answers, "Hey you, I will get the tea brewing." Nikki knows the routine too well. If I'm calling this late, then it's time for tea.

"Great," I sigh, "I'm on my way now, see you shortly," then end the call.

Nicolette isn't fond of her formal name; thus, she prefers Nikki. Nikki is a very attractive woman. Like many of the women in our family, Nikki has a voluptuous, full-breasted build. She has short, brown hair that's cut in a Pixie style.

When I have a rough day at work, I stop by Nikki's place on my way home for a cup of Nikki's special tea to help me unwind and relax. Our city knows and respects Nikki for her own somewhat practice of medicine.

Nikki has a medical degree too, but she believes in Holistic Medicine. She opened a holistic health store called Soul Candy in the French Quarter on Dumaine Street near Congo Square a few years ago. Whenever asked why that name, she states "I provide herbal supplements to sweeten your soul".

Nikki and I spent several years of our childhood together. As I mentioned earlier, Nikki and her mother, had to move in with our grandmother, whom we call Gran for short, after Nikki's father died in a car accident. Nikki was seven years old at the time. She was heartbroken over the death of her father.

One of the most rememberable things about Nikki's father was his gypsy heritage and his family's ring. As the eldest son of his family, Nikki's father had inherited a ring from Nikki's grandfather. It was a family heirloom passed on from generation to generation. The ring had a thick band with thirteen gems used for healing arranged in a design that resembled a wing of flames.

According to tradition, he should have given his ring to his eldest son, but he died before he and Nikki's mother could have any other children. Nikki had a hard time dealing with her father's death. She felt guilty for not being able to save her father.

Ever since Nikki can remember, she has had dreams of a raven appearing then manifesting into a graceful woman. She has described her as a tall, delicate woman with hair as black as a raven's feathers. Her lips are the color of blood and her skin pale white.

I always pictured someone such as Snow White from the fairy tale when I thought of her. Nikki named the woman Raven. Raven gives Nikki warnings of future dangers but the messages are encrypted in the form of rhymes. Nikki says the woman reminds her of a small child the way she speaks and behaves.

Nikki thought the dreams were random, lucid dreams until her father's death. She had never spoken to anyone about her dreams of Raven before her father's car accident. After her father died, she realized they were warnings of future events. Dreams such as these may sound odd to most people, but growing up in New Orleans where Voodoo, legends of vampires, and tales of ghosts are an everyday happening, not so strange here.

Nikki never knows what the message means until after the event has occurred. Hindsight being 20/20 as people say. Two weeks before her father's fatal car accident, Raven had visited Nikki as she sometimes does in a dream. Raven gave her this message:

"I do so fear,
That I can hear,
The Grim Reaper is near,
He will bring you many tears."

Even at Nikki's young age, she felt if she had told people Raven's message, she could somehow have saved her father. After the car accident, Nikki fell into a deep depression from the loss of her father.

Nikki's mother did something special for her by having his ring made into a necklace. Since Nikki's father's ring was large and made for a man, the jeweler made the delicate chain of the necklace out of the gold from the band. He then made the medallion from the thirteen healing gems of the ring leaving it in the form of the wing of flames.

Nikki fell in love with the necklace the moment she saw it and has worn it every day since. She finds comfort in wearing something that meant so much to her father.

After Nikki received the necklace, she gradually started to act like the child she was before the accident. Later, Nikki confided in Gran and I the details of her dreams of Raven along with her guilt over her father's death. She thought of Raven as a curse.

Gran told Nikki to think of Raven as a Guardian Angel instead of a curse. She explained to Nikki that death comes to everyone when their time on this earth reaches the end. Gran believed even if Nikki had warned her father, death still would have taken him, regardless.

Nikki considered what Gran told her. She decided Gran was right, but she thought Raven was more of a defective Guardian Angel who can only speak in code and rhymes. Now, we treat any messages from Raven as a puzzle to figure out.

Most of my memories of childhood include Nikki. Both of my parents, Charles and Monica Black, are doctors that worked long hours at the hospital and on call. Now, my parents take part in Doctors Without Borders overseas. They usually only come home for my birthday and for Christmas.

While growing up when my parents both worked, I stayed with Gran. After Nikki moved in with Gran, Nikki and I spent most of our time together. We even attended the same school. We developed a sister-type relationship and did everything together, including mischief.

Years later, after we graduated high school, Nikki's mom remarried and moved out. Nikki still lives with Gran, but now it's to help Gran out around the house. Gran felt comfort when Nikki didn't move away and leave her alone.

My grandfather passed away before I was born. Gran never seemed interested in the thought of remarrying. She said my grandfather was the love of her life and wasn't replaceable. I've always been a little jealous at times of how close Nikki and Gran are but, I am glad they have each other.

Gran and Nikki live in the French Quarter in a Creole Townhouse built in the 1830s. It's been in the family since being built. The first floor is shop space and houses the Holistic Medicine store that Nikki owns, called Soul Candy. The front windows have lighted displays in them with a variety of items on display.

The shop is spacious with a large room in the front and an open storage space in the back where Nikki creates her holistic medicines. The right side of the store houses glass shelves on the walls filled with bottles of lotions and potions along with mixtures of herbs for many ailments.

She also sales a variety of items for spiritual healing such as spiritual colognes, fresh herbs, and Palo Santo just to name a few. In front of the shelves is a display counter with charms and crystals housed in a glass enclosed case that has a cash register sitting on top of it.

My favorite part of Soul Candy is on the left side of the store where Nikki has a built-in bar style counter that includes bar stools. It's where she serves the fabulous teas which she mixes herself. She designed the bar with glossy finished barge-board wood. The stool tops are a chiffon pattern with New Orleans colors of purple, green, and gold.

In the center of the wall behind the bar is a mural of a fleur de-lis. In the middle of the fleur de-lis, Nikki has a picture of her father's ring. The rest of the wall behind the bar is painted in a light crème color with local artists' paintings hanging on display for sale. The counter behind the bar is where she brews the teas. Most of our friends enjoy coming here. The store is a popular hangout for locals as well as tourist.

The Townhouse still has the original ceiling medallions, plastered walls, crown molding, and marble mantels upstairs. They've done modern updating to keep the townhouse one of the nicest in the Quarter. The living space is on the second floor. You can access the upstairs using either the stairs in the back room or the outside stairs located to the left of the building. The outside access for the living space opens into the kitchen.

The kitchen is a moderate size with a square granite countertop island in the middle of the room. It has four stools, one on each side of the island. This is where Gran, Nikki, and I have our heart to heart chats while sipping one of Nikki's teas.

Baskets of herbs hang from the kitchen ceiling. On the left side of the kitchen, is a deep country style sink, a stainless-steel gas stove, and stainless-steel refrigerator. The kitchen cabinets are modern but look rustic. There is a window over the kitchen sink that overlooks a small enclosed courtyard surrounded by adjacent buildings.

The kitchen has an adjoining dining area with a small table and four chairs. There is an antique china cabinet built into the left wall which houses Gran's antique china. A doorway from the kitchen leads into the living room where comfortable modern furniture awaits along with a flat-screen TV hanging on the wall. A hallway to the right of the living room has walls covered with family photos. It also has doors to the two bedrooms and one bath. Gran's and Nikki's bedrooms both have balconies that overlook Dumaine Street. This place is my home away from home, and I can't wait to get there to relax with my favorite people.

Chapter 3

Nikki

"Keeping It on the Down Low"

I place my phone on the kitchen counter, then walk over to the entrance of the hidden stairwell. The entrance of the stairwell is adjacent to our dining room, and is hidden behind the china cabinet. It's only accessible by pulling a handle on the side of the cabinet that releases a lock which allows the cabinet to slide to the left to expose the doorway.

Through the doorway is a spiral staircase that leads from the second floor down to a room on the ground floor that is hidden and only accessible from the second floor. You can wonder around the store area on the ground floor and never know the hidden room exists.

The hidden room has antique bookshelves on every wall that stand from floor to ceiling housing hundreds of ancient journals that contain our family's dark history. Half of the journals are full of historical events that influenced my family for generations. The other journals contain strange legends, instructions on how to mix potions, and magical spells.

Knowledge of the journals is only granted to one family member per generation. Present day, three family members alive know of its existence. My grandmother, my mother, and me. I am now training to become the overseer or keeper of our family's dark history. As keepers, we oversee keeping the journals safe and hidden, along with updating them on current events. Gran has been in here cleaning and writing for the past few hours.

At first, I had issues keeping this secret from Willow. It felt dishonest, seeing as how we had never kept secrets this big from each other before. I think everyone has a right to know their heritage. Our ancestors feared history could and would repeat itself.

If history has a chance to repeat itself, I don't want to be the one to bring anguish to my family by confessing our secrets. You see, we are direct descendants of a race known as the Fae. Our clan is known as the Willow Clan, named after the trees my ancestors lived by in Ireland.

We are supernatural shapeshifters punished by Karma. The punishment was due to unfortunate events in the past involving werewolves. At one-time, our clan could shape shift into small, fairy-like creatures. We possessed the supernatural abilities of magic, knowledge of how to use herbs to heal, and other unique abilities such as being able to learn foreign languages with little effort. For centuries, my ancestors passed knowledge of how to master these abilities on from generation to generation.

According to the history in the journals, our clan had a falling out with werewolves belonging to the Rougarou tribe. The Rougarou could shape shift into the form of a human or a wolf. They had supernatural strength with heightened senses, regardless of the form they chose. In one of the oldest historical journals, a series of tragedies occurred which caused major changes to our clan and the Rougarou.

The author of the journal describes how the Rougarou did not trust the Fae and wanted to get rid of them. One member of the Rougarou seduced a young female Fae. After luring her away from her clan, he gave her the choice to betray her clan by giving up their location or face death. She chose death. The girl's grandmother sought retribution using dark magic to punish the Rougarou by taking away their ability to shift shapes, leaving them stuck in human form and making the Fae their soul mates.

This led to a disruption in the balance of nature causing the Laws of Karma to intervene with an eye for an eye. These Laws exist in nature to maintain harmony among creatures. Karma trapped our clan in human form, and their soulmates became the Rougarou they had cursed.

As a reminder of the consequences of breaking the Laws of Karma, both the Fae and Rougarou descendants are born with a birthmark. The Fae have a birthmark of a butterfly while the Rougarou have a wolf paw print. Other than not being able to shape shift, both races maintained their other abilities.

Unsatisfied with the punishment dealt by Karma, members of the Fae tried to reverse the curse but only caused more mayhem in the process. The failed attempt to lift the curse ended in destroying the Rougarou. Members of our clan were desperate for peace. War seemed to follow them like a plague. War in their homeland and the war with the were-wolves in the new land had taken a toll on them.

Due to the natural born mischievous nature of the Fae, and the ability to perform magic, the elders of our clan thought it was best to no longer pass this knowledge to future generations. They chose to hide their identity from everyone, including their own future generations. In other words, they wanted to give future generations a clean slate to find the peace and tranquility they strived for but never could obtain.

As far as I know, Rougarou no longer exist. Though according to legend, other werewolf tribes are still around. I'm not aware any other clans of Fae that survived. Presently, most people have no knowledge we ever existed.

Just like the Rougarou of the Louisiana swamp, my heritage turned into myth and legend. So, I understand why the elders thought secrecy was for the best. Even though I hate "keeping it on the down low", my mother and Gran drilled this rule into my brain from the first day they showed me the hidden chamber.

I've been researching the journals for years now. Gran is strict concerning the rule of no magic, but I suspect she has dabbled into it more than a time or two. After many debates with Gran over using the knowledge in the journals, she allowed me to use the knowledge of mixing potions, lotions, and herbs for healing. Most of the products I make and sale in my store come from the journals.

As I reach the bottom of the spiral staircase, I find Gran sitting in an old antique high-back chair. She is updating one of the newer journals. "Willow will be here in about twenty minutes for tea, rough workday and all," I inform Gran on a sigh.

Gran peers up, she narrows her brow when she sees my face. "Why are you frowning so child?"

"I wish Willow could find a man. She spends too many long hours working, then goes home to that large empty house every night. Willow won't admit it, but she misses having someone to go home to. She keeps talking about buying a damn dog, but a dog can't spoon with you in bed plus they shit in the floor!" I hear Gran chuckling under her breath. My Gran is one of those cool grandmothers, so I don't use a filter on my mouth.

I wonder over to the shelves that house the journals which contain magic spells. I pick up the journal I've been studying for the past couple of months and flip through the pages. Even though I'm forbidden to practice magic, I still can't shake the fascination I have with it. In this journal, I've discovered a spell to help someone find their true love, their soul mate.

"Gran, what harm would you expect to come from a spell to find one's true love?" I ask, staring at the journal I'm holding trying not to make eye contact with Gran for fear she will catch on to what I have in mind.

In the corner of my eye, I see Gran pause from what she is doing. "For Willow?" She asks while studying me.

"Well, for anyone including Willow," I answer while shrugging my shoulders trying to appear nonchalant as I turn to face her direction without making eye contact.

Gran puts her finger on her chin appearing to ponder the best way to answer my question. After a minute, a smirk appears across her face. Even though I try to hide my thoughts,

Gran can see right through me. She knows I have a purpose in asking my question.

"Contemplate the worst consequence you can think of, then double that tenfold. It's best to leave these kinds of matters alone." My eyes drift to meet her wiser ones. Gran gives me a loving smile as she stands. Her hands rub her lower back before she takes steps closer to me. "I will set out my oatmeal cookies to go with our tea," she says as she gently pats my shoulder which is her way of ending this discussion. "Are you coming?" Gran asks as she starts up the spiral staircase leading back into the dining room.

"In a minute. I need to put the journals I looked through this morning back on the shelves."

"Well, don't be too long, Willow will be here soon," Gran warns as she reaches the top step of the spiral staircase.

"Be right out," I say as I search through the journals trying to determine which one had what I needed. Once I find the journal, I rush to put the remaining ones back on the shelves. I want to get a closer glimpse at the spell I've been studying.

After hiding the journal under my shirt, I head back up the stairs. I push the china cabinet back in place to hide the secret entrance once again. I take a quick glance at Gran, noting her back is turned, then race to my room with the journal, quickly shutting the door behind me. While taking a deep breath, I climb onto my bed, settling against the pillows to read the journal.

I flip the pages of the journal and stop on the page that contains a spell I hope will work to find true love. I speculate about what Gran had said. "What could be the worst thing to happen?" I wonder under my breath. "Well, if I use it for Willow or myself what can go wrong is the real question to ponder."

After a few minutes lost in my muse, I sit straight up in bed as a horrible image enters my mind. The entire Willow Clan had their soul mates killed off centuries ago trying to lift their curse. What if summoning true love brings our soul mates back from the grave? "Hmm, that's all New Orleans needs is a tribe of zombie werewolves running around." I gasp at the horrible images racing through my mind.

With New Orleans being below sea level, most graves are above ground. I shuttered at the image of a bunch of love-struck zombies crawling out of their crypts. Or better yet, what if it summons their souls and they end up haunting the family? "Hell no," I say out loud to my empty room. For once I've got to agree with Gran and just abandon this crazy idea. As I sit here lost in my imagination, I hear Willow in the kitchen. Crap, I don't have time to put back the journal. For now, I will leave it here until after Willow goes home.

Chapter 4

Willow
"What the Fuck"

When I turn onto Dumaine Street, relief washes over me to discover a parking spot in front of Soul Candy. It's not surprising to have parking issues in the French Quarter. Most people, both tourist and locals alike, opt to take a streetcar or bus to travel around the city whenever possible to avoid the parking issues. Or, you can just go on a walkabout.

On the days I work, I use my car to get around the city because of the odd hours my job demands. On my off days though, I enjoy using the streetcar to get around New Orleans, which is very convenient since one of their stops is located right outside my door.

On the days I ride the streetcar, I get off on the Canal Street stop and walk the rest of the way to Nikki's shop enjoying window shopping on my way. The French Quarter or Vieux Carre (Old Quarter) is the heart of the city. The well-preserved historical homes and buildings are designed in a mixture of French, Spanish, and Creole styles with beautiful wrought iron balconies.

The French Quarter is home to many unique stores, modern boutiques, and the French Market. For people not interested in the shops, there are a variety of other things to see and do such as historical tours, fortune-tellers who will do readings, along with artist who paint and display their work around Jackson Square, excellent restaurants, pubs that can make any drink you would like, and plenty of street performers to watch. If sitting still to people watch is more your style, Café

Du Monde is the place to go.

As I open the car door in front of Nikki's shop, I hear jazz music playing in the distance. I peer down the street towards where Bourbon Street crosses Dumaine and see people coming and going from both directions. It reminds me how alive this city is night or day. There are festivals for everything, from food festivals to celebrations of the dead. I love this city; it's the only place you can be yourself without being criticized by others.

I make my way up the outside stairs on the side of their townhouse, enter the door, and stroll into the kitchen. Gran is resting at the kitchen island with a platter of her special oatmeal cookies waiting. I walk over to Gran and kiss her on her cheek as she reaches up and pats mine. Gran is an attractive elderly woman. She has long flowing gray hair which she keeps in a bun on top of her head. She has blue soulful eyes that still sparkle with love. I imagine gran was a heart breaker in her youth.

"Rough day dear?" Gran asks in her sweet soft voice with her brows pulled together and her lips pressed in a thin line. I know Gran worries that I work too much.

"You can say that again, but no worries. It's nothing that your cookies and Nikki's tea can't make better," I reply with what I hope was a reassuring smile. I throw my car keys along with my cell phone on the island and take a seat on my usual stool beside Gran.

Nikki waltzes into the kitchen, then stops dead in her tracks when her eyes meet mine. She scrunches her eyebrows together as she takes in my appearance from head to toe. "Damn, Willow! You look exhausted. You have dark circles under your eyes. It's just like I've been preaching, you spend too much time working and not enough time enjoying," Nikki gripes as she makes her way over to the stove to heat the kettle for tea. They keep the antique tea kettle on the stove for long nights such as tonight.

I roll my eyes at Nikki when she turns from the stove to

study me again. From the concerned expression on her face, with brows drawn together while chewing on her bottom lip, I can tell "The Talk" is coming. For months now, she and our close friend Arianna LeBlanc, or Ari for short, have been coaxing me to go out with them to "cut loose," as they call it.

They have convinced themselves getting me laid, as in a one-night stand, will get me out of this slump I've drifted into since Bill the rat-bastard left me. Since the breakup, from time to time I get what I refer to as "The Talk" from either Nikki or Ari.

My thoughts travel to Ari, who is the closest childhood friend Nikki and I share. Nikki and Ari hit it off, developing a tight bond when Ari moved in next door to Gran. Ari was nine years old when she came to live with her older cousin. I think Ari and Nikki's tight bond stems from them both having childhood tragedies. Nikki lost her father, and Ari lost her mother. They both have treasured necklaces that remind them of their lost loved ones. Ari's experience was more heartbreaking. At least Nikki still has her mother, Ari is an orphan. Ari's father passed away before she was born. Then, her mother passed away shortly before she moved in with her cousin next door to Gran.

When Ari first moved in, she was a mousy, shy little girl with auburn hair, light freckles on her nose, and bright green eyes. Right after her arrival, she would spend her days sitting on her front porch watching Nikki and I play together in the street. Whenever we tried to approach her, she ran inside.

As time passed, we were able to engage Ari in small conversations without her bolting back into her house. Once we got her talking, I don't think she ever stopped. She was like a Chatty Kathy doll. Not long after, we were like the three musketeers. All for one and one for all!

We spent an abundance of time together while growing up and still do. Nikki and I adopted Ari as our surrogate sister. We share everything together, except for toothbrushes, underwear, and boyfriends. There are some things you shouldn't share with anyone. If I had to classify our personalities as adults, I would say Nikki is the flirty one, Ari is the shy mother hen one, and I guess I'm the practical one.

After we had Ari talking, she told us why she had to come live with her cousin. Ari never knew her father, and her mother was a single parent for Ari's entire life. The small one-story home they lived in caught on fire one night. Ari awakened to her mother's screams of terror. She tried to get to her mother, but the doorknob of her bedroom door was too hot and scorched her little hand. She still has a scar on her palm as a constant reminder of that dreadful night.

In a matter of minutes, Ari began choking on the thick black smoke filling her lungs as it consumed the air in her bedroom. Ari was forced to crawl out her bedroom window, which faced the backyard. She could feel the heat of the flames dance across her skin as she ran to the front of the house. She heard the deafening wail of a sirens as she reached the front yard.

As Ari approached the steps to the front porch, her mother's screams stopped. Without thinking, she took off running up the front steps to go back into the burning house to find her mother. But just as her foot touched the top step of the porch, a strong arm wrapped around her waist stopping her. Startled, she stared up to discover a fireman holding onto her. She tried to pull away, pleading with him that she needed to help her mom.

As she fought to free herself from his grasp, he tightened his hold on her, carrying her away from the fire as the other firemen were running through the front door. Flames engulfed her home as she sat helplessly watching. Through tear blurred vision she watched her home reduce to nothing but ashes and charcoal. Her mother never made it out of the house alive. Ari says she still has nightmares of her mother screaming in agony.

The only belongings Ari owns that survived the fire were a necklace and a few pictures of her with her mother. Her necklace is unique like Nikki's. The chain is made from titanium and has an orange crystal that has rays of red streaks. In the center of the crystal is a strange symbol.

Ari was sent to a group home for children directly after her mother's death while authorities tried to locate the few remaining living relatives she had. Her grandparents had passed away and she had no living aunts or uncles. After a few months, they located her cousin Judith. Judith had lived next door to Gran for years. She was delighted to take Ari in to live with her.

You could describe Judith as an old cat lady, but without the cats. She is a petite, older but still attractive woman with a kind heart. Judith was always pleasant when we were around, but she kept to herself before Ari came to live with her. She never married. Judith couldn't have children of her own but desired to have one. Ari filled a void in Judith's life.

Present day, Ari is still on the petite side. Her description would be a sexy, meek and mild nerd. She could be a man's ideal fantasy in a dirty librarian wet dream, with her slender legs, wavy auburn hair that ends midway down her back, and bright green eyes. Her eyes are vivid green like emeralds.

She has a shy disposition towards people she doesn't know, which has limited her boyfriend choices over the years. She has a mother hen personality, wanting to either fix your problems or to comfort you when she can't fix it.

Ari is a professor at Delgado Community College in the History Department. She specializes in ancient civilizations. Her other passion hits closer to her heart. She's been helping at a local children's shelter that provides temporary housing for children. The shelter's primary goal is to get kids off the street, whether the kid is a runaway or a throwaway. The shelter has social workers that work with families in order to place the kids back into their homes. If home is not an option, they try to place them with a foster family. Volunteers, including Ari, help by being positive mentors for the kids.

The whistle of the kettle on the stove draws me out of my muse. Nikki fixes each of us a cup of tea, then joins us at the kitchen island on her usual stool. The fourth and last stool at the kitchen island is where Ari sits when she's here for our chats. I didn't call Ari on my way to Gran's house to invite her.

Tonight, is one of the three nights a week she volunteers at the children's shelter. Ari says she is a kindred spirit to the kids there. She once said if it wasn't for her cousin, she could have been one of those kids that couldn't find a home. She's a mentor to them and is a living example that even though rough times may come their way, you shouldn't give up on your future.

Gran, Nikki, and I catch up on the goings-on in each other's lives as we sip tea. I describe my day at the hospital, sharing the details of the boy I saved. Nikki tells us details of her latest dream visit she had from Raven a few nights ago.

"I had another visit from Raven," Nikki informs us.

"Oh?" replies Gran with a curious twinkle in her eye.

"What crazy message did she give you this time?" I ask with excitement laced in my voice. Unlike Nikki, I've always enjoyed the messages since most of them aren't related to death. It reminds me of a mind-bender game, a challenge to find the answer to her riddles.

With a sigh, Nikki recites the coded message:
"Love can be wicked,
Love can be sweet,
Be careful of what one speaks.
The wolves are coming under a veil,
But these wolves have no tail."

"Well hell, that's as clear as mud," I say with a huge smile on my face. Nikki rolls her eyes at me which makes me laugh.

"Maybe it has something to do with that puppy you want, Willow. A tail-less puppy," Nikki says causing me to laugh even harder. Nikki shakes her head in disbelief at my enjoyment.

After my laughter dies and I catch my breath, I watch Nikki. She's biting her lower lip again while staring at me with brows drawn together. I know what's coming, "The Talk."

"Have you given any more thought to going out with Ari

and me this weekend?" Nikki asks as she starts in on me. "Ari and I want you to go with us to a place called The Club to celebrate Ari's birthday. Please, just think about it. It's been too long since the three of us went out to have fun," Nikki pleads.

"Even if I could, I have nothing to wear to a club, and I don't have any time to go shopping," I reply, thinking this was an excellent reason to not go.

"I knew you would say that. When I was out shopping the other day, I just so happened to pick up a cute little black dress that just so happens to be your size. It's hanging in my closet. Go look at it while I clean up our dishes. I will be in there in a minute," Nikki responds with a smug smile. I must have used the 'not having anything to wear' excuse too many times trying to get out of going in the past.

"Okay, okay, I'll go look at the dress," I tell her with a sigh. I'm wondering just how "little" the black dress is. I drag myself off my stool and head towards the hall.

"Well, ladies I am heading off to bed now," Gran announces through a yawn. She gives both of us a hug before leaving the room. I follow Gran down the hallway heading towards Nikki's bedroom.

I love Nikki's room. She has a natural ability to create a mood of peace and relaxation by the colors along with the décor. The head of her bed is against an exposed interior brick wall on the right. The other walls are made of wood and plaster covered in a medium grey paint.

The ceiling is twelve-foot tall and painted cloud white with massive exposed wooden beams running across that she painted grey to offset the white and match the walls. Straight ahead from the doorway beyond her bed is a door leading out onto a balcony. The balcony has a cast iron railing and overlooks Dumaine Street.

My favorite part of the entire townhouse is Nikki's balcony. When Nikki and I were kids, we used to sneak out onto the balcony late at night to lean over the cast iron railing to watch the passersby stroll along the street. The people were coming and going to the many clubs that call New Orleans home. Nikki's balcony has a view of Bourbon Street crossing Dumaine in the distance. We discovered early on that New Orleans attracts the most unusual variety of people. Actually, New Orleans breeds a different type of people all together.

Even with the variety of different people, they had one thing in common- most everyone was pleasant towards us and would wave as they passed. During the weeks of Mardi Gras, the locals from our street tossed beads up to us as they went past our balcony on their way home from attending the many celebrations or parades that happen during this time. I have to say we learned a lot about human anatomy by sitting on that balcony. We found it was better entertainment than any television program.

After entering Nikki's room, I walk by the bed heading towards her closet. Out of the corner of my eye, I see something laying on the bed that catches my attention. Curious, I walk over to investigate. It's an old-looking book laying open near the pillows. I lean in to get a closer look, then pick it up in my hands.

The book appears to be a hand-written journal. I take notice of how soft the leather that lines the hardcover feels. The pages of the journal are thicker than a standard piece of paper, and the hand-printed words are dulled from time. It has a remarkable old English style of penmanship. It is evident by the calligraphic lines that a feather quill was used to write the old English letters. As I wonder just how old this journal could be, I take in the details of the page. The page has weird instructions, and a poem written at the bottom. Mesmerized with the journal, I follow the instructions as I read the words out loud:

"A true love to love is what my heart needs,
  I call out for my true love to come to me,
To fill my heart and set me free,
  To love me now and let our love be,
  Stronger than the strongest bond,
Let our love unite us both as one."

"A book of poems?" I ponder out loud.

Meanwhile... back in the kitchen, as Nikki is putting the last cup in the dishwasher, a sudden chill rushes up her spine from an electrical charge that appears to be growing in the surrounding air. "Shit!" Nikki exclaims out loud. "I forgot about the damn journal on my bed," she continues to growl at herself. As she races to her bedroom, she says a prayer to herself that Willow hasn't noticed the journal.

Willow back in the bedroom... I'm lost in my thoughts, still examining the old journal when Nikki rushes into the room like hellhounds are on her heels. She snatches the book out of my hands, slamming it shut with a wild look in her eyes. The only response I can manage is standing with my mouth hung open in shock at Nikki's bizarre behavior.

"Did you read any of this book?" Nikki asks with a panic laced voice.

For a few seconds, I open and close my mouth like a fish out of water as I try to form a response. My mind is hard at work trying to process what's going on. Nikki asks me again, as her voice gets louder with each word, "Did you read..."

Finally, my mind reconnects to my mouth. I cut her off in mid-sentence and reply, "What the fuck?"

"Did you read..." Nikki asks again and again I cut her off.

"Oh no, no, I was just admiring the cover and the paper that the pages are made out of," I answer her with what I assume is a shocked expression still on my face. I rarely lie to Nikki, but her behavior over this old book of poems has me feeling startled and alarmed. I feel like a teenager that's gotten caught looking at porn by an upset parent. What I admitted to was half true though, so that should count. "Why?"

"It's one of Gran's old private journals, and... and you know how she likes no one reading her private thoughts," Nikki tries to explain. I can tell she's stumbling over what to say to cover up the truth.

"But she allows you to read her private journals?" I ask Nikki while raising one eyebrow and looking straight into her eyes. I believe the book belongs to Gran, but I know damn well Gran didn't write that poem. Unfortunately, calling Nikki out on her lie means I have to admit mine. Gran adores antiques and is possessive with the ones she owns, not wanting anyone to damage them, so her not wanting the journal touched isn't surprising.

"Well.... allowing and not knowing are two different things. Forget about the book, where's the dress?" Nikki asks trying to divert the conversation. I let her drop the subject of the journal, thinking Gran must have forbidden her to look at one of her so-called private journals and I caught Nikki with her hand in the cookie jar so to say.

"I was just about to get it," I reply as I turn my body away from the bed to walk toward the closet while never taking my eyes off Nikki. I'm still in shock at her behavior. Of all people, Nikki should know I have her back in any situation, including helping her cover up sneaking a peek at an old book.

Nikki walks past me to her closet and pulls out the little black dress. I guess I wasn't moving fast enough for her. I inspect the dress and love it, forgetting about Nikki's mini freak out. I can't wait to try it on. Since I've been at work the entire day, I am contaminated with germs. I don't want to try on the dress without taking a shower first.

"I knew you would love it," Nikki exclaims even though I haven't spoken a word about it yet. I am sure she can tell just how much I love it without saying it by the huge smile that is spread across my face as I examine the details.

"I do love it! Thank you," I say smiling back at her.

The night is getting late. I say my goodbyes to Nikki. Then. I head out the door with my new little black dress while promising Nikki that I will consider going out with her and Ari.

Chapter 5

Willow
" Oh, Hell to the No"

The visit to Gran's and Nikki's house was on Monday. The next few days went as I expected: all work and no play. I did take a break to visit with the boy I saved on Monday. I was pleased to find him doing well with his recovery. Today, Friday, didn't go as expected. I do not expect hospital administration to honor me for doing my job, but at least I think they should congratulate me on a job well done for saving a boy's life. But, was the hospital grateful? "Oh, hell to the no!!"

Instead, this evening at the end of my shift hospital administration summoned me to an urgent meeting. I received a lovely 45-minute lecture on how I'd violated hospital policy by operating on someone in the trauma bay in the emergency department instead of the operating room. They seemed uninterested in the fact the boy would not have lived long enough to make it to the operating room.

Now, as I leave the hospital and get into my car, I'm so pissed that I'm seeing red. On the drive home, the details of the meeting I attended keep replaying in my mind. I'm appalled by the meeting. I work long hours and bust my ass trying to do the best job I can. I've put my time into serving the needs of the hospital, then get a reprimand instead of a thank you.

Now, for the first time, I'm second guessing if I'm working in the right position. My Plan B to devote myself to my work in place of a man has gone to "Hell in a Handbasket" along with the 20-year plan that went to "Shit in a Hand Bag." I wish hospital administration appreciated my performance for once. I need a well-deserved break.

"Fuck it! I will reward myself!"

I want a carefree night of frolicking and fun. Ari and Nikki have been pestering me for months, telling me that all I need is a night of no strings attached good, no, fantastic—no breath-taking, mind-blowing sex with multiple orgasms given by a man, not by my own doing. I need a night that produces not one, but many orgasms that wash over me with waves of ec-stasy leaving me lying on the bed, breathless, with my heart pounding.

Now, I agree with them. Since its Ari's birthday, tonight is the perfect night to go out. Nikki is taking her out tonight for the yearly celebration. I will call Nikki and include myself. A night of escape from this stress-filled lifestyle I've been living is what I want. I've had my fill of hospital administration's bullshit. How dare they chastise me, for saving someone's life? He would not have made it to the operating room alive. Is it the policy to let a kid die? Screw them!

This career self-evaluation has got me reevaluating my re-lationship with Bill the rat-bastard. Why did I take it so hard when he left me? I've never had multiple orgasms with anyone. In fact, I seldom had an orgasm with Bill, much less multiple ones. Come to think of it, I'm not sure what I experienced with Bill would classify as a mind-blowing orgasm, more like below average. There were no waves or pounding heart. No spooning afterward to enhance the experience. Bill would slump over to his side of the bed and mumble thanks right before drifting off to sleep. Bill lacked passion.

I'm beyond tired of being Willow Black, MD. There is more to life than just a career. I want to enjoy myself. I don't want to settle anymore for ordinary. I want extraordinary. I want, no correct that, I need to have multiple orgasms with a hot, sexy man who knows the correct way to pleasure a woman's body.

Since I'm strolling across memory lane, I might as well do a self-analysis. I can't depend on anyone or anything to make me happy. Who could be happy with me if I'm not even happy with myself? Thinking back, I realize no one has asked me out on a date since Bill the rat-bastard left, unless you count the drunken patients in the ER.

I'm not an ugly duckling. I never take the time to fix myself up anymore. I've been in more of a slump than I realized. I've been using the excuse that makeup takes too much time in the mornings to apply then disappears during the long shifts I work. In reality, I haven't cared enough about my appearance to put in the effort.

As far as my hair, it's either pinned up on top of my head or in a ponytail most of the time. After all, it's not like I'm going for a night on the town. I work in an emergency room where sick people are looking for a cure, not a date. Not that I ever considered dating a patient. I need to put more effort into my appearance, venture out and meet people again. Put myself out there if I want to date again. I develop a Plan C to go out to get laid. So, I do the one thing I do when I need reinforcement. I pick up my phone and call Nikki.

"Hey, you," Nikki greets as she answers her phone.

"I'm going out with my BFFs tonight. I have the entire weekend off to enjoy, and that's what I plan to do! Go pick up Ari and meet me at my house," I instruct Nikki. "We can get ready at my house over drinks. I'll stop at the store to grab some wine to get our evening started," formulating Plan C in my mind as I'm talking.

"Will do, that bad of a day?" Nikki asks knowing something major must have happened to bring on my new mindset.

"You have no idea. I'll fill you in as we get ready for tonight. I desperately need a night out!"

"We'll resolve that problem tonight. One of Ari's friends from the shelter is co-owner of a club that just opened in the Warehouse District, the one I mentioned Monday night, so we are going there."

"OK, see you in a few."

"See ya," Nikki says back right before I press the end call button on my phone.

I stop at the liquor store that's near my house. I decide to get Sangria wine after scanning the many choices available. It's Ari's favorite wine, and it's her birthday. I grab a bottle then grab a second for good measure. After leaving the store, I drive the remaining short distance home and park in front of my house. As I walk about halfway up the cobblestone walkway toward the porch, my heel catches causing me to stumble.

"Damn, I'm tripping, and I've not even had a drink yet," I say out loud with a giggle. I realize the thought of spending quality time with my BFF's has brightened my mood. "Girl power!" I shout out loud, laughing again. I regain my composure as I open the door and proceed into the house. I go straight into the kitchen, put one bottle of the wine into the refrigerator and grab wineglasses out of the cabinet.

After opening the second bottle of Sangria, I pour myself a glass. I inspect the glass of wine thinking "what the hell," and continue to fill the glass full. I'm not a big drinker, but some liquid courage might help me step out of my comfort zone tonight.

No sooner than my lips tasted the fruitiness of the Sangria, the doorbell rings. Nikki and Ari walk straight into my house. We've never waited for one another to answer our doors. It's an open-door policy for each other. Each of us have a copy of one another's house keys in case of emergencies.

A bottle and a half of Sangria with many giggling episodes later, Nikki says "Okay, let's get you ready to rock some guy's world!"

Knowing they always have my best interest in mind, I allow Nikki and Ari to fix my hair and apply my make-up. I conclude that if they think I need a night of great sex with a hot guy, they will make my looks fit the bill.

"Since you have flawless fair skin, I will apply a light base," Ari says as she applies my make-up. "The gray eyeshadow and charcoal mascara will highlight your blue eyes, making them appear large but at the same time sexy. A medium blush called Barely There will bring out your cheekbones. As for lipstick, a bright red color to enhance your full, thick lips," Ari says as she does her finishing touches on my make-up.

I take one final glance at the mirror, then step into my bathroom to change my clothes. I slip into my black lace thong. I adjust my breast into a matching push-up strapless black lace bra. Sexy underwear is a great tool to arouse a man. Then, I shimmy into the silky little black dress Nikki bought for me to wear tonight. I love how the material glides over my body, reminding me of a lover's touch. I pull the front open to position my breast before I push the spaghetti straps over my shoulders. "Wow," I say to myself as I stare at my reflection in the bathroom mirror. I must admit, I barely recognize myself. I can't believe how stunning my reflection is.

The dress Nikki bought me is fantastic. She always has good taste. The dress is form fitting, showing off my full breast with enough visible cleavage to appear sexy but not slutty. There's a fine line between sexy and slutty, and Nikki's taste always leans toward sexy. The silky black material clings to my voluptuous curves like wax on a candle. It looks as if I poured myself into the dress—a perfect fit. The bottom dress seam hugs my thighs about four inches above my knees—short enough I can't bend over without baring the edge of my round ass cheeks. I make a mental note to myself to not bend over tonight.

I slip on the shoes I brought into the bathroom with me. As for the shoes, Nikki picked out three-inch black stilettos from the back of my closet I'd forgotten I owned. As I inspect at my legs, I notice the black stilettos accentuate my legs giving them an appearance I only see on models.

Earlier, Ari and Nikki insisted I ditch my "geeky glasses," as they called them. Instead, I replaced them with contact lenses. That was a smart choice on their part. The icing on the cake is my perfume. It's an ambary, jasmine scent reminiscent of tropical flowers and summer passion. A scent that invigorates me.

I give myself one last once look over in the bathroom mirror. I make the final adjustments to my hair that Nikki styled earlier. She curled the ends of my wavy hair, which added volume. She left it down flowing over my shoulders.

I step out of the bathroom to go find Nikki and Ari, who are getting themselves together in the bathroom down the hall. As I step into the room with them, they stop speaking to each other as they catch my reflection in the mirror. They turn in unison with both mouths open.

"Well?" I ask as they continue to stare without making a sound.

Ari is the first to speak. "Wow! You look stunning tonight!"

"It's been so long since we've gotten you out for a night of fun that I actually forgot how damn well you clean up," Nikki adds.

I can't help it, but a huge smile streaks across my face. These compliments help give me the courage I need to put myself back out in the dating world. My best friends always know what I need to hear. They are more effective than the liquid courage I've been consuming this evening.

"Thanks, guys for making me beautiful tonight, and for doing this for me. I really do need this," I tell them.

"Don't thank us Willow. You're a beautiful woman. We only added a little make-up to highlight your beauty. And as far as the dress goes, a dress can't make you look sexy if you don't already have a sexy body," Nikki starts a rant.

"Okay, Okay," I say to get her to stop ranting. I lean over and give them a group hug.

I take a seat on the stool that goes to a make-up table in the corner of the bathroom to watch as Nikki and Ari finish getting ready. As I continue drinking Sangria, I tell them both the lecture I received today from hospital administration as I promised Nikki earlier. As I finish my story, it's obvious they are both pissed off on my behalf. They finished getting ready, then stand in the middle of the bathroom for their inspection the same as I did for my inspection earlier.

Ari has on the green satin form-fitting mini dress Nikki gave her for her birthday, which matches her green eyes and compliments her auburn hair. It's accentuated by a pair of black suede 2-inch closed toe pumps which I paid for, but Nikki picked out as my birthday gift to Ari. Nikki has on a form-fitting black spaghetti strap dress with a black lace choker that blends well with her short pixie cut brown hair. Nikki's shoes are 2-inch open toe black leather heels with a gothic look. Both ladies are much more used to dressing for the club atmosphere and thrive there. After inspection, I yell out, "all for one," and they yell back, "and one for all."

As we are getting ready to leave, I go to my bedroom and retrieve the little cocktail purse I chose earlier. It matches my dress. I walk over to where my makeup is still laying out and pick up my lipstick to carry with me tonight for touch-ups. I double check I have my cash, cell phone, and ID. After confirming I've got everything, I turn to go find Nikki and Ari but am surprised to see them standing right behind me. I didn't hear them come in to my bedroom. Ari snickers while Nikki stretches out her arm to hand me something. She has a massive grin on her face.

"What's this?" I ask as I reach out my hand to take whatever she is handing me.

"You need to pack these, safety first you know," Nikki informs me as she places something into my hand. I look into my hand to find condoms. As I hold them up into the air, I realize it's a roll of ten condoms attached at the ends.

"Seriously? Ten condoms Nikki? I doubt any guy can get it up ten times in one night," I tell her as I roll the condoms up before I shove them in my purse.

"You never know," Nikki says with a smirk and a wink.

I roll my eyes saying "Whatever. Let's go my ladies; we are wasting serious party time. Did anyone call for a cab yet?"

"I will call for one now," Ari says.

Since the three of us started drinking before the transformation process started, by the time the cab arrives I'm too ecstatic to worry anymore over my appearance. I have confidence that my appearance looks as good as I feel. I insist we take a cab to the club called The Club. How original, The Club. It's a newer dance club that's opened in the Warehouse District. It seems to be the hot spot for people our age. The cab ensures that we get there, Sangria and all. I'm refusing to become a patient in my emergency room after the day I had at work today.

Chapter 6

Willow
"Eye Candy" and "Sex on a Stick"

As the cab pulls up, I glance out the window and notice a line stretching along the sidewalk with at least twenty people waiting for entry at the front door. The Club is new, and the line is evidence it's the newest millennial hangout in the city.

I can hear the muffled thumping of the music coming from the building before I even open the cab door. The Club is in an old brick one-story building on Tchoupitoulas Street. There's a large black metal door that has "The Club" painted on it in red paint in Gothic style lettering, with a doorman controlling entry into the building.

I exit the cab, first by placing my feet on the sidewalk while keeping my legs closed not to give an accidental peep show. As I stand up tall on my three-inch black stilettos, I notice the doorman checking me out from head to toe with an appreciative smile on his lips. He's a large muscular black man with tattoo sleeves on both arms that disappear under his shirt sleeve and reappear at his neck. He gives the vibe of someone you don't want to mess with.

As Ari steps out, he does the same to her. By the time Nikki is out and standing tall, he's got a huge smile on his face, almost drooling.

As the cab pulls away from the curb, he walks over to us and says, "right this way, ladies." He escorts us away from the entry line straight into the club as if we are getting VIP treatment. I'm not used to this attention. I would normally be in line watching other people enter. Not this time. It's beauty before brains. For the first time in my life, I'm being ushered past the front of the line. It's an exhilarating, almost empowering feeling.

I turn to thank the doorman before he walks away. "Thanks for allowing us in so quickly."

"No problem, little lady. Owner's instructions are to allow all the eye candy in to keep the men in the club smiling and drinking. It's good for business," he explains as he runs his index finger across the side of my cheek in a flirty gesture. I keep smiling as he turns then walks away. Eye candy should sound insulting, but tonight it's a total compliment.

As I turn back toward Ari and Nikki, I notice the place is crowded. It's a large, open room with tables from the front door to the middle. There's a large free-standing bar area in the middle of the room that has bar stools surrounding it. In the back half of the room there is a large dance floor with a DJ booth and speakers located along the back wall. There's a short hallway off the right wall that leads to the bathrooms.

This place is a melting pot of urban millennials dancing and socializing. At first glance, a third of the people are using cell phones to talk, text, or take selfies. I've never gotten involved with social media like other millennials. In fact, at 28 years old I don't even consider myself to be a millennial. The only things I could post on social media would say "working at the hospital" or "still at work," so what's the use? Now, with Plan C I'm at least going to join Facebook.

As we walk further into The Club, we notice that all tables within our view are full. If this was earlier in the night, it might concern us, but considering the Sangria we've already consumed we migrate toward the bar. We order a round of Apple Martinis. As we wait for our drinks, I scan the people in the bar for my hot guy.

I notice a group of women staring in the same direction. I follow their line of sight that land on the guy straight across from where we stand that is oozing "sex on a stick" sex appeal. The man has dark brown hair in one of those just got out of bed intentional messy styles- very hot. I can't tell how tall he is because he's sitting on a stool talking to another Mr. Hotty sitting beside him.

Mr. Sex on a Stick has a sharp flawless jawline. It's the kind I can imagine myself running my tongue along until I reach his lush, full lips. His eyes appear to be dark from this distance. He has broad shoulders which allow the white dress shirt he is wearing to hug his chest just enough to tell there's muscle underneath. He has an air of authority to him. He has the bad-boy vibe. Not the type that makes you want to run from him, but the kind that makes you want to run to him.

That's the type of man I would love to go home with! I don't care how good I feel about myself or how much liquid courage I consume, I can never approach someone like him without feeling like a babbling fool. I wouldn't even know what to say to him to get him to talk. It's not like he doesn't have a variety of women to choose from, considering the attention he's getting from the other women here. I stare at him until he takes notice and smiles at me. I return the smile, then glance back at Nikki who is talking. I feel my face flush as embarrassment takes over my body at the fact a hot guy caught me ogling him.

After we receive our drinks, we stand by the bar and people watch. Nikki informs me to browse for a man because she's not allowing me to leave the bar without one. I smirk at her for that little comment because I've already found what I want. I just don't know how to get it yet. As I glance around the room, my eyes along with my mind keep going back to Mr. Sex on a stick. I notice he keeps looking my way too, probably wondering why the hell I keep looking over at him like a stalker.

After standing and looking around for a few minutes, towards the middle of the room Ari spots a table of people she knows from the shelter. They have three empty chairs, so she suggests we sit with them to keep from standing all night. One of the women at the table jumps up with excitement when she spots Ari. She meets us part way to greet Ari by pulling her into a tight hug. When they stop hugging Ari introduces everyone.

"Lindsey, these are my friends I grew up next door to that I've told you about, Nikki and Willow. Nikki and Willow this is Lindsey. She volunteers at the shelter too," Ari says as introductions.

"Nice to finally put faces with the stories Ari tells me. Don't worry it's all good stories," Lindsey says with a chuckle. "Dominic and his cousin just left our table to check to make sure this place is running smoothly tonight, so that leaves our table with empty chairs. Would you three like to join us?" Lindsey asks.

We all agree and make our way to the table. Ari finishes the introductions with the other two women at the table before we sit. Their names are Rachel and Erica.

"You all just missed our up-close eye candy. Dom brought his cousin over to introduce us to him tonight, and he is as fine as Dom," Erica tells us after we sit down. The other women giggle and fan themselves.

I've heard Ari mention Dom, short for Dominic, a few times. Besides investments like this club, he volunteers at the children's shelter. He also runs a home that houses children for more extended time periods than the shelter which Ari volunteers. He's involved with the shelter because of his rough childhood and has a big heart for kids in need. There seems to be one small detail Ari forgot to mention- that's how fine Dom must be according to these women. So, on top of having money, a big heart, and loves to help children, he's fine as hell too!

It seems my meek and mild friend has been holding out on us. I glare at Ari while raising one eyebrow. She blushes then looks away. She knows I want to know why Dom's fineness wasn't discussed before tonight. I won't bring it up now because it will embarrass her shy ass on her birthday, so that will be a topic for another day-like tomorrow.

After a couple of rounds of lemon drops in honor of Ari's birthday along with singing the happy birthday song to her, I'm feeling over the moon good. I can't help myself and turn to take a glance at Mr. Sex on a Stick, noticing he keeps looking my way. I wish he would make a move, ask me to dance, come over and talk or even better come grab me up into his strong arms, take me to the back and fuck me against the wall. Wow, where did that last part of my thoughts come from? I think it must be the lack of sex and the much-consumed alcohol.

Leaning in close Nikki asks, "Why don't you go up and talk to him, you know, introduce yourself?"

"Who?" I ask pretending I don't already know who she's talking about.

"Who?" Nikki asks, "Are you serious? Whichever one of those two hot guys you keep scoping out at the bar, that's who."

"Guys?" I peek back up towards Mr. Sex on the Stick. I forgot he was sitting by another good-looking guy.

"The guy on the right. What do you expect me to do? Look at him, he's sex on a Stick. I can't approach him. I wouldn't even know what to say," I whine to Nikki in a whispered rant.

"Well, you need to woman-up and figure it out. You're not the only one those two have caught the attention of. You snooze you lose," Nikki says with a lecturing tone.

"Drop it, Nikki. You're killing my buzz," I hiss.

"Whatever," she responds, then turns back to face everyone at the table. I know she's only trying to help, but I'm out of my element with him. I need to find a cute guy to get back in the saddle of seeing men again, not one full of hotness. Then, maybe I can get the courage to talk to a pure alpha hot guy next time.

After another round of drinks, I realize I'm enjoying myself this evening. It's been way too long since I've gone out with my girls. I didn't realize just how much I miss this. The DJ plays the song Cheap Thrills. Nikki, Lindsey, and I decide it's time to hit the dance floor together. I love to dance. When I stand up, I realize just how much alcohol I've consumed tonight. I notice how tipsy I am when I feel the room start to sway.

After we've danced for a few songs, I decide the more I drink, the better I think I can dance. I then laugh, causing Nikki to burst out laughing even though she doesn't understand why I'm laughing.

"It's good to see you laugh Willow," Nikki yells over the music.

"I can't remember the last time I laughed so much. I feel tipsy and free from thinking or caring about anything. And you know what?" I ask Nikki, slurring words as I try to communicate over the music.

"What?" Nikki yells back with a huge smile on her face.

I kind of think she may be laughing at me instead of with me, but I continue, "The more I drink, the better I dance, so I'm wondering if the more I drink, the better I can fuck," I tell her not realizing just how loud I'm talking to make sure she can hear me over the music.

Nikki's eyes open wide as she bursts out into laughter. Now, I know she's laughing at me. The next thing I know, a giant pair of warm hands wraps around my waist, and a hard body presses into my backside. I tilt my head to glance up. Not Mr. Sex on a stick as I hoped, but this guy is almost as sexy looking. He looks more like GQ model hot, not the bad boy hot. Taller than I am and smiling down at me when I glance up, he has the cutest dimples I've ever seen on a man. For some reason, I think it's good to inform him of this by blurting out "I like your sexy dimples."

He laughs, then replies "Thanks, and I like your sexy laugh. I've been listening to it while you've been dancing." He grabs my hips and swings me around to face him, making me laugh again. "Dance with me," he whispers in my ear.

Proceeding with my getting laid plan, I agree to a dance. He keeps his body close to mine, as close as a person can get to another without touching, except for his hands which stay on my hips. We danced for a song. With all the moving and laughter, I notice that the drinks I've consumed are hitting my bladder.

"Uhmmm….," I say to this guy then he interrupts.

"Jack," he tells me as he leans his head down to better hear me over the music.

"Willow," I respond. "Jack," I start again. "I love dancing with you, but I really need to run to the restroom. Do you think we can continue this dance in a few minutes?"

"Sure, why don't I walk with you then I'll buy us another drink at the bar as we head back," Jack offers.

"Sounds like a plan, and you know what Jack? I like plans," I blurt out again.

"You are so damn cute," Jack replies smiling while shaking his head.

"Thank you," I tell him, I then turn around to face Nikki and mouth the word bathroom to her, so she knows where I'm going. She raises her eyebrows as if asking do I want her to go with me. For reasons unknown to me, when women are out, we travel around in groups when going on bathroom trips.

I shake my head at her then glance back and forth from Jack to Nikki to indicate he's going with me. She smiles at me and nods her head in understanding. I turn then walk off the dance floor with Jack following.

Chapter 7

Connor
"Go the fuck on"

Earlier the same evening...... "Connor, lighten up man and find some pussy," my brother Drake whispers in my ear. While nursing my beer, I wonder again how my brother Drake, who's sitting beside me engaged in conversation with a hot blonde with big tits, talked me into coming out tonight. Then, I remember why. Since my team arrived in New Orleans, Drake's stayed on my ass complaining there's no way he will survive this assignment without getting laid.

Even though we live just outside of New Orleans, our work takes us all over the place and to many states. Sometimes we're gone for months at a time. We're on our first assignment on our turf. We've been here in New Orleans on the job assignment for two-and-a-half weeks. Drake thinks his dick will malfunction if it doesn't get a weekly work out, and with us working nonstop since we arrived, he feels deprived.

Our assignment is right in the middle of a city known for enjoyable sin, and Drake will not pass up the opportunity to find some serious female action. I knew to survive this assignment without killing my brother, I needed to meet him halfway. I know Dominic Almonester, one of the co-owners of this club, which appears to be the favorite place to hang judging by the crowd here. One call to Dom and we bypassed the line outside with no problems. I have known Dom for quite a few years now. He runs a shelter for half-breeds, and I help him with locating absent parents or missing children.

My name is Connor Boudreaux. I own and run a company

called Cerberus. I chose the name Cerberus for my private business. Cerberus is a name found in Greek mythology. It's the name given to the three-headed dog that protects the gates to the underworld, keeping the two worlds apart, which is why I think the name suits my company so well.

My company provides services to humans and non-humans while keeping the two apart. We provide locating services, security, and protection for individuals when we're not on assignment for The Guardians. The Guardians are a group of non-human races that work as law enforcers for the Leadership Council of non-human races. We're like regular police officers, FBI agents, and CIA agents all rolled into one. The difference is we do whatever it takes by any means possible to get our job done. We exist so the non-human races can live in peace.

My family lines originated from a Native American tribe of shape shifting werewolves called the Rougarou. We used to be able to shape shift into wolves. Due to a misfortunate run in our ancestors had with some demonic fairies known as Fae, our family line almost ceased to exist. The Fae placed a curse upon the entire family line and future generations robbing us of our ability to shift forms. It traps us in human form. Around the same time, we almost became exterminated, the Fae went extinct, and a cure for the curse disappeared along with them.

The history of the Fae has since turned into myths and legends. As a reminder of our curse, each family member has the same birthmark. It's in the shape of a paw print. We kept all the other abilities associated with our kind, including supernatural strength, speed, and heightened senses. Because we have homed in our abilities, the Council has appointed my brother and I to be members of the elite group, The Guardians. It's a group made up of different teams with the same purpose- to keep the peace between humans and non-humans.

I'm the commander of a team of five. Our current assignment has brought us to New Orleans. We're tracking down a gang of Wendigos. They are the primary suspects for a string of recent killings around the city. The victims have the markings of a Wendigo bite, but to the average non-human it would appear an animal had mauled and eaten on the body.

Wendigos are shapeshifters that can transform from a human form into their true form of a monstrous demon. Their demonic form still maintains the shape of a human but has green and orange scales, sharp teeth, and horns. Their faces have the appearance of a hollow skull, rumored to be the origin of the Calavera painted faces of The Day of the Dead celebrations. Wendigos have superhuman strength, but not as strong as a wolf shifter. They're much stronger than humans though. Their taste palate gets them into trouble. Their favorite choice of food is human meat. Harming humans is forbidden by the Council. It forbids anything that brings unwanted attention to the existence of non-human races, a vital part in protecting non-humans.

My team functions like a well-oiled machine. We're a force to be reckoned with when on assignment. Second in command is my brother Drake, who has the same abilities I do. The only difference between us is that I have stronger leadership skills. I've got a natural gift to read any situation that my team encounters and go with my gut feeling on how to deal with it. I'm dead on with knowing what to do and to handle the situation. Drake is better at being able to read individuals and predicting their next move. He also has an uncanny ability to judge if someone is telling the truth or hiding something.

Another team member, Daniel Melancon, is a werewolf from a different tribe. He can shift into wolf form at will, along with all of mine and Drake's other abilities. Daniel has developed strong tracking skills and is a skilled sharpshooter who can shoot unheard of distances and never misses.

Drew O'Brien is another team member. He's a Druid. He's not as strong as a werewolf, but he's able to hold his own in most fights. Drew knows all things about technology and computers. Because of his Druid heritage, he knows a lot of magic including using spells, symbols, and potions.

The last team member is our only female. Her name is Valentina Montgomery or Val for short. Val is a Cat Sith, a creature of a human form with the ability to transform into a black cat with a white spot on her chest. In cat form, she's slightly larger than a house cat. Val handles the research for the team. She transforms into cat form to help with surveillance. She's a powerful Empath as well.

An empath can pick up on people's emotions, and on the emotional vibe in any room. Emotions in a room take on physical characteristics to her. For example, people say they can feel tension in the air, but she can feel the tension in the air like a physical touch. She's short and petite in human form but never underestimate her fighting skills. She's sent many human males home holding their balls after they've pissed her off.

I have an ulterior motive in accepting this assignment in New Orleans. I've got a more personal matter to investigate while we're here. For years now, in my spare time, I've been trying to get the curse lifted off my family. A few months ago, I heard part of a myth about the Fae that I've never heard.

The myth spoke of books containing magical spells that the little demon Fae used to use. It's probably a lost cause, but since I'm in New Orleans, I want to look around and see if I can find any truth to what I heard. Since the last known Fae was living in this area, I thought this city the best starting point in my search. I'm hoping if I can find the books, they may have information on reversing the curse.

While sitting here drinking my beer and listening Drake talk smack to the blonde, a vision across the bar catches my eye. Across the bar on the opposite side, I notice three gorgeous ladies walk up to the bartender to order. The blonde one grabs my attention. She's hot, sexy as hell, and I can't take my eyes off her. I check her out from head to toe noticing her sexy long legs that disappear under the short hem of her little black dress. She has a perfect heart-shaped ass that's just begging to be caressed, along with full breast begging to be squeezed and played with. She has beautiful, succulent, full lips I'm longing to taste. Damn, the sight of her almost made me groan out loud. This woman looks amazing!

As I gawk across the bar at her I realize I don't think I've ever been this turned on by how a woman looks before. I want, no, I need to get closer to her. I can say for the first time tonight I'm glad I let Drake talk me into coming here.

All three women order drinks and continue to stand at the bar looking around talking to one another. I want to know more about the blonde in the middle, so to prevent distraction I look down and try to concentrate to see if I can hear their discussion. This is one situation I'm glad I have a heightened sense of hearing. It's too crowded and noisy with all the music and people in the club talking to pick up the whole conversation, but I hear at least a few of their words.

The beautiful blonde's friend just called her Willow. As I glance back up at her, I could swear I caught her checking me out. When Willow makes eye contact with me, I give her a coy smile. She gives me a small smile in response, and I notice that her neck and face blush in the cutest light pink color when embarrassed. Oh yeah, I caught her checking me out, which I find interesting. She looks over at her friend, which they call Nikki if I heard right. Nikki informs her to look for a man because she's not allowing her to leave the bar without one. I see Willow smirk at Nikki. This bit of information is interesting. I decide in an instant I will be that man. If Willow's goal is to leave with a man, then dammit I will step up to the plate and volunteer. I don't mind helping a beautiful woman. Willow continues to glance around, but her eyes keep coming back to me.

I notice another woman approach the one they call Ari and invite them to sit at her table. I glance to the table the woman is pointing at and see only females sitting around it. I'm not in the mood to sit with a table full of women and listen to them talk all night because I don't like to hear about some shit that a group of women want to talk about. Some things are just not meant for a man to hear. I decide I will make my move closer to leaving time, so I will sit and watch for now.

Over the next couple of hours, Willow keeps glancing at me, so I know the interest is mutual. With the smoky looks she's giving me, I would say the lust is mutual too. Willow gets up with two women at the table and approaches the dance floor. When she shakes that perfect heart-shaped ass the hard-on I've been sporting since I first saw her gets harder and tighter against my jeans. I can't say I remember my cock ever being this hard and full. It's as if I'm fixing to cum in my pants. As the three of them are dancing, they move closer to the speakers that the music is blaring from, so I can no longer hear their conversation.

I notice a man that was dancing close to Willow's little group turns and places his groping hands on Willow's waist. I see fucking red. "Oh Hell No," I say with a low growl. I can see Drake turn towards me out of the corner of my eye, but I don't fucking care. I have an overwhelming possessive feeling consuming me now, and only one word comes to my mind, "mine," which shocks the hell out of me.

I've never felt this possessive over any woman, especially one I've never spoken to. There's no way in hell I will sit here and watch this ass-wipe paw at her. As I stand up to storm over to the dance floor to remove the little ass-wipes' hands, I notice Willow smiles and says something to the ass wipe. She then walks off the dance floor.

That fucking dip shit is following her like a desperate puppy. The dip shit places his hand on the small of her back in a weak attempt at claiming Willow as his territory. "I Don't Think So," I say with another low growl, causing my jaw to clench. That's all I can fucking stand. I lean toward Drake as he turns away from the blonde he's been trying to talk into his bed all night. In a low voice, I inform him, "I'm heading out the door and not planning to leave alone. Hopefully, I won't see your ass until sometime tomorrow afternoon."

"It's about damn time brother. I was getting exhausted watching you stare at that fine piece of ass all damn night.

It's past time for you to make your move," Drake tells me then turns back to the woman he's talking to. I walk away from the bar to go after what's mine. I see Willow entering the women's bathroom. The dip shit stops in his tracks but remains standing near the door waiting. I don't waste time and walk right up to him.

"Hey man, what is your name?" I ask the dip shit.

"Jack," the dip shit responds.

I hold my hand out in a gesture to shake hands. "Connor," I reply as Jack grabs my hand to shake it. We shake hands, but as he tries to pull his hand back, I tighten my grip not releasing his hand. Jack's head snaps up as he looks at me with a puzzled look mixed with a little fear. I'm a good four or more inches taller, not to mention at least fifty pounds heavier of pure muscle,

I lean down and forward, so our eyes are at the same level. "Here's the thing Jack, the woman you're trying to claim has already been claimed. That woman is mine. So, you need to go the fuck on," I say, squeezing his hand a little tighter for good measure. I see his Adam's apple bob up and down as he swallows hard and his eyes widen.

"Um, sh. sh. she didn't say she was here with anyone, man. I didn't know she's here with you," he says as he stumbles over his words as if trying to figure out what to say.

"Well I guess then it's my job to inform you, so consider yourself informed," I tell him. I release his hand and turn sideways to give him room, so he can go on. Jack is a smart man because he doesn't hesitate to go the fuck on and never look back.

Chapter 8

Willow
"A Ho Fo Sho"

After a quick visit to the bathroom stall, I stand at the sink to wash my hands. I check my lipstick in the bathroom mirror and notice I need to do a touch up when I get back to the table where I left my purse. My mind keeps drifting back to Mr. Sex on a Stick. I think he's interested in me. I've seen him looking at me at least half of the times I've glanced in his direction. Maybe he's trying to figure out why I keep looking at him like a stalker and he's really not interested in me at all. No, he smiled at me. I need to stop over analyzing this. I take a deep breath to calm my thoughts before leaving the bathroom.

When I step back into the hallway, I glance around to see if Jack is still waiting. He's nowhere in sight. Assuming he's at the bar ordering our drinks, I turn that way and walk straight into a hard chest. I step back a couple of steps and glance up to apologize to the head that belongs to the chest and realize it's Mr. Sex on a Stick. This is the first time tonight I've seen him standing. His size is impressive. He's so much taller than me. He must be well over six-foot tall. His eyes are the color of melted chocolate with the seductive power to have a woman lose herself in them.

Mr. Sex on a Stick raises up his hand and gently runs the back of his thumb across my cheek, causing a tingling sensation to shoot thru me, making me realize I've been standing here checking him out without saying a word to him. What the hell is wrong with me? I need to say something before he thinks I'm a complete idiot. My mind is searching, for something to say, but before I can form a word out of my mouth Mr. Sex on a Stick steps closer.

With our body's inches from touching, he leans his head and brings his face down closer to mine. He places his fingers under my chin. Just as I think he's about to kiss me, he gently guides my face to the left with his fingers. I feel his warm, moist breath on my neck. It sends a shiver down my spine and makes my nipples rock hard. I wonder if he felt me shiver, or if he can see my nipples protruding thru my silky dress. Do I even care if he felt me shiver? No, no, I don't. I've never had a man have such an effect on me or my body.

"Your friend, Jack, remembered he had somewhere he needed to be, so he went the fuck on," Mr. Sex on a Stick explains in a low whisper that causes chill bumps to form on my arms. I catch my groan before it leaves my throat. I'm so out of my element here. I'm craving this man like a drug addiction and don't know a thing about him. I don't even know his name.

"Jack?" I ask confused for a moment before remembering it's the name of the other guy. Mr. Sex on a Stick doesn't answer my question; instead he ever so lightly runs his nose from the base of my neck up to my ear. I hear him taking a deep breath and realize he's inhaling my scent.

"Damn, you smell as good as you look. I bet you taste even sweeter," Mr. Sex on a Stick whispers in my ear as he groans with his deep voice. I think I melted in my panties. I'm sure the moisture is palpable. His deep voice makes the little hairs in my ears tingle.

I take a deep breath and inhale his yummy masculine scent. He smells of sandalwood, spice, and masculinity. Again, I realize I've only spoken one word to him. I open my mouth to speak, "Let's get out of here and go someplace a little more private," I blurt out. Did I say that out loud?

Mr. Sex on a Stick growls, leaving no doubt in my mind, I did say it. I'm mortified the first thing I said to this man is let's get out of here and go somewhere more private. I should've asked his name, told him mine, or said something. He must think I'm a slut, or a "Ho-Fo-Sho," as my friends say. Now, my face is burning from blushing and there's no way he will not notice it with him standing so close.

"I love the light pink color your skin turns when you blush," Mr. Sex on a Stick says in a low whisper that makes me shiver again.

I pull my head back, and peer into his eyes as I explain, "I guess I'm a little embarrassed. I've never done anything like this before. I've never asked a man, especially one I don't even know, to leave with me before," I say. Great, now I'm rambling; totally not sexy.

Mr. Sex on a Stick closes the distance I've created between our faces, so our lips are as close as can be without touching and replies, "I got that idea already by the blushing. We can easily resolve part of that issue. My name is Connor," he says with a gentle smile. He's so close that when he speaks, the warmth and moisture of his breath caresses my lips.

"Willow," I reply just as breathy with a small smile.

"It's a pleasure to meet you Willow. Now that we know each other why don't we go somewhere a little more private?" he replies and then places a gentle kiss on my lips.

This time I release a groan from my throat and my lips separate further apart while doing it. Connor takes advantage by deepening the kiss, sliding his warm tongue into my mouth. His tongue is dancing with mine, and it feels unbelievable. The sensation of electric shock waves moves through my core ending with wetness at the apex of my thighs. My lacey thong is definitely moist now.

As his arms wrap around my waist, I run my hands up his rock-hard abdomen to his chest and grab onto his shirt. I pull him in as close as I can to my body before wrapping my arms around his neck and running my fingers through his thick, silky soft hair. Connor clamps his large hands firmly on my ass cheeks, crushing my body into his. I feel the stiffness of his cock through his jeans. His cock is huge. I can't help myself and start to grind against him.

Connor pulls his lips back from mine, leaving me panting. As his nostrils flare, he says, "Willow, baby I need to get you out of this place, and I mean right now." Nothing else needs to be said.

Panting so hard I can't form words; I nod my head in agreement. I take a deep breath to try to slow my rapid heartbeat, "Let me go inform my friends I'm leaving and grab my purse."

Connor grabs my hand, lacing our fingers together, then heads toward the table where my friends are sitting. I notice as we reach the table that Nikki and Lindsey have rejoined the group. I take a step around Connor to grab my purse causing everyone at the table to stare up at me. Nikki's eyes look past me over my shoulder. I'm sure she's looking at Connor because I can feel the heat of his body pressed against mine. I take a glance at everyone else at the table. They're all looking at Connor with their mouths open, which I assume is the effect of his hotness. I move my eyes back to Nikki and Ari. I make introductions, "this is Connor…" I say when Nikki interrupts me.

"Mr. Sex on a Stick has a name? Well, Connor, I'm Nikki and this is Ari," she says. As she continues with the introductions, I tune her voice out and glare at her for calling him Mr. Sex on a Stick. He caught onto her little comment too, because as soon as it left her lips, I felt him place his large hand on my hip and squeeze. I wonder, could the saying be true concerning large hands? When she's through with the introductions, Nikki looks back at me with a smirk across her lips.

I clear my throat, "Connor and I are leaving to go get coffee somewhere quiet." I start my excuse of why I'm leaving, not wanting to announce that I've found my inner slut for the first time and plan to fuck the hell out of this complete stranger for the rest of the night.

This time it's Ari who interrupts me. "Coffee?" she says with a smirk on her face. I roll my eyes at her.

"Whatever, I just wanted to let you know I'm leaving," I continue.

66

"Ok, see you later. Have fun," the women say in unison.

Connor takes my hand in his and pulls me away from the table as he tells everyone with a smile on his face "It was a pleasure meeting you all. Goodnight."

I hear Lindsey saying, "Honey, believe me when I say the pleasure was all ours." Then I listen to laughter coming from their direction as we walk away.

As we approach the front door, I pull Connor to a stop and ask, "Don't you need to tell your friend at the bar you're leaving?"

He gives me a puzzled expression, then realizing who I'm talking about replies, "He isn't my friend, he's my brother Drake, and he can figure it out on his own." With that statement, we leave The Club.

Chapter 9

Connor
"Lose My Load"

The Club has an open agreement with one of the local cab companies to keep two or three cabs lined up across the street from the entrance of The Club to encourage people to not drink and drive. In return, if someone needs a taxi, this cab company gets all the business, an arrangement my buddy the co-owner of this club arranged.

Luckily, there's one cab left when we make it out in front of The Club. Any delay in me sinking my cock into Willow won't be tolerated. I've had my fair share of drinks tonight, so I have no intention of getting behind the wheel of my truck and fucking it, one of us, or someone else up tonight.

I grasp Willow's hand and hurry her across the road as if hell's hounds are at our heels. She breaks out into a fit of giggles while asking, "anxious much?"

I open the back door of the cab, sit down, then swirl Willow around as I snatch her downward. After she lands in my lap, I shut the cab door. I lean in close, placing my mouth next to her ear, and with a growl give her my reply, "You have no fucking idea. My cock went rock solid when I first saw your beautiful face which was several hours ago, and it's remained hard watching you shake that heart-shaped ass of yours on the dance floor." As I lean in closer, I nip her over the pulse spot at the base of her neck causing her body to melt into my lap. Oh, you are so mine I think to myself. Peering up I realize the driver of the cab has a cocky grin and is staring at us through the rearview mirror like he knows what's going on. I couldn't care any less right now about what he thinks. I glance back down at Willow and ask, "Where to sweetheart?"

"I'm not sure. I've done nothing like this before, but I'm thinking the closest damn hotel," Willow replies in a sultry voice.

"You heard the lovely lady," I tell the driver, "and an extra twenty dollars if you push the damn rearview mirror in the opposite direction and don't turn around," I say. I stress the last part more as a command than a request. The driver gives me a chin lift, pushes the rearview mirror in the opposite direction then pulls away from the curb.

I look back down at Willow and she's got a "fuck me look" written all over her gorgeous face. She's got half-hooded eyes and red, pouty, swollen lips from the kisses we've shared. Without saying a word, I grab the nap of her neck and guide her face up to mine to kiss those luscious lips again.

I trace the outline of her bottom lip with my tongue causing her to gasp, gaining access to her mouth when it slightly opens in response. She shivers as I take full advantage of her mouth with my tongue. I kiss her hard and deep, just the way I plan to fuck her when we get to the hotel.

I ease up the intensity of the kiss after realizing the need to calm down and take a slower pace before I lose my load in my pants like a horny teenager. I don't want to scare her off by being too aggressive.

As I begin to pull back, Willow's hand slides over my cock and slowly strokes the shaft through my jeans. I lose what little control I'm maintaining and deepen the kiss again. As I explore her mouth with my tongue, she matches the stroke of my tongue with hers.

My other hand is resting on Willow's bare thigh where the damn sexy as hell little black dress ends. As I deepen the kiss, further devouring her mouth, I feel her legs spread apart. I slide my hand up her soft, creamy white inner thighs. Willow gasps as I knead the smooth skin of her inner thigh inches from her pussy. She kisses me harder and spreads her legs wider in response as an invitation.

I accept the invitation by slowly caressing a path and working my hand farther up her inner thigh. She tilts her neck and leans her head back to give me better access to her neck. This causes her sweet tits to rise in response. Her breasts are a perfect size. They're, a bit more than a handful, with nipples protruding like tight, small pebbles underneath the silky material of her dress. As I take a moment wondering whether they're pink or light brown, I growl from anticipation of finding out.

I begin to alternate kisses with gentle bites on the curve of her delicate neck. Her neck smells of an amber scent that's driving me crazy. When my hand makes it all the way up her thigh to her warm pussy, I discover her panties are already wet for me. I stroke her cunt through lace panties that seem to disappear into the crack of her ass. This earns me a groan from her. Damn, with each stroke of my fingers her sweet little cunt grows wetter through the material of her panties.

I place my mouth to her ear so she's the only one that can hear me and whisper, "Damn baby, your sweet little pussy is dripping wet and ready for my cock. Your panties are fucking soaked." She grabs my hair, pulling my head back to make us face to face, and forces my lips to collide with hers again.

I plunge my tongue into her wet mouth and vigorously kiss her while easing the material that is blocking my fingers from her juicy cunt over to the side. With the tip of my finger, I gently rub the tops of her soft pussy lips until they open like the petal of a flower. I slide one finger slowly into her dripping, tight pussy causing her to moan. I release a growl of my own when I realize just how tight she is. I work my finger further inside her luscious little cunt, crooking it upward to allow my finger to rub across her g-spot.

She pulls away from our kissing and stares into my eyes. From the look she's giving me, I'm guessing no one's ever hit her magical spot before. I place my thumb over her clit and slowly work it in circular motions, while massaging her g-spot. Her breathing becomes erratic and heavy. A few more swirls of my thumb and she fucking explodes. I stare at her beautiful face and finger fuck her cunt as she cums all over my finger. I take pride in the moans I'm causing to escape from her delicate throat.

She leans her head back and rocks her hips as she rides my hand. Her pussy starts rhythmically pulsating as if trying to suck my finger. "You're so fucking beautiful when you cum," I tell her. Just as her pussy slows the rhythmic pulsations, the cab brakes to a stop.

As I slide my finger out of her warm wet pussy, I rotate it in a circular motion at the same time while putting gentle pressure on her clit. This little gesture earns me a few jerking motions from her hips along with one last moan. I pull her dress back over her thighs, then push her body up into a sitting position on my lap again. Willow gazes into my eyes while grinding her ass against my painfully hard cock. I place the finger I used to pleasure her with into my mouth, sucking her sweet essences off it. I lean in to whisper into her ear, "Just as I thought, you taste as sweet as you smell, like honey."

Chapter 10

Willow
"50 Shades of Grey Girl"

I can't help but stare in fascination at Connor. I am surprised at the bold words that flow effortlessly from his lips. My breath catches in shock as I watch him place the finger coated with the release of my orgasm into his mouth. He sucks his finger clean. His action causes a surge of heat to course through my body down to my core.

Connor smiles as if he knows how he is affecting me. His devilish smile makes his appearance even more spectacular. "Damn, you're even hotter when you smile, if that's even possible," I blurt out. Apparently, the filter from my brain to my mouth still hasn't recovered from the numbing sensation of the alcohol.

This cab ride experience is the most erotic, sexual thing I've ever done in public. I wonder if this is normal for him. I'm so out of my comfort zone, but I'm so fucking aroused. I've never been with a man that wanted sex out of the bedroom.

I never thought of being a 50 Shades of Grey girl, but damn I would be so down with some hand tying, blindfolding, and a little ass slapping if that's what Connor's into. I put a stop to gags, canes, and slave collars though. Everyone has their hard limits, so I guess those are mine.

"Up and out gorgeous," Conner orders me and then kisses the tip of my nose as he opens the door of the cab.

After we step out of the cab, I bend over to grab my purse that had fallen off my shoulder during our escapade. I feel the feather touch of the cool night air on my upper thighs. I recall a little too late how short my dress is and consider the view I must be giving Connor. I let out a little squeal as he gives me a playful swat on my ass, as though he read my mind. I jerk back into a standing position. He then places his hand on my ass as he tucks my body into his side. He pulls out a wad of cash from his pocket to pay the driver.

I feel awkward about the cabby having a front-row seat to everything we did in his back seat. When Connor kissed the hell out of me, nothing else existed. It was like all my surroundings disappeared. His kiss has the power to melt away the rest of the world. I tilt my head to peer through the side window of the cab to glance at the driver. He's inhaling and exhaling at a fast pace indicating heavy breathing. He reaches between his legs and adjusts his crotch. Before he drives away, he wipes sweat beads from his forehead with the back of his hand. Obviously, we gave him quite a show.

We head to the hotel's reception desk for Conner to get us a room. My thoughts keep focusing on Connor's mouth and hand. I've never been kissed, or finger fucked like that in my life. My body feels like a vibrator because it will not stop humming. I glance up at Connor and find him staring at me like a predator that's about to enjoy his prey. Damn, I'm glad to be his prey tonight. I want him to feast on my body. I want him to hit that magical spot again and again. I can't believe how much my body craves the touch of this man.

As we approach the elevator, I whisper to Connor, "I've never done anything like this before."

He smiles as he leans his head to my ear and whispers, "Babe, I know. You might have already mentioned that a time or two tonight." He then nibbles on my earlobe causing my body to shiver, which I know he felt. By the time we enter the elevator, my pussy is throbbing with the need of his cock or skillful hand. I'm glad to find we have the elevator to ourselves, as Connor pushes a button to our floor. When the doors close, I catch him off guard by taking both of my hands and shoving his chest causing his back to collide with the elevator wall. Not wanting to waste any time, I unbuckle his belt.

"Connor, I've never been fucked good in my whole life. Now, I need to be fucked really good, and after that cab ride I know damn well you can fuck me good." Again, no filter between mouth and brain, but at this point who gives a shit. I explain my new 'fuck plan' to him, because even drunk and horny it seems I still need an organized plan. "Are we on the same page here, Connor?" I ask with an unexpected demanding tone in my voice.

Connor gives me a coy smile and asks, "So your cunt's craving my cock?"

His dirty mouth should repulse me, but it does the opposite. None of my other lovers were dirty talkers. For the first time, I realize how a few dirty words can amp up the excitement. This man drives me wild with every inch of him, even his words. His presence, his touch, his smell, how powerful it must feel to have so much control over someone. I wish I possessed that talent. I'm brought out of my inner muse when Connor pushes me backward out of the elevator doors, which have opened. He has the demeanor of a predator claiming his prey, only stopping his pushing when my back hits the wall in the hallway.

That's it! I can't take this aching need I sense in my core for another second. As my back hits the hallway wall, I make my plea in a breathy, sultry voice I don't even recognize. "Connor, I can't wait a second longer. I've never been this turned on. Your lips, your hands, hell even the little dirty words you say. I never knew words were this powerful... I AM ABOUT TO EXPLODE!" I exclaim.

He pulls back away from me to stare into my eyes asking, "Has no one ever used words to get you all hot and bothered before?" I shake my head no while biting my bottom lip getting embarrassed. Having no filter between my mouth and brain is embarrassing but having to analyze my spoken words is mortifying.

"Well, in that case, let me be your first," he says with his devilish smile, then continues, "Let's get you to the room so you can sit on my face as I suck on your clit with my mouth. I want to flick my tongue back and forth over your sweet little nub as I finger fuck you until you cum in my mouth.

Then, I'm gonna fuck your cunt so hard that your clit is going to quiver and your tits and ass will bounce from the sheer fuck force being imposed on your pussy. I'm gonna make your pussy purr and then it will cum all over my cock and drip down my balls," Connor says with a cocky grin. He knows exactly what he's doing to me. By this point, my mouth has gone dry. His words cause my panties to become wetter as tingles of pleasure shoot through my body down to my core.

I'm panting so hard I may hyperventilate. "The walk to the room will take too long. I haven't felt the touch of a man in two years, Connor, two very long damn years. Now! Connor now! Don't make me beg," I plead.

"Then wall sex it is. Baby girl you'll never have to beg me to pleasure your beautiful body," Connor declares as he unbuttons then unzips his jeans.

I reach into my handbag and pull out the roll of condoms Nikki and Ari gave me. His eyes widen as he sees how long the roll is. Connor grabs one, tears it loose from the bottom, then rips it open with his teeth. He even makes that move look sexy. He pushes his underwear down in the front, giving me the first look at his thick cock as he rolls the condom on it.

I don't think I've ever seen a cock that big and I'm a doctor. I'm not even sure it will fit in me. It's not just long, but thick with an angry red head standing at attention. I've never been one to give blow jobs, but my mouth is watering at the thought of sucking his massive cock. Connor grabs me by the hips and presses my back against the wall. A small squeal escapes me as he lifts me. I spread my thighs and wrap my legs around his waist, forcing the hem of my little black dress to rise.

"I see you're planning an all-nighter with that many condoms. Let's see if we can work our way through your supply and turn you into a cock loving slut by morning. MY cock loving slut that is," Connor says, emphasizing the word my. He grabs my lace panties, rips them off, and stuffs them into his pocket. He grabs my right ass cheek with his left hand to steady me against the wall, and with his right hand pushes the head of his cock against my opening. I whimper as he slides the head of his cock in, spreading open my dripping wet pussy.

He continues sliding his cock inside between my velvet-soft walls, slowly and tediously working my pussy down the shaft of his rock-hard cock causing my senses to explode. I grasp his muscular shoulders tight as I moan with the full exquisite stretching sensation I have inside me. His cock is so thick he must stop after about half the length of his shaft is inserted to allow my body to adjust. I know it's been awhile, but I never remember feeling this full as my pussy stretches and grips his cock.

"Damn, your pussy is so fucking tight. My personal sunshine pussy," Connor whispers into my ear. He then begins to fuck me good and hard as I'd requested.

He starts thrusting his hips at a painfully slow speed. Once I get adjusted to his massive size, I let out a desperate whimper signaling him to go a little deeper and harder. Connor seems to read my body like a familiar book. Without me having to say a word he thrusts in and out harder, deeper, faster. It's just what my body needs. All I can do is lean my head against the cool wall, holding on for the ride as all my senses awaken.

My body feels like a live wire energized with electricity. I feel his right-hand slide between us, stopping when it meets my swollen clit. He applies pressure and rotates his thumb in a small circle over it. It doesn't take long before I feel the walls of my pussy start tightening up in a pulsating rhythm. I know I'm close now. Connor must be able to feel it too because right as I start my orgasm, he encircles his mouth over mine and absorbs the moans escaping from my mouth into his. The wave of the most intense, rolling orgasm I've ever experienced explodes and washes over my body.

As I'm coming down off what seemed like a Tsunami wave

of pleasure, I realize Connor is staring at my face and talking, "Damn, Sunshine, I love watching you cum on my cock. It's a view I could get used to."

I let out a gasp as he pulls back, leaving my body. Connor tries to zip his pants with one hand and hold me up with his other. He takes a quick glance up and down the hallway. When he focuses his chocolate, brown eyes back on me, he smiles a very sexy, hot smile. "Baby, we've got to make it into the room unless you're into voyeurism," he says. I nod my head in agreement still too out of breath to speak

. I glance down at his hand as it seems he's having trouble with his zipper. I look back up at his face. "The damn condom is stuck in the zipper, fuck it," he growls. With his pants up but still unzipped, he places my feet back on the floor, leans in pushing his shoulder against my stomach causing me to bend at the waist over his shoulder. He scoops me up into a fireman's hold making me squeal, then carries me toward our room. It's a good thing I'm not expected to walk because my legs are still quivering from my intense orgasm.

As he carries me down the hall, Conner swats my ass and explains, "Quiet; we're in a hotel." I giggle. I feel his hand on my bare ass, which must be exposed since my dress is so short. As we enter the room, he massages it, causing me to moan. Once the door is closed behind us, I'm thrown into the air, landing flat on my back on the bed. Another squeal escapes.

"Babe, I said quiet. I guess I'll have to show you what happens to naughty girls who don't behave," Connor says, stalking towards the bed, removing his clothes as he moves.

When he gets to the edge of the bed, he leans over and kisses my leg above my ankle, slowly working his way up towards my thigh with kisses leaving chill bumps in their path. As he gets to my inner thigh, he grabs my dress with both hands, in one swoop it's off and thrown to the floor. I reach behind me, unfasten my bra and collapse back onto the bed. He stares at me, raking his eyes up and down my body.

"You're beautiful Willow, from your head, to your

pretty little shaved pink pussy, to your sexy little feet," he says as he lowers his body between my legs, allowing only his warm breath to blow on my throbbing clit as he moves across my mound to kiss my other thigh.

I decide to end this sweet torture and grab his head mid shift, shoving him face first into my throbbing pussy. I start grinding my hips shamelessly, letting out a loud moan as his tongue delves into my opening, exploring at will. He tilts his head, focusing his tongue on my clit. He slides one of his fingers into me, bending it upwards as he does. He again massages my G-spot, licking and sucking on my clit as he finger fucks me like he said he would.

I grab his hair and hold him firm as I vigorously grind his face. I moan as I have what can only be described as the biggest orgasm of my life. I feel like I am climbing up a cliff as a pulsating sensation takes over my entire body. Every muscle in my body tightens, and my legs quiver as my body drops off the cliff in pure ecstasy. I feel my velvet walls convulse, gripping, and milking his finger as I climax. When I float back into my body, I realize Connor is staring at me with a look of pure satisfaction.

"That felt amazing. Thank you," I struggle to say as I try to calm my racing heart.

"Not as amazing as it was to watch, but don't thank me yet. We're far from done. I intend to show you what happens to naughty girls who can't be quiet in the hallway. Remember, we have more condoms to go through to make up for your last two years without sex," he says through his sexy smile while winking at me.

Connor proceeds to show me exactly what happens to naughty girls who can't behave. He does everything he said he would do to me when we were in the hall, plus a lot more. I'm finally getting fucked good, no I'm being fucked out of my mind! I never knew sex could be so amazing.

Chapter 11

Drake
"Man-Whore"

As I sit here taking a deep breath, trying to calm my irritated nerves, I notice I've developed a twitch in the corner of my right eye. This sexy little hot number I've been sitting by has not shut her fucking mouth the entire night, and her squeaky little voice is driving me bat shit crazy. I can't seem to drink enough alcohol to numb my ears. Damn, the things I must endure for the sake of pussy. I smirk at my own thoughts.

Since the deep breathing doesn't help, I glance around the bar trying to tune out the sound of her voice altogether. It's not like I've had to put a lot of input into our conversation. It's as if someone has placed her on autopilot and all I must do is smile and nod my head every ten minutes.

While glancing around, a chick standing across the bar catches my attention. She arrived with the woman Connor left with. She has short brown hair and a smile that makes my mouth water. I rarely pay much attention to dark headed women. Blondes are my type, but there's just something about her that's intriguing.

Judging by the number of shot glasses being filled in front of her, I guess she's buying a round of shots for everyone at her table. The redhead from the same table comes to stand by her. They are whispering and laughing together. Damn, she's got a sexy laugh. The tone of her voice is a soothing balm to my tortured ears. It's getting late, and the crowd has thinned out somewhat, so I'm able to listen in on their conversation.

I discover the brunette's name is Nikki and redhead's name

is Ari. They're talking about men. The redhead, Ari, is cute in a girl-next-door kind of way. She's to meek, mild, and all around too sweet of a look for my taste. I like the feisty, spirited looking brunette, Nikki. Their names are the only thing of interest I've heard in their conversation so far.

I find Nikki's body language more my taste for conversation. She's twisting her slender neck while taking her hand and massaging lightly. Then, she slides her fingertips down her neck, stopping right before she gets to her luscious full-sized breasts. Her hand zeroes in on a medallion on her neckless. She twirls it between her fingers.

As I'm wondering how her skin would taste if I traced the same path along her neck down to her breast with my tongue, she slides her tongue over her luscious plump bottom lip. As she brings her tongue back into her mouth, she sucks in her bottom lip. Damn, thinking of things I could do with that mouth is making me hard.

I wonder how her mouth and tongue would feel wrapped around the head of my cock. I almost groaned at the image I've created in my mind. I glance over at Ari who is now watching me, and by the small smile upon her lips, I can tell she knows I've been checking her friend out.

"Nikki, there's a really hot guy across the bar that can't seem to take his eyes off you," Ari says snitching on me.

I was right, busted. Nikki looks my way until our eyes meet. I put on my panty wetting smile raising my beer bottle to tip the top in her direction. Then, I give her a chin lift, the universal sign of hello.

Nikki tells Ari, "He's the guy that Willow's new man was here with. Uhmm... wait here with the shots for a minute, I want to go over to say hello."

Just as Nikki turns and sashay what I'm assuming is a fine-looking ass over in my direction, the sexy blonde I didn't remember was sitting next to me, much less remember her name, leans her head on my shoulder asking, "Babe, are you even listening to me?" It seems I've missed my every ten-minute nod and smile.

I tilt my head to glance at her and mutter "No, baby I'm not."

Women have called me many things I can admit to, but the one thing I'm not is dishonest. I have no reason to be. I don't want a girlfriend and the headaches that comes with relationships. I make a point not to lead a woman on. I make it clear if it's a relationship they want, they will not find it with me so search elsewhere before the sex. There are too many women willing to have a night of fun to put up with the clingy ones.

The blonde sticks her bottom lip out in an overextended pout right before placing a kiss on my cheek, which at once makes me think of Nikki and her plump bottom lip. I glance back up in Nikki's direction to find she's glaring at me with slit eyes with a grim line on her lips. I smile at her while winking my eye, which if her expression is anything to go by, has the same effect as if I lit a fire under her ass. She glares at me while mouthing the word man-whore. It's a word I'm well acquainted with because I have heard it on more than one occasion. She then turns stomping back toward Ari. I realize that I assumed right- she has a beautiful, sexy little round ass. It's got a heart shape, which makes my cock even harder.

"Never mind, let's head back to our table," Nikki tells Ari as she loads the shot glasses into her hands.

"What? What happened to change your mind?" Ari asks.

"Man-whore!" is Nikki's only reply.

Then Ari turns to look at me noticing the blonde that still has her head on my shoulder. She shakes her head in disbelief while gathering the rest of the shot glasses, then follows Nikki back to their table. I can't help but laugh. I know what I'm doing pisses most women off, but I can't seem to stop myself. I enjoy watching their response too damn much to behave. The ones that my behavior doesn't faze are the perfect ones for me because they know I am not interested in a relationship.

Chapter 12

Willow
"The Walk of Shame"

I wake with a pounding headache from the bottomless pit of hell. My eyes don't want to open, but I know its morning since the sunlight is seeping through my closed eyelids. I pull the blanket up to shield my eyes from the light and snuggle deeper into my pillow to sleep this headache away.

As I'm waiting for the bliss that only sleep can create, I realize my pillow is radiating with heat and has a heartbeat. "What the…. Shit! Shit! Shit!" I mumble. The memories hit me like a boulder hitting my aching head. Now that my mind is awake, I try to remember where I am and what happened last night. I wonder what I'm about to sit up and face.

The human pillow I'm lying on twitches, causing my legs to shift. I can't help but smile at the delicious soreness suddenly felt between my legs. I haven't felt this way in over two years. Wait, I can't remember ever being this sore. The soreness causes memories of Connor and of last night to rush through my mind.

I'm mortified at my behavior. I've never been a very sexual person. What the hell came over me? I could blame my predicament on the alcohol, but I would be lying to myself if I did. I never knew I had an inner slut waiting for the right guy to wake her up. Shit, how will I face him after last night. Face, what a word.! With the thought of that one word, face, I remember where his was on my body, where I had mine on his body, the cab ride, the hallway, the room, and bending over the table in the room. Oh, the things this man did to my body! The spanking, the dirty talk, I enjoyed every damn minute.

Wait, what if he thinks I'm an easy ho? I can't face him knowing he thinks that. Though with him, I am an easy ho. I need to stop panicking. What I need is a plan. First, I need to assess the situation. By Connor's rhythmic breathing pattern, I know he's still asleep.

I move my shoulder that's not pressing into his side to make sure he doesn't have an arm around me, which he doesn't. Okay, the plan is to ease up out of bed, dress, no... find my clothes then dress. The goal is to get the hell out of here before he wakes, and I'm forced to face judgment. I know this is the coward's way out, but I have no experience in a situation like this. For future reference, I need a plan in place so if my inner slut retakes possession of my body I'll know what to do.

I ease my head up and study Connor, who is still sleeping. He looks hotter than he did last night. Last night he had a bad boy, alpha-male hotness about him. Now, watching him sleep I see his face has an innocent boyish resemblance, but still hot. His dark hair is a tossed mess on top of his masculine face.

There should be a law against a man looking this good in the morning. I can imagine my appearance right now. I decide not to lift the covers to get up; instead, I slide over to the edge of the bed feet first underneath the covers. When I reach the edge, I slip down until I'm sitting on my ass in the floor beside the bed. I take a chance and sneak a peep up over the side of the bed to make sure my escape plan is working. So far so good, he hasn't moved.

As I stand my head swims causing my stomach to flip upside down. I get back on all fours and crawl around the room to find my clothes. Crawling instead of standing keeps my head from spinning so much. Careful not to make a sound, I crawl around on the floor and locate my dress, one shoe, my bra, then the other shoe, but no panties. After searching for a few minutes, I remember Connor ripping them off my body. The memory makes me quiver sending a wave of pleasure to my core.

I crawl into the dark bathroom where the only light is the few rays of sunlight filtering in from the bedroom. I force myself into a standing position and gag from the nauseating sickness caused by the alcohol. I put on my bra, my dress, then get my shoes on in record time.

As I turn to go to the bedroom and search for my purse, I catch my reflection in the mirror. Damn, I look terrible! If mortification weren't the reason for keeping me from waking Connor, my looks would be. My hair is worse than my usual bed-head hair. The back of it is standing up as if I stuck my finger in an electrical outlet. Strands of hair are sticking out everywhere, giving my hair a teased style. I've heard people use the phrase 'freshly fucked look' before, but I've never had that look. I guess there's always a first.

My eyes are even more frightening. My smoky eye makeup has smeared all around my eyes making me resemble a raccoon. I grab a tissue from the tissue box sitting on the bathroom counter and wipe off as much of the makeup as possible, then run my fingers through my hair to smooth it as much as I can.

I peer down at my dress and try to smooth out the wrinkles. Realizing this is as good as I can fix my appearance, I tiptoe out of the bathroom, thankful my stomach has settled down. I locate my purse on Connor's side of the bed on the floor. After reaching down and picking it up, I pause for a moment. I want to look at him one last time, so I watch him sleep as I try to memorize every detail about him. After a final gaze, I turn then tiptoe across the room and slip out the door.

A sigh of relief escapes my mouth as the cab pulls up in front of my house. But as I glance around, I realize neighbors are out doing domesticated things in their yards. The dark shadow of dread consumes my relief as I contemplate the walk of shame I am about to perform. I've never done the walk of shame before.

I peer down at my dress, and yes, you can tell I've been out in this dress all night. With my sex hair, and the little bit of smeared makeup that's still left on my face, it screams "walk of shame." I feel like a teenager caught trying to sneak in after a night of partying. I need to pull my big girl panties up and walk with my head held high, except I remember I can't because I'm going commando at the moment.

I pay the cab driver and thank him. This time I remember to keep my legs together as I slide out of the cab, so I don't give my audience a peep show. Just as I expected, old Ms. Jones starts waving at me, screaming "Good morning," bringing the other neighbors' attention in my direction.

I give a quick wave, then haul ass into my house as gracefully as I can. I rush in so fast I trip over a table that's been knocked over just inside the door. Grabbing the wall is the only thing that keeps me from face planting on the floor. Startled to see the table on the floor, I glance around and wonder if someone has broken into my home.

I calm down when I see two pairs of high-heel shoes lying on the floor by the overturned table. It's the same shoes Nikki and Ari were wearing last night. I was in such a rush to get the "walk of shame" over I never noticed Nikki's car sitting in my driveway. I'm thankful they stayed here last night considering how much we all drank.

I yawn and realize I need a toothbrush and a long, hot, relaxing bath. As I enter my bedroom heading toward my bathroom, I unsurprisingly find Nikki and Ari passed out in my bed. I guess I'm the only one that left with a man last night. Not wanting to sit through an interrogation session before my relaxing bath, I tiptoe to the bathroom without waking the drill squad.

I close the bathroom door and lock it, so they'll leave me in peace for a little longer. Once the tub is full and I've added scented bath oil, I slide down into the steaming, hot, relaxing bath water. I can't believe how awesome the heat is on my sore girly bits.

I never knew how much energy it takes to sneak around. As I lean back against the tub, the aching of my sore spots causes memories of last night to rush back. I relax and allow myself to reminisce through every detail. The more I reminisce, the more I wish I didn't sneak away this morning. I would like to see him again. I should've at least left a note.

When the hot bath water starts to cool, I decide it's time to face my drill squad. Wincing, I drag my tender girl bits out of the tub and towel off. While slipping into my favorite fluffy blue robe that I keep hanging on the back of the bathroom door, I decide I'm willing to share some details with them, but plan on taking the most embarrassing parts to my grave.

I open the bathroom door to find Nikki and Ari awake and sitting on the edge of my bed staring at me. The aroma of coffee hits my nose. Ari must have anticipated my need because she hands me a fresh cup of coffee.

"How was your night?" Nikki questions, as she starts the interrogation.

"It was nice, REALLY nice," I respond. I can't help the devious smile that forms across my face as I walk over to my dresser, put my coffee mug down, get out my favorite pajama pants with a pink tank top and put them on. I grab my coffee off the dresser then walk over and join them on the bed. As I ease down onto my sore ass, Ari burst out into laughter.

I glare at her with furrowed brows wondering what's so funny when she says, "Oh, hell no, you're not gonna get by with a just 'nice, really nice' comment. You can't even sit down. Spill it!" Ari demands.

We all three burst out laughing. After regaining my composure, I tell them about my fabulous, sensual night with Connor and all his hotness, leaving out the details I plan to carry to my grave. I even tell them about Connor being a master of dirty talk, and how it's a shame no other man has ever talked that way to me before.

"Yeah dirty talk is a fading art that men shy away from, but who can blame them? When a man talks dirty to a woman its sexual harassment, but when a woman talks dirty to a man, its $2.99 per minute," Nikki comments as Ari nods her head agreeing.

"Did you make plans to go out again?" Ari asks with a huge grin while bouncing on the bed and doing a little clap like an excited child.

"No," I mumble, then throw myself onto my pillows with a long sigh.

"Why not?" Ari asks with a frown on her face.

"I was embarrassed by how eager and slutty I must have appeared last night. I was too much of a coward to face him this morning," I explain, feeling stupid. I grab a pillow to cover my face to avoid seeing their disappointment. For the second time this morning I regret not leaving a note. I feel one of them grab my coffee mug out of my hand before I spill it.

"What? Why?" Nikki asks as she grabs the pillow out of my hands and forces me to face them.

"Because! I don't do one-night stands. He must think I'm a slut. I didn't have a plan on how to deal with the morning after," I explain.

"You and your damn plans. One day, Willow, your gonna have to learn to wing it. You can't plan your entire life. For a smart woman you sure can be stupid," Nikki lectures.

"Thanks a lot, Nikki! Why don't you tell me how you really feel?" I say.

"Ok. First, it's not a big deal to have a one-night stand. People do it all the time. Second, if you freak out and leave without as much as a note, it looks worse," Nikki explains as she tells me exactly how she feels, which I didn't want to hear.

"Well, on top of being embarrassed, I looked like crap. I had sex hair, which wasn't sexy, and my makeup was a mess. I'm sure he wouldn't have thought that look was too sexy, I don't think so. Not to mention how wonderful, sweet and sexy he looked, lying there asleep. He would've been like a coyote wanting to chew off his arm instead of waking me had the tables been turned and he woke up first," I snap back.

"Don't be a drama queen. If he's the one who gave you the sex hair, I'm sure he wouldn't mind seeing it. He probably would've even taken pride because he made you look so well sated," Nikki snaps back at me.

"Well, it's obvious you like him. Just call him and see if he would like to have coffee or something. Coffee would be a quick and easy meet-up, if you want to cut it short, then you can. Nikki and I will do a role-playing pretend phone call with you, so you'll feel comfortable enough to make the call.

Now that you've gotten out there and got your feet wet again in the dating pool, don't backtrack to dry land. The last thing this world needs is another lonely cat woman, or in your case, a dog woman since you love dogs," Ari suggests with excitement on her face lightly bouncing again. She's like my personal cheerleader right now.

"Hey, it's not a bad thing to be prepared with a plan," I complain grabbing my coffee from Ari before she can spill it.

"It is when you can't function without one," Nikki continues with her lecture.

"Well, I can't call him; I didn't get his phone number. I was too preoccupied with last night's festivities to think about asking for it," I say in a whiny voice.

"That's ok. We can try to locate his phone number. We'll stalk him on the internet using his name," Ari suggests.

"Grrrrr! We can't. I don't even know his last name. Damn, I sound like a country song," I confess.

"We can plan to go back to The Club this coming weekend to see if he's there," Nikki suggests.

"Can't, I'm on call this weekend," I say. I take a deep breath, sigh, then continue "Guys, last night was one of the best nights I've had in a long time. Best sex I've ever had in my life, but let's face it I messed up by not getting any personal information besides a first name. I don't even know if he's interested in seeing me again. It's a lost cause. I do agree to no backtracking though. I need to move on and learn from my mistakes. Next time I'll remember to get contact information, or at least leave a note before making a run for it."

"Well, at least there's a silver lining- you agreed to go out with Nikki and me again. Getting you laid and interested in having a social life was the goal for last night's plan, and that's what we did. Goal accomplished!" exclaims Ari, the forever cheerleader of our group.

"Enough about my night, what about you guys? What happened after I left? Meet anybody?" I ask as I start my own interrogation.

"We hung out and danced for a little while after you left. Oh, the other hotty that was sitting at the bar next to your man flirted with me from across the bar while some blonde was groping him! A complete Man-Whore!" Nikki says while scrunching up her face in distaste when saying Man-Whore.

"That Man-Whore is Conner's brother," I inform my two friends.

"You're joking!" Nikki gasps as I shake my head no at them.

"Well, hopefully, Connor's apple fell far from his family tree and rolled down the hill into the next orchard. Hopefully, he's not like his brother," Nikki says with wide, surprised eyes.

"For all I know, he could be a Man-Whore too. It's not like I was playing the hard to get virgin school girl last night. Instead, Slutty Willow woke up and came out to play. He probably thinks I'm a whore after the way I behaved last night! You know the saying if it looks like a duck and acts like a duck, then it is a duck?" I ask as I turn and throw myself face down into my pillows, almost spilling my coffee.

"I don't think Connor thinks you are a duck," Ari says as she takes my coffee away. I turn and glare at her. "Lighten up, worst-case scenario Connor thinks you're a slut. If you ever see him again and he spends time with you, he'll be able to tell how not slutty you are. He's the first person you've had sex with in two years. That's a very poor slut resume, honey," Ari says with a smirk.

I sit back up to focus the interrogation back to them. "What else happened last night and why in the hell have you not told us how fine Dom is? You've been holding out girl!" I say to Ari.

"Yeah, he is fine, but I've always looked at him more as a

brother than a guy. It would be like me wanting to date a close family member. Gross! So, no, I don't look at him that way," Ari explains with a look on her face that matches what she's saying.

"We took a cab here last night to wait for you. We didn't consider you could've come back here until after we unlocked your door. So, we crept in, leaving the lights off in order not to disturb you. I think Ari was a little too drunk to be quiet though," Nikki says with a chuckle.

"Me! You were the one falling in the dark, so I think you were just as drunk as me if not more!" Ari snaps at Nikki then we all laugh.

"So, that explains the mess by the door," I tell them while still laughing.

"I'll go clean it up, you two go cook breakfast," Nikki orders as she gets off the bed. I shake my head and stand up, then hold out my hand offering it to Ari to help her up. She takes my hand, pulls herself up, and we head to the kitchen to cook breakfast.

Chapter 13

Connor
"Fuck Fest"

I wake up from the best night's sleep I've had since starting this assignment. With my eyes still closed, I begin to stretch when I'm hit with Willow's scent, which immediately makes my cock grow hard. I can't control the urge of wanting to feast on her body. I reach over to pull her body against mine only to discover she's not in the bed. I sit up, rub my eyes and look around to find I'm alone in an empty hotel room.

"Sunshine, are you in the bathroom?" Only silence returns. I get up, sit on the side of the bed and glance around the room, hoping to find a note, sign, or something. There is nothing. I walk into the bathroom, nope, no note in here either.

After I finish my morning pee, I give up all hope of seeing her this morning and begin searching for my clothes. Seeing them spread out all over the floor is a friendly reminder of all the sex we had last night. Wall sex, bed sex, table in the corner sex, we really worked the room.

Damn, I can't seem to wrap my mind around why she took off without waking me or leaving a note. Last night was like a fuck fest with a sex-starved temptress. Our bodies were so in tune with one another. I imagine she felt the same. No woman can fake that many orgasms.

I reach down, grab my boxers, then locate my pants. As I try to slip my pants on, I can't seem to get the zipper to come down all the way. Upon closer inspection, I realize a portion of the first condom we used during the hallway sex is still trapped in the teeth of the zipper.

Damn, that was the first time I've had sex in a hotel hallway. Images of Willow flash through my mind. She was so hot with her swollen lips and fuck me eyes. I shake my head trying to clear my thoughts. If I keep thinking like this, I'll end up having to take care of this hard on with my bare hand before I leave this room.

As I free the condom from the zipper, I notice there is a rip down the side to the tip. Great, just my fucking luck. I head back to the bathroom, throw it away, then wash my hands. Hopefully, it didn't rip until after we were through fucking. I push that disturbing thought out of my mind and finish getting dressed. I stop to check my pockets, making sure I've got my wallet, cell phone, and keys.

When I reach my hand into my right front pocket, I feel lace. I grab hold and pull out a pair of panties. It's the panties I ripped off Willow's sexy ass last night. I hold them up to my nose and inhale deeply, taking in the smell of Willow's sweet essence. I decide there's no fucking way I'm throwing these away. I shove them back into my pocket, then head to the front desk to check out. Outside the hotel, I catch a cab back to The Club to get my truck.

After paying the cab driver, I get into my truck. As I crank it, I decide to check on Drake before heading back to my place. I'm going with the pretense of checking if he made it home ok last night; but honestly, he's got a house-keeper that cleans his place and keeps his fridge stocked full of food. I'm starving, and I haven't shopped for food for my house since we came to New Orleans for this case. All we've eaten since arriving in New Orleans is fast food, which I don't think I can stomach this morning. New Orleans has the best food in the world, but since arriving in town, we've been too busy to enjoy the more elegant restaurants.

We're renting an office building just outside the French Quarter while we are here for this assignment. The office space came with the option to rent a two-bedroom one bath apartment above it, which we did. This allows us a quick response time. All my team members live in Louisiana, but we all live in different areas away from New Orleans. The closest member to New Orleans is Drake, who owns a bayou home about an hour drive south from New Orleans. My team has the weekend off, so everyone else went home for the weekend.

Drake lives in an old one-story waterfront house off Bayou Rigolettes in Lafitte Louisiana. The home has three bedrooms, two bathrooms and was built in the mid-1800s. The outside is painted light green with forest green Bahama shutters. Over-size wide steps lead onto the front porch which spans the length of the house. Colossal fern plants are hanging from the porch rafters.

Drake's front door is unlocked as it usually is when he's home, so I walk right in. He's in his living room going through some case files for our current assignment. He's a workaholic. We both are, but work is the last thing on my mind after my recent fuck fest.

"About time you show up and help me with this case," Drake says as I enter the room.

"What? It's my weekend off, and if I remember right, it's your weekend off too," I remind him.

"So, when did you start taking off days? We don't actually take off days, remember?" Drake asks while looking at me suspiciously. He's right, we usually don't take time off even when the team has off time.

"Only by choice brother," I smirk, as I head for his kitchen with him staring at me with a puzzled look plastered on his face.

As I pull items from his cabinets and refrigerator to cook breakfast, Drake enters the kitchen. "How did your after-club date go last night?" Just the mention of last night triggers thoughts of Willow, bringing a smile to my face that I can't stop from forming. "Judging by the smug grin on your face it appears to have gone well brother.".

"Let's just say the best damn night of sex I've had in a long time; no change that, best damn sex in my life and let's leave it at that," I tell Drake as I continue making breakfast.

"That damn good? So, you'll be seeing her again?"

"Can't, didn't get a phone number or a last name." He stares in disbelief.

"So, let me get this straight… best sex ever, beautiful woman, dopey ass grin, and you didn't bother to get a phone number or a last name? And I'm the one that got called a man-whore," Drake says while shaking his head.

"Hold up. You're called a man whore because, well, you are one and you also like to irritate beautiful women by acting like an ass. I'm just an inconsiderate prick who was too preoccupied last night during a fuck fest to get a last name or phone number," I correct him.

"Wait, fuck fest? It's not like you to go after the slutty ones. That's more my type."

Not liking Drake comparing Willow to a slut, I point the knife I'm holding in his direction threatening, "Watch your mouth brother. Willow's not a slut. Judging by how many times she told me she's never done anything like that before, and based how tight her sweet little cunt was, I believe her."

"Hey, hold up. Let's back up to the fuck fest part."

"Not a chance in hell." I turn back around ignoring him to finish making breakfast.

Chapter 14

Willow
"Are You Shitting Me?"

Six weeks later......... With a disappointing growl, I wake early to start another day. Every time I dream of Connor, I'm awakened right before the most deliciously amazing and best part of the dream, which would be me having a mind-blowing orgasm.

"Damn," I say under my breath as I crawl out of bed and stand. I didn't get much sleep with working late last night and now getting up for an early shift today. I need to stick to one shift, this flipping back and forth is taking a toll on my energy level. My back feels stiff, so I kneel on the floor in the middle of my bedroom to do a few quick yoga stretches.

Just as I stretch into a downward dog position, my stomach rolls and a wave of nausea hits me like a derailing train. I cover my mouth with one hand while making a wild dash to the bathroom. I barely make it to the toilet before the persuasive force of my body causes projectile vomiting. I feel like the girl in the Exorcist movie scene. I half expect my head to rotate around like the girl's did in the movie.

After my up close and personal time with the porcelain prince has come to a close, I lay back on the cool tile floor to catch my breath. "What the hell!" Like most people, I hate vomiting. I hope I haven't caught a stomach virus. I do a mental replay of the past twenty-four hours to figure out why I'm so sick. I think back to my long shift yesterday at the hospital. It was late when I headed home. I was exhausted, starving, and every fast-food place I passed on my way home was closed.

When I arrived home, I found two-day-old seafood left-overs in my refrigerator. I did the quick smell test and decided it was okay to eat since it didn't have a bad odor. After scarfing down the food, I managed a quick shower before collapsing onto my bed. Damn, the seafood must have been bad. No more smell tests in the future. Mental note to self, throw away after a day is my new policy on left-over seafood.

After several minutes, I'm able to peel my body off the cold tile floor. After a quick shower, I dress in a pair of clean scrubs-all without having to vomit again. On my drive to work, I'm relieved to discover I feel somewhat better. My mind drifts back to the dream of Connor I had this morning, causing me to almost miss my turn.

I arrive at work and head straight to the employee break room for some much-needed coffee. I bypassed my usual great eye-opening first thing in the morning coffee when I woke up sick this morning. I pride myself on my coffee making skills. They rival any Starbucks.

The aroma of coffee hits my nose as I open the break room door. The smell is beckoning me to drink it. I have high hopes the coffee will clear my head. I can't get this morning's vivid dream of Connor off my mind. I wish I hadn't woken before the best part.

I walk over to the coffee pot and notice my friend Hank sitting at a table drinking coffee while reading the paper. I met Hank my first day on the job. He was an odd character from the start. Hank runs the ER lab. He's taller than I am, has sandy blonde hair, a cute smile with dimples, and a year-round tan.

From the start of our friendship I thought we were polar opposites. I can't count the many times I've walked into the lab and found his head bent over a table studying microorganisms, trying to discover everything possible about them. Unlike Hank, I'm all into killing off microorganisms before they kill off their host, otherwise known as my patient.

Hank's received many research grants to help in developing treatments against various diseases over the past few years.

Because of his unusual personality, it surprises most people to discover how intelligent he really is. He once told me he grew up in Southern California, and when he didn't have his head in a book, he had it on a surfboard surfing.

He's kept that SoCal accent while living here in New Orleans. Hank originally came here for a temporary position to help the hospital with a research grant and ended up accepting a permanent position. He still travels to find the perfect wave on his vacations though.

"Dude you look, um... totally pale. Sure you need to be here, dude?" Hank asks while squinting his face towards me as if my appearance disgusts him.

"Actually, I feel better than I did when I first crawled out of bed this morning. I think it was the two-day-old left-over seafood I ate last night."

"Totally understand that concept. Had my fair share of bad grub on the beach growing up," Hank says, agreeing with me it could have been the seafood.

Three hours later.... I'm now resting in the call room where the on-call doctors go to rest when they're not treating patients in the Emergency Room. I felt sick again after my shift started and thought it best to come in here to rest my head after embarrassing myself in front of a patient. I had to turn around and vomit in the trash can right in front of the patient during her exam.

This caused the patient I was treating to gag. I've never been so embarrassed in front of a patient in my whole career than that unbelievable moment. The nurse assisting with the exam rushed me out of the exam room with trash can in hand while apologizing to the patient for me.

I went by the lab on my way to the call room and had my blood drawn by Hank to see if I can self-diagnose. Then, I grabbed a can of ginger ale from behind the nurse's desk on my way to the call room to rest my spinning head. I'm hoping the ginger ale soothes my upset stomach.

Hopefully, its food poisoning and not a virus. At least with food poisoning, I won't worry that I've spread whatever it is to the patients I've already seen this morning or to the other staff members I'm working with today.

As I'm lying here on a bunk in the call room waiting for my lab results and for my head to stop spinning, my mind drifts back to the fabulous dream I was having this morning.

It amazes me that even though I only spent one night with Conner, I still can't get him off my mind. No one's ever had such an effect on me. I'm surprised that even feeling sick doesn't stop my mind from thinking of him.

During the last few weeks, I've went to The Club several times hoping Conner might be there. I've even recruited Nikki and Ari to help in my pursuit to find him.

They too have made many stops by The Club, scoping it out for Conner or his man-whore brother, as Nikki prefers to call Drake instead of using his actual name. At least if they found Drake, they could get a message to Connor giving him my phone number or at least maybe learn his last name.

When I'm not on-call, I've been going out with Nikki and Ari.

I laugh under my breath every time I remember Ari's comment about me finally getting out of the house with them. She said all it took was fantastic sex with a hot guy with no last name. So far, all attempts to find Conner No Name have ended in disappointment.

As I'm lying here, lost in thought, Hank slips into the room without me hearing him.

I'm startled and jump when he announces, "She lives!" I glare up at him to find he has a smile on his face.

"Sorry Will, dude, you're like in space in your mind. Results are in," Hank announces while waving the paper printout of my lab results high in the air.

"You didn't tell me you were stepping back out and dating again," Hank states with a smirk on his face.

"I'm not. I'm always working. With this lifestyle, I don't have the time to date, and you know that," I complain, furrowing my brows together confused of why he's thinking of my social life when all I want to know is what the lab results are.

The few times I have gone out with my girls doesn't fall under the label dating. I need to go out with a man for that title.

"Well, you've been doing the nasty with someone, maybe on the down low which is like totally cool. The body has needs you know," Hank replies while holding the papers up high in his hand flapping them back and forth with the movement of his wrist.

All I can think is I must have some STD with the comments Hank is making. Oh God. Oh no, Connor, I think as my mind races. I knew that night was too perfect. Just my luck, my first one-night stand and I catch something, even with the protection of a condom. Well, several condoms that is.

This must be some sort of divine punishment. My mind is on high alert with dozens of thoughts crashing around in my head all at once. I hope there's at least an antibiotic out there to get rid of it. Maybe Nikki has an herbal cure.

"I ran a complete panel of lab work on you just to make sure we know what, if any, little buggers are crawling through your system making you sick," Hank says as if he's pulling my thoughts out of my head.

"For heaven sakes Hank, what do I have and more importantly, can medication or some other treatment kill it?" I ask as desperation and anxiety sets in, causing chills to work their way up my spine.

"Dude, calm down a notch. In your condition, you need to try for total relaxation and calm. I used to do this meditation thing first thing every morning when I lived on the coast for total relaxation and focus......" Hank says as he describes his meditation ritual causing me to growl at him.

"Hank! Please focus on the current issue here and tell me the damn results please," I demand.

I'm sitting up ready to jump up to grab the damn papers from him. Hank senses this as he holds the results higher in one hand while putting his other hand in front of me to stop me from trying to take them from him.

"No worries dude. Your condition will cure itself in a few months," Hank says trying to keep from smiling.

Even though I try to hide it, he knows I'm a germ freak by the way I act when I'm in his lab. I'm always walking in with a pair of gloves on, and I hang out near the door, staying as far away as I can from his research. It's ironic I decided to become a doctor.

Once when he asked me about it, I just mumbled something to the effect of you shouldn't trespass on the zone of the enemy of humankind.

"What?" I ask, confused by his comment about my "condition."

"Dude, you are fine and congrats to you on having a little dude," Hank says with a chuckle, as he's unable to contain his laughter any longer.

"What, what little dude?" I ask with a confused look on my face that matches the confused state in my head. I can feel the color draining from my face.

"Your little dude. You are what I like to call prego," Hank announces.

"You've got to be shitting me! Pregnant? Pregnant! Um.... no, no I'm not pregnant. I would know if I'm pregnant, I'm a doctor after all," I say as a small feeling of panic grows inside my chest.

"Right, well labs don't lie, so no, I'm not shitting you. Dude, you are most definitely prego."

I sit feeling shell-shocked, staring off at the wall across the room. This can't be happening, this can't be happening, I keep repeating in my head. When was my last period? Shit, I can't remember.

Since I don't have a boyfriend now, and haven't for a long-time, I don't keep up with it. I stopped taking birth control because I don't need to be on it due to the lack of a sex life. Shit! There is no way, then I remembered Connor!

"Dude, your face is turning a lighter shade of pale and looking kind of sickly again. Might be best if you lie back down. My sister's morning sickness was a real bitch when she was prego with her little dude," Hank says as he assists me in laying back down.

He walks into the small bathroom connected to the call room then returns to the bunk where I'm now visibly deep breathing. He hands me the cool, wet cloth. It feels soothing when I place it on the back of my neck. He confesses, "I don't do so well with the upchucking stuff, so I'm going back to the lab. Want me to send in one of the nurses?"

"No, I'll be fine. I just need to lie still for a few more minutes. Thanks for everything," I reply as I give Hank the best fake smile I can form in my current state of mind. Hank gives a small laugh, shakes his head, then heads for the door.

Before he walks out, he turns back to face me, "Will, congrats again on the little dude. I'm guessing this is a surprise, so I'll keep it on the down low. And Will...." Hank waits until I look up at him before he continues.

"Yeah?"

"Everything has a way of working out. Hang in there," Hank says in a consoling tone.

"Thanks again," I tell him as he opens the door then leaves.

I can't believe this shit. It can't be right. Labs don't lie as Hank says, but people do make mistakes and errors do occur. This must be a mistake. Maybe Hank got my lab work switched with someone else's. That must be it! I remember seeing a pregnant patient sitting in one of the exam rooms earlier when I passed by it in my mad dash to the call room. That has to be it.

There's no way I'm "prego" after one night. Granted, it was a night full of multiple times with multiple orgasms, but we used condoms that were new. Several in fact. We used them each time we had sex.

A little voice in the back of my mind creeps up to remind me condoms aren't 100% effective. "Oh, shut up," I tell that little voice out loud as I push myself up off the bunk to gather my stuff with a bit of newfound hope.

There's only one way to clear up this mistake, and the sooner the better. Since my shift ended the moment I vomited in a patient's room, I will take care of this ASAP.

I head out of the call room and notice they've called in a replacement for me. After saying a prayer of thanks, I can leave without the guilt of my coworkers being short staffed. I say my usual goodbyes to everyone as I pass in a hurry to the exit and head straight to my car.

I hear a few staff members wishing me get wells on my way out the door, but I don't lose focus. I'm on a mission determined to get this cleared up as fast as possible. I get in my car and head to the nearest pharmacy that's on my route home.

When I finally arrive home, I go straight to the bathroom, carrying my pharmacy bag in one hand and a sack full of water bottles in the other. I dump the bags out onto the floor of the bathroom. I stare in awe at the pregnancy tests mixed together with the multiple water bottles rolling across the floor. Ten pregnancy tests to be exact, each one of them a different brand. I may have gone overboard buying so many tests, but I've got to be sure without a doubt.

I look through the tests to decide which one I should use first. There are tests with results that have blue lines, results that have pink plus signs, and results with the words pregnant or not pregnant. I like the words I decide. Words are simple, they are straightforward with an answer leaving out any confusion.

I sit on the toilet to begin the test. I pee on the stick, then place it face up on the counter like the instructions say. I've never taken a pregnancy test before. I didn't realize how hard it is to complete without getting pee all over your hand.

I try to distract myself by washing my hands. After the longest three minutes of my life, I turn to look at the results. Pregnant. I decide I don't care for words after all, so I start drinking my second water bottle to take another test.

After what feels like hours, I've completed all ten tests.

Standing in my bathroom clenching the white pedestal sink, I glare at myself in the mirror.

"You had a plan" I mutter to my reflection. I release my grip on the sink, and with trembling hands pick up the last pregnancy test to take one more look to see if I've read it right the first time. Yep, just like the other nine tests- positive. I turn on the cold water and lightly douse my face with it.

After having a mini mental meltdown, I leave the bathroom in a stunned state. I mindlessly wander through my home, thinking of how I've ended up being a single mother.

I slowly ease back into an antique leather chaise lounge next to one of my front windows overlooking the streetcar route. Thoughts of how I ended up in this situation clutter my mind.

After what seems like hours have passed, the dinging bell and clanking of a St. Charles streetcar brings me back to a sobering reality. All the water I consumed has left me feeling waterlogged and sick to my stomach with a need to lie down.

I walk to my bedroom in a daze. When I reach the bed, I lie down hoping to relax and figure out how to get control over my emotions. I feel exhaustion setting in. My body is slowly relaxing, but my mind is still in high gear.

I need to figure out a plan of action. I like plans. They give me a sense of control over my life. I'm an educated woman for heaven sakes, and well capable of figuring out how to handle this situation.

I go over the facts: I'm pregnant, I have no clue of the father's last name or how to get in touch with him, I have a crazy ass work schedule, I'm single, and I live alone.

Oh hell, what am I going to do? I am so fucking screwed. In a panic, I decide to call in reinforcements, so I pull my cell phone out of my pocket to call Nikki. By the time Nikki answers, I'm a nervous wreck and burst into tears at the sound of her voice.

"Willow? What's wrong honey? Are you ok?" Nikki asks in a rushed voice laced with concern.

"I…. I…. need tea," I manage to say in between sobs.

"Honey, calm down and talk to me. You're freaking me out. I will bring you tea, but you've got to give me more information here. I won't be able to drive like this," Nikki says.

I can tell by the high pitch of her voice she's getting nervous with every second that goes by with the only sounds on the other side of this call being my sobs. I can't help it; I can't seem to stop. "Breathe Willow," Nikki encourages trying to calm me.

I take a few deep breaths to calm down then begin again, "I… I… need you to come, (sniff). Bring Ari (sniff) with tea here. I need (sniff) help to come up with a plan of action. I… I don't know what to do," I say as I finally get the words out.

"A plan of action? A plan for what honey?" Nikki asks still in her high-pitched voice.

"I…. I…. I'm pregnant!" I confess before bursting into tears again.

Nikki lets out a breath of relief. "Is that all?" she asks.

I sit stunned at her comment, then with a growl I ask, "Is that all? Is that all! What the hell do you mean is that all!"

"I didn't mean it like that, but you were scaring the hell out of me. I had a hundred ugly thoughts of what could be wrong racing through my mind, and well, a baby is the least of all the terrible choices, so to say. Still, a biggie, but not doom or death," Nikki tries to explain.

"Let me hang up, then I will gather my tea and swing by to pick up Ari on my way. Don't call her for heaven sakes, you'll scare the shit out of her with all your crying. After I pick her up, we'll head straight to your house. Are you sure you're pregnant? What if I run by the pharmacy on the way to your house and pick up a few bottles of water and a couple of pregnancy tests to make sure?"

I gag at the thought of anymore water. "No! No! I can't drink anymore water. I've already taken ten different types and brands of pregnancy tests. There are pink pluses, parallel blue lines, and the little bitch of the one that has the nice word pregnant glaring at me. I need my friends and tea," I explain in a mini rant.

"OK, ok. Calm down! I'll be there as soon as I can. Try to stop panicking. We're a family. We got this. I'll be there soon. I love you, sis," Nikki says reassuringly.

" Love you too. Hurry and get here as fast as you safely can." I hang up the phone to wait on my girl posse to arrive.

I grow restless lying in bed waiting. Thoughts of Conner enter my mind, as they always do when I'm relaxing, or better yet trying to relax. I try to imagine how he might respond to the news of my pregnancy if we had kept seeing each other. I want to think he would overall be happy, but scared at first of course. That's expected. Look how well I'm taking the news.

I imagine that he'd be excited after the initial shock. A voice in the back of my mind asks what if he didn't want kids? The next images that pop into my mind are of him becoming angry at the news of the unexpected pregnancy, demanding I end the pregnancy, screaming it was a mistake.

The thought of this causes anger to swell in my chest. Oh, hell no! I would tell him that he's the mistake, not the baby and that I'm keeping my baby. He's the one I would need to get rid of.

I snap out of my daydream or daymare when the realization I'm carrying a little human slam into me. The word pregnancy isn't just a medical term to me anymore.

Even though I'm scared out of my damn mind, and have a ton of issues to figure out, I love this baby and want him or her. I'm amazed that a mothering instinct has already kicked in. I don't know how, but I'll find a way to make this work. I have a good family and friends to lean on. We will be ok.

Unfortunately, I don't get to rest much longer because all the water I've consumed for the tests is going straight through my body filling my bladder. As I make my way to the bathroom, I figure I will probably spend most of my night in there between the water consumption along with the all-day "morning sickness" I experienced today.

With the thoughts of going back and forth to the bathroom, I wonder if I should save myself time by sleeping in the tub. It would save me from all the walking back and forth. The image causes a giggle to escape.

This is the first laugh I've had since I woke up today. "Yeah, I'll be ok. No, let me correct that baby," I say out loud while rubbing my stomach in the area where the baby should be. "We will be ok," I tell my baby.

Chapter 15

Willow
"Misery Loves Company"

Today started out as every other day has since finding out I was pregnant six weeks ago. I've exchanged my great eye-opening first thing in the morning coffee for hellacious and constant morning sickness.

After I'm able to get off my knees from praying for mercy at my new porcelain altar, I stagger over to the sink to brush away the awful taste of vomit with some minty toothpaste.

As I brush my teeth, I inspect my reflection in the mirror and realize how terrible I look. I'm not one of those pregnant women that glow, unless I count the green tint to my pale face. No, definitely no glow for me.

After the continuous struggle to not vomit in front of my patients last week, I decided I should take this week off. Somehow, I've got to find a way to make dry-heaving look professional before I go back to work.

I brush my teeth and determine I've got just enough energy to grab some crackers along with a bottle of water before crawling back into my bed. Not only has this pregnancy taken over my stomach, it has drained my energy too.

The worst part of being pregnant isn't nausea, vomiting, or exhaustion though; it's the extreme bouts of horniness that hit me at random times caused by my raging hormones. I don't know how I will survive the next few months if this keeps up.

I've read in my "What to Expect When You are Expecting" book that my Gran gave me that the adverse effects should end around my second trimester, which is five weeks away.

Five weeks doesn't sound like a long time; but living it makes it feel like a lifetime. I'm more than grateful I have the support of my whole family. My parents were excited about the baby but disappointed with no baby daddy in my life.

I realize I must have fallen back to sleep when Ari wakes me. "Good afternoon baby mama," Ari says as she opens the blackout curtains I use to help me sleep during the day when I have to work night-shift.

"What time is it?" I ask, as I stretch and yawn myself awake.

"Noon. They canceled my afternoon meeting, so now I have an extra-long lunch break. I need to run an errand and thought you might join me. How are you feeling? Do you think you can stomach getting out of the house for a little while with me and getting some fresh air?" Ari asks while looking at me with her brows pulled tight together as she takes in my appearance once the sunlight spills into my bedroom.

Since the mental meltdown I had when I found out I was pregnant, Ari's mother hen tenancies have kicked into overdrive. She's been coming over three times a week to check on me, which I appreciate. I can't help but feel bad that my pregnancy has taken over her life too.

Not only do I wish I had the baby's father to help me raise my baby, but now I wish I had him around to help with my pregnancy as well. I guess the saying "misery loves company" is true because I don't want to do this alone. I cautiously sit up. I'm relieved that the morning sickness I had earlier has subsided.

"Actually, I feel much better than I did this morning. Let me clean up and throw on some yoga clothes, then I would love to go with you," I inform her as I jump out of my bed.

"Slow down we have time. Are you hungry? Do you want to eat something before we go?" Ari asks while I'm running around her in a circle getting ready.

"Like hell we have time. You don't seem to understand; the morning sickness can turn into afternoon sickness at any moment. It's a no to the food for now, I'll eat when I get back. I don't want anything coming up if the nausea returns at the store," I explain as I put on the much-needed makeup to camouflage my pale face. "Where are we going?"

"We're going to a mommy and me store on Chartres Street. They have a princess dress I need to buy. A little girl living at Dom's named Bailey wants to be a princess for her sixth birthday. Not a fairy princess though, she wants a real princess dress," Ari explains.

At the mention of Dom again I question Ari, "Has he ever hit on you?"

"He doesn't see me that way, and I don't see him in that way either. I mean he's easy-going and fine as hell, but I've known him since I came to New Orleans as a kid. We have more of a brother, sister, or cousin relationship. What I'm trying to say is he's more family material than dating material."

"Ok, just checking."

After I look human again and Ari finishes her lunch she fixed while I was getting ready, I gather my keys, cell phone, and purse before we head out the front door.

At the store, Ari finds the pink princess dress with the lace and beading she was talking about. It comes complete with a standout slip that would make any princess proud to wear it. She even found shoes and a tiara to match.

After finding the perfect dress, we look through the newborn clothing, which makes me excited about my baby. This boutique has unique children clothes. I pick through the selection of neutral gender outfits and find a few to purchase. I can't wait to dress my little one.

These are the moments I need to remember during the rough morning sickness times. I need to focus on the positive and not dwell in misery. When we're at the checkout counter, I see bags of lollipops for morning sickness. I grab two bags and buy them.

As we leave the store, I notice the time. "Damn, I didn't realize how much time we spent inside shopping. It's like those baby clothes have the power to hypnotize us into staying," I say with a giggle.

"Yeah, but it was fun looking plus I'm glad to see you laughing and smiling again," Ari says as her mother hen personality comes out. "I was going to take the dress out to Dom's house for Bailey, but now I'll call to let them know it will be tomorrow. I have just enough time to take you home then get to my late afternoon class."

Now I feel bad as I realize I'm the reason a five-year-old little girl won't get her party dress today. I spent too much time looking through baby clothes.

Since Ari's been doing so much for me lately, I decide it's time to give back. "Ari, text the address to my phone. I'll take a cab out to Dom's house to deliver the dress myself, and you can get back to work."

"I can't ask you to do that Willow. You need to go home and rest."

"First, you didn't ask, I volunteered to do it. Second, I need to get back on my feet again, so I can return to work. Last, you've been doing so much for me lately that I need you to let me do this," I demand stomping my left foot down to help show my determination.

Ari cuts her eyes to the side giving me a long look, then consents. "Ok. I appreciate you doing this. I think Dom will appreciate it too. If I know Bailey, which I do, she will worry Dom to death until tomorrow asking when I'll be there. She's so excited about this outfit. I'm texting you the address now, then I'll text Dom, so he'll expect you. Due to the family issues surrounding some of the kids staying with him, Dom is cautious about who comes to visit." Ari sends the text to my phone, then sends Dom a text as I call a cab.

Chapter 16

Willow
"Cream your panties"

When the cab turns up Dom's drive, my mouth drops open. The house sits back off River Road, so unless you go down the driveway, you wouldn't know it's there.

Old Oak trees line both sides of the drive leading to the house. The limbs of the old oak trees go up and curve over the driveway meeting in the middle. It looks like you are driving through a tunnel of trees.

The sight of the long driveway with the canopy of leaves and branches overhead is breathtaking. At the end of the tree line the driveway opens into a huge yard with a circular drive leading to the front of a large house.

The house is one of the old plantation homes from years gone by. In the middle of the circular drive is a three-tier water fountain with water cascading down the edges of each tier ending in a circular shallow pool at the base. Beautiful, vibrant multi-colored flowers surround the fountain.

Dom's house is a white two-story plantation home with six tall white columns in front. The house appears to have been built around the turn of the 19th century. There is a cobblestone path leading from the fountain in the circle to a set of wide wooden steps front center of the house.

Small round shrubs line the front of the house on each side of the steps. The steps lead onto a wooden porch that spans the entire width of the house. In front of the steps is a large wooden door. On each side of the door are three tall windows framed with tall wooden shutters. The door and shutters are dark green. Over the front door is a second-story balcony surrounded by black wrought-iron railing. The whole scene is breathtaking.

.

When the cab stops, I step out, then turn back to pay the driver who is staring up at the massive home with his mouth hung open. His reaction mirrors mine.

"You have a very beautiful home ma'am," the driver comments with awe in his tone.

"It's not my house, but I have to agree with you," I tell him with a smile. I thank him as I pay. I place my own purchases in my purse before heading up the cobblestone path to the steps.

I take my time walking up the steps, focusing on the details of the grand old house. There are four white wicker rocking chairs two on each side of the door with small glass top tables in between each pair. To the far right, sits a white wicker glider that can fit at least two people. It's lined with green floral print cushions that match the shutters.

I can picture myself curled up on the glider reading a book on a bright sunny day. Its obvious Dom took care of the details when restoring this plantation to its original glory. I can appreciate the effort and time this must have taken, since I did the same to my home, except on a smaller scale.

As I step onto the porch, I look down taking in the details of the natural Cyprus wood. The startling sound of the front door causes me to jump as it swings open. A small little girl steps out and freezes in her steps when she sees me. She seems as startled at my presence as I am of hers.

She has the most beautiful hair I've ever seen on a child, with long blonde ringlets cascading down the back of her delicate framed body. Her soulful, emerald green eyes are glued on me and wide with shock at seeing a stranger.

"Umm… hello, I'm Willow. Dom is expecting me, I came here to help our friend Ari deliver a dress for a princess named Bailey," I explain, as I bend to her level. It's obvious she's afraid of me as she backs into the doorway of the house to put more distance between us.

When she realizes the words I said, she beams a bright smile that stretches across her face, brightening her features showing her natural beauty. "That's me," she says in almost a whisper. "But I'm not really a princess," she adds then giggles as she covers her mouth with her small hand.

"May I come in to speak with Dom? He's expecting me."

"Uh-hmm," she says while staring at the bags in my hands. "Is that my princess dress?" I smile and nod my head, mesmerized by her enthusiasm.

"You can wait in there," she says, pointing toward a room to her right. She suddenly exclaims, "My baby!" then runs back out the door past me to the closest rocking chair on the left to grab a doll I hadn't noticed earlier.

As I stand back up straight. Bailey runs back to where I am just as fast as she ran to her doll. She grabs my hand and gently pulls me inside. I give her a soft smile as she glances back at me with those emerald eyes. Bailey gives me a huge smile in return that would melt anyone's heart.

As I walk through the door, I stop to look around the room at the period furniture and ornate wood trim. The place reminds me of the movie "Gone With The Wind." There's a large open foyer with a wide staircase coming down in the middle. The stairs have white railing instead of the brown railing in the movie though.

Vases of flowers sit on top of the end caps of the railing instead of the candelabras in the film. The stairs have a ruby-red carpet runner coming down the center which is similar to the movie. The floor I'm standing on is a white marble tile with black swirls.

I focus my attention back on Bailey. "Can I try my princess dress on then show it to you?" Bailey pleads with her hands clasp together under her delicate chin. She is standing on tip-toe staring wide-eyed trying to peer into the bags in my hands.

"Well of course. I would love to see a pretty princess all dressed up." I giggle at Bailey and her excitement. It must be contagious because now I'm excited for her.

Visions of playing dress-up with my own little girl run through my mind as I watch Bailey. We could even invite Ari and Nikki over to dress up with us, then have a tea party. If I am having a girl that is.

I'm pulled out of my thoughts of playing dress-up when Bailey's hands grab onto the bags. I hand them over to her.

With bright eyes, she informs me, "You can wait in there," pointing to the arch way to the right again.

As she runs up the stairs, I remind her "Bailey, honey, be sure to tell Dom I'm here ok?"

"Ok," I hear her small voice say as she runs down the hall from the top of the stairs.

I laugh while shaking my head, then turn to walk into the room where she instructed me to wait. I am back in awe as I enter the room.

It's a grand parlor room with tall, floor to ceiling windows on both the left and the far wall that have heavy, thick, pleated drapes. Vintage light green Victorian wallpaper covers the walls.

There is a large fireplace centered on the right wall. A desk sits in the corner just inside the doorway to the left. There is a white coffered ceiling, and the floor appears to be the original hardwood flooring. An antique Victorian couch with Victorian chairs sitting on each end create a cozy seating area facing the large fireplace.

As I continue to walk around admiring the details, I see movement out of the corner of my eye. I turn to see what's moving and my mouth drops open as I salivate. Damn, my hormones seem to be stuck in overdrive.

Just in front of the staircase where I'd been standing a few minutes ago is a hot guy that has a bad-boy appearance. Not in a bad-boy a scary way, but in that "cream your panties" kind of way.

This must be Dom. Now I see why women at the bar were lusting over him. I've got a strong desire to crawl up his body and have my way with him. He's standing still and doesn't notice me gawking at him, so I take full advantage by checking him out from head to toe.

He's over six-foot-tall, wearing a pair of basketball shorts with his shirt in one hand instead of on his body. The other hand holds a piece of paper which his masculine face is gazing down at.

He looks like he just finished working out. The tips of his dark, shoulder-length hair are damp from sweat. His muscular chest has a thin patch of dark hair and is covered with a visible sheen of sweat.

A tattoo covering his left shoulder and peck travels down the length of his left arm, forming a sleeve of artwork. He has an eight pack which I've only seen on one other man that looks that good- Connor.

I continue my visual tour of his body and notice a large bulge in the front of his shorts. Taking a deep breath, I continue my tour finding his legs are just as muscular as the upper half of him and are also a tantalizing golden-brown.

Suddenly, his weight shifts from one leg to the other causing me to dart my eyes up to his. I'm so busted. He just noticed me and if the frown on his full lips or the furrowed brow along with the glare of his dark eyes is any sign, he's not happy to see me.

I was right with my first observation. He's an alpha male, now stalking straight toward me with the intensity of a predator after his prey, but not stalking me in a good way like Connor did, though. My eyes widen with each step he takes towards me. My mind quickly moves from lust to fight or flight, which I choose flight and back up a step for every step he takes in my direction.

When my back is firmly pressing against the far wall behind me, he quickly cages me in by placing his massive thick arms against the wall on either side of my body while leaning into my personal space. He's much taller than me, which in this position puts my eye level at his chest.

I can't help but inspect the fine close-up details of his tattoo I couldn't see from a distance just a minute ago. I have an overbearing desire to trace those tattoos with the tip of my tongue, damn hormones. He even has a pierced nipple. I wonder how painful that experience was.

"Hey, my eyes are up here," I hear a deep masculine voice say, snapping me out of my muse and visual inventory of his tattoo. Busted again!

I jerk my head up to find myself peering into his dark chocolate eyes at the same time I feel a deep red blush creeping up my neck to my face. On closer inspection, I realize his eyes are not dark chocolate but are a breathtaking deep brown with a reddish tint.

"Who the hell are you and how did you get in here?" he says in a harsh, pissed off tone. I'm about to answer but I realize how his face is just as hot close up as the rest of him. I notice the dark whiskers that are surrounding plump, kissable lips. His nose is sharp with just a little crook to it.

"I'll ask you one more fucking time woman, who the fuck are you and how the hell did you get in here?" he asks again looking angrier as his jaw starts to clench.

I'm stunned almost speechless by all the anger directed toward me. "Walked?" is all I can say, but it sounds more like a question as my voice cracks. His scent is surrounding me, and it's so intoxicating it makes my head swim.

My pregnancy hormones must be on the warpath because his predatory attitude is not only scaring the hell out of me, it's also turning me on. What the hell is wrong with me?

Instead of lusting, I need to explain. By the time my common-sense kicks in, he's leaning down with his face so close to mine that our noses are almost touching. I feel his breath on my face. His eyes stare straight into mine. The reddish tint in them seems to be getting darker the angrier he becomes.

"Walked? Woman now is not the time to be a smart ass. If I find out you're here to harm one of the kids, I'll make you wish you never got out of the fucking bed this morning," he growls through his clenched jaws.

"What? Harm? No! The text! Are you Dom?" I try to explain, but my mouth and brain are having miscommunication issues causing me to babble incoherently.

"I am, and you better start making sense......." Dom says just as Bailey comes into the room talking.

"Willow, look! Do I look as pretty as a real princess? I feel like a real princess," Bailey says swirling around in the princess dress while looking down watching it flare out as she spins. She is too focused on the dress to noticed I am caged to the wall or the tension growing in the room.

"Willow?" Dom asks with furrowed brows.

"Yes, I'm a friend of Ari's. She sent you a text message letting you know to expect me?" I inform him, but it comes out more like a question again.

"I've been working out, and I don't keep my phone on me when I'm downstairs in the gym, so I didn't see a text message," Dom says while still keeping me caged against the wall.

"Ari didn't have time to bring Bailey her princess dress, so I told her I would do it for her," I continue to explain.

"Uncle Dom, look at my dress!" Bailey says finally looking up at us while still appearing oblivious to the tension between Dom and me. He takes a deep breath while scanning me from head to toe like he's assessing me, then takes a few steps back to release me from the cage his arms created. I instantly breathe a sigh of relief.

"You look beautiful, baby," Dom says as he turns around to face Bailey. Now he's smiling with a softness to his eyes that wasn't there a second ago.

"You look lovely in that dress, just like a real princess," I say to Bailey which makes her beam a bright smile again.

"I bet Flame will like your new dress too. Why don't you go find him, and show him?" Dom instructs Bailey. Flame? What an unusual name. I wonder who would name their child Flame.

"Ok!" Bailey exclaims with excitement as she runs out of

the room. Dom walks over to the dark mahogany, wooden desk that's in the corner and picks up a cell phone. He appears to be scrolling through his text messages. He has a half smirk on his face when he looks up at me.

"I have a text message from Ari, so I guess your story checks out. I apologize if I frightened you., but it shocked me to see a stranger standing in here. Protection of the children left in my care is something I take seriously. No harm will come to anyone on my watch," Dom states.

"That's ok. I thought Bailey went to tell you I was here before she tried on the dress. Bailey opened the front door before I was able to ring the bell, so she let me in as soon as I told her why I was here. I asked her to let you know I was here. In all her excitement she must have forgotten," I continue to explain.

Dom frowned at the part when I told him Bailey let me in and then mumbled under his breath about having words with Bailey later. Feeling awkward and like an unwelcome intruder, I decide it's time to get the hell out of here.

"I guess I'll go now. I'm glad Bailey loves her dress," I say as I head to the doorway leading out into the foyer. I'm planning on calling a cab while I'm walking to the end of the tree-lined drive to River Road then wait to be picked up there. Dom's not thrilled to have a stranger in his house, and it's probably best I leave at once.

After walking three steps, the room starts to spin. I feel my body sway. I hear Dom say my name. He sounds further away than he is though, with what sounds like concern in his voice. I feel as light as a feather floating down before the room suddenly goes black.

I wake up and open my eyes to see Dom's face staring down at me. "What?" I ask as I try to sit up. I notice I'm lying on the sofa that's in the same room I was talking to Dom in before the blackness took over.

"You passed out for a few minutes. Take it slow. Don't try to stand," Dom who is kneeling beside me says as he helps me to a sitting position. I'm embarrassed again.

"How is she?" I hear a feminine-toned male voice ask. I look up to see a man standing beside Dom dressed in a shirt with wild colored swirls print that he paired with bright orange pants. He's wearing dress boots that have heels. I look back up to see he's smiling at me.

"Honey, I'm Flame. How are you feeling? Do you need a doctor? I think she needs a doctor Dom," Flame says in a rapid rant that's hard for me to keep up with due to the speed he's talking.

"Flame?" is the only thing I get out of my mouth before he interrupts me again.

"I help out here with the kiddos. Honey, they call me Flame cause I'm so hot, baby girl," he says while popping his hip out slightly and grinning from ear to ear. This makes Dom roll his eyes while shaking his head.

"They call you Flame because you're flaming, as in flamboyant," Dom says, turning his head to look at Flame as he corrects him.

"Whatever! Back to our patient, honey do you need a doctor?" Flame asks again.

"No, actually I am a doctor. I didn't have much to eat for breakfast, and I skipped lunch. I think I need to get some dinner on my way home. I'll be okay," I explain as Dom turns his attention back towards me.

"No, you aren't going anywhere alone," Dom says, sounding more like a command that will not allow any arguing.

"Honey is there someone we can call? Are you single or do you have a husband or boyfriend to come to get you?" Flame asks. "By the way, Dom's single," he adds, which earns him another eye roll from Dom.

I can't help but chuckle a little at Flame before I respond. "No, I'm NOT single, and no I don't have a boyfriend or a husband to call."

"Dom, did she hit her poor little head when she passed out?" Flame asks. Dom shakes his head raising his brow with concern while looking at me.

I reach up to rub my temple trying to clear my head so I can start forming sentences that actually make since, then explain, "I meant, I'm not single because I'm pregnant."

"Oh," is the only thing Flame says.

"Well, I'll drive you home and pick up dinner for you on the way to your place. There's no way I'm letting you drive taking a chance on you passing out again. Ari would kill me," Dom says still like a command.

"I came here in a cab, so I'll call for a cab. I'll be fine," I inform them.

"Nonsense, what if you pass out again in the cab? Dom can take you, can't you Dom," Flame says as he shoves him on his shoulder.

"I'm taking you home Willow, or you can stay here. Maybe Ari can come pick you up if you don't feel comfortable with me driving you home, which I can understand since I scared the hell out of you earlier. I've already told you no one gets harmed on my watch, even if self-inflicted," Dom says with a small smile.

Not having the energy to argue nor wanting Ari to drive out here since the whole point of me coming was to save her the trip, I nod my head yes. "I would greatly appreciate you taking me home, but I need to use the restroom before we go," I tell them both, giving in because I know I can't win this battle.

Dom stands, then helps me to my feet. Flame takes a hold of my arm to walk me to the bathroom.

After escorting Willow to the bathroom, Flame returns to talk with Dom. "Did you notice how beautiful she is even while passed out and pale?" Flame whispers to Dom. "I wonder what's up with no active baby daddy?" he continues.

Dom takes a deep breath, exhales slowly and responds, "For once Flame, let your match-making tactics go."

Just as Flame opens his mouth to continue ignoring Dom's request, Bailey comes skipping back into the room still looking down admiring her new dress. She runs right into Dom's legs causing her to stumble then falls back onto her bottom. "Sorry

Uncle Dom," she says as she looks up at him.

"That's ok baby, but you've got to watch where you're going before you hurt yourself by running into stuff," Dom replies as he bends over to pick the little girl up into his arms from the floor where she landed.

Bailey leans her head close to Dom's ear before whispering, "Is Willow's baby going to come to live here with us Uncle Dom?"

"How did you know Willow has a baby in her tummy, and why would you think she would leave her baby with us? We only take in our kind who don't have a mommy or daddy to look after them," Dom whispers back.

"I can hear it and smell it. The baby is like you," Bailey whispers in response to Dom's questions. Bailey is not like the other children staying in his home. Her senses are stronger at a younger age and even more advanced than his in ways, this being one.

Dom isn't surprised Bailey could pick up on the fact Willow is pregnant when he couldn't. But, what's surprising to him is the fact the baby is a half-breed meaning a half werewolf if Bailey is correct.

Dom is a half-breed. Half-breed is a term used to describe someone born half human and half something else. Dom's father is a werewolf with Alpha status in Tennessee. Dom's mother, a human, was just a sexual play toy for his father. When she became pregnant, Dom's father rejected him as his own because Dom is a half-breed, which most werewolf tribes look down on. His mother fled to New Orleans to escape his father once he demanded her to get rid of "the bastard" she was pregnant with.

Unfortunately, Dom's mother never knew his father wasn't human when she was sleeping around with him. That realization came later when Dom hit his preteens. When Dom showed signs of being part werewolf, his mother turned him away out of fear.

Not understanding what he was, Dom lived on the streets

trying to avoid people and their reactions to him from age ten until around thirteen. Those were the toughest years of his life., and he barely survived. Fortunately, for him, Dom met an elderly woman who ran a shelter like the one he currently runs that takes in unwanted non-human children who mostly are half-breeds.

When Dom was twenty-four, his mother died as a victim of an arm robbery gone bad. She never had any other children, leaving Dom as the sole inheritor of her estate. A lawyer tracked him down. To his surprise, she was born of money which left him a sizable inheritance.

Because of what he had endured growing up, he used the money to help children that found themselves in situations like his. He did this by buying an estate and opening his home up to half-breed children who experienced the same or similar reactions as he did from their families.

To help locate these kids, he works with the shelter in town. Half-breeds can inherit some or all of their parent's gifts. In Dom's case, he has the gifts of a werewolf except he cannot transform into a wolf. On demand, he can change his eyes, teeth, and claws to werewolf form, but nothing else. He has the other gifts of strength and heightened senses too.

Dom has eleven children now staying with him. All of them are half-breed werewolves. If he can't find suitable foster parents who can cope with their unique abilities, he allows the children to live with him until adulthood for their protection.

Bailey and Flame are the exceptions. Flame is a full werewolf, or pure breed, but never fit into the hierarchy of his tribe. Most werewolves have alpha personalities. Flame doesn't possess any alpha traits and was treated like an outcast. He left his tribe to find happiness elsewhere.

Bailey is a pure breed also, but she is a rare breed altogether. She is in constant danger from tribes either wanting to own her or other tribes just wanting to destroy her. Dom plans on keeping her safe until she's capable of keeping herself safe, which means she rarely leaves his estate.

She is always kept close to home, including being home schooled while the others attend a private school. She has sharper senses than anyone else living there. Therefore, Dom and Flame take her claim about Willow's baby seriously.

"Are you sure Bay?" Flame ask as he moves in closer to join their conversation. Bailey nods her head yes in response. Almost as soon as she nods her head, the front door bursts open with the other children arriving home from school and bringing with them daily chaos.

"Go put up your stuff, snacks are waiting on the table, then homework time!" Flame yells towards the children as they enter the foyer. The children groan at the mention of homework but follow Flame's orders.

Bailey begins to wiggle wanting down to join the others. As soon as Dom places her feet on the ground, Bailey takes off after them.

The children hurry off in the direction of the kitchen leaving Dom and Flame staring at each other. Flame breaks the silence. "She's a human having a half-breed, Dom. Do you think she knows?" he asks.

"I have no idea, but I plan on finding out," Dom declares.

Flame begins another one of his rants. "Well, ain't this just a cluster-fuck of a situation. The poor baby girl needs to know so she can be prepared to handle what's coming her way. If not, we'll have another pitter-patter of little footsteps gracing our halls. Dom, the ones we have already work my nerves. They do I tell you; they do. So, do something now is all I've got to say," Flame says ending his rant with a flamboyant jerk of his head and snap of his fingers causing Dom to roll his eyes again.

Chapter 17

Willow
"Shit-eating Grin"

As I walk down the hall from the bathroom heading back to the room where I left Dom, I'm suddenly surrounded by a stampede of children who don't seem as alarmed about a stranger being in their home as Dom was. They zoom by in a flash with an occasional hello and a smile as they pass me.

I entered the room to find Dom and Flame talking. When they see me, their conversation immediately ends. They keep staring at me as I approach them. Feeling self-conscious, I smooth my shirt down and wonder what's out of place.

Dom breaks the silence by asking, "Ready to go?"

"Yes. I'm feeling better. I noticed all the kids seem to be back, so I don't mind taking a cab," I say in a last-ditch effort to leave alone.

"No," is the only response Dom gives me, then holds out his arm toward the foyer with a smile. I guess that's my cue to its time to head to the car.

"Ok then, I guess I'm ready. It was lovely meeting you, Flame. Please tell Bailey I said goodbye, and I'm glad she's happy with her dress," I say to Flame then turn to walk toward the foyer.

"Take care of yourself and that baby. Come back and visit us sometime," Flame says as Dom and I make our way to the front door to leave.

The ride back to my house is an uncomfortable silence along with the glances Dom occasionally gives me. I gave him my address when we entered his SUV, which he programmed into his GPS system, so I wouldn't have to give him directions. Out of the blue Dom turns his head toward me asking, "Do you like pizza?"

"Yes, I like the plain cheese, which drives Ari crazy. She says it's kid's pizza, and I need to grow up to at least a couple of toppings," I tell Dom which causes a genuine laugh that reaches his eyes. Damn, he looks even hotter laughing.

Dom focuses on the road again as he pulls his cell phone out to make a call. When the person on the other end of the line picks up, Dom places an order for pizza delivery then ends the call by giving the person my home address. My mouth drops open as I stare at him.

He turns to face me with a shit-eating grin on his face. "What? I'm hungry, and you're passing out from hunger. I told you before we left, I would pick you up something to eat, but this way is easier. We should arrive at your house before they deliver. And, babe, close your mouth," Dom says as he turns his head to face the road still grinning.

We arrive at my house just as the pizza's arriving. Dom pays for the pizza as I unlock my front door. He follows me into the kitchen then sits the pizza box on the island while I go to the cabinets to get glasses out to fix both of us a drink.

"Tea ok?" I ask.

"Beer?" he asks.

"Yes," I respond and pull out a bottle. I can't drink alcohol anymore, but I keep a supply of beer along with wine for my BFFs.

Dinner with Dom is anything but boring. We're sitting on my sofa close to one another with me turned sideways facing him while he has his back against the sofa. Once I learned to relax around him, I discover not only is he fine to look at, big-hearted, and loves children; he's also quite charming. We seem to be compatible. I've laughed more in the last two hours than I have in a month.

I get up halfway through eating the pizza to refill our drinks. Right before I turn to go into the kitchen, I steal a glance at his profile and catch him chewing on his bottom lip while staring at my ass. I turn my head back around before he sees I caught him checking me out. I sway my hips the last few steps into the kitchen to make sure he gets a proper show.

These hormones are creating an alter ego, I'm afraid. My libido is in overdrive. I better get Dom out of here soon before I start dry humping his leg. I wonder had I met Dom that night at The Club, would I have ended up with him instead Connor?

After Dom and I finished off the pizza, we stayed sitting on the sofa in engulfed in conversation. Dom asks the question that's been sitting like an elephant in the room. I knew he would ask me eventually, but I wasn't expecting it this soon.

"Willow, I know I'm asking you something personal, so don't feel like you have to answer if you don't want to, I will completely understand. I'm curious for my own selfish reasons than just being nosey. Where does the father of the baby fit into your life?" Dom asks.

"That's ok to ask, but first explain the selfish reasons before I give you my answer," I reply, now curious myself.

The sides of his mouth go up a little, and as a devious look appears in his eyes he replies, "I've really enjoyed this evening with you and getting to know you better. I'm wondering if I keep coming around, am I going to have a chance with you?" he asks.

I feel heat forming in my face with embarrassment from the flattery of his comment, and shame from dealing with the possible judgment of admitting to not knowing Connor better. I'm surprised he's interested in a pregnant woman but I'm sure as hell not going to complain.

"Well, I met my baby's father the night Ari, Nikki, and I went to your club to celebrate Ari's birthday," I explain. When I mention his club, his eyebrows raise in surprise. I pause for a moment looking down at my fingers while biting my bottom lip, trying to figure out how to word the next part.

I must have taken too long to continue causing Dom to ask, "Willow?" When I look back up, he has a concerned expression on his handsome face.

I throw my hands over my face to cover my eyes (because that's the mature thing to do, NOT!). I ramble, "I don't know how to say this without sounding slutty, but I promise I've never done anything like that before," I stop talking and peek out between my fingers at him to see what look is on his face before I continue.

"Willow?" Dom asks as he grabs my hands with his much larger ones pulling them away from my face. Then he places our clasped hands in his lap and begins brushing his thumbs over the backs of my hands in a comforting gesture.

His hands feel strong and much rougher than my own. My mind drifts to thoughts of all the places on my body I would rather his hands be right now. Oh hell, my hormones must be waking up my inner slut. I need to learn to control her. Last time I allowed her to run free, she left me single and pregnant.

Dom speaks again pulling me from my muse, "First off, even with the short time we've spent together the label slut doesn't register when I look at you. I've met many slutty women in my time, actually more than I've wanted to. So, based on my experience, slut doesn't apply to you. Second, we all have at least shadows if not skeletons in our closets."

I let out a long sigh then begin my story, "I met a guy, a charming guy at your club that night. I had a lot to drink. But, honestly, I can't blame my actions on the alcohol. All it did was give me the boost of liquid confidence I was lacking."

I pause to take a much-needed deeper breath. I try to pull my hands away from his to cover my face before I give the last part of my confession, but he keeps a firm hold on them. So, I continue, in a rushing rambling rant to quickly get the admission of shame over with.

"The alcohol combined with a long sexless dry spell took over my better judgement and we spent the night at a hotel. The next morning, I was too embarrassed to face him. You see, he's the first and only one-night stand I've ever had. I didn't know how to deal with the morning after awkwardness, so I snuck out and left without getting his name. I've tried finding him because I would really like to get to know him and to tell him about the baby. I've even recruited Nikki and Ari to help, but we've had no success." I finish my confession feeling winded.

I was able to say all that in a rushing rant all in one breath. I take in a deep breath through my nose and blow it out through my mouth sitting still watching Dom, waiting for the judgment to begin. To my surprise, it never does. After he studies me for a moment, a big smile breaks out on his face.

"What?" I ask, getting annoyed at him finding humor in my shame.

"As stressed out as you're becoming, it's like you're trying to confess to a murder instead of a hookup. Like I said before, I would like to spend time getting to know you, and I'll even try to help you find your baby daddy to make sure I have no competition to deal with in the future. I have a buddy of mine that does investigation work. He was there that night as well. If you're interested in really finding this guy, I'll ask my buddy to help, if you don't mind me sharing your story with him that is."

The urge to locate Connor overcomes my embarrassment, so I take him up on his offer. "I would love your friend's help."

"He's working on a local investigation right now. I'll get in touch with him within the next couple of weeks to ask for his help. Then set up a meeting between the two of you to go over specifics."

"That would be wonderful," I feel a new spark of hope in locating Connor. An unexpected colossal yawn escapes my mouth at that moment.

"I need to go so you can rest," Dom says as he picks up our now empty glasses along with the empty pizza box to take them into the kitchen. I get up to follow him. After throwing our trash away, I follow him out onto the front porch. To my surprise I don't want him to leave just yet, so I continue to talk. He must be enjoying himself too because we schedule another dinner get together at my house for next week. Forty-five minutes later, we say goodnight. He leans in to place a feather light goodbye kiss on my cheek before walking to his SUV. I stay out on the porch and watch him drive away. When I can no longer see the tail lights of his SUV, I turn around and walk back into the house.

As he is driving away, Dom reaches into his pocket to pull out his cell phone to call Flame.

"You got Flame," Flame says in greeting as he answers the phone.

"Hey, it's me. I am heading back to the house. Look up the number for Cerberus. I need to get in touch with a buddy of mine to see if he can locate Willow's baby daddy. He was a nameless one-night hook up," Dom tells him.

"Really, I would have never guessed that about the girl!" Flame says with surprise and excitement in his voice.

"Me either. She said she'd never done anything like that before, which I can believe. She didn't want to tell me. We not only need to locate him for Willow but also to make sure he isn't making it a habit of breeding," Dom says while feeling anger towards the man for not only creating a half-breed with an unsuspecting woman but also on behalf of Willow.

"Wait, you really like this girl, Dom. I can hear it in your voice. I thought I detected a spark in your eye when you looked at her earlier."

Dom rolls his eyes even though Flame can't see. "Let's just say I am planning on seeing more of Willow in the future and we'll leave it at that."

Chapter 18

Connor
"Ain't No Sunshine"

Two Weeks later…. After my team finished up tonight and hidden out, I decided to stay at the office for some needed alone time to mull over our evidence to see if I can get any fresh leads on our current case we might have missed. But focus is not my best quality tonight and I can't keep my mind on task. Frustrated, I sit back in my chair, then pull out a hidden bottle of Patron gold tequila I kept in the bottom drawer of my desk. I pour some of the golden liquid into my empty coffee mug sitting next to the files I've searched.

Finding a killer is difficult when I'm focused more on a hot little number named Willow. I can't figure out what is wrong with me. It's like her sunshine pussy has put a spell on me. No woman has ever consumed my thoughts like this before. Giving in to the moment, I hit the playlist saved on my iPhone then lean back in my chair, rest my head on the head rest while I close my eyes.

I allow my thoughts to travel back through time to the night I spent fucking my sunshine pussy. The song "Ain't No Sunshine When She's Gone" begins to play when I realize I'm no longer alone. I hear a familiar growl, but I don't bother raising my head. I open my eyes to see my brother, Drake. standing in front of my desk shaking his head.

I eye him suspiciously. "Why are you here, brother?"

Drake starts shaking his head with a look of disgust on his face like he just tasted something rotten. "Well, it sure as hell wasn't to play witness to this pathetic excuse of a man scene.

Do I even want to know why you're infatuated with sunshine on your new playlist? 'Ain't no Sunshine when she's gone,' 'You are the Sunshine of My Life,' Oh! Let's not forget my personal favorite 'Pocketful of Sunshine'; you didn't even realize I knew about that one did you, bro? Pathetic, just pathetic."

I shoot daggers at him with my eyes for his comments and for being so fucking observant. "Again, why are you here?"

Drake reaches over to turn my iPhone off. "Dom called. Needs help on another case of locating someone, so get off your pussy whipped ass. We're meeting him at his club." I make a dramatic sigh like this is a hardship, gather my phone, keys, and wallet then follow Drake to his SUV.

We arrive at The Club fifteen minutes later. We head straight to the bar to order a beer and to let ask the bartender to inform Dom we're here. "Two beers, and let Dom know Connor and Drake are here." He nods his head while chewing gum and never speaks, just points with his finger toward a VIP booth.

I turn to see Dom sipping on a beer, leaning part way over the table lost in deep thought. Judging by the look on Dom's face, this job isn't good. I look at Drake and raise my eyebrows to him when he takes his eye off Dom to look at me. He shakes his head in response to my raised eyebrows, both of us having the same feeling of concern by the way Dom looks. We head in his direction. Dom doesn't notice us until we're three steps away from him. When he sees us, he sits up straight, and gives us a chin lift as in a greeting.

"Hey man, how's it going," I ask as Drake and I take a seat across the booth from him.

"Could be better," Dom replies.

I decide to get straight to the point of our meeting. Dom looks as pathetic as I feel, so I don't think he'll mind if I cut to the chase. I'd like to head home as soon as possible before Drake tries talking me into staying and being his wingman. "Drake said you have another job you'd like for us to do."

"Yeah," Dom sighs then continues, "I've come across someone else's baby momma of a half-breed, and she would be the human half who has no clue what her child is." Dom spits out the last part of his reply is through clenched teeth.

"Don't take offense, but you seem more tense with this case than normal. Are there more issues with this case than usual?" I inquire.

"No offense taken. The problem is, I can't get someone else's baby momma out of my head," Dom replies.

"Shit! What a pathetic couple you two make. Ask Connor here about his sunshine," Drake whines like a bitch.

I give Drake a deadpan look then, turn back toward Dom to get back on track. "How old is her kid?"

"I guess I would have to agree with Drake's observation of pathetic. She's still pregnant with said baby, and apparently still hung up on this guy because she's trying to locate him. The father doesn't know she's pregnant. I feel guilty for saying it, but I'm hoping he wants to stay gone once he hears the big announcement. That way I can slide right into the position he's giving up," Dom says with a strained smile on his face.

"You want to tell me how you came across the knowledge she's carrying a half-breed? You know werewolves can't sense something like that," I comment while raising an eyebrow at him.

Dom sits tapping his finger on the table for a minute mulling over my question. "No, that part isn't important. What concerns me is the father's having unprotected sex with unsuspecting women and leaving a trail of potential half-breeds."

"You mean you're more concerned with staking a claim to the baby momma," Drake says with a smirk.

We both ignore Drake's comment. "What's this guy's name? Any details that could help us locate him fast?"

"Well, did I mention she doesn't really know the guy? He was a random one-night stand. She met him here a few weeks back. I have all the footage from the security cameras saved. I'm planning to ask her for the exact date, then either watch the film until I see her with this guy or have her come in to point him out. Also, I can bring her into your office, so you can interview her to see if there're any details of that night she might remember that could help you. I'm going over to her house to take her dinner in a couple of nights. She's been struggling with morning sickness. I haven't figured out how to tell her that being pregnant with a werewolf requires an increase in calories and eating more will help stop her nausea. For the last couple of weeks, I've been randomly showing up to coerce her into eating more until I tell her. The quicker we locate this guy the quicker I can come up with a plan of how to tell her," Dom says.

"Hell, it sounds like the two of you have it bad for a couple of humans. If you both can fix your pathetic love lives, you guys should get the women together. They'll have a lot in common finding out about the existence of non-humans and all, except for the baby on board thing. Connor here could be the poster child for safe sex. He not only buys himself condoms but also has a supply at work for all of his employees," Drake says with a smirk.

After having had enough of my brother's comments, I reach up and slap him on the back of the head. "Ignore him, he's just jealous."

"Yeah, that's it. I'm jealous that I haven't found a woman to fuck up my head and turn me into a pathetic, lovesick bastard," Drake says with a snarl. Suddenly, I have a desire to stay here at the bar longer with Dom than to share another car drive with the prick that shares my DNA. I end up spending the rest of my evening drinking across from Dom while the both of us watch Drake do his lap around the bar looking for the next woman he wants to charm out of her pants. I'm thankful that Drake always practices safe sex like I do, and that we're not leaving a trail of half-breeds in our wake.

Chapter 19

Ari
"Scared little girl"

That same night...... "Damn, I hate leaving work so late," I say to myself as I place my computer bag on the ground next to my feet while locking the door to my office. As I reach down to pick my bag back up, I notice how eerie this place is after dark. I'm the last one to leave tonight, and when I make it out to the faculty parking lot, my car is the only car left. The sky is darker than usual due to the moon being covered by clouds.

I shrug my shoulders as I try to get the tension to leave my body before I have a panic attack like a scared little girl. It doesn't work. I can't shake the feeling something's not right. I feel like I am being watched. It's not helping that all the recent dead bodies found around New Orleans keep popping into my mind. The news declared them to be animal attacks, but I have my doubts.

I pause for a second when I hear something in the distance. Shit! I hear footsteps! It sounds like couple of sets of footsteps are closing in on me from both sides. I feel my heart racing as the adrenaline starts pumping through my veins. I speed up the pace to my car. I'm a few feet from the car when I realize I still have my keys in my hand from locking the office door. I place each key between my fingers with the jagged side outward like a weapon while keeping the keyless entry in my palm. I hear the footsteps getting closer as I get closer to my car, but I think I can make it before they reach me. At least I pray I can. As I close the distance to the safe-haven of my car,

I hold out my hand to press the keyless entry to unlock the doors. I feel a hand grab on my shoulder from behind halting my next step.

Damn, I never heard him coming up from behind, but I can feel his breath on my ear as he says, "What's the rush pretty little thing? All we want to do is invite you to dinner," then I can hear three men laugh as they close in on me, just before all hell breaks loose.

Chapter 20

Nikki
"Shit Happens"

Early the next morning…… I wake from a deep sleep and hear whispers coming from the direction of the kitchen. I glance over at my cell phone laying on my bedside table to check the time. It's one a.m. I wonder what's going on? Gram was in bed before me tonight. I'm tempted to roll back over; pretend I heard nothing and go back to sleep.

As I start to follow through with my plan, I begin to worry that Willow is here this late, if so, then something must be wrong. Either she had a bad shift at work, or she's struggling with morning sickness, better known as the twenty-four whenever sickness when talking about Willow. If Willow is here, I will offer to make her a tea to help settle her stomach, half expecting her to say don't worry about it and to go back to bed. Reluctantly, I pull myself out of my warm, comfortable bed then put on my robe before I go to investigate.

I head out of my room, take a few steps then stop dead in my tracks when I can identify the voices. I recognize Ari and Gran whispering, but I can't make out the words. I continue the short distance towards the kitchen trying to be as quiet as possible. It is not until I turn the corner that I finally can make out the words they are whispering.

"You will have to tell them one day," Gran tells Ari.

"I know, but I'm not ready yet," Ari responds.

"Tell who what?" I say as I walk into the kitchen closing my eyes while yawning. When I open my eyes again, I find Gran and Ari staring at me. I forget about what I asked when I see

Ari's face. She has a bruise on her left cheek with scratch marks on her neck. I look farther down her body and realize she is shirtless, sitting on her stool in her bra, while Gran is standing behind her taping cotton gauze onto her left shoulder. "What the fucking hell happened to you? Were you in a wreck? Shouldn't you be at the hospital?" I run over to her to assess her injuries myself.

"Calm down Nikki, I'm fine. I worked late tonight, and someone mugged me on the way to my car. Physical injuries are easily healed. It's…" Ari says until I interrupt her.

"Yeah, yeah, it's the broken pieces of the soul that don't mend," I finish for her. I can't tell you how many times I've heard Ari say that, but this time it's pissing me off. "Don't downplay this mugging like it's not a big deal, it is a big deal; I see your injuries! What's under that gauze on your shoulder?" I reach to lift a corner of the gauze not tape down to take a peek.

Gran swats my hand away. "Calm down Nikki. It's just a road rash abrasion. It'll heal."

I move to stand in front of Ari. "Did you at least make a report with the cops?"

Ari reaches up to pat my shoulder in a gesture attempt to calm m me down. "I did. There's not much they can do. The only thing the thief got away with was my necklace. I'm banged up, but fine."

It is that moment I realize what is missing. "Your mother's necklace?" I hate that for her because I know what it means to her. It would devastate me if I lost mine. Ari nods her head yes.

She sighs; "Shit happens," is her only response, but I can see the grief in her eyes from the loss.

"At least see Willow tomorrow and let her check you out," I say as I grab the kettle from the stove and head to the sink to fill it with water. I need the damn tea now. It pisses me off to see someone I care for get hurt by the hands of an asshole. When I get to the sink, I notice the brown antique bowl we keep in the hidden room along with other forbidden objects that are used to do magic.

What the hell is going on here? I've suspected Gran dabbles with magic for a while now. Did Ari interrupt Gran when she showed up? I decide to confront Gran after Ari's gone. I casually reach down into the sink to feel the black paste residue in the bottom of the bowl, rub it between my fingers then realize its henna tattoo ink. Interesting.

I never get the chance to confront Gran because Ari ends up staying the night with us and sleeping in my bed. My discussion with Gran will have to wait for another time, but it will come because it's past due.

Chapter 21

Willow
"Life throws you curve balls"

Two weeks later...... I take a deep breath trying to ease my nausea before it turns into vomit. I'm back at work, having a day from hell. The morning sickness is kicking my ass. All I want to do is go home, take a hot relaxing shower while trying not to vomit, then head straight for my bed. If the morning sickness doesn't stop, this pregnancy will feel more like nine years than nine months. I'm now four months in, with five to go. I have no idea how other women do this, or why they would want to do this more than once.

As I sip my ginger ale in the break room, trying to feel human again, my pager alarms. "What now," I mumble with a sigh as I pull the damn thing out of my pocket to check the message. It reads ETA fifteen minutes unconscious male with a gunshot wound to the chest. I jump up to run to the trauma bay while taking the last few sips of the ginger ale and sending up a prayer that my nausea subsides long enough to save a life.

The patient arrives by ambulance, and the paramedics bring him straight into the trauma bay. There are three nurses, a respiratory therapist, along with me awaiting the patient's arrival. As they move the guy over from their stretcher onto our table, I get the first look at his face causing the breath to rush out of me in pure shock. It's a face I'd given up looking for, thinking I would never see again and sure as hell never imagined seeing again under such dire circumstances. I hear one nurse ask the EMTs if they know his identity.

"His name is Drake," I respond without a conscious effort.

The words leave my mouth as the shock of the situation seeps into my bones.

"Yeah, Drake, do you know him?" the EMT asks me.

I shake my head as I try get a grip on my emotions. "Not really. Do you know any details about the shooting?" I ask hoping Connor wasn't with him when it happened. God, please let Connor be ok, I pray in my head.

"Only thing I know is they think it was gang-related. Two people were injured, this one is the only one still breathing when we arrived," the EMT replies. I stumble at the news of the other victim's death. Connor! I gasp and at once feel like I can't catch my breath. I feel the color draining from my face. I never got the chance to tell him about the baby. I still held on to the hope of locating him to let him know he is a father, hoping we could somehow come together and be a family.

Even if we weren't together as a couple, my baby could have at least known his or her father. Thoughts of my child growing up fatherless rush through my mind and I know deep in my heart the incredible responsibility I now have. I will be both a mother and a father to my child. I feel a hand grip my arm, and glance over to see who's touching me to find its Sharon, the charge nurse, holding onto me, staring at me with concern.

"Are you okay Dr. Black?" she asks in a whisper that only I can hear.

Damn, I've got to pull it together. I take several deep breaths. "Morning sickness right before I got the page, but it's easing up," I tell her in a whisper as I give her what I hope is a reassuring smile. There's no way in hell I'll tell her the truth about how I'm feeling in this situation right now and not break into a million pieces. I've got to push my fears into the back of my mind and focus on saving Drake.

"Okay," Sharon whispers back again nodding her head with furrowed brows and a concerned look. She can tell I'm lying, but thankfully doesn't call me out on it.

The EMTs gather their stuff onto their now empty stretcher and are about to leave when the one giving us the information turns back to face us and says, "One more thing, his brother was at the scene with him. Conner is his brother's name. He said he would meet us at the hospital after he notifies his family."

A wave of relief washes through me as a warm sensation signals the color returning to my face. That's when it hits me and the relief I felt is gone as I think back to the first part the EMT said about the shooting. After the EMTs are out of the room, I look back to Sharon. "Did I hear him say this was gang related?"

Sharon nods her head. "Yes, I believe that's what he said."

"Yeah, that's what he said," another nurse confirms.

Great! Just fucking great! My baby daddy wasn't shot, is alive but mixed up in some gang. Just my luck, I have a thug for a baby daddy. He's not only a thug but a thug that has bullets flying around him. I don't think they make a bullet-proof vest in infant size.

Ironically, I've gone from praying that Conner isn't dead, to thoughts of killing him myself in less than a five-minute time span. Well, that bit of information just made up my mind about telling Connor about the baby. There's no way in hell MY baby will be raised with a thug for a father, especially a thug with bullets flying around his head. I've patched many gang victim's bodies back together, so I can do it again months later when they have a return visit to the Emergency Room.

I love my baby too much to put my baby through a life of danger by falling in love with a father that will be ripped from the his or her life when he gets shot. Connor has chosen this lifestyle, not me. With that decision made, I take a deep breath to still my racing mind then work to save Drake's life.

The only wound I find is a bullet hole in his chest next to a birthmark shaped like a paw print, which causes a flashback to the life-altering night I spent with Connor. The same birthmark is on Connor's back. I forgot about that. I recall tracing it with my tongue during the throws of passion. The monitor connecting to Drake alarms, pulling my mind away from Connor and bringing me back to the present. I look up to discover Drake's blood pressure is rapidly dropping and his heart rate is speeding up. Drake is crashing.

"We need to get him to the OR stat!" I bark in a tone that causes everyone in the room to move at warp speed. We get him to the OR in record time, and for once my nausea holds off, so I can do my job. I'm thankful for the small bit I luck I've held onto.

After two long grueling hours in the Operating Room, I feel exhaustion reaching down into the depths of my soul. I don't have the energy level I did before I was pregnant. In the past, I could do a sixteen or twenty-four-hour shift before exhaustion like this hits me. Now, I'm ready for a long nap after an eight-hour shift. This surgery was not just physically exhausting; it was emotionally exhausting as well. It was touch and go for a while, but we saved Drake with no long-term damage.

Now comes the part I've been dreading since I stepped foot into the OR. As Drake's surgeon, I'm the one that has the responsibility of updating the family on his condition, which means seeing the face of the man that's altered my life forever. That same man has been haunting my dreams and invading my thoughts daily since we met. The man I've been searching for to deliver the news of our unexpected bundle of joy.

It's funny how life throws you curve balls. Now, all I want to do is run and hide from him. If I focus on Drake's other family members in the room instead of Connor, I might pull this off. With any luck, he was too drunk or not interested in me enough that night to want to talk now. Hell, he didn't take the time to learn my last name either, so maybe it's a habit of his and I'm just another notch on his bedpost.

Chapter 22

Connor
"Shooting the Shit"

In the surgery waiting room..... I'm sick to death with worry. What the hell is taking so long? It feels like hours have passed. The only information we've gotten about Drake's condition so far is that he's holding his own and having emergency surgery. Being werewolves, we rarely worry about fatal wounds due to our ability to heal quickly. This situation is unique. How the hell did tonight go so wrong?

We were sitting in our office just shooting the shit, ready to wrap up our day when the call came in from our human contact on the police force that's helping us with this case. He received a tip of three suspicious looking guys harassing a female just a few blocks away near an abandoned building in the Warehouse District near where one of our victims was last seen. To rule out a connection, we investigated.

The Warehouse District is near the French Quarter. The area began as an industrial part of town in the 19th century when the port of New Orleans was the primary source for transporting goods. When the trade practice changed, and containers replaced warehouses, they left some buildings abandoned. When contemporary arts became popular in this area, the abandoned warehouses became the perfect place to create art galleries. Now, there's over twenty-five art galleries in this area among the few buildings still left abandoned.

After the call, Drake, Daniel, and I went to investigate. The rest of our team held back. Every team member including the ones staying at the office wears an earpiece, so we can have open communication with all team members during investigations in the field. This allows us to inform everyone on the team of any suspicious activity we encounter. In return, anyone in the field needing information can ask the ones remaining in the office.

Before we headed out the door, we grabbed our weapons to help capture any Wendigos unwilling to cooperate. Experience has taught us that nine out of ten times they're uncooperative and fight to the death instead of being caught. Like humans, you can kill a Wendigo; they're just faster and stronger than humans. We won't hesitate to use our weapons if the need arises.

We saw no signs of activity as we approached the abandoned building. Fire damaged the building years ago, and they never restored it. There was a smaller building on the property that sat across an alleyway close to the front side of the original building. It looks like an outside storage building added to the property years after they built the original building.

The original brick two-story building was a warehouse back in its day. I'm familiar with the place because I used to come here. The bottom half was a bar/restaurant until it caught on fire several years ago. Most of the second-floor windows that burst during the fire remain boarded. All remaining windows have holes and cracks from vandalism. There's a wire fence surrounding the whole property, but it has several sections missing leaving gaping holes along each side of the fence.

When we arrived, the only visible light was moonlight. Being werewolves, we have a much better eyesight than humans. Although we can't see clearly in the dark, our vision is better than the average person, and more importantly better than Wendigos. We carry flashlights for the darker places when we go out at night for fieldwork.

We fan out and go separate ways to scan our surroundings for any signs of trouble. Daniel lets out a low whistle, his signal to get our attention without having to shout to alarm anyone of our presence. When we approach him, he points to the ground.

"Blood," he whispers, as he illuminates the area with his flashlight. I look at the ground, and there're splatters of fresh blood with a line of drops leading toward the warehouse.

"Sulfur," I say and the other two nod in agreement. The blood of a Wendigo has a sulfur smell to it.

"At least we know how to handle these bastards. Hopefully, the woman seen with them got away, but the odds are against her," Drake comments. We know one woman against three Wendigos doesn't stand a chance, but at least she seems to have given them a run for their money based on the Wendigo blood trail. We follow the droplets to the closed door of the warehouse where there's a handprint formed out of blood on the wall beside the door handle.

I inform every one of my plan. "Drake and I will go inside and check it out. Daniel, you stay out here and make sure no one leaves the warehouse undetected." Daniel is the best choice to leave outside watching the perimeter. In a worst-case scenario, if a Wendigo tries to run away from us, Daniel is the only one that can transform into wolf form. His wolf eyes are able to see clearly in the dark. He could catch and subdue the Wendigo before it can escape into the neighboring crowds of people. The last thing we need is an audience witnessing us catching or killing one of these bastards.

Drake and I enter the warehouse with our guns out, safety off, ready for anything that might come our way. These creatures will fight to the death, which is fine by me since there are no jury trials in the world for the crimes these Wendigos committed. This group has been regularly feeding on humans.

Any Wendigos that feed on human flesh regularly are like rabid animals after consumption of human flesh. There will be no rehabilitating them. Their addiction will always be human flesh, which we cannot tolerate. Execution is what's in store for them, and they damn well know it. They never used to hunt in groups and usually behave violently towards one another over food. Knowing their eating habits led to the Guardians taking notice of their victims, they've wised up over the last decade and figured the best odds of survival is to hunt in a gang.

Inside the building is dark, and scattered debris cover the floors. The rancid smell of sulfur hits me like a freight train, making me gag, reminding me again how awful these mother-fuckers smell when they're injured. I point a finger to Drake, then point the direction I want him to search. I then point to myself, then the opposite direction to show him where I plan to search. He nods in understanding and heads off in his des-tination as I turn to head off into mine. I update Daniel on our plans thru my earpiece. I speak at barely a whisper which I know he'll be able to hear.

"Roger that," I hear Daniel respond back. Outside, Dan-iel is staying in the shadows and keeping a close eye on the warehouse for any movement. After a few minutes of silence, Daniel informs me he hears the sudden sound of movement and smells the overpowering smell of sulfur emerging in the air. "Guys, our injured Wendigo has moved out of the building. I hear movement and smell sulfur," Daniel announces thru the earpiece cutting the silence.

"I have movement on my side of the building too, going to investigate," Drake says.

Outside, Daniel hears a slight noise in the alleyway toward the outside storage building. He then hears another strange sound, a faint high-pitched whistle, followed by break-ing glass. A loud thud with a moan comes from the front of the warehouse. Daniel quickly makes his way to the front of the warehouse and sees a Wendigo lying on the ground taking his last breath. He glances up to see a shattered window on the second level of the warehouse that was only cracked when we first arrived.

"Whichever one of you shot at the Wendigo on the sec-ond floor, you hit your mark. He fell out of the window, is down and not getting up. I think he's what I smelled and heard a minute ago when he came near the cracked window," Daniel informs his team.

"Not my hit," I respond.

"Not mine either," Drake says.

"Well, what the hell? Sure as hell isn't mine," Daniel announces.

"Maybe the bastards really can't get their shit together and get along. Hopefully, they're killing each other," Drew comments from the office over the earpiece.

Daniel moves in closer to examine the body. The disgusting smell rising from the fatal wound in the Wendigo's chest is so strong Daniel has to cover his nose. He takes out his flashlight, leans over the body, and shines it on the chest to get a closer look at the wound. He notices something odd about the injury. It's not round as if a bullet hole, but more like a straight line over the heart. He glances on the ground around the body for a weapon, but there's no sign of any object that could inflict such a wound.

Daniel focuses back on the dead body and notices the tip of something metal sticking out of the wound. After pulling his knife out of the side of his cargo boot, he uses it to spread the wound wider, discovering what appears to be a shuriken or ninja star type of weapon. As he dislodges the shuriken from the wound, he notices an intricate design engraved in the center of the shuriken. He takes a plastic bag out of his pocket then bags the shuriken as evidence. He further searches the body and finds a cell phone along with an odd stone on a broken chain in the Wendigo's pants pocket. The medallion has a similar intricate design engraved on it as the Shuriken. His gut tells him this kill is not made by another Wendigo and in this type of profession you learn quick your gut feelings are usually right.

"It appears we're not the ones who killed this piece of shit, and my gut tells me it wasn't another Wendigo based on the evidence I'm finding," Daniel informs the team over the communication system. He remembers the noise he heard across the alleyway towards the storage building just before the body fell out of the window. Without moving his head,

Daniel glances toward the storage building out of the corner of his eye trying to see if he can get a look at whatever made the noise without alerting anyone that might be hiding.

Due to the difficulty his human eyes have seeing that far in the darkness, he switches to his yellow wolf eyes. Wolf eyes have a special light-reflecting surface behind the retina which allows better night vision than his human form eyes allow. This is one of the advantages he has over Connor and Drake due to their curse and the inability to transform into wolves. He glances around with his head down, hoping no one notices the yellowish glow his eyes emit. He sees someone hiding against the building. Other than having a small body frame, he can't make out any other details of the person.

"Guys, we're not alone out here. From what I can tell by the small body frame, it's probably a teenage boy, and probably human. I doubt the woman the Wendigos were after earlier would hang around if she's even still alive," Daniel says updating his team.

"We've got it covered in here. See if you can get a closer look at whoever's there," I instruct Daniel.

"Roger that," Daniel responds.

Chapter 23

The Mystery Woman
"What the Hell"

I watch as three men enter through the broken fence surrounding this deteriorated building I've chased the Wendigos into. I injured one of the three, the one I'm after, the one who took what belongs to me. Come hell or high water, I will get back what's mine. The men look and dress like SWAT members on the police force. I must put my plans on hold until these guys either get themselves killed or leave.

I spot a small storage building sitting beside the main building and run over to hide against it to wait them out. I'm wearing a black hooded jacket, so I tuck my ponytail into the hood and pull the sides of the hood close around my face to hide my facial features. In the darkness, I can't make out any features of their faces. I don't dare change my eyes to see in the dark because they shine a bright emerald green and would be seen. The three men are large, as in muscular, and are moving with stealth quickness towards the warehouse as if searching for someone. I wonder if they're after the Wendigos too. I don't care what they do with them as long as I get back what's mine.

They've stopped over the spot where I injured the one wendigo just moments before I saw the men coming towards the fence. They are whispering. Thanks to a past tragedy, I lost my heightened sense of hearing and can't make out what they're saying. Thinking of my hearing causes the memories of that night to resurface. It was the worst night of my entire life. I shake my head to clear them away and stay focused on the present moment. I can dwell on the past later.

Two of the men enter the building while one stays outside and moves into the shadows by the warehouse for the cover of complete darkness. Standing as still as I can, waiting for what seems like forever for something to happen, I spot the thief I know has what I want back. He's standing in one of the second-story windows of the warehouse. The sight of him enrages me. I refuse to let anyone or anything turn me into a victim ever again.

With fury racing through my veins, I don't even think before reacting. I grab a shuriken, my weapon of choice, from a compartment I had made in my hooded jacket then I throw it with all my might. I hit my target dead-on. Not surprising since I've been training for years to protect myself in this fucked up world that people don't know exists around them.

I hit the Wendigo causing him to fall through the window and land on the ground. This causes the man in the shadows to stir. That's when I realize the consequences of my action. Somehow, I forgot he was outside with me when the thieving bastard Wendigo entered my sight.

I press my body as close to the side of the building as I can, hoping I didn't just give my presence away but fearing I did. I stay quiet as I watch the man investigate the body with a flashlight. This allows me to see his features. I already know the man is over six feet tall after watching him. Now, with the light from the flashlight, I can tell he has a chiseled jawline, dark-colored hair, and broad shoulders. He is good looking in a bad boy kinda way.

I watch as he digs my shuriken out of the chest of the Wendigo. I close my eyes for a moment as I think how gross it must be to dig into one of their nasty, smelly bodies. That's the reason I work with shurikens. They're quiet, you can use them from a distance, and they are deadly effective as evidenced by the dead Wendigo. You don't have to get up close and personal with your intended target when using them. I open my eyes in time to see the man putting the stuff he bagged and put in his pockets. Damn it! I wonder if he found what belongs to me.

I can tell he's speaking again, but to whom I don't know. I can't see anyone else around, so he's either talking to himself or the dead Wendigo. I notice him go still. I look at his eyes, which glow bright yellow and are looking at me. Shit! Shit! Shit!

By those eyes, I can tell he is a shapeshifter, probably a wolf, and he's looking at me. I have on black pants with a black Henley covered with my black hooded jacket. I hope it's enough of a disguise. It's time for me to get the hell out of here, fighting one of my worst enemies is the last thing I need right now.

Keeping my head tilted toward the ground, I raise only my eyes to keep a watch on him. Staying pressed against the wall, I work my way down the side of the building to escape this situation. As I get to the edge of the building, the man stands up straight staring at me with his yellow eyes. I freeze in my steps for a second, then turn the corner of the building and bolt away as fast as my legs will take me, which is damn fast considering speed is one of my gifts which I've enhanced through training.

I reach the end of the block and turn left without ever slowing, daring not to look back for fear he may see my face. After running a few more blocks, I hear a group of people laughing and partying outside a local bar, so I turn in their direction hoping to get lost in the crowd. I'm now on a street that's home to several bars. People are everywhere, so I stop running when I reach the crowd.

I'm surrounded by people now, and the smell of alcohol is thick in the air. I pull my hood closer around my head and walk with the crowd thinking I'm home free with my escape when I feel a strong-arm wrap around my waist from my right side, pinning my right arm to my body. My back is pulled tight against a muscular, hard chest.

The smell of leather, spice, and masculinity encases me, making my senses aware of how long it's been since I've been intimate with a man. I feel his head getting closer to mine, then feel his breath on my right cheek as he leans in past the edge of my hood.

He inhales a deep breath. "Human," I hear him say with disgust in his tone. He leans in near my ear then speaks in a low growl of a voice so I'm the only one that can hear him as he says, "I'm assuming you know what the hell you killed back there, boy. Explain what the fuck you think you were doing following creatures like those. You will get yourself killed; this isn't child's play. I suggest you get your ass home to your parents, behave and grow up to be a man. If you keep this shit up, you'll end up dead or even worse, end up a meal."

What the fuck? At least I know he hasn't gotten a good look at me, otherwise, he sure as hell wouldn't mistake me for a boy. At least I know the cloaking spell used to hide what I am is still working. I've got to get the fuck away from him before he turns me around. I struggle to break his hold on me and sound out through my locked teeth, "LET ME GO."

He doesn't let go. In fact, his right arm that's around me becomes tighter as he pulls me into the small side alley beside the building we're struggling in front of. He brings his left arm and wraps it around my chest making escape even more impossible. I go completely still when I realize the hand attached to the arm around my chest has landed on my right breast and has a tight grip on it. He must have noticed too because I feel his hand relax then squeeze again.

"What the hell?" he says with confusion in his voice.

"Do you mind letting go of my breast?" I ask with sarcasm dripping off every word.

"Shit! You're a woman!"

"Way to point out the obvious. I see you have a brain to go with those muscles."

"Smart ass!" he growls.

He at once pulls his left arm away from my breast but holds it inches in front of me as to block and discourage me from struggling to get away. Shit! There's blood on his index finger. I glance down and see there's a hole about a half inch long in my jacket with blood smeared around it. I didn't realize I got injured fighting the damn Wendigo. Damn, plus this is my favorite jacket to wear out when I'm on a hunt! The fucking Wendigo has not only stolen from me, but he has now fucked up my favorite jacket. If that motherfucker wasn't already dead, I would hunt him down and kill him again for this shit.

"You're hurt," the man says, apparently seeing the blood on his finger. "Turn around, let me see how bad it is."

There's no way in hell I'm letting him see my face. "Physical injuries are easily healed, it's the broken pieces of the soul that don't mend," I tell him. I heal fast. The cut is no longer bleeding, and by tomorrow morning it should be nothing but a faint pink line that will eventually go away. Still staring at the blood on his finger the thought occurs to me that my DNA is on his damn finger. There's no way I can take a chance of him discovering what I am, the truth I keep cloaked.

When the shock of me being a woman wears off, he will realize that I'm probably not human, especially if I have to kick his ass to escape. I will not give him the chance to have my blood tested. Praying it's not the hand I saw digging into the nasty dead Wendigo, I do the first thing that pops into my mind. I reach up with my free hand and grab with a light hold his left hand to bring it closer. Before he can react, I put the finger in my mouth, wrap my warm wet tongue around it and apply light suction as I slowly pull his finger out, sucking off every last drop of blood. I feel his body stiffen behind me. I then wipe his finger off with the sleeve of my jacket.

"There it's all better. See, nothing to worry about," I stupidly say not understanding how to explain my actions without blurting out the truth. As the memory of this guy putting things pulled off the dead Wendigo into bags comes to mind, I wonder if he has what was stolen from me in one of the them. I casually try to reach back behind me to steal it from his pocket but fail.

"I...." he says but is interrupted as I hear a faint voice shouting words I can't make out. I realize he is wearing an earpiece, so whoever is at the other end of that earpiece is who I've been watching him talk too. He jerks his body in response to whatever they say to him. I take full advantage of this and jerk myself loose from his hold. I take off running once I'm free.

"Wait!" is the only word I hear him yell. I don't stop until I've run for several blocks. I then turn to make sure he didn't follow me. I don't see him. After taking a deep breath, I decide it's time to head home and come up with a plan to get back what belongs to me.

Chapter 24

Daniel
"Copping a Feel"

The smell of the dead Wendigo is burning my eyes, but I don't dare move because I can see whoever is hiding in the shadows edge slowly down the side of the building. He is small, so I'm guessing it's a stupid teenager. Human too, because I can't sense or smell anything from him. It's that, or the stench of the Wendigo is masking his smell. My best guess is a human that stumbled across our reality, who now wants to play hero until it catches up to him and he finds himself dead.

The kid takes off running the second after he reaches the corner of the storage building, so I give chase. I must hand it to him; he's fast for a human. I almost lose him until I hear people around the next corner. If the kid is smart, he'll try to blend into the crowd. After going a block down the street, I spot the black outfit he's wearing.

His gear was good for hiding in the dark, but here in the open around other people, it helps me spot him easily. He has slowed his pace, so I'm guessing he thinks he's ditched me. As I get closer to him, I decide it's time to end this cat-and-mouse game and grab his right side with my right arm. I secure him up close so maybe I can scare the fuck out of the little shit and get him to stay home where he belongs. He needs to leave this reality to the grown-ups trained to deal with it.

I feel his body go rigid and still. I lean in to smell his scent. "Human," I declare, not hiding the irritation in my voice. I lean my head closer to his ear to keep others from hearing me, "I'm assuming you know what the hell you killed back there, boy.

Explain what the fuck you think you were doing following creatures like those. You will get yourself killed; this isn't child's play. I suggest you get your ass home to your parents, behave and grow up to be a man. If you keep this shit up, you'll end up dead or even worse, end up a meal."

The little shit struggles. "Let me go" he growls out. I see a small alley off to our side, so I drag his ass over to it before he brings us unwanted attention. I feel like beating his ass, but instead, I need to get him to stand still so I can try to talk some sense into him. If that doesn't work, I might go ahead and beat his ass. I wrap my other arm around his chest trying to subdue him. When my hand grabs hold of him, I feel something familiar in my palm, but it can't be. I release and squeeze again.

"What the hell?" I ask with confusion in my voice.

"Do you mind letting go of my breast?" the woman, not a boy, says in a sarcastic tone.

"Shit! You're a woman!" is the first thing that flies from my mouth.

"Way to point out the obvious. I see you have a brain to go with those muscles," she responds.

"Smart ass," I reply.

I let go of her breast and move my left arm but keep it close in case she tries to bolt away. For the first time, I notice the smell of vanilla perfume radiating from her. My cock pays attention. I guess copping a feel of her tit along with her scent and feisty attitude are too much for my cock to handle at one time, so it woke up. I hope she can't feel my growing hard-on pressing against her. After moving my arm, I catch a glance at my hand and realize there's blood on my finger. "You're hurt. Turn around and let me see how bad it is." Like a typical woman, she ignores my demand.

Instead, she responds, "Physical injuries are easily healed, it's the broken pieces of the soul that don't mend."

Before I can give a response, she shocks the hell out of me by pulling my hand to her face and placing her mouth around my finger. I can see her thick full lips as she wraps her tongue around it, gently sucking as she pulls my finger out of her mouth. It's the best finger suck I've ever had. The only thing that comes to mind is her thick lips sliding over the head of my engorged cock as her warm wet tongue wraps around the shaft. The mental image makes my cock harder. I've got to see the face belonging to that sexy mouth.

"There, it's all better, see nothing to worry about," she says as if I'm the one who's hurt and not her.

"I..." is all I get out before I hear Drake moaning like fucking hell over the radio. Connor hears it too because now I hear Connor calling Drake's name. While I'm caught up in what I hear over the earpiece, my grip on the feisty woman loosens. She takes full advantage of this by yanking out of my hold and racing off again.

"Wait!" I yell after her. All I can do is watch her disappear in the distance because my team needs me. I turn to head back to the warehouse to help my team.

Chapter 25

Connor
"Fuck Monkey"

As I inch my way forward, I spot one of the Wendigos lurking up ahead. When I'm close enough for a clean shot, I stop and aim my pistol at the smelly bastard. Just before I pull the trigger, I hear the faint whistling sound of a bullet cutting thru the air. I quickly glance around to see if I can pin point where the bullet originated from. A moment later, I hear Drake moaning in my earpiece causing my blood to run cold. I turn back to finish off the Wendigo in front of me only to find him gone.

"That fuck monkey shot me!" I hear Drake say as he groans out the words.

"Drake, I'm heading your way." Drake continues moaning as I race toward his voice. I hear a door open and then slam closed, which I assume is the Wendigos escaping from the building. That's fine. I'll make it my personal mission to hunt both those bastards down to make them pay for this.

It doesn't take long for me to reach Drake. I put down my gear as I bend over to assess him. I can't believe how much blood is draining out of the hole in his chest. I shake my head to clear my thoughts. I need to push the fact that this is my brother out of my head and focus on the task at hand to keep from losing him. As I look into his face, I see he is struggling to keep his eyes open.

"Man down, I repeat man down," I bark into the earpiece. "Drake's been shot in the chest."

"Already heading your way," I hear Daniel say. Something is fucked up with this injury. With our ability to heal fast, the flow of blood should have shown signs of slowing.

"We're heading your way," Drew says over my earpiece from back at our office.

"Silver... it.... burns like silver," Drake says, gasping for breath in between words and struggling to speak. That's why the wound looks so fucked up, silver is our kryptonite. Drake's eyes close again only to stay closed this time.

"Drake! Stay with me, Drake! Help's coming," I say trying to encourage him to keep his eyes open. I place my hand on my pistol as I hear footsteps heading towards us. I realize a second later that it's Daniel.

"What the fuck happened? How the hell did a fucking Wendigo get the drop on him?" he asks. "What the fuck! Why is he not healing?"

"I think the bullet is silver. Try to see if you can get to it without doing any more damage while I call Kira," I order Daniel as I take out my cell phone to make the call. I hit Kira Sharman's number, which we keep programmed on speed dial on all our phones. Kira is a physician for non-humans.

"I can't get to it without doing more damage. The bullet lodged near his heart. Another half inch to the left and he wouldn't be breathing," Daniel says as I wait for Kira to answer my call. She finally picks up. I quickly run through the details of Drake's wound.

"I agree the bullet sounds like its silver laced or made from silver from the description and the fact he's not healing. I'm too far away, he needs immediate treatment so get him to the hospital closest to you and let them treat him. He doesn't have long before the silver destroys the surrounding tissue, then it will progressively get worse until it kills him. With it that close to the heart, getting it out quick is the only choice. Once the silver is out of his system, we will run into a hell of a mess trying to explain how he's able to heal so quickly, so I will get started on having him transferred to my care once he's out of surgery," Kira Instructs.

Daniel must have heard our conversation because I hear

him on his phone confirming the address with 911 for an ambulance. Seconds later, the door bursts open with Drew and Val charging towards us. I thank Kira and hang up.

"How bad is it?" Val asks.

"It's bad enough we have to get him to the local hospital. An ambulance is on the way. We need to hide the dead Wendigo's body before they get here," I say barking out orders. Drew stands to head back out to do as I ordered, but the EMT's are already pushing through the warehouse door, running our way.

"Too late," Drew states the obvious. "I'll call in our connections to the county morgue to make sure they cover our tracks by concealing the fact the body is non-human," Drew says as he heads outside to do just that. I stand back helplessly watching them load my younger brother into the back of the ambulance in record time.

"Hold on little brother," is the only words I can get out of my mouth before the doors of the ambulance slam shut. Val is up front in the ambulance riding with them to watch over Drake while I stay behind for a few minutes. As the team leader, it's my job to make sure everything is taken care of and the scene secured before I head back to the office.

When I get to our office, as I grab my motorcycle, I call my family in the process to let them know about Drake. My mother breaks down, but my father is there with her, so he'll make sure she gets to the hospital safely. I can tell from the slip of emotions I hear in his voice how the news of Drake has affected him, but I've never seen him lose his shit in any situation.

My team and family crowd the hospital's emergency department waiting room. I'm mentally reliving the night's events when the sound of a female voice breaks through the silence of the waiting room, pulling me from my thoughts. I hear the woman announcing that she is Drake's doctor, and as I lift my head to look at her my mouth falls open.

I stand up with the rest of my family and team to gather around the doctor, so she can update us on Drake's condition. My mind is so overloaded with thoughts I almost miss her announcement that Drake is critical but stable. Finally, I shut my mouth closed. It can't be, can it? Willow? Dr. Willow?

Chapter 26

Willow
"Diarrhea of the Mouth"

When I reach the doorway of the waiting room, I pause to take a deep breath. Adrenaline is coursing through my veins from the knowledge of knowing within seconds I'll be face to face with the man I've been searching for since our one night together. I would never have thought I would say this, but the man I'm about to face is not only my baby's father but, is also a gang member who carries around guns, and gets shot at with real bullets.

After one more deep breath I hold my chin up high, keeping my mind set on the plan to focus my attention on Drake's other family members rather than Connor. Before I take another step, I glance down to assess my stomach, ensuring my scrubs are concealing my baby bump. As I step through the door, only a couple of people notice my presence. I clear my throat which causes everyone else to jerk their heads up to look at me too.

"Drake's family?" I ask, knowing the answer but asking to be polite. After a few nods of heads, a yes, and a woman stating, "we are his parents", I continue to finish with the introduction part. I quickly decide only to use my last name with a spark of hope that Connor will not remember me and also, not wanting to jog his memory by using my first name. "I'm Dr. Black. I'm the surgeon who operated on your son," I say to the man and woman that introduced themselves as his parents. As my report to them of the details of Drake's condition continues like a robot, I see Connor out of the corner of my eye but keep my eyes facing forward. I feel his eyes trained on me with such intensity I know he recognizes me. As I'm concluding my report, I steal a quick glance in his direction causing me to stumble over my words, but I quickly recover with the next sentence. He looks even sexier than I remember. His dark eyes and messy brown hair with his muscular build sends chills down my spine to my lady bits.

Just as flashbacks of our night together race through my mind, his mother startles me by grabbing me and hugging me tightly, showing her gratitude. As I give her a quick hug and a light pat on her back, two thoughts slam into my mind. One- would this woman still be hugging me if she knew the things I did to her son and allowed him to do to me with his mouth, fingers, and cock? Two- I realize the woman hugging me is my baby's grandmother.

That realization causes me to glance around at the people in the waiting room, realizing that all of them could be relatives of my child. They're here because they care for Drake, which makes me feel guilty because I might be robbing my baby of a loving family.

As his mother steps back from our hug, I feel the need to hurry and get the hell out of this room. The walls feel like they are closing in on me as his family crowds around us. My forehead breaks out in a sweat. Time to exit, "If you will excuse me, I need to finish rounds on my other patients," I say while smiling a smile that must have looked as strained as it felt to make. As I turn and walk out the door into the hall, I release a breath as the anxiety leaves my body with the thoughts of a clean getaway from Connor. As that thought enters my mind, it rushes out just as quickly when a strong, large hand wraps around my upper arm, pulling me to a stop. Damn! I thought as Connor spins me around to face him.

"You're just going to run off without saying a word to me?" Connor accuses with a look of confusion.

"I did talk to you. In fact, I talked to your whole family," I snap at him.

"That's not what I meant, and you damn well know it,"

Connor replies just as snappy as I did.

With a softer approach to my voice, I try to give what I think sounds like a believable excuse, "Look, your brother was just shot, and I didn't think it was the time or place to discuss us in front of your family. Plus, do you realize how awkward it was hugging your mother while flashes of us that night were running through my mind?" Damn did I say that last part out loud?

With the smirk on his face as evidence, I realize yes, yes, I did. I need to get away from this man, otherwise I may keep having diarrhea of the mouth and let other things slip.

"Well," Connor says, "I would like to discuss us. I had an amazing night with you and I thought the feeling was mutual. Everything was good until you bailed on me while I was asleep. I didn't even get your last name. Have you ever tried to find someone by only their first name? Let me just say, it doesn't work. I know you're busy, but I would love to sit down to discuss future possibilities over lunch or dinner. Hand me your pen." Connor reaches his hand behind him, pulls out his wallet to gets something out of it. I reach into my front pocket pull out my pen then hand it to him. When he reaches for it our fingers touch, sending an all too familiar shiver from my hand down my spine that seems only to happen when he touches me.

"This is my cell phone number I'm writing on the back of my business card. I would love for you to call me in the next few days to either meet for coffee or to go out on a date. I'll let that be your decision of what we do, but I want to get to know you better Dr. Black," Connor says as he reaches up to my front scrub pocket and slides his business card down into it.

I remind myself to stay focused on the fact he belongs to a gang before I turn to goo and melt into a puddle on the floor while staring into those gorgeous eyes of his. His gang has business cards? How professional.

"I do have to go," I tell him, needing to get away from him before the desire to jump his body overtakes the logical side of my brain.

Chapter 27

Connor
"Sucker Punch"

"Call me," I remind Willow as she turns and walks away. I have a sick feeling in the pit of my gut she will not call, but that's just too fucking bad Dr. Black. After searching for her without success then stumbling upon her by accident tonight, I'll be damned if she will dismiss me this easily.

A moan almost escapes my mouth as I watch her ass sway when she walks away. The feel of her ass in my hand as I braced her against the wall and pounded her tight, sweet tasting little cunt is forever burned in my memory. I reach up with my hands to rub my face and block the vision to regain control of my cock when I see her pen still in my hand. Now, I have an excellent excuse to chase her down and touch her again even if it is only her hand.

I start after her, as I turn the corner of the hall as she did a second earlier, I stop in my tracks. She's standing a few feet away behind a long desk talking to a nurse. I stay where I am to wait for my chance to speak with her alone again. If I approach her now, she could dismiss me after I hand over her pen. So, I prop myself up against the wall to wait.

She's smiling at the nurse as they speak quietly to each other. Damn, her whole face lights up when she smiles. It makes her appear more beautiful if that's even possible. Curious about what's making her smile, I concentrate and eavesdrop on their conversation.

"It's good to see you too Melinda," Willow tells the woman.

"You look well. Not as pale as the last time I saw you," Melinda tells her.

"I've been doing better than I was in the beginning. I haven't been as nauseated," Willow informs her. What the hell, is Willow sick? Should she even be working if she's sick? How is she going to get better if she takes care of everyone but herself? I'm surprised that I'm feeling real concern for her well-being, in a possessive kind of way, when the next words I hear her say feel like a sucker punch to my gut.

"Morning sickness morning, noon, and night," Willow says.

"I had morning sickness till I was around five months pregnant, then it just disappeared," Melinda tells her.

"Well, I'm four months. After I passed the first trimester, I gave up hope, afraid I would be one of those pregnant women who stay sick the whole nine months. Who knows, maybe there's hope for me yet," Willow says with a slightly weaker smile on her plump lips this time. "I'm heading home to get some rest. Page me if you need anything," Willow instructs Melinda as she walks away again.

"Will do, have a good night," Melinda replies.

Pregnant? Willow's pregnant? I quickly do the math in my head. The amazing night we spent together was about sixteen weeks ago. Just for good measure, I recalculate in my head again coming up with sixteen weeks. Could Willow's baby be mine? Am I going to be a father? Why the hell didn't she say something? Is she planning on having MY KID and NOT even informing me? The lust I was feeling quickly disintegrates, transforming into anger.

I push off from the wall I'm leaning against to pursue her ass and confront her over the shocking betrayal I feel. It'll be a cold day in hell before I let her get away with my kid. Knowing Drake has made it through the worst of it and will heal quickly since Willow removed the silver, leaves nothing holding me back from the confrontation that's coming.

I follow her out the exit doors of the hospital into the parking lot. I watch as she makes her way to her car, stopping once to pass a greeting on to another employee of the hospital before she enters her car. This gives me a moment to make it over to my motorcycle. I turn on my bike and crank it up, making the engine roar, as I wait for Willow to leave the parking lot to follow her.

I'm able to follow far enough behind Willow's car to keep her from noticing, not that she would suspect anyone following her since her lifestyle is so different from mine based on our career choices. I plan on finding out exactly where little Miss Dr. Black calls home. If she thinks she can dismiss me so easily and be rid of me, she's got another thing coming. When Willow turns on her blinker to pull over in front of her house, I pull to a stop two houses away. I wait until she's out of the car and safe in her home before driving by the house heading down St. Charles Street back toward the Quarter. I plan on confronting her, but first I need to run an errand to prepare for what is to come.

Back at the hospital parking lot…. Connor had been so preoccupied and pissed off that he didn't notice the figure standing in the shadows watching from a distance. Jay, one of the three Wendigos from the warehouse, followed the ambulance. The Wendigo killed earlier this evening was his brother.

Jay

I am not per se heartbroken over my brother's death, more like pissed off. He irritated me to the point of wanting to end his life myself often. When I saw the ambulance transporting that fucking werewolf Drake, I followed it. Drake and his brother, along with the rest of the fucking Guardians, have been like a festering abscess on my ass for years. I was hoping to gain undetected access to Drake to finish him off but abandoned the idea once I spotted a waiting room full of werewolves. After all, I'm not that stupid.

I fell back to watch from a distance, looking for any opportunity that might occur allowing me to rid myself of one of the Guardians. I know they've come to town to put a stop to my little clan of Wendigos from helping ourselves to the free meat on the streets. Getting rid of an injured werewolf is much easier than a healthy one. The bullet that hit Drake contained a lethal dose of silver. I should know, I created it myself. How my idiot partner could get a shot in without being detected is something I haven't been able to wrap my mind around yet.

Apparently, it missed his heart, which would have caused immediate death. I know having silver in the werewolf's body will keep Drake weak for a few hours up to a few days, depending on how long it remained in his body. When I spotted Connor coming out of the hospital, I froze in the shadows from the buildings on the other side of the parking lot. I watched Connor glare at some female doctor as she was getting into her car. I'm surprised that with all those damn heightened senses of his, he didn't notice me. I watch as Conner gets on his motorcycle and follows the car, keeping his distance in the process. "Interesting," I say in an almost whisper, "very interesting indeed." With that new tidbit of information, I leave.

Chapter 28

Willow
"Fish out of Water"

I'm physically and mentally exhausted and can't wait to crawl into bed for some well-deserved sleep. My goal is to not dream of Connor. During the drive home, I kept replaying the events of the day in my mind. Out of all the people I could imagine being wheeled into my emergency room tonight, I wouldn't have guessed Connor nor his brother. Especially not from a gang shootout that killed one person. I wonder who shot the other victim, Drake or Connor? Could my baby's father be a murderer? Will he get arrested?

Now that I've made it home, my mind is racing with so many thoughts I know there's no way I'll be able to go to bed and fall asleep as planned. I take a deep breath and consider my options. I could go for a cup of Nikki's tea, but I don't want to drive to her house. The short drive would feel like an eternity. Plan number two is to take a hot shower and fix myself some warm milk to drink. Perfect! I like Plan two, it might do the trick to help relax me, so I head to the shower, peeling my clothes off as I go.

After I'm finished washing my hair and body, I stand in the shower allowing the hot water to cascade down my body. As I feel the tightness in my muscles give way, a wonderful feeling of relaxation comes over me. My mind keeps wandering back to thoughts of Connor and how much better he looked tonight than I remembered him looking the night we were together in the hotel. The expert way he touched my body with his hands, fingers, and tongue though, I remember like yesterday.

I glide my right hand over my thigh while the left massages my breast, trying to mimic his sensual touches.

As I remember the way he held me up against the wall and ripped my underwear free from my body, I slide my hand over from my thigh onto my mound and slip my fingers through the swollen folds of wetness, causing me to moan as my index finger brushes my clit. My other hand caresses my breast as I pinch my hardened nipple between my forefinger and thumb.

The wetness grows from my fingers working their way in and out of my opening as my hand glides over my clit, increasing the pressure without ever breaking contact. I remember Connor's piercing eyes looking up at me as he devoured my pussy with his mouth. My body trembles as the walls of my pussy contract around my fingers as they slide in and out.

I moan and bite down on my bottom lip as the orgasm takes control of my body. Still panting as I float back down into my body from my orgasm, cold water washes over me indicating its time to get out of the shower. Well hell, so much for getting Connor off my mind.

As I'm getting dressed, I realize my options for clothing are dwindling. I will have to shop for maternity clothes soon. I will be the size of a house at the rate my lower abdomen is growing. My cute, sexy, short-short PJs are already uncomfortably snug. Looking through my closet, I decide on an oversized shirt and loose-fitting boy shorts I still feel comfortable wearing. I dress, then grab my hairbrush off the dresser and brush through my hair. My plan for the rest of the night is to fix myself a cup of warm milk while I settle into my bed. Then read a book as I sip the warm milk. Once it's gone, I'll turn out the lights and hopefully fall right to sleep. The shower along with the self-induced orgasm relaxed me quite a bit already.

As I step into the kitchen, I hear my doorbell ring. "What now?" I ask out loud, feeling a little irritated that someone is disrupting my plans for the rest of the night. I walk over and look through the peep hole. I can't believe my eyes. It's Connor. With a confused look, I open the door. "What are you doing here and how do you know where I live?"

"I followed you because we need to have a little chat," Connor replies with a deadpan glare in his eyes.

Not wanting to deal with whatever this is about, I politely try getting rid of him, so I can have my freak out in private. "I'm exhausted," I speak, but he cuts my words short.

"Are you pregnant Willow?" I feel the color drain from my face and think I'm going to be sick. Why the hell does he think I'm pregnant? Maybe I'm showing my baby bump through my scrubs more than I realized.

I do the only thing I can think of doing which is lie, lie, lie. "Umm… no, no, what on earth gave you that ridiculous idea?" I'm such a terrible liar that even I can hear it in my voice.

Connor steps around me to get inside without even waiting to be invited. Now what the hell am I going to do? I shut the front door because it's not like I can force him back out the door, anyway. I take a deep breath then turn slowly to face him noticing he is struggling to get something out of his pocket with his left hand. After a moment he pulls an elongated box out of the pocket, and my mouth drops open when I read the print on the box.

"Then you won't mind going into the bathroom with me and pissing on this stick to prove it," Connor says while glaring at me as he opens the side panel and pulls the actual test stick from inside the box. I can only stare at the stick with bug eyes while opening and closing my mouth like a fish out of water, trying to figure out what the hell to say.

"I don't have to pee right now," I exclaim.

Connor gets a devilish grin on his face, "I've got all night baby, in fact I can give you all day tomorrow if I need too."

"Shit!" I say as all other responses elude me.

"Yeah, my thoughts exactly. What the hell Willow! I can understand not knowing how to get in touch with me. Hell, I've unsuccessfully searched for you since that amazing night too, but tonight I was right in front of you and you couldn't get away from me fast enough! Do you honestly think I don't have a right to know? Just so we're very clear, don't open your mouth and tell me it's not my kid you're carrying unless it's the truth, because there's a test for that too. I'll drag your little ass into a lab with the baby and have that one ran if I need too," Connor threatens as he paces back and forth.

His face gets redder with each word leaving his mouth, and his voice louder with each sentence he speaks. He stops pacing and stares at me while panting with each breath as if trying to calm the anger or hurt that is radiating off him.

My mind tells me I should be afraid of this raging man in front of me, but somewhere deep in my soul I know he would never physically harm me. I'm guessing he wants me to respond now since he keeps staring at me. The only thoughts I can muster after the lecture is the fact that he said he had searched for me and that he called our night together amazing.

Those thoughts cause an unwanted fluttering sensation down low in my body. I don't know what pisses me off more my traitorous body or the lecture on morals I just got from a gang member. I've got to get a handle on my hormones. I glare at him, then storm off to the kitchen to fix my milk, wishing it was something a hell of a lot stronger like a shot of whiskey.

Apparently, my night isn't going to end as early as I'd planned. Connor is fast on my heels following me into the kitchen which isn't surprising. I get the milk from the refrigerator, grab a mug from the cabinet, and then head for the stove- all while keeping my back to him.

Finally, Connor breaks the silence, "I'm waiting for an explanation woman, and I damn well deserve one." Now, I'm the one getting annoyed. It's late, and I'm tired. I slam the milk on the counter next to where I placed my mug, then take a couple of steps away from the counter.

"You're not good enough to be my baby's father!" I yell as I turn toward him, surprising myself a little for that outburst. I see a trace of hurt in his eyes, then just as quickly I witness the anger return.

"How the hell would you know that? You don't know me

well enough to judge me!"

That's it! Feeling the need to get all my frustrations out about the disappointing revelations I discovered about him today, I start a yelling rant, "I know enough! I know that what happened to your brother was gang related, and out of two people shot, your brother is the only one that's still alive. I don't want my baby growing up with bullets flying around; thinking its normal being around only God knows what. My baby needs and deserves a happy, peaceful home with a white picket fence and a puppy in the yard, not a barbed wire fence with thugs in the yard as playmates!"

I start to feel dizzy and stumble a couple of steps as I try to grab hold of the edge of the counter. I realize I'm not close enough to reach it and close my eyes as I hold out my hands, waiting for the impact of the floor to hit my hands and knees, but it never comes.

"Fuck!" Connor says as I feel his arms catch me to steady me on my feet. "Damn, I shouldn't come off as an ass no matter how pissed off I am right now. It can't be good for the baby, MY BABY that is," he says, sounding more like reassurance to himself than a statement to me. Standing right beside me now, he is bracing me by my arm, so I don't tumble over again. As he takes a couple of deep breaths that I assume are to calm his temper, I feel the air he's exhaling against my neck, causing me to become more light-headed for other reasons now. Damn hormones! Connor must have felt me sway because one second, I'm trying to stand up straight and the next I find myself swept into his arms in a bridal hold. I feel an electric shock travel through my body when his hands and arms touch my skin, causing me to gasp.

Connor freezes in his steps to stares down at me. I wonder if he felt the shock from our contact as well? The look on his face disappears before I figure out what it meant, and after a couple of seconds he storms out of the kitchen with me still in his arms. I then remember I'm not supposed to be mesmerized by this thug of a man. As I open my mouth to demand he put me down, again he speaks and cuts off my words before I can get one syllable out of my mouth.

"We need to get a few motherfuckin' things straight, but first you're gonna calm the fuck down. We both are," Connor amends with a growl through clenched teeth as he takes me into the living room, walks over to the sofa then sits down with me in his lap.

The feel of his firm cock against my ass signals I'm sitting directly on top of it, almost causing me to let out the groan that's forming in the back of my throat. I have flashbacks remembering the details of his cock from our night together; its thickness, bulging veins, and almost angry looking head.

The strong urge to grind my hips down so my pussy can rub the length of his shaft to ease the hungry throb I'm feeling between my legs is almost more than I can contain. I realize that he's stopped lecturing me and is now staring at me with bewilderment in his eyes.

"Woman, are you paying attention?" As soon as the words left his lips, a look of realization crossed the beautiful features of his face, indicating he knows exactly where my attention is. My face heats up from the embarrassment his question is causing while praying I'm wrong about his all-knowing look. I feel like a child caught making out with a boy by her mother. With a smirk on his luscious lips, he asks, "What were you thinking about just now?"

Damn my traitorous body. "Nothing, I was just listening to you." I try looking innocent, but I know I'm failing as I feel my face becoming even more flush. The look on his face along with that question tells me he knows what I'm thinking. His smirk turns into a cocky grin which annoys me. Not wanting to sit in his lap any longer, I try to stand. He clamps his hands together awhich brings his forearms down above my hip bone, caging me in and forcing me to stay in his lap. "Whatever," I say, faking a bored sigh as I roll my eyes.

As soon my roll my eye is completed, his grin disappears from his lips and is replaced with a thin line as he presses his lips together with a look of aggravation reappearing back into his eyes. He continues our discussion in a lecturing tone. "First, you're gonna calm down that temper of yours. Second, you watch way too much damn TV to come up with all those ideas you have floating around in that pretty little brain of yours. Third, my kid will not have a dog as a pet. And lastly, did you even look at the front of the business card I gave you tonight?" Connor asks as I feel him release his hold on my hips. I no longer have a desire to vacate his lap, so I pretend not to notice.

"No," I respond in a whisper while looking down at my hands. I feel ashamed from not even reading the card. With the anger he's showing, I'm getting a small feeling that maybe I let my imagination run away from me earlier. "I didn't read the card," I continue with my confession.

He leans his left hip up slightly while reaching into his back pocket to pull his wallet out for a second time tonight to get another one of his business cards. He holds it out for me to take. This time, I take the card and read it. Afterward, I feel confused. "I don't understand what this is or what you are trying to tell me."

"We're the good guys, babe. My company, Cerberus," he points to the name located on his card, "we hunt down and take care of the bad guys by helping law enforcement when they ask us to get involved. So instead of assuming you know everything, you should have taken the time to find out. My baby," he says as he places a hand over my lower stomach and starts to rub gently while continuing to talk, "needs a father and that's me, whether you like it or not. I'm not planning on leaving behind what's mine. I was raised to put family before anything. Do you understand what I'm saying to you woman?" he asks as he leans closer to my face to look directly into my eyes.

For a moment, all I can do is stare back into his beautiful milk-chocolate colored eyes. I could stare at them all day. At this moment, I realize for the first time I'm in deep shit. I could lose my heart to this man. It hurt when Bill left, but I got over it. I feel if I fall for this man in front of me too fast, it could break me. Maybe it's just my hormones, but I genuinely don't believe it is.

I know I need to respond to his comments, so I try coming up with something to say other than do you want to have make-up sex. All I do is open and close my mouth like a fish out of water, not knowing quite what to say. I notice this is becoming my typical reaction to him. I see his eyes staring at my lips as he sucks in his bottom lip and rubs his top teeth across it as he drags it out again.

"Well good, I'm glad we both agree," he says as he stands up with me still in his arms. He then turns and sits me down in the spot his ass was just sitting in. Just like that, my lust filled mind has turned to annoyance by his cockiness. "I will fix you and my baby the warm milk I assume you were trying to fix while you lay here and rest. By the looks of your swaying earlier, you've probably been working too damn much."

He then walks out of the living room heading toward the kitchen. I take this opportunity to sneak a peek at his ass, and then quickly look away as I notice his body turning back in my direction. I don't want to get caught ogling his body parts. "When I get back with your milk, we will need to talk about how you need to move in with me," Connor announces, then turns and leaves my sight heading to the kitchen.

"Wait! What?" is all I manage to ask as his words soak into my brain. He can't be serious, can he? Suddenly, the words of the old Twilight Zone show run through my mind, "You are traveling through another dimension, a dimension not only of sight and sound but of mind. A journey into a wondrous land of imagination. Next stop, the Twilight Zone!" I must have fallen at work and hit my head. Yes, that's got to be it. That's where this all started tonight. Thinking back through everything Connor said tonight, the first thing that pops into mind is his comment about no dogs. "What do you have against dogs?" I yell.

"No dogs! A wolf is okay as a companion, but definitely no damn dog!" Connor yells back from the kitchen. What the fuck? A wolf? Now, I know for sure I must have hit my head at work. The best plan of action is just to lay my head back on the sofa cushion and wait until I wake up back in the Emergency Department at work.

Chapter 29

Connor
"All up into my Stuff"

I use this momentary reprieve in the kitchen as an opportunity to clear my mind. My brain feels cluttered from the events of the day. I need to prioritize the events and decide how to handle everything from the case, from Drake being shot, and from me discovering I'm going to be a father. Just one of those events is enough to blow anyone's mind, and now I must deal with all three. Since I know Drake is stable and just needs time to recover, I will put my focus on Willow and the baby.

I reach for the milk that Willow left on the counter earlier, then walk over to pour some into the pan already sitting out on the stove. As I dig through the first drawer I open, I find a wooden spoon. I take it out and continue my thoughts as I stir the warming milk with it. I don't know a damn thing about birthing babies. A thought slams into my mind. Willow is a human carrying a werewolf baby. I mean I knew this little fact, but I seemed to have buried it in the back of my mind. The ramifications are now front and center.

There's no way in hell she'll be able to use a regular doctor. I do know enough to know Willow must use Kara as her Obstetrician. A human being pregnant with a werewolf baby could be more complicated, and that's one of the reason's relationships with shape-shifters and humans aren't just discouraged, they're frowned upon. Telling Willow mine and my family's secret identities is not an option now. I'll have to tell her eventually, but I have a few months before I must, so I'll figure that part out later. I've dealt with half-breed children when assisting Dom and I'll be damned if that shit happens to my kid. The plan is to find a way to tell Willow without scaring the hell out of her in the process. The focus now is to make sure they both are getting the best care possible, so I will have to convince Willow to see Kara.

One thing I know for sure, Willow working too much is causing undue stress on her and the baby. If how exhausted she looks isn't an indicator, then almost falling is. Had I not been here to grab her, she would have hit the floor. So, the second thing we need to discuss is her not working as much. She can quit her job for all I care. I make plenty of money to support her and the baby. If she doesn't listen to reason, then it's not beyond me to just tie her to the damn bed for the next few months, my bed that is.

My cock immediately takes note of the idea of restraining Willow to my bed. I take a deep breath and try to get control over the damn thing. He seems to have his own agenda. My cock is the last thing I need doing my thinking for me.

As mad as I am at Willow for trying to keep her pregnancy from me, I'm surprised I have this overwhelming possessive, protective need to keep her safe. Even more startling is that even if she wasn't pregnant with my baby, I suspect the need to possess and protect her would still be there. I push those thoughts to the back of my mind for another day.

I look down at the milk in the pot I've been absentmindedly stirring and notice the milk has steam rising from it, which pulls me out of my muse. I carry the pot of milk to the sink to pour it into the mug I saw Willow retrieve out of the cabinet over the coffee pot right before her ranting started.

A flash of light in the night sky catches my attention out the window located over the kitchen sink. Great, the last thing I needed to add to tonight is a drive home on my bike in a thunderstorm. Maybe the storm won't last long, but with the amount of lightening developing in the distance, I know my chances of it clearing before I leave are slim to none.

I turn around with the mug of milk in my hand and walk

back to the living room to give it to Willow. I realize she's been very quiet during my time in her kitchen, causing me to wonder if she fell asleep. As I walk into the room, I stop for a moment to watch her lying still with her eyes closed. I note how beautiful and peaceful she looks as she lays against the arm cushion of the sofa.

"Willow, baby, are you awake?" I inquire in a hushed tone in hopes of not waking her if she is asleep.

Willow turns her head in my direction without lifting it up and opens just one eye to look at me. "No, apparently I'm not awake yet," she says then closes her eye again.

"What?" I ask, confused as hell with her answer as I approach the sofa with the milk.

Willow opens both eyes and peers up at me. She sighs heavily while rising to a sitting position. "I was assuming I must have fallen and hit my head at work and this whole night must be some bizarre, delusional dream I'm having, but it appears that's just wishful thinking." She reaches for the mug of milk. As I sit down, I feel a little taken back a little by her comment. Is she wishing I didn't figure out the about pregnancy?

Willow must have noticed the hurt look on my face and elaborates, "I didn't mean it like that. I now realize it will be nice having someone around that's just as invested in this pregnancy as I am. It's the bizarre comments of us moving in together and the wolf comments that are making my head spin. It's hard for me to tell if you're joking or being serious. You know, we didn't exactly do a lot of talking that night to get to know each other."

"We would have if you'd hung around the following morning," I snap causing her to wince.

"Touche, you're right. I took the coward's way out instead of facing the awkward morning after scenario. I was too embarrassed and didn't know exactly how to act because I'd never had a one-night stand before."

That confession makes me feel a little better as deep down I hoped that was the only reason she bolted that morning. "I kind of figured that was the reason. To clear up any confusion you have, I'm serious about the moving in," I say with a smug look forming on my face as I see the shocked look that spreads across her beautiful features.

"Were you dropped on your head when you were a baby?" Her response causes my smirk to turn into a full-on smile while shaking my head.

"Maybe, but just hear me out."

"No, we can't live together. We barely know one another. I've lived on my own for a while now and I'm set in my ways. Living together would put a strain on getting to know each other," Willow states as she lets out another heavy sigh.

"Calm down. We can talk all that out later before you agree." The before you agree comment earns me an extra eye roll from her. "For now, I want you to keep me updated on your pregnancy. I missed out on everything so far, which is going to change as of right now. I plan on being around for the long haul, not just after the baby is born but throughout the pregnancy as well."

Willow snorts as she informs me, "The only thing you've missed out on is a whole lot of nausea and vomiting, so consider that a positive thing. Believe me, it hasn't been all sunshine and roses. I wish I could've missed out on that part myself. Anyway, having someone watch as you hang your head into the toilet while you vomit is not something most people want witnessed, especially not me."

It is my turn to wince. "That bad huh? What's your doctor said about all the morning sickness?"

"Umm...," Willow says. My brow frowns with her comment as the realization that she hasn't gone to see a doctor yet hits me.

"What?" I ask. "You've been to see an Obstetrician haven't you, Willow? I mean I know you're a doctor, but even I know you need to see a doctor who delivers babies. With you being a doctor, you sure as hell should know better than that." I don't know whether to feel grateful that it should be easier to talk her into seeing Kara or pissed at the carelessness of her not taking care of herself and the baby better. I decide to go with the latter, pissed off feeling. I sense she can feel the air around us filling with tension from the anger radiating off me, causing her to feel defensive and embarrassed since she does know better.

"No, I haven't seen a doctor! I took a blood test at work along with the multiple home pregnancy tests to confirm I'm pregnant. I started over-the-counter prenatal vitamins right afterwards. I usually see a GYN in Baton Rouge, but I know I need an OB doctor closer than an hour and a half away."

"Hour and a half away? Why not use one at the hospital where you work?" I ask shaking my head in confusion yet again.

"Well, I don't want to be at work and run into someone that's been, you know, all up in my stuff," she says as she gestures with her hand in a circular motion between her legs. As the redness of embarrassment slips up from her neck onto her face, she continues, "I don't want someone looking at my vagina today, then have to greet them as I pass them in the hall tomorrow."

Willow looks down, busying herself by picking at the bottom hem of her top as we sit in awkward silence for a moment. She looks up when she hears me take a deep breath and exhale. I can only stare in disbelief. It's difficult for me to fathom how modest Willow is after our wild night of sex. She sure as hell didn't care about baring it all then. After about a minute I realize what a blessing the weirdness over her modesty really is.

"I may have a solution to this current problem," I inform her trying not to appear manipulative. Willow raises her eyebrows as a sign for me to continue when I pause for a moment. "My family has used the same physician for years now to deliver babies."

Willow furrows her brows as she considers this option. "Male or female?" she inquires.

"Female," I respond.

"Located where?" Willow continues with her interrogation.

"Just right outside of New Orleans," I reply. Willow pauses for a moment, appearing lost in thought and pondering her decision.

"I've known her to make house calls," I add for good measure.

"OK," Willow agrees.

"OK?" I ask, needing to verify because this seems a little too easy. Willow nods her head in agreement.

"Well, now that we agree, we can go tomorrow so you can meet her, and you can have your first appointment. I'll pick you up in the morning, so we can ride together," I inform her.

"But," as Willow speaks, I reach up and place a finger over her lips to silence her protest. She takes me by surprise when her wet pink tongue snakes out of her mouth appearing to lick her lips. I pause, staring intently at her mouth watching her tongue slip out further, barely tasting my finger, then back in.

It takes a great deal of self-control to keep me from moaning. I stare at her mouth as I remember how it felt to have her warm tongue sliding down the shaft of my cock. This woman's going to be the death of me if I don't get away from her. Even with everything still unsure between us, I want to be balls deep into her sweet little pussy.

In a husky voice, I tell her, "I don't care about your work other than where my brothers concerned. I do care about this baby though and starting right now you'll be taking better care of yourself and my baby." By the tone and texture of my voice combined with the serious look I'm giving her, I know she realizes I mean every word I said like a vow.

I move my hand away from her lips, reaching for a strand of her hair that's fallen onto her cheek and brush it behind her ear while not taking my eyes away from those luscious lips. I can't help but notice how soft Willow's hair feels. It's like soft silk between my fingertips.

I gaze at her beautiful face, taking in all the little details

I'd missed the night we had sex. The fine details were missed as I was preoccupied devouring her sweet little pussy with my mouth. My cock stiffens with that memory. I quickly push those thoughts out of my mind. I know I need to move slowly with Willow. I want to do things right to keep her because I know there will never be a way to let her go. It's startling as the realization of just how much I want this woman hits me again.

After taking a deep, shaky breath like she's struggling with her emotions just as much as I am, she agrees to my plans. "I have the day off tomorrow. I need to get some errands done, but they can wait. So, are you going to be one of those bossy, over protecting baby daddies?" Willow asks. She tries to look put out and annoyed but looking deep into her eyes, I can tell how affected and emotionally moved she is because I want to be involved.

"I am glad we agree," I say smiling. Finally giving in to my desire, I lean my head forward to kiss her. Just at that moment, a loud clap of thunder sounds causing Willow to jump and ending the kiss before it ever began.

"It's just a storm," I say to reassure her as I gently rub up and down both of her arms hoping to calm her with a gentle touch. I vow to myself this very moment to always chase away her fears as the need to protect her seeps deep into my body down into my soul.

My touch seems to comfort her. I feel the remaining tension in her body relax as she gives into a yawn, reminding me just how exhausting this incredibly long day has been on her tired body. We sit quietly together as I continue to rub her arms.

Willow speaks first, interrupting the compatible silence between us. "It's hard to believe just this morning I woke up not knowing where to find you, and now we're sitting together in my living room. This day's been so long it feels like a week has passed."

I have to agree with her because it feels the same for me. She then yawns for the second time. I can't ignore Willow's yawn. I'm feeling guilty for keeping my pregnant woman from going to bed. "Look, I need to let you and the baby get some rest." I reluctantly let go of her. "Plus, I need to try to stay ahead of this storm. It can be a bitch riding a bike in bad weather." I stand and reach out a hand to help Willow stand up too.

Willow stands up, leans back a little to stretch her tired back. "Bike? You came here riding on the back of a motorcycle?" A look of fear creeps over her face as she continues, "I've had to take care of numerous motorcycle crash victims. I can't count how many trauma patients I've taken care of in the past that had serious life threating injuries from those wrecks."

Noticing the concerned look on Willow's face with her brows furrowing together I try to reassure her. "Yeah, but don't worry I have an SUV too. There's no way in hell I'll be putting my baby momma on the back of my bike. So relax, no need to get worked up." Then I smile at her hoping to further sooth her concerns.

"That thought hasn't even entered my mind," Willow informs me now with a pissed look on her face.

"What's wrong then?" I ask feeling confused.

"It's you on a motorcycle riding around in this weather! How are you supposed to help with the baby if you're laid up in a hospital hurt from a motorcycle wreck, or better yet lying six feet under after killing yourself on that death trap!" Willow says as she blows out a frustrating sounding breath.

I suppress my smile with a small cough as I realize how cute she looks when she's pissed off, and I take note of the concern she has for my wellbeing. "Baby, I'll be fine. This isn't my first storm on my bike. Not really got a choice, I'm not calling a cab."

Seeming to get more irritated at my remark than she already looked, she throws her hands on her hips for emphasis before her next remark. "Maybe not your first ride on a bike during a storm, but your first one with you back in my life and I'm not having it! Do you hear me! There's another choice. You're staying here! Besides, if you wreck who do you think the hospital will call to come put your ass back together. Me! Then, I will have to carry my tired ass back to work in the middle of a storm!"

"Stay here?" I ask as I reach up cupping her cheek with my palm. I can't help but notice how large my hand is when compared to her petite face. I caress her soft skin with my thumb. "Figured you'd want to slow things down between us," I say with a small smile on my lips. Though I meant what I said, I can't deny the desire to have her again.

"You did? I...I mean I do," Willow replies as I watch her eyes dilate with scorching heat. "Spare bedroom, you can sleep in the spare bedroom," Willow continues to say as she pulls away from my touch, putting the much-needed distance between us to take it slow. I'm glad she did. The last thing I want with this woman is a relationship built on sex. "Come on, I'll show you around the house and then show you the spare bedroom you can use," she says while walking away not looking back to see if I follow. I follow as expected.

"This is the kitchen as you know," she says as she points toward the kitchen. She keeps walking and talking as we make our way down a hallway until she's standing in front of an open doorway. She reaches in to turn the lights on for the room but doesn't dare enter it. "You can sleep in here. There's a private bathroom through that door," she says as she points to a doorway across the room.

Even though I haven't touched her, I can tell she knows I've stepped up right behind her by the gasp and shiver her body takes. Still not turning to look at me, she points down the hall saying, "My room is at the end of the hallway. Make yourself at home. If you need anything, just let me know."

I lean in closer, still not touching her, but close enough to make sure she can feel my breath on her neck. I watch as goose bumps cover her arm. A sign I'm affecting her like she is me. "Good night, Sunshine," I say in a deep voice.

She replies, "Goodnight," in an almost whisper as she turns toward her room and walks towards it.

Only when she reaches the safety of her doorway does she dare turn around. She sees I'm still standing in the hall watching her. In a shaky voice, she says, "See you in the morning," and then shuts the bedroom door behind her.

Hours later, I'm startled awake by a horrible noise. I bolt straight up into a sitting position in a bed that I realize is not my own. It takes me a moment to take in my surroundings and recall exactly where I am. Memories from last night of my brother, Willow, and the baby come rushing back.

Glancing over at the clock on the bedside table I see it's still early, only 5:22am. I rubbed my hands through my hair and down my face to try to remember what had startled me awake. Without coming up with an answer, I lie back down to try to get a couple more hours of sleep.

As I close my eyes, I hear a retching sound like someone gasping for breath that ends in a deep groan. "What the fuck? Shit Willow!" I bolt out of bed, this time grabbing my jeans off the chair in the corner of the room and slipping into them with lightning speed. I don't waste time to stop to button them, nor do I put my shirt back on. I'm in too much of a hurry to check on Willow and the baby.

I head straight for Willow's bedroom door. Not bothering to knock, I open the door. The room is dimly lit by a light coming from a doorway connecting to her bedroom. With my heightened sense of sight, I can tell that Willow isn't in the room. I look toward the lit doorway, figuring it's the bathroom, and head that way to continue my search for her.

Chapter 30

Willow
"The Realist"

After showing Connor the spare bedroom, I go back to my room, to put some much-needed distance between us. I hold my breath in anticipation until I get my bedroom door closed. I lean against the closed door and slowly exhale as I slide down onto the floor with my back still pressed to the door. So much has happened tonight that I need to take a few minutes to wrap my mind around it and reign in the flood of emotions Connor stirred up in my heart.

I fear my heart is swelling with false hope, so being the realist I am, I need to mentally lecture myself. The last thing I need is to jump in with my heart, thinking this is some fairy-tale romance where mommy, daddy, and baby all live together happily ever after. I need to stay focused on keeping my head straight and not giving in to what my heart wants to see is going on here.

Remembering how Connor comforted my fears when the storm startled me makes me melt a little more. That must be how Connor will soothe our baby when he or she is afraid. The tenderness displayed by this tough, all bossy, alpha male makes me want him that much more.

I was scared to look back at him when walking down the hall to my bedroom because I was afraid that I would melt like goo if I saw the heat in his eyes one more time. We don't need a relationship built on sex. No, I want a real lasting fairy-tale re-lationship. The one I've hoped for since I was a young girl.

It's been hard not focusing on the sexually charged chemistry that was almost palpable between us this evening. I could tell when Connor stepped up behind me in the hallway even though he wasn't touching me. I felt the heat radiating off his body engulfing my own.

When he leaned in closer, the feeling of his breath on my neck gave me goosebumps and sent an electric spark straight to my girl parts. When he said, "Good night, Sunshine," in his deep sexy voice, the tiny hairs inside my ear tingled. Only when I reached the safety of my bedroom doorway did I dare turn around.

When I did, he was still standing in the hallway watching me. The only thing I could think to say was, "See you in the morning." I then shut the bedroom door behind me. He really has a unique effect on me. As I sit here remembering the way Connor called me sunshine just now, and how he referred to my pussy as his sunshine pussy those many nights ago, my panties become wetter. I'm glad he can't see the heat rushing into my face.

I push myself up the door into a standing position and take a deep breath to clear my mind of all thoughts of how my body aches for the man down the hall who's determined to take things slow. Too tired for anything more, I walk over to the bed then collapse onto my back. Despite how worked up my mind is, I can feel the darkness of sleep surrounding me within minutes. As I drift off to sleep, my thoughts are encased around the man sleeping a few feet down the hall.

"Don't stop, oh, please don't stop," I whisper to Connor almost in a plea as he stops devouring my mouth with his starving kisses to kiss my jawline. He gradually moves down my neck to my breast.

As he sucks my aching nipple into his mouth, I feel one of his hands moving further down my body with a feathery touch that sends a streak of goose bumps across my skin. A pool of wetness develops between my legs. Right before his fingertips reach my throbbing nub, I feel my stomach churn. A second later, I'm fully awake bolting for the bathroom door hoping I make it to the toilet in time as I quickly flip on the bathroom light.

After my body forcefully empties every last drop of contents inside my stomach, I begin to retch again seconds later. Afterwards, I lean my head on the edge of the tub, not daring to get up. I've learned from trial and error of dealing with my morning sickness it's better to be safe than sorry and just to wait it out a few minutes to see if it's safe to move away from the toilet. The last thing anyone one wants to do after vomiting is to clean up vomit.

I try to focus on more pleasant thoughts while I give my stomach time to settle. My mind immediately drifts back to the dream I was in the middle of before the morning sickness abruptly pulled me from it. Why couldn't my stomach just hold off a little longer? I was just getting to the best part. I let out a frustrating groan, thankful at least that Connor is sleeping down the hall and not having to witness this moment.

A noise at my bathroom door startles me from my muse. Oh, hell no! Please don't be Connor, please don't be Connor, I pray silently as I cut my eyes in that direction while not raising my head up just yet. The first thing I see is his bare feet, and for the first time, I'm amazed at how sexy bare feet can be.

As I start the gradual climb up his body with my eyes, I see he is still in his blue jeans, but they are no longer buttoned affording me a full view of the V-shape his lower abs make. Still gradually climbing his body with my eyes, I see the trail of hair from his lower abdomen darting up from his jeans. When my eyes work their way to his chest, my mouth goes dry. Finally, my eyes reach his to find him staring at me with furrowed brows with a concerned expression that has taken over his face. I'm sure my appearance right now isn't having the same effect on him as his is on me.

"Sunshine, are you okay?" he says while taking a step toward me. He halts when I hold my hand and gesture him to stop.

"There're some experiences people don't like to share with

anyone and vomiting is one that definitely makes my top ten list," I declare in a whisper of a voice. Ignoring my declaration, Connor continues walking towards me. Irritation washes over me now causing me to raise my head up to inform him just how irritating he's being, "Really! Leave Con…" is as much of my rant I'm able to get past my lips before realizing my big mistake with the quick movement of my head. I quickly turn to the toilet as the dry heaving returns, causing me to gasp with each jerk of my body.

I vaguely hear the bathroom sink water running when I feel a hand gather my hair and a soothing, wet, cool washcloth is placed on my neck. After what feels like hours of humiliation and gasping for breath but knowing it couldn't have been but a few minutes, I decide to save what dignity I have left and go back to bed.

As I try to stand, my knees give out from under me causing me to collapse into Connor's embrace. He again scoops me into a bridal hold and gently carries me back to bed, easing me down with such care it's as if I'm so fragile I could break. He then walks back to the bathroom. Groaning with embarrassment again, I place a pillow over my face.

"How humiliating," I say into the pillow. I hear Connor returning from the bathroom to my bedside.

"Sunshine?" Connor says with more emphasis as a question than addressing me. I peek out from around the corner of the pillow that's still covering my face to find Connor standing over me with my toothbrush with toothpaste already on it in his hand along with a glass of water from the bathroom sink. After a quick brush of my teeth, I hand the toothbrush back to Connor then reach for the cup of water. I freeze right before I take a drink when I see Connor place my toothbrush into his mouth.

"I don't know whether to be grossed out or turned on," I proclaim.

"What?" Connor asks as he takes the toothbrush out of his mouth. "I think we can safely say we've definitely passed the point of not swapping body fluids. Our baby is like the poster child of how condoms fail to work." As I lean back in bed against the pillows, my eyes are drawn back to Connor's zipper.

"The zipper," Connor says almost as if he's talking to himself. Feeling warmth forming in my cheeks and afraid of being caught ogling his body, I jerk my eyes back up to his and see he's staring off into space in deep thought.

"Zipper?" I ask.

"The day after we had sex, the day you bolted from the room without waking me."

"What about it?" I ask.

Looking back down at me he continues, "When I went to put my pants back on, I found one of the condoms we used had gotten caught in the zipper of my pants and was ripped. I assumed it ripped afterward, but I guess it's possible it got caught on the zipper and ripped before or during our wall sex." Those two words leaving his lips, wall sex, send a shiver down my spine.

I look from Connors' lips to his eyes hoping he didn't see my reaction to his spoken words, but if the hooded look of his eyes is any sign, he didn't miss a thing. After a few seconds of staring at each other in silence, I lick my lips, thinking nothing of it. This earns me a deep growl from Connor. Well good, at least I'm not the only one feeling the electric charge of sexual tension in the air.

"Scoot over Sunshine," Connor says, breaking the spell between us as he places the cup and toothbrush on my nightstand.

"What?" I ask, not sure if I heard him right or if my mind just interpreting the words it wants to hear.

"We both need some more sleep, and I'm not going down the damn hall knowing you might be in here sick to your stomach. We both know there's no way you'll call for me, so scoot your little ass over I'm sleeping in here," Connor says in a matter of fact tone.

Knowing there's no use in fighting him plus feeling the exhaustion seeping into every muscle in my body, I do as I'm told and scoot over facing away from him. A second later, I hear the rustle of what can only be his jeans coming off then feel the indention of the mattress as he slides into the bed. A big arm wraps around me with a large hand that's placed gently onto my stomach as he slides up behind me with his front flush to my back. I open my mouth to say something, but I'm cut short.

"Sleep baby that's all we're gonna to do," Connor declares. That declaration is the last thing I hear before the warmth of his body encircles mine, and I drift off into a deep, restful sleep.

Chapter 31

Connor
"No Shame in my Game"

I awaken still snuggled in an embrace with Willow and notice sunlight is slipping through from around the window blinds lighting the room. I lift my head to find she is still fast asleep. Continuing my gaze around the room, I realize it's as if I stepped back in time. Someone has restored this place to its former glory. I was too preoccupied earlier to notice the details of Willow's bedroom.

The bed we are in is a large 4 post bed. It appears the ceiling is ten or twelve-foot tall, is painted white, and a wide crown molding surrounds the room. The walls are a light mint green. Two large floor-to-ceiling windows have plantation style shutters that are allowing the light into the room. They must face St. Charles Avenue, as I can hear the street car passing.

I glance down at Willow just to watch her sleep. At some point while I slept, she has turned around to face me and ended up resting her head on my chest. I realize my hand is resting on her ass. Damn, I love the feel of her ass. I'm tempted to squeeze my hand and get a good feel, but fight the urge knowing Willow needs all the rest she can get right now.

I'm still floored over the shocking sense of possession and protection that's developed over this woman. Change of plans, if she doesn't move in with me, then I'll be moving in with her. A smile crosses my face as I remember her telling me to make myself at home last night. I know this isn't what she meant when she spoke those words, but I will not miss being here for her and my baby.

Slowly I move my hand from her ass then carefully lift her beautiful head to place it on her pillow. I've never seen a more beautiful woman. I could lie here all day looking at her, but I have to coax myself into getting out of bed. After slipping back into my jeans, I head for the kitchen to make breakfast while I make some necessary phone calls.

"Good morning son," my mother answers.

"Morning mom, how's Drake?"

"He's doing well. He was awake for a few minutes this morning, but he was groggy and drifted back to sleep after the staff insisted his ornery ass take some pain pills. He'll be up and running quicker than they think, though. It doesn't take our kind near as long to heal, you know. Kara has been by to inform the staff she's assuming his care, so our secret should be fine," my mother replies.

"Mom, I need to tell you something, and I want you to hear it from me first before the word gets outs. I have a baby on the way…" I pause when I hear a gasp from my mother. Trying to gauge whether her response is good or bad, I wait a few seconds before continuing. "Remember the surgeon who operated on Drake?"

"She's the one?" my mother asks.

"Yeah, we were seeing each other a while back and lost contact," I say wincing a little at the white lie I'm telling. There's no way I would cause Willow any embarrassment by announcing it was a one-night stand. If she couldn't face me the next morning, there's no way in hell she could face my family if they had that kind of knowledge.

"But isn't she human?" my mother inquires.

"Yes, she is," I declare with no hesitation in my voice. Let's face it, there's "no shame in my game" so to speak. I want this woman like I've wanted no one else. I might as well get the full reaction before I place Willow face to face with any members of my tribe. There's no way in hell I'll tolerate any disrespect towards her for being human or towards my baby for being a half-breed.

She must sense my longing for acceptance, as she continues, "Well, this baby maybe only half wolf, but it's 100 percent my grandchild, so you get any negative thoughts out of your head. I will speak with your father at once. He'll not say a negative word if he knows what's good for him and believe me, he knows. Being alpha, the rest of the tribe will follow his lead. That baby is and will be well loved," she finishes.

"Mom, I'm not telling Willow what I am right away. I want to ease into this discussion with her. She's important to me, and I don't want to mess this up."

"I understand. This'll be quite a shock to say the least," my mother says agreeing with me.

"I need to let you go so I can call Kara; but thanks, I knew I could count on you."

"Always. A grandbaby, oh all the shopping and preparing we need to do! Connor, don't mess this up for me!" my mother says in an authoritative voice.

"Yes, ma'am. Bye now," I chuckle as I disconnect the call. I can always count on her for support; it appears especially if a grandbaby is involved.

Next, I call Dr. Kara Sharman's office. Surprisingly, Kara answers the phone instead of her assistant. I explain the situation to her concerning Willow's lack of knowledge of me being a werewolf. This isn't her first dealings with this kind of situation.

She warns me not to delay for too long in telling Willow the truth. The faster Willow knows, the better prepared she'll be to deal with this type of pregnancy, Kara informs me. I give her reassurance that I indeed understand and end the call with a 1:00 PM appointment scheduled for today.

I cook a simple but delicious breakfast consisting of eggs, bacon, and buttered toast completed with a glass of fresh orange juice, then return to the bedroom with the meal in my hands to wake up my sleeping beauty. I mentioned to Kara how sick Willow's been with this pregnancy. From being around pregnant she-wolves from time to time, I know one of the best ways to keep nausea away is to eat.

According to Kara, the same goes for humans pregnant with a werewolf. Werewolf babies demand more nutrients than human babies while in their mother's wombs. If the she-wolf doesn't eat enough, it brings on a nauseated feeling, which is worse for a human pregnant with a werewolf baby. Men from our tribe complained about being eaten out of house and home while their mates were expecting. Now, I need to figure out how to convince Willow to eat more, which is the opposite of what she thinks she needs. I brace myself and prepare for the upcoming argument.

Chapter 32

Willow
"Know it All"

The smell of food awakens me as Connor sits a tray on the bed beside me. I gently give Connor an explanation of why I regrettably can't possibly eat what he cooked. But he doesn't listen to a word I say as he keeps pushing me to eat. Finally, I have had enough.

"I don't want to eat anything Connor!" I swear this man is an all-alpha caveman. It's kind of like I am man, you eat woman. I already tried to explain to this thick-headed man calmly. Since he didn't get it the first time, I will try again but less calmly.

"Especially not this kind of food. I just want a few crackers before I get up. It's so thoughtful of you to go to so much trouble, but honestly I usually just eat something light until my stomach settles, which is rarely ever," I complain as I sit up in bed. Connor is still not listening and again tries to get me to eat.

"Well, now that's the problem. You haven't been eating enough. Just try eating as much as you can this morning. If it makes you sicker, then I will shut up and let you go back to eating like a bird tomorrow," Connor counters which earns the best glare I can muster.

"Fine, obviously you've been pregnant how many times? So, of course, you're an expert," I reply snottily. After vomiting so much early this morning, I don't want to relive that anytime soon.

"Please, it's for the baby," Connor says with a pleading look on his face. Damn it! He had to bring the baby into our battle.

"Fine!" I growl at him. How can I refuse when he is obviously trying to be useful in an overbearing, demanding, caveman kind of way? The food smells wonderful. I say a little prayer of hope to not have a repeat embarrassing performance of close encounters of the toilet kind.

Starting with the eggs and toast, I eat as instructed. After the first few bites, I do start feeling better and pick up the speed of my eating. I sneak a quick glance at Connor's face to see if he's watching, not really wanting to admit I was wrong, and he was right.

My eyes are met with a smug "know it all" look on Connor's face. Smug bastard. Before long, I manage to eat everything on the plate, and I'm tempted to lick it for good measure but decide not to, leaning back against the headboard of my bed instead to rest and digest.

Glancing up again at Connor, he now has a smile on his face which causes my stomach to flutter in the excited way, not the oh shit I have to vomit again type of way.

"You need to get up and get dressed. We have a doctor's appointment at 1:00 PM and I don't want to be late," Connor says, putting me in a state of shock over how quickly he's able to get an appointment. I decide to ignore his bossiness for now.

"You were able to get an appointment that quickly?" I ask in amazement. "Wait what time is it?"

"Yes, I did, and it's fifteen minutes till twelve," Connor says.

"What? I can't believe I slept this long. That doesn't give me much time to get ready," I declare as I jump off the bed and hurry to the bathroom. I decide on a loose-fitting sundress and my strappy sandals. The dress says sensible but matched with my strappy sandals it has a hint of sexy. With my ever-increasing pregnancy induced breast size, the swooping neckline shows more cleavage than it used too.

I decide on a messy bun style for my hair and add mascara along with lip gloss to finish my look. When I leave the bathroom, I find Connor sitting on the bed leaning against the headboard looking all delicious in his tight-fitting jeans with his legs crossed. He's wearing a Henley shirt that hugs his sexy chest and arms.

"Sunshine, stop," Connor says causing me to jerk my eyes to meet his.

"What?" I ask, pretending I didn't just get caught ogling his body.

"Stop staring at me like your starving and I'm your next meal."

"Whatever," I reply as I walk toward the bedroom door to leave, trying to play off his comment as I hear a light chuckle from him that sends another shot of electricity right to my girl parts. Damn these hormones. I've got to get my body under control before I jump him and devour him like he is my next meal.

When we get outside, "I'll drive," Connor announces in a matter of fact take charge kind of way as he snatches the keys out of my hand. Typical move for a man.

"Umm... You do realize this is my car. I'll drive," I inform him as I reach to get my keys back. He's quicker and raises his damn hand way above my head out of my reach. If he thinks it's beneath me to climb his body like a tree to reach them, then he'd better think twice. He must be reading my mind because he folds his hand out toward me, stopping me dead in my tracks.

"Not happening, Sunshine. Your name is on the paperwork for this car, but possession is nine-tenths of the law, and right now I have the keys in my possession. The way I look at this situation is currently we are cohabiters of this automobile," he says while smiling and jiggling the keys to taunt me as he speaks. I give him the best glare I can muster up.

My glare has no effect on him. He opens the passenger door and ushers me into the passenger seat, then places my seat belt around me. I go along with his plans because realistically what other options do I have? I receive one last kiss on the cheek before he closes the door.

"Do you always get your way?" I ask Connor with a huff as he enters the car on the driver's side.

"Are you always this difficult?" he asks with a growl to his voice. Yes, an actual growl.

I try my glare again. "Are you always this bossy?" I say, snapping back.

"Yes, he replies as he props his left hand upon the steering wheel after he adjusts the driver seat back to allow room for his legs, then turns his upper body to face me. "I told you last night I plan to be here to help you while you are pregnant, so sit back, relax, and let me help you. Yeah?" he says with the most serious face I've seen on him yet. Well damn, those words were sweet, how can I say no to that?

"Yeah," I say on a sigh, hoping he can't tell how much his words move me.

We arrive a couple of minutes before 1:00pm at my new doctor's office, Dr. Kara Sharman, which is printed on the office glass door. The office is a bit on the small side, but quaint and cozy with a blue carpet and light tan leather chairs in the waiting room. I've put little thought into what it would be like having my own practice, but I imagine if I had an office it would be a lot like this one. This has a warm, homey and inviting feel to it.

If I had my own practice, I too would create an inviting atmosphere to bring comfort to my patients. After signing in, I walk over and sit in a chair against the wall facing the open waiting room. As I keep taking in the details of the place, one surprising thought hits my mind- we are the only ones here. Maybe it's Dr. Sharman's lunch hour, and that's why we got an appointment so fast, she cut her lunch break short.

"Sunshine?" Connor says pulling me out of my inner muse.

"Yeah?" I ask as I turn and notice the clipboard with papers clipped to it he's holding out in my direction. "Oh right, sorry, not used to being on this side of the doctor-patient relationship," I say as I reach out and take the clipboard to fill out the new patient packet.

Connor sits beside me, and together we filled out the information about the father's health history. I'm amazed at how right it feels being here doing all of this with him and now realize how nice it is to have the baby's father with me. I know Ari, Nikki, and even Gran would have come along with me had I asked, but it seems so much more intimate and surreal with Connor.

"Are we going to find out what we're having when we can?" Connor asks out of the blue. I glance up to see him staring at a 4D ultrasound photo on the far wall.

"I think I want it to be a surprise," I tell him. "What about you?" I ask staring at him while he stares at the photo.

He turns to face me. "Surprise it will be," he replies, then leans in and kisses me on the forehead.

Just as I add the last of my signatures needed to complete the forms, a nurse enters the waiting room through the door next to the sign-in window. She's a short, middle-aged woman with graying hair and glasses. She introduces herself as Nancy, Dr. Sharman's nurse. After asking me to follow, she ushers me through the door she had just came from, then steps in front of Connor to block him from following.

"I'm going back there with her," Connor says straightening up to his full height while glaring down at Nancy in his alpha-male macho status. I don't know whether to laugh or be in awe of how sweet it is for him not wanting to miss anything.

"Nancy, it's fine with me if he wants to come with me, I don't mind," I tell her.

"Honey, are you sure? Remember, it's a full exam the first visit," she states with a kind smile.

"Full exam?"

"Yes, that's why I thought you might want to keep him out here and have him come back when it's time to discuss everything," she clarifies.

"Umm... Connor, you need to stay out here," I instruct him.

"Hell no, I said I'm going to be by your side helping and sitting out here is not by your side Willow," he declares.

"Look, some things can't be unseen and some things I wouldn't want to share with you even when we'd been together 100 years," I snap back. I see a funny look flash across his eyes for only a second, then disappear before I'm able to figure out what it means. Then I realize the words that just escaped my mouth. Did I just declare we're going to be together for years to come? I've got to slow my emotions down before my heart is engulfed by this man. Reluctantly, Connor agrees to stay in the waiting room.

Nancy shows me into the exam room. It's a small room with a desk height shelf across the far wall that has a charting area for the doctor on one end. The rest of the rack has medical supplies organized down to the desk. There are cabinets over the counter. Just inside the door is the infamous Gynecology Table with the stirrups to aid with vaginal exams. There is a paper gown lying on the exam table. Nancy instructs me to put it on and cover up with a paper sheet that she hands me before leaving the room.

I undress and put on the paper gown. It's not much more than an oversized paper towel. This is one thing I would change if I had my own practice. Really, does anyone not make decent cover-up gowns and sheets for these types of exams?

The exam room door opens as I'm trying to figure out how to sit in this oversize paper towel without ripping the damn thing, all while keeping my lady parts covered at the same time. An attractive woman walks in and shuts the door behind her. She has long, brown wavy hair and a voluptuous build, much like my own pre-pregnancy body. She has on a white lab coat and is carrying my chart in her hand.

"Hello, I'm Dr. Kara Sharman, and you must be Dr. Willow Black," she says as she reaches out to take my hand in a small handshake gesture.

"Yes, but just call me Willow, and thank you for fitting me in today on such short notice."

"Call me Kara. No problem, I go way back with Connor's family, so this is no big deal. I'm happy you're here, so let's get started shall we."

During the exam, while feeling for lymph nodes on the back of my neck, Kara pauses and traces something at my hairline with her fingertip. As she pushes my hair to one side to get a closer look, it dawns on me at what she is feeling and looking at.

"That's just a birthmark. I forget it's there half the time. No one ever really notices it because my hair usually conceals it. It's funny, most of my family members have the same mark, except in different places," I explain.

Chapter 33

Kara
"The cat's out of the bag"

I separated Willow's hair to get a closer look at the mark I've discovered in her hairline. As Willow explains her birthmark, I'm frozen in the same spot for a moment, somewhat shocked, as I'm trying to come to grips with what I see. The birthmark is shaped like a butterfly. I'm all too familiar with the different markings of the supernatural, and there's only one that has this marking. I'm stunned, and it's taking a moment for me to regain my senses. It's the mark of the Fae.

It's surprising I have a Fae in my exam room. Most people believe these creatures became extinct, or that they are just a myth or legend. I have only come across a couple of Fae in the past who still call New Orleans home. I also know that most Fae don't know their own family history or what they truly are.

Keeping their history secret is a bunch of nonsense related to them wanting to protect their children, which I firmly disagree with. Knowledge is power and hiding it only causes more trouble. Case in point- a Fae unknowingly pregnant by a werewolf.

"Kara, is everything ok?" Willow asks, interrupting my thoughts.

"It's fine. I was just looking at your birthmark. It's not every day I see a birthmark in the shape of something I can actually recognize." I feel a little rattled and hope my excuse for my behavior is believable. I continue with my exam while deciding the best way to approach the subject. I decide to dig a little for information to see if Willow knows who and what she is or if she's one of the unfortunate untold Fae.

I come up with an idea to see how she reacts when I question her about Connor's mark. Any Fae that has any clue at all about their history should know about werewolves. After all, if she knows what she is, we can stop pretending everyone is human and deal with the unknown effects of a hybrid offspring. Even if she knows she's a Fae, she may not know Connor's a werewolf. It appears Connor hasn't seen her mark, so it's possible she hasn't seen his. What a shock this will be when this "cat is let out of the bag."

"You and Connor have something in common," I begin.

"What would that be?" Willow asks as she raises one eyebrow in my direction with an inquiring look.

"Unusual birthmarks. Have you seen his? I believe it's on his back." I have patched Connor and Drake up so many times with their "work injuries" that I know the location of their marks all too well.

"You mean the paw-print looking mark on his back?" Willow then blushes as if her knowing this information is embarrassing. With us both being doctors, I'm surprised Willow is embarrassed to talk about Connor's body. If just talking about Connor is embarrassing, I'm surprised she's pregnant at all with that much modesty.

"Yes, that's the mark." A dreamy look appears on her face like she is lost in delightful memory. She is clueless. There's no way she knows what Connor, or she really is.

"Did you know his brother has the same birthmark on his chest? I wonder if anyone else in his family has the same mark. I assumed it was rare that my family members have the same birthmark, but I guess it isn't as unique as I thought."

"That's right! You're the one that operated on Drake. I know his family well, and I'm the primary physician for most of them. I spoke with his mother today to check on his condition. They requested I take over his care since I've treated him for years and know his medical history all too well. I hope you don't mind. They're very grateful to you for saving his life," I inform her as I watch her face light up with a smile.

"I would just say that's my job, but I feel like by saying that I'm telling people their family member isn't important and is just another patient. That's not what I mean when I say that, but I'll say it to you since you can relate. I don't mind you taking over and completely understand," Willow replies.

"I know exactly what you mean," I tell her with a light, comforting squeeze to her upper arm.

"The answer to the question you asked before I got off track with our conversation is yes, most people in his family share the same birthmark. What did Connor think of your birthmark when he saw it?" I ask knowing that Willow's answer to this question will get rid of any doubts that they both are clueless to the situation at hand.

"I don't think he's noticed it," she says while shrugging her shoulders and smiling.

I'm not surprised at all to hear that answer. Connor would've flipped his lid over the sight of that mark. Looking at Willow, I'm sure her hairline was the last thing Connor was looking at. So, Connor doesn't know what Willow is, and Willow is clueless to all of it. Damn, I've got around five months to figure this cluster fuck out and get everyone on board with this hybrid baby.

I finish the exam and ask Nancy to bring Connor into the exam room. Nancy brings in the ultrasound machine that gives Connor and Willow the first glimpse of their baby. Nancy measures and confirms Willow is around 16 weeks along in her pregnancy.

Willow and Connor thank me again as I follow them out to the reception area. I set them up for the next appointment, and they leave the office oblivious to the situation. I go back to my office and start to finish my charting when Nancy comes in.

"You look worried and lost in thought. Is something wrong?" Nancy asks with a look of concern on her face.

With a heavy sigh, I explain, "Two worlds are about to collide, and I need to figure out a plan for the fallout. Also,

I need to do a little research to see if there are any potential dangers I need to look for when you mix the DNA of a Fae with a werewolf." I watch Nancy's eyes become bigger and bigger with each word I speak. Nancy has been with me since I started my practice. She's the one person I know who will take information like this to her grave before she would ever tell anyone. She understands we live in a different world that most people don't realize exists. I'm thankful I have her working for me. It's hard to find good people willing to keep information to themselves, which is essential when dealing with this realm of the world.

"Fae! I wasn't aware they even exist anymore. Wait, doesn't Connors's tribe despise Fae because of their rough history?" she asks with a concerned look that replaced the excited one she displayed just seconds ago.

"That's putting it mildly. Well, Fae do exist, and this little fairy has landed in the lap of the big bad wolf," I reply with another large sigh while shaking my head.

"What are you going to do, Kara?"

I can't help but sigh again. "I don't know yet. I really don't know."

Chapter 34

Willow
"Gone to Hell"

Connor pulls over to the curb parking the car in front of my house. I step out of my car, then look up while bending slightly backward to stretch my back. I notice how clear the sky is today and how comforting the warm sunlight feels on my skin. It's amazing how everything can change in twenty-four hours; even my nausea is better. The drive home from Dr. Sharman's office was quiet. Not an awkward quiet, more like a comfortable silence. The silence gave me the opportunity to do some self-reflection.

My life plan has changed again during the past twenty-four hours. My revamped life plan, just like the others, has blown up and disappeared! I'm wondering if planning one's life is even a good idea anymore. Every plan I came up with has gone to hell; and not over a long span of time. It's more like an atomic explosion destroyed them in minutes.

The newest plan is not only now in pieces, but the pieces themselves no longer exist. The clanking of the street car going by pulls me out of my muse. I straighten back up then turn to find Connor walking around the front of my car towards me with a concerned look across his face.

"You ok Sunshine?" he asks as he gets closer. He surprises me by pulling me in close wrapping his strong, muscular arms around my body. No one has ever shown this kind of affectionate display to me before, especially out in the open for anyone to witness. My body melts into him, absorbing his warmth like we've been cuddling for years. It feels right and natural.

"I'm fine, I was thinking about how much my life has changed in the last twenty-four hours."

"I hope that's a good thing," he says with the concerned look still on his face.

"Yeah, it is," I say with a smile, hoping to ease his worry. Connor kisses my forehead, then releases his hold on me. I immediately feel the loss of his warmth. He places my hand in his much larger one, keeping them joined as we begin to walk toward the house.

Once inside, he follows me into the kitchen and watches as I pour a glass of orange juice for myself. I offer him a drink, and we settle down at the table to discuss our plans for the rest of the day.

"I need to leave to check on a few things, are you okay with that?" Connor asks. What, am I disabled now that he knows I'm pregnant? The question annoys me but it's thoughtful of him to ask.

"Of course, I'll be fine. Besides, I want to go to the hospital and drop in on your brother to see how he is doing. I know Kara is his doctor now, but I want to check on him."

"He's one thing on my need to do list. I need to check on my mother too while I'm there to make sure she isn't wearing herself down. Knowing her, she hasn't left Drake's side. Tell them I'll be up there later today, will you?" Connor asks.

Shit! Shit! Shit! I feel a sudden wave of panic wash over me. I haven't even thought about coming face to face with his family again. If I don't tell them I'm pregnant with their grandchild and they find out later, how will that make me look? When I saw them in the waiting room, there was a lot going on, so not telling them then was excusable. I stand up to pace the kitchen floor.

"Babe, what's going on in that beautiful head of yours?" Connor asks as he comes over to stand in front of me, grasping my shoulders to halt my pacing. I take a deep breath to calm myself. I don't want him to see how unhinged I am becoming, so I stare past Connor over his shoulder, trying not to look at him.

"Eyes babe," Connor commands.

I reluctantly look into his eyes. "What?"

"Eyes on me and talk to me," he explains in a calm, sooth-ing voice I've heard people use when trying to calm a small child. He will be a great dad. "Sunshine?"

I take a deep breath and explain, "Your mom will be there!" I tell him like that should explain it all, but if his raised eye-brows are any sign, he doesn't seem to get it.

"And?" he says to prompt me to continue explaining.

"And, I'm pregnant with her son's baby! What do I say when I get there? Remember me? Hey, I'm the surgeon who operated on your son; and oh yeah, by the way, your other son knocked me up when we had our one-night stand together. She'll think I'm a slut, a ho. A ho Connor!" I take another deep breath waiting for his response. He isn't saying anything, just staring at me. "Are you listening to me?" His shoulders begin to shake. My mouth opens to continue my rant, but I clamp it shut when I realize he's laughing at me. I can't help but notice how much hotter he looks when his full smile meets his eyes. "Stop laughing at me! It's not funny!" He may be one of the hottest guys I've seen, but that doesn't give him a free pass to laugh at me.

"Sorry babe. I'll go to the hospital as my first errand, so you won't have to face my mother alone. You should know though I've already told her about the baby, and by now everyone in the family should know. My mom loves babies, and this is her first grandchild, so I'm sure she's told everyone she could," Connor says in a matter-of-fact way.

"What? So, she already knows I'm a ho. Great!" I blurt out.

"You're not a slut or a ho, as you call it. No, I didn't tell her every detail. As far as my family goes, they think we were see-ing each other for a while and lost contact before you knew you were pregnant. Except Drake that is. He was at the club that night; but he knows better than to tell my business, especially if he doesn't want me to tell mom his. I never went into the details with my mom. That's none of their business."

That announcement calmed my nerves a lot, but not entirely.

"Let's get ready and head out." I nod my head agreement. We might as well get this over with.

An hour later, Connor and I walk into Drake's hospital room hand in hand. I notice it's just Drake and his mother. Thank goodness there's no one else here; I don't think I could take on the whole family right now.

Drake appears asleep, and his mother is sitting on a small sofa across the room looking down at a magazine. She looks up at our faces then glances down at our joined hands, then back up to our faces again with a huge smile. I automatically try to pull my hand away, feeling uncomfortable with our situation and our display of public affection, but Connor tightens his grip refusing to release my hand.

"Dr. Black," she says.

"No, please call me Willow." Her eyes brighten as she stands and walks toward us. When she gets nearly into my personal space, I take a step back. I'm unsure of what to expect or do, but she's fast on her feet and grabs me pulling me into a tight hug that seems to last for a few seconds.

I feel the loss of Connor's hand as he lets go. I hug her back as I look over at Connor. He has the same smile on his face. He has her smile. I can't help but wonder if our baby will have their same smile too. His mother pulls away but grabs onto my hands as she does.

"You can call me Irene. Oh my, I'm so excited you're here! When Connor told me the grand news, I thought I was going to burst from excitement. The news couldn't have come at a better time with all that's going on," she says as she tilts her head in Drake's direction. "News of a grandbaby just brings light to a dark situation," she continues, which puts me even more at ease. I slowly exhale in anticipation as she pats my hands and lets them go.

Then, she turns and walks back to the sofa while still talking. "We need to plan a girl's day and get to know each other, and then plan some shopping trips for baby stuff," she says as she sits down. She places her pointer finger onto her chin, looking lost in thought, as she lists things to put on our to-do list.

"Mom, don't overwhelm Willow all at once," Connor states in a gentle voice.

"It's fine," I say to Connor, "I want to get to know your mother and I would love to shop for our baby." His eyes beam with a possessive look when I say the words our baby. He reaches and brushes the back of his thumb down my cheek. I think he's about to kiss me in front of his mother when I suddenly hear Drake.

"Hey man, what's going on?" Drake asks in a hoarse voice as he looks at Connor. Drake then looks at me with an intent look like he's studying me. A smirk appears on his face as he recognizes me.

"Hey, Ms. Willow. It's nice to see you again."

"How are you feeling?" I ask as I pull away from Connor to walk over to Drake's bedside.

"I've been better. The chest is a little sore," Drake replies as he reaches up with his hand and rubs over the bandage on his chest. "So, my brother finally tracked you down. I'm glad he did! If I had to listen to that Ain't no Sunshine When She's Gone song again, I might have had to shoot him to end my misery." I turn my head towards Connor to find him glaring at his brother. I turn back to Drake to see a gleam in his eyes. I can barely contain my smile.

"Willow is actually Dr. Black, as in Dr. Black that did your surgery and saved your life," Connor informs Drake. I personally think he uses this information as a diversion to shut Drake's mouth. Drake reaches out for my hand, and once he has my hand in his, he pulls it close to his mouth.

"Thank you," he says, then kisses the back of my hand.

"You're very welcome," I respond, noticing Drake isn't releasing my hand but holding it in his.

I hear Connor growl, "Drake, get your hands off my woman." His woman? I kind of like the sound of that; maybe a little too much considering it has caveman silently written all over it.

"Boys, behave! So, help me if you two upset Willow, it'll be me the two of you will have to deal with. Remember, she's pregnant and doesn't need any added stress," Irene declares from across the room from where she's still sitting. Drake's mouth falls open. I'm guessing he's not one of the people his mother has kept in the loop concerning the announcement of my pregnancy.

"Wait, what? Just..." he says as he stares out the window with a confused look on his face. He looks back at Connor and continues, "Just how long have I been out of it? When did this happen?"

I couldn't help but laugh at his expression. Nor could I help to say, "While you were sleeping," which happens to be my favorite line out of one of my favorite movies. His mother chuckles, and I look over at her. She gives me a knowing look. Apparently, it's one of her favorite movies too.

Connor gives both of us a look I can't decipher as he shakes his head.

"What?" I ask him. "Oh, come on; don't tell me you never saw the movie *While You Were Sleeping*."

"Sunshine, it was a chick flick," he responds like that explains it which I guess it does. I guess macho guys don't watch chick flicks.

"Bro, you were shot yesterday," Connor explains while coming closer to put an arm around my waist. "The baby came about when Willow and I were seeing each other before," Connor says to Drake with a raised eyebrow communicating something private between the two. I'm guessing that means keep your mouth shut about it being a one-night stand.

On that note, I decide it's my time to leave. "I think I'll leave now and let you get some rest," I tell Drake, who through the confusing situation has finally let go of my hand.

"I have to go too so I'll walk you out to your car," Connor says. We say our farewells to his mom and I exchange phone numbers with her, so she can call me after they release Drake from the hospital to plan a girl's day. She gives Connor her promise to rest and not stay at the hospital 24/7.

As we walk back out to the parking lot located across from the emergency room entrance, I can't help but wonder what's next for Connor and me. Do I wait for him to ask me out? Are we considered dating now? Do I invite him over? When we reach my car, Connor turns and asks, "Let me feed you dinner tonight?"

"Ok," I say, maybe a little too eagerly if his smile is any indication. I do love his smile.

"Good, this will give me the opportunity to talk about our future plans and living arrangements."

"Connor, I'm not moving in with you," I tell him with a tone of annoyance in my voice.

"OK, have it your way," he says way too quickly. I raise my eyebrow to him in disbelief.

He leans over and kisses my lips lightly before saying, "I'll see you tonight. When will you be home?"

"It's 4:35 now, I am going to Nikki's shop to update her and Ari. They are my cousin and best friend. Remember the girls I was with that night?" He nods, and I continue, "I need to update them on my life status, or I'll never hear the end of keeping the news of you silent. They're also invested since they helped me search for you," I inform him. "So, around seven?"

"Ok see you at seven, Sunshine," Connor says right before he gives me a long, passion filled kiss that causes my toes to curl and sends tingles to all the right places. He pulls away, leaving me breathless. Finally, he kisses me somewhere other than the cheek or forehead! He then takes my keys out of my hand, unlocks my car door, and opens the door for me. A girl could get used to this kind of attention.

On the drive home from Nikki's shop, I couldn't help but smile as I thought back to their reaction to my news. I called

Ari on my way to Nikki's shop to tell her to meet me there, so I could tell them both at the same time that Connor is back in my life.

Ari bounced up and down like a schoolgirl from the excitement of my news. Nikki was excited too but didn't bounce. They took a little too much enjoyment out of the story of how Connor confronted me about my pregnancy.

I pulled in front of my house to find an SUV parked in my normal spot, so I pulled up behind it. I'm assuming the SUV belongs to Connor. I look down at my watch to see if I'm late, but it's only 6:30, so he's early.

As I make my way to the front of the house and onto my front porch, I'm surprised when I don't see Connor sitting there waiting. I hear noises coming from inside my house as I approach the front door. Alarmed, I turn the front doorknob to find it unlocked. As soon as I open the door, a delicious Italian aroma of garlic and spices hits my senses causing my stomach to growl loudly, indicating the fast-food lunch we ate on the way home from Dr. Sharman's office is long gone from my system.

I know I didn't have ingredients for an Italian meal in my kitchen, so he must have brought his own. That thought puts a dopey smile on my face. I can't help but appreciate the jester he's making. As I walk into the kitchen, I notice the kitchen island is a laid out in a salad bar style, with lettuce and various salad fixings in small bowls. I look over at Connor to find him standing near the sink with his back to me fixing something that has the appearance of a yummy dessert with whip cream and strawberries on top.

"What is that delicious Italian smell?"

Connor faces me, "My family's secret recipe for lasagna."

"Secret, huh?" I ask as I slowly walk towards him.

"Yep," he replies with a wickedly sexy smile. I plant a quick appreciative kiss on his lips that leaves my lips feeling tingly.

"Not that I'm complaining, the dinner smells divine, but I thought we were going out to dinner?"

"No, I asked you to let me feed you tonight," Connor answers. "Besides, I thought this would allow us the privacy for the conversation we need to have. Why don't you go on into the living room, put your feet up and relax while I finish up our dinner?" Well, it really wasn't like a suggestion, it was more like an order which I decide to overlook since the thought of putting my feet up and relaxing sounds so good.

"What conversation?" I ask. Connor looks at me with an eyebrow raised while displaying one of those 'what the fuck do you think' looks. "Right," I say. I turn to leave the kitchen and pause when something out of the corner of my eye catches my attention. I begin to look around with a concerned look on my face.

"Sunshine, you ok?" Connor asks as he notices my reaction.

"It's clean."

"What?"

"The kitchen, it's really clean other than the bowls that you have food prepared in!"

"OK," he slowly responds, indicating he probably thinks I'm crazy.

"I mean you didn't create this huge mess when you cook. It's impressive," I tell him, and it really is. On the rare occasions when Bill used to prepare our meals, it took at least an hour for me to do damage control, cleaning and wiping splatter messes off everything including the damn walls. I turn and head to the living room to do exactly what the bossy alpha male told me to do, relax. Not because he ordered me to, but because I really like the idea of being able to relax in the evenings. This pregnancy seems to suck my energy level down to zero by evening time.

Later, after we finished our dinner and moved onto dessert, a thought occurs to me. A question comes to mind that I can't believe I haven't considered asking until now. "I appreciate this delicious meal, but exactly how did you get into my house?" I'm grateful for not having to fix my meal. Also, I'm surprised at myself for how much food I consumed and for not feeling sick to my stomach for once, but curiosity has gotten the best of me.

"Umm, well, you did say last night to make myself at home, so I noticed the extra keys hanging in the kitchen and took the spare house keys," Connor awkwardly informs me with an innocent expression on his face.

"That's not exactly what I meant when I said that," I respond with an added roll of my eyes.

"Well, how else would I make myself at home," he questions with a sheepish look in his eyes.

"Oh, I don't know. Maybe like normal people who would understand the meaning to be like to take a shower or to fix themselves something to eat," I say, educating him on the actual meaning of the kind jester.

"Well, too late now to get all specific. Anyway, we have more important things to discuss right now," Connor says conveniently changing the subject.

"Connor, I already told you I'm staying here. I'm not moving in with you," I repeat to him for what feels like the hundredth time.

"Oh, I remember. That's why I moved all my stuff here while you were gone," Connor replies with a smug look.

"Here! Here as in my house here?" I feel my heart rate speed up slightly. He can't possibly be serious.

"Well, yes, your house. You said no to my house and of course, you said make myself at home."

My mind flew back to the "ALL" part of his announcement. I jump up to look for myself to see what ALL means and not trust just asking him.

"You know as I said earlier, that's not what I meant, and I believe you know it!" I say, growling as I march down the hall to my spare guest room. I walk straight to the closet, open it, and to my surprise see none of his clothes hanging there. I spin around and notice there's not a suitcase or overnight bag in the room. I then march into the bathroom connected to the bedroom to find only my stuff and nothing of his.

Confused, I walk back into the spare guest bedroom to see

Connor in the doorway leading back to the hall, propped up looking smug again. I raise my eyebrow at him in a questioning look. He laughs a little like he's enjoying himself.

I watch as he raises his hand from his side and points his index finger toward my bedroom down the hall. I scrunched up my face in confusion. The smirk on his face turns into a full smile the minute he realizes I understand what he's indicating with the pointing of his finger. He has moved his stuff, no wait 'all his stuff' as he had phrased it, into my bedroom.

"No, no," I say to him as I begin my march again, this time toward my own bedroom. As I enter the room, I see several things lying around that don't belong. I march onward to my closet to discover a few of his clothes hanging beside mine and a duffle bag open on the floor of the closet with more clothes inside. Beside my shoes sit a pair of very cool looking men's motorcycle boots, dress shoes, and a pair of running shoes. As I turn, I notice Connor in the doorway, but march on past him into my bathroom to discover his toothbrush along with other male products such as shaving cream and man soap. I ignore the little flip my stomach did, caused by the intimate display of our toothbrushes standing side by side.

I hear Connor's footsteps coming up behind me. I look up into the mirror, and my eyes met his eyes. He gives me a sympathetic look and says, "Really, you did say make…"

I interrupt him mid-sentence to growl, "DO NOT FINISH THAT SENTENCE!" as I march around him and head back to the living room.

Chapter 35

Connor
"Poke the Bear"

I walk toward the living room, which is the direction I saw Willow storming to. I try hard not to smile, knowing it will just rile her up more; but damn, I can't seem to help myself. She looks so damn cute when she's all riled up and fiery mad. I know it must make me a sick fucker, but my cock jerks every time she growls at me.

I walk into the living room to find Willow sitting on the sofa again looking distraught and exhausted. I saunter over- and sit down beside her, being careful not to 'poke the bear' as they say. She's quiet for a few minutes, then turns toward me and asks, "Seriously, were you dropped on your head as a baby?"

I can't help but chuckle as I respond, "Like I said before maybe, but just hear me out. I know I sound like a broken record, but apparently, I need to repeat myself until you either hear me or believe me. I want to be here to help anyway I can with this pregnancy, which I can't do when I'm miles away from you.

Even sleeping down the hall from you there is a 50/50 chance I wouldn't hear you get up in the middle of the night or early in the morning to vomit. I can and want to be here for you and MY baby. We are adults. We can coexist in the same bed without sex.

And as far as personal space goes, we bypassed that little jester months ago. There are no personal space boundaries when a part of me is growing inside you. I sleep on my side of the bed, and you stay on your side of the bed if that's what you want. Now, I know what you're thinking, that you will have trouble keeping your hands off my body," I say trying to lighten the mood which succeeds causing Willow to snort with an added eye roll.

"Humble much?" Willow asks.

"That's me, humble. I can give you my word I will not sexually touch you until you beg me too." I hope I'm not telling a lie because I already know I'll be having a case of blue balls after spending a few days in her beautiful presence. There's just something about her that makes me want her like I've wanted no one ever.

"Ok, ok. I'm willing to give this a try. You did help this morning. I'm really exhausted, so I'm going to go get ready for bed," Willow says as she gets up and stretches.

"I have an early morning start, so I'll head to bed with you," I tell her as she leaves the room.

I give her a few minutes of privacy to get ready for bed before I head in the direction of the bedroom. As I enter the room, I notice Willow is already lying down with the lights out. As quiet as possible. I slip off my clothes then I slide in the vacant side of the bed. I usually sleep bare ass naked most nights, but tonight I leave my boxers on.

I rest on my back with my hands behind my head staring up at the ceiling listening to the rhythmic breathing that indicates Willow is sleeping. After a while, much to my dismay, Willow rolls over and curls her body up to my side with her head in the curve of my arm. She's apparently not asleep. She places one hand on my chest, drawing a small circular figure with her finger around one of my nipples. I cautiously put my arm around her back and cradle her to my body being careful not to place my hand on her ass even though that's precisely what my cock is instructing me to do.

"Connor," Willow says so softly that it's barely a whisper. The feeling of her breath on my chest is causing a fierce reaction in my cock.

"Yeah, Sunshine?" I ask after a minute of silence.

"When my ex, Bill the rat bastard, left me it hurt," Willow begins. I give her a little squeeze, trying to comfort her while my blood boils at the mention of how her ex-boyfriend treated her. Willow pauses for a moment, then raises her head slightly to look directly into my eyes then continues, "I know we just found each other again, and this could just be my pregnancy hormones, but the potential feelings I have for you," she says, then goes quiet without finishing and looks away.

"Eyes Sunshine," I say to get her to look back at me. When she does, I continue, "What are you trying to say?"

"Bill hurt me by leaving, but you have the potential to break me," she finishes.

"I'm not here to play house with you Willow. I can't promise you a future filled with roses and rainbows, but I can promise you if we make a go at this relationship when you're ready, I plan to be in it for the long haul and not just for the baby. Do you get me?"

"Yeah, I get you," she says right before she curls back up to my side, and we both fall asleep.

Chapter 36

Willow
"Don't Egg Him On"

The next day I wake to my usual morning sickness. This time instead of handling it alone, to my mortification and against my protest, Connor sticks to his promise by staying at my side holding my hair in one hand with a cold, wet washcloth in the other. I hate to admit it, but even this humiliating act is better with a partner.

After I brush my teeth, Connor orders me back to bed in his bossy, manly, sexy way then goes to prepare breakfast. This time I eat slowly without complaints or refusals. Before I leave for work, I notice my nausea is completely gone, and I feel like I'm getting my energy back.

Connor and I say our goodbyes. He tells me he'll probably have a late day at work. I'm finally able to convince him it will not starve the baby or me to death if we have a late dinner together of delivery pizza after he gets home. I give him my word I'll feed our baby a late afternoon snack to hold him or her over until pizza time.

The first stop I make at work is the break room for my one cup of caffeine a day I've converted to for the baby's health. As I walk in, I find Hank sitting at a table reading the sports section of the paper. I sit with him for a minute to see how he's been doing.

"Will, how's my favorite dudette and her offspring doing?" Hank asks.

I can't help but smile, and not just any smile, but a huge dopey smile as I reply in Hank's lingo, "Totally awesome."

"Excellent. With that smile I would guess you've been spreading some love."

"Yeah, the young offspring's daddy is back, and it seems to be totally rocking," I respond earning me a high five.

"Yeah, that's righteous Will! Picking up my ways too I see. I knew I would totally rub off on you one day," Hank says with a smile. Before we have time to catch up with any other details of each other's lives, my pager alarms and with a weak smile I say farewell to my friend to go out to begin what looks like another busy day.

I spend the rest of my eight-hour shift on my feet, except for the lunch I promised Connor I wouldn't skip. My day seems to fly by, with my mind consumed with thoughts of Connor when I'm not focused on the sick. I feel like a teenager again with the butterflies fluttering in my stomach, and a smile plastered to my face. My head is in the clouds.

At three, my shift is over. I say my goodbyes and head to the house, buying myself the promised late afternoon snack on the way. I stop by my favorite restaurant for a large order of red beans and rice with a large bowl of gumbo to go. I know I won't be able to eat all this food, but I plan on sharing the leftovers with Connor as a snack in case he's starving while we're waiting for the pizza to be delivered tonight.

At the rate I'm eating, it won't be long before I start putting on the pounds and getting rounder. I'll need bigger maternity clothes sooner rather than later. That thought now has me worried. Do men find pregnant women attractive? Will Connor stay attracted to me as I grow as big as a house? All my insecurities about relationships in general creep into my mind.

By the time I'm at home I'm too tired for even a shower, so I opt to take off my shoes and put on a sundress. I head to the living room to lie back onto the sofa, sinking into a dark pit of depression. Surprisingly, my house now feels lonely. I stare at my untouched late afternoon snack that's currently sitting on my coffee table when the doorbell rings.

I roll off the sofa then walk over to the door to see who's

here, knowing it can't be Connor since number one he stole my house key and number two it's too early for him to be off work. I open the door and to my surprise see a hot sexy Dom standing there. Crap! I completely forgot Dom was coming over tonight to eat dinner with me. We've eaten on the same day of the week every week since the week we met.

He looks all yummy while I'm standing here feeling like a bloated pig. He's wearing faded jeans that fit just right in all the right places, with a tight black t-shirt that enhances his muscular stature, topped off with a killer pair of biker boots. I glance over his shoulder to see his motorcycle parked in front of the house. I'm surprised I didn't hear him drive up.

"Hey gorgeous, why the long face?" Dom asks as I step aside to give him room to enter the house.

"I'm finally getting my appetite back," I tell him expecting him to understand, but he just looks confused.

"That's a bad thing? I thought morning sickness was the evil villain in the pregnancy department," he says, acting as confused as he looks.

"No, that's good; but well, now I'm going to get as round as an olive and huge too," I whine on the way to back to the sofa. I hate hearing this whiny tone in my voice. I was never a whiner before.

"Babe, you're pregnant, not fat, and when your baby grows, that's his or her weight, not yours. Besides, baby you are beautiful no matter what," Dom says as he softly reaches up and tucks a strand of hair behind my ear after sitting down next to me. I know there's been an attraction between Dom and me since we met, but nothing like Connor and I have. I need to be straightforward with him so there's no miscommunication. I want Connor.

"I have some news about my baby daddy," I start.

"I do too," he says.

"You do?"

"Yeah, I talked with my friend I told you about that could help locate him. He said he wants to meet with you and to

226

try to help," Dom informs me. "What's your news?"

"Well, a funny thing happened at work. We had an emergency case come in a couple days ago, which was the brother of my baby daddy. Small world. Anyway, we talked, and he wants to be a part of my life and the baby's."

"It's what you want, right?" Dom asks.

"Yeah, it is."

"Then why the long face and the worried look babe?"

"This may take a while," I glance over at my food still sitting on the coffee table. The sight of the food causes my stomach to growl, and we both laugh. "Wait here. I'll grab you a beer and orange juice for myself, along with plates, bowls, and spoons. I bought too much food earlier, so there's plenty for the both of us," I say as I head towards the kitchen.

I return, and we get situated again sitting on the sofa, this time with our food in our laps. I turned sideways to face him.

"Ok, now spill it, Will," Dom demands with a pointed look.

"OK." I take a deep breath and sigh as I begin the discussion of my worries. "Now, that the baby's father is back in my life, everything seems to be falling into the right places. I think I like him more than I thought I did. I know it's corny to think of love at first sight. OK, I guess in this case love at second sight, but I can see myself falling for this guy fast and hard.

I know with him it'll be so different from Bill, my ex. If I fall for this guy and it doesn't work out, it'll not only hurt me but break me. Now I'm getting my appetite back so not only do I have to worry about falling too hard and fast, but now I'm worried about him thinking I'm fat and ugly," I rant while Dom stares at me. "Am I even making any sense to you?"

"You're falling in love with this guy, and you're afraid he doesn't feel the same as you, or that he'll lose interest in you because you'll be growing with the pregnancy," Dom states.

"Well, yes, I guess that sums it up," I say with a surprised look on my face. Damn, he gets it. We finish my late afternoon snack and place the dishes on the coffee table, then sit back to finish our drinks.

"Willow, you're a wonderful, beautiful, smart woman and this guy would be a fool to let you slip through his fingertips. I think when a woman is pregnant with a man's baby, the man doesn't see fat and ugly, which you're not and never will be. They see you as a woman carrying their baby. They see mom and baby," Dom says softly. Damn this man is not only hot but sweet. He'll make some lucky woman very happy one day.

"Do you think it's possible to fall in love with someone in a matter of days or is this just my pregnancy hormones in overdrive? Is it possible that he could feel the same way about me?"

Dom sits straight up and looks toward the front door. After a few seconds he turns to me then reaches up with his hand to cup my cheek. "What are you doing?" I ask, startled by his behavior and touch.

"Trust me, just go with it," is the only explanation he gives me. Still confused I hear the front door open and see Connor coming into the living room.

I look down at my watch and see that Connor is home early, then state the obvious, "Hey, I wasn't expecting you until later."

"Apparently," he says in a deep growl of a voice.

What the hell? I look up from my watch to see Connor's eyes focused on Dom's hand on my cheek, which I somehow forgot all about when I saw Connor.

Connor glares at Dom, then me, and then back at Dom's hand on my cheek. It's obvious from the clenched jaw and the twitch of his cheek that he's pissed off. Well, shit, this might look bad. I decide I need to hurry and make introductions to smooth the situation over. I move away from Dom's hand and stand.

"Connor this...." I start to say, but Connor cuts my words short.

"Dom, what the hell are you doing sitting in my woman's living room fucking groping her?" Connor asks, still in his deep growl tone of a voice.

"You know each other? Wait, groping, really?" I say in a surprised tone as I move closer to Connor. I come to a stop a couple of feet away when Connor's angry eyes focus on me instead of Dom.

"Stay out of this Willow," Connor says which really pisses me the hell off.

I start to open my mouth, but Dom cuts me off this time before I can get a word out.

"Connor, so you're the mystery guy who knocked up Willow?" Dom asks standing up, then positioning himself between Connor and me like he needs to protect me. Really? I can't believe this shit is happening. I couldn't find a guy to even go out with not too long ago, now I have two hot guys in my house apparently arguing over me.

"Hold the fuck up. Are you telling me Willow, my woman, is the pregnant woman you were discussing with me the other night who your planning to stake a claim to if the baby's father didn't surface?" Connor roars. Wait, what does Connor mean stake a claim to and why are they discussing me like I'm not in the room?

"Sunshine, come over here," Connor demands.

"Not a damn step with that temper flaring," Dom says as he holds out an arm in front of me to halt my steps.

Do they think I would really obey a command you would give a dog in the first place? Fed up with the amount of testosterone floating in the air, I step around Dom's arm to stand in the middle of the two cavemen and hold my arms up. This seems to quiet them, but it does nothing to stop the glaring.

I turn to face Connor, "Really Connor? Why don't you just piss on me to mark me and get it over with? Dom is just my friend so back down."

I then turn to Dom who is now giving Connor a devious grin. "Dom, stop that!" I snap which causes Dom to stop glaring at Connor and look at me. "Don't egg him on like that."

"It's getting late. I need to head back to the house anyway to help Flame with the kids," Dom says. He then walks up close to me, places a finger under my chin and says, "To answer your last question, Willow, Yes. Yes, I do think it's possible." He then gives me a wink as he walks around Connor and I to leave. Before he walks out the front door, he turns back to speak to Connor one last time, "Man, if you fuck up, I plan on being there to step up, keep that in mind." He smiles at me, turns and shuts the front door behind him as he walks out the door.

I stand in place shaking my head, trying to wrap my mind around what the hell just happened. I think back to what Dom said right before Connor walked through the front door. 'Trust me, just go with it' was his exact words. He must have heard Connor walking up on the front porch. I guess his hand on my cheek was a test of some sort for Connor who must have passed if his fit of jealousy was any indication.

Judging by the surprised look on both their faces, I don't think knowing each other was part of the plan. I can't help it and bust out laughing because of how childish it all was and how relieved I am that Connor flew into a jealous fit. I laugh so hard that my eyes tear up. I glance over at Connor. He seems to not find any humor at all in the situation and is now glaring at me. I try to straighten up and hold my laughter in.

"You think this is funny, Sunshine?" he asks in a not so calm voice. "I work hard all day to finish up early, so I can rush home to be with my woman just to find her with another man's hand touching her beautiful face," he continues to say as he stalks one step at a time closer to me like a predator stalking their prey. This causes me to take one step backward for every step he takes.

"You're mine Sunshine," Connor continues to say. As my back hits the wall, Connor stops right in front of me. "No one touches this face but me," he continues, but the tone in his voice has lost the anger. His eyes bore into me like they're piercing my soul. He now has one hand cupping my cheek while his other arm is caging me in.

Just the touch of his hand to my cheek causes my body to shiver, which doesn't escape his attention. My breath picks up speed causing my breast to move up and down quickly, which doesn't miss Connor's attention either. His eyes look down at them. He looks back up into my eyes with his hooded eyes full of desire and his nostrils flaring.

"Are you done lecturing me or is there anything else you feel you need to say, caveman?" I ask trying to look put out about the possessive caveman badass claiming remarks that secretly turn me on.

"Just one more thing, Sunshine. Most importantly, this sweet pussy is mine," he says then moves his hand from my cheek to cup my pussy, applying just enough pressure to make me wet my panties.

"Connor," I say in a breathy voice.

"Yeah baby?"

"Shut up and fuck me," I blurt out. To hell with holding back, I want him, and I want him now. I guess this caveman routine turns me on more than I realized.

Connor takes the hand that was forming a barrier against my escape and buries it into my hair. He firmly grasps my hair causing my head to tilt slightly to the side for easy access. "Fuck, I thought you would never get around to asking," he says right before his lips slam into mine in an almost violent, punishing kiss.

He releases my lips and relaxes the hand in my hair, pausing our kiss to ask, "I know we were gonna take things slow, so are you sure about this Sunshine? If I go any further, I may not be able to stop. I don't want you to have any regrets."

I look into his lust filled eyes and see true hunger, which causes sparks to shoot straight through to my core energizing my body like a live wire full of electricity. I'm panting so hard I can't form words to answer him, so I nod my head instead.

"Sunshine, I need the words," he responds in a delicious, rich, husky voice.

"I want this. I want you, please Connor, now shut up and fuck me," I say in a sultry whisper of a voice I barely recognize as my own.

He gives me a devilish smile, "I was hoping you'd say that,

but you aren't begging yet."

Once again, he tightens his grip on my hair as our tongues collide into a dance of a battle of wills. Our kissing engulfs my mind and transports me into our own little world where just Connor and I exist. My body seems on autopilot.

Without thought my hands grab hold of his shoulders and my legs wrap around his waist causing the sundress I'm wearing to gather at my hips. I feel Connor taking full advantage of this by sliding his hands up my thighs to my ass. He grabs my ass with both of his large hands squeezing each cheek as he grinds the sweet spot between my legs against his coarse pants. It creates agonizing friction that has my body throbbing with the need for more, oh so much more. While he lightly traces the underlining edge of my panties up around my hip bone towards the front, he asks, "Are you wet and ready for me Sunshine?"

"Yes," I declare, barely even audible with my panting breath.

Connor's hand moves directly between my legs and I let out a desperate groan as he slowly slides one finger through the wetness of my slick folds. He slides his finger in and out, "Babe, your pussy is so fucking drenched."

"Please…. Connor, please," I beg between pants of breath. It's been way too long since I've felt his touch. I feel like an addict must feel, desperate for my next fix with Connor being my body's drug of choice. I feel his thumb apply circular pressure to my swollen, throbbing clit. "Oh, please," I gasp.

"Please what, Sunshine? Would you like for me to press my tongue to your clit, then lick your sweet little pussy with my mouth? Or maybe gently suck on your clit as I slide my tongue down into the folds of your juicy lips working my tongue in and out of your tight pussy?" Connor asks.

He continues his circular pressure on my clit with the masterful strokes of his finger as he finger-fucks me. His words are like honey dripping with pure sex. Damn, the way he talks dirty makes the flames of the fire that's flickering through my body rise high and engulf me completely. I feel the all too familiar flush of my skin beginning on my chest then slowly crawling up towards my face as the walls of my pussy clench, rhythmically milking his finger.

"That's it sunshine, cum for me baby. I'm gonna take you into the bedroom and throw your beautiful ass onto the bed and devour your sweet tasting little pussy with my mouth. I'm not going to stop until you beg me to!" Connor says, giving me just the push I need to tumble over the orgasmic cliff into ec-stasy. My body bucks and white-hot bolts of pleasure consume me. I hear my voice repeating his name over and over again, but it sounds like it's from a faraway distance.

As I start the post-orgasmic descent back down into my body, I become aware of my surroundings. I realize I'm in my room with my back pressing into the mattress as my legs dan-gle off the bed. His rock-hard body is encasing mine again with his forearms on either side of my upper body with his hard cock pressing into the apex of my thighs.

He slowly kisses me again, but more gently this time like his mouth is making love to mine. Our tongues are entwined in a slow, sexual dance. He moves his mouth, applying kisses down my jawline until I can feel his hot breath on my ear.

"Mmmmm…. Connor," slips from my lips, as he traces his tongue from behind my ear to the pulse point on my neck, giving the spot light suckles. He places his warm hand on my shoulder, and with a featherlight touch he slowly brings the strap of my sundress lightly down my arm setting my skin on fire in its wake. He catches the strap of my bra, taking it down too as his fingers descend further down pinning my arm to the bed with the strap and exposing my breast. When the cool air hits my already tight nipple, it hardens even more, standing up at attention begging for his touch.

He slowly licks down over my collarbone causing goose bumps along the path. When he reaches my nipple, he sucks it into his mouth, gently playing with it with his tongue. My back begins to arch and my limbs tense as my already sensitive clit starts the aching throb again.

He reads my body like a book, knowing what it needs without me saying the words, He takes his other hand and lightly brings down the other strap exposing my other breast and pinning that arm down too. He then moves to my other nipple giving it the same exquisite attention as he pinches the first one between his forefinger and thumb, giving it a twist causing a moan to escape my throat.

I feel the increased wetness soak my panties as pure desire for the man rushes like hot lava through my veins. Not being able to touch him with my pinned down arms, I call out his name in an almost plea while wiggling my arms and shoulders trying to set them free.

Chapter 37

Connor
"Balls Deep"

Willow says my name like a begging plea. I give my woman what she wants; no, correction, what she needs. I stand up between her dangling legs and remove her sundress as she slightly lifts her hips, leaving her wet panties in place. I purposely position her ass close to the edge of the bed for an easy access feast for my mouth. I take a few moments to admire her beautiful body, with her beautiful flushed face and thick lips. It makes my chest swell with pride knowing how hard I can make her get off.

Her gorgeous tits are the perfect shape and size. It's as if they were made for my hands. I continue taking in the rest of her body as I see for the first time the small swell of her stomach. It may be primal, but I take great pride in knowing I put our baby in there. Willow brings up one of her delicate hands to shield the area from my view earning her a stern growl of, "Don't," from me.

I see her relax her hand back down as she turns her head to the side and whispers, "I feel self-conscious lately because I'm getting fat."

I take off my boots then bend down onto my knees, staying between her legs as I place my hand gently onto her stomach to cradle our baby in the palm of my hand. "Look into my eyes Sunshine," I demand in a firm voice, so she'll know I'm serious about what I'm about to tell her.

She slowly turns back to face me whispering, "Such a caveman," under her breath.

When our eyes meet, I continue, "You're not fat Sunshine. I think you look sexy as fuck. Knowing I'm the one who put our baby in there, caveman or not, turns me the fuck on." Her expression turns from a look of awkwardness to a look of pure desire.

Enough fucking talking, I mentally declare. I reach up between my shoulder blades and grab a handful of my shirt, yanking it off over my head then toss it to the floor as I prepare to let my mouth take her pussy to the next level.

I peer into her eyes one last time before I begin and notice them raking across my bare chest and abs. "Glad you like what you see," I say as my mouth twitches from holding in an arrogant smile. I reach for her left leg and bring it level with my face, placing my mouth close to her knee.

I start with light kisses, working my lips up the inside of her thigh. By the time I reach the top of her thigh my kisses have turned into gentle bites. I stop right before reaching her cunt. "You're so fucking wet for me," I declare as I notice how wet her panties are.

I drape her leg over my shoulder and repeat my actions with the other leg until my face meets her cunt once again. I dig my nose into the material of her panties and inhale the sweet musk that's unique only to Willow. The smell of her nectar is intoxicating.

"Oh, Connor…. please," I hear her beg. Not wanting to waste any more time, I grab her panties with both hands and rip them off. I take a moment to admire her shaved cunt with its shiny, drenched, pink slit. I can't help but notice how swollen her sweet little clit looks. When she squirms, I lean forward and suck the swollen little nub into my mouth earning an "Oh, Connor!" cry from Willow's luscious lips.

I flick her clit with my tongue while gradually flattening it applying pressure at the same time. She grabs two fists full of my hair in her hands and shoves my face into her pussy then grinds my face with her juicy little cunt. Like a madman, I lick and suck like there's no tomorrow. She pants and starts a rhythmic motion signaling she's ready to cum.

Not wanting this to be over so quickly, I back my face away. Using my thumb and forefinger, I spread her juicy lips and slowly slide a finger into her fleshy wetness. I crook my finger upward to apply pressure to her g-spot, knowing I have hit her sweet spot by the increased speed of her grinding and the deep moan she releases.

I can't help but remember how sweet her tight little asshole looked when I ripped off her panties and decide to see how receptive she is to anal play. I remove my finger from Willow's pussy. The suction her tight cunt has on my finger makes my cock throb in anticipation.

Willow lets out a whimper from the loss of contact. I slide my tongue into the empty void left from the removal of my finger and suck up her juices as I do. She grabs my hair again and starts rhythmically fucking my face with her juicy cunt. When I feel her clench down onto my tongue, I know her body's about to explode. I take the finger coated with her essences and paint her little asshole with the sweet liquid. I press the finger covered in wetness against the tight little hole and slide my finger slowly into her ass up to my knuckle. Willow lets out a groan, then grinds even harder.

Realizing she is receptive to anal play, I begin to work my finger in and out of her ass, slowly at first, but speeding up to match the motion of her grinding hips. Soon I'm finger fucking her ass at the same pace she is grinding my face.

Willow moans loudly and chants my name as she explodes again into another massive orgasm. I continue with my double penetration of tongue-fucking her cunt and finger-fucking her ass until she comes down from the most extended orgasm she's had yet. I make a mental note my Sunshine takes pleasure and delight with anal play.

My cock is painfully rock-hard, feeling like its being strangled in these pants. It needs to be balls deep in my woman, so I decide it's my turn. I stand and rid my cock of its restraints by removing my jeans. As I slide the jeans and underwear down, my cock pops out over the top of my jeans garnering a slight gasp from Willow as she stares at it in anticipation. I throw my pants onto the floor. This is the point I usually grab a condom, but hell we're way past that point with a baby on board already. I want her bare so I can bury my cock balls deep into her longing cunt as I fill it with hot cum.

"Baby, I want to take you bare. I'm clean. Are you ok with that?" Willow nods her head yes, but that's not good enough. "Baby, I need the words."

"Yes, Connor I'm good with that. I'm clean too," she responds with the words stretched out on a groan.

"Sunshine, are you ready for me?"

"Yes," she moans as she nods her head. That's all the discussion I need on the subject. I grab her by the waist, picking her body up to bring it entirely on the bed. I push the head of my cock against the folds of her wet lips of her cunt, which instinctively open like the petal of a flower. I slowly slide my cock into her warm, sweet, tight folds causing her to moan with pleasure as I work the shaft in.

I start off gently sliding my shaft in and out as her cunt applies suction as if trying to milk the cum from my cock. With each thrust I go deeper with longer and harder strokes. She thrust her hips upward and with her receptive cunt matches my pace and rhythm.

I grab her ass cheeks with both hands to lift her up at an angle, so I can feel my balls slapping her ass. She moans loudly every time my balls slap her ass as my cock bottoms out in her tight cunt. The wetness is so intense now that creamy, white juices are gathering at the base of my shaft and dripping down onto my balls.

As I strain for control, I feel her pussy grip my cock in a tight hold causing my balls to tighten. I hear my woman chant my name once again as she rides out her third orgasm, causing me to give in to my own release. I slip my tongue into her mouth and kiss her passionately as I thrust my cock one last time as deep as I can when the orgasmic waves shoot cum into her longing cunt. I feel the walls stretch with each squirt of cum. As I slowly withdraw my cock, cum squirts out of her pussy and runs down her crack creating the look of a well-sated pussy.

I collapse down next to her instead of on top of her, not wanting to put the pressure of my body weight onto our baby. I grab Willow by the waist positioning her on her side with her back plastered to my chest, her ass against my wet cock, and our legs entwined with each other. I haven't thought about it before, but with her growing abdomen I'm guessing Willow and I will have to get creative in our fucking positions.

After my breathing slows down to normal, I get up to go get a wet cloth to clean Willow. I take a good look at my sated woman who's already asleep. I take pride in knowing I'm the cause of that very sated look. After I get us both clean, I turn out the lights and lay back down to resume our spooning position while covering us both up. I've never been a spooning type of guy; but for the first time, spooning doesn't feel like a chore, more like a need.

Chapter 38

Willow
"Falling in Deep"

A few weeks later...... Connor and I seemed to slide right into a daily domesticated routine composed of Connor making sure I'm well fed, that I'm resting often, and providing me with lots of sex. He didn't seem burdened or put out from helping me with this hormonally induced desire for sex; in fact, he appeared very creative in finding ways to satisfy my every craving, whether it be food or his body. We seem to have the same mindset with everything with the baby. We decided not to find out the sex of our baby; instead, letting it be a surprise which upset a few family members.

Tonight, when I got home, Connor had dinner ready with his Louisiana-style fried chicken and red beans with rice waiting for me. His delicious meals and love of cooking are a perfect complement to my no desire to cook.

After dinner, we laid on opposite sides of the sofa, so I could rest my tired feet on him while he rubbed them. This is something he excels at, taking his time, he rubs each toe separately and applies pressure to each one before working his way down to the ball of my foot, then doing the same to the heel. By the time he's through with the second foot, I feel like a melted puddle of goo. The evening news has ended and although I try to stay awake to spend time with Connor, I can't keep my eyes open.

"I'm going to get ready for bed, I'm exhausted," I announce as I stand and stretch my back.

"Go ahead. I'll clean up the mess, lock up, and be right behind you. I need to have an early start in the morning, so I'm going to bed with you," Connor says giving me his sexy as hell smile. Perfect, a man who doesn't mind the clean-up!

After finishing my nightly routine, I wait for Connor to come to bed before falling asleep. I've become addicted to his arms around me as I drift off. He's been spending as much time with me as he can. I suspect his team's been taking on extra responsibilities to free him up, so he can spend time with the baby and me to make a go at this relationship of ours.

I must admit, I've learned a lot about this man. About everything except his job that is. It seems to be classified information. All I'm told is they hunt bad guys which they are excellent at, at least that's what he tells me every time I express my concerns of the possibility of him getting hurt like Drake.

Not wanting my mind to go there and think of losing Connor right after we've found each other, I focus my mind instead on our baby. I pull the covers down to my hips and lift my short pale-pink nightie exposing my ever-growing baby bump. I slowly rub my hands over my abdomen and close my eyes waiting to feel the baby move. All day I've been feeling light flutters, but unfortunately it seems Connor's touch not only soothes me but calmly influences our baby as well since the flutters have now stopped.

I'm so focused on the baby I haven't realized Connor has entered the room until I feel the indention of the bed between my legs. I immediately spread them wider giving him easy access to my body and open my eyes to find his eyes glued to my baby bump. He stops moving when his face is right over my baby bump, making himself comfortable between my legs by stretching his large body out between them.

Ignoring me, he begins to rub over my abdomen with his rough callous hands while talking to our baby, "Hey baby, its daddy. How are you doing in there? Are you behaving and letting mommy rest? I bet it's nice and comfortable in there. I know if I could stay in mommy's body all day I would too, but for different reasons." The last comment earns him a slap on the hand from me.

"Connor, you can't say stuff like that to our baby," I begin my lecture trying to hold back the laughter because I know the last comment was to get a reaction out of me, which worked. Before I can continue lecturing him, he cuts off my words.

"Shhh.... woman, the baby won't be able to hear me over you," he remarks adding an eye roll playfully. A giggle escapes my mouth, but I settle down and try to keep still so he can have his daddy-baby conversation while rubbing my stomach. This tender moment causes my heart to swell as I realize for the first time, I'm getting my fairy tale ending. This strong all alpha caveman has a very loving, tender side to him. He will make the perfect father for our baby. My fairytale dreams end when I do the hormonal unthinkable; I burst into tears.

With a horrified look of alarm, Connor crawls beside me and places his arms around me, "Sunshine, what's wrong? Are you in pain?"

"No," I manage to say as tears run down my face like a waterfall. The tears are falling quicker than I can wipe, which makes me feel like a blubbering idiot for crying.

"Then what's wrong?" he asks in a soothing voice as he gently rubs my baby bump.

I take some deep breaths, trying to reign in my emotions so I can form words. After a minute I blurt out, "Nothing's wrong. You're a bossy, arrogant, stubborn all alpha caveman with sweet mixed in the middle." I am failing miserably in my explanation.

Connor pauses the hand that's rubbing my stomach, looks deep into my eyes with confusion and worry written on his face, "Are you saying I'm making you unhappy?"

"No! I'm saying I'm in love with you Connor," I clarify, then watch as the worry on his beautiful face is replaced by a tender smile.

"Well, it's a good fucking thing you feel that way sunshine, because I've fallen in love with you too. It would be awkward never being able to get rid of me if you didn't feel the same. And before you say it, I promise to do my best never to break you," he declares, making me laugh. I grab his beautiful face with both of my hands pulling his lips to mine, then kiss him with all the love I feel coursing through me. Our moment is interrupted when I feel a strong kick in my stomach under his hand still resting over my baby bump. I pull back from Connor to ask if he felt it too, but before I can get a word out my question is answered as Connor moves to position his head right above my stomach, placing a kiss right over the area where I felt the kick.

Watching him, I realize the love I feel for this man is stronger than any love I've felt for anyone in my whole life. The feelings I had for Bill seem like puppy love in comparison. Panic begins to set in with my overwhelming emotions.

The concern I feel must be written on my face because Connor asks, "Willow? What's wrong Sunshine?"

"I realize watching you with our unborn baby how much I really love you, which scares me to death," my voice is barely a whisper.

"Why does that scare you, Sunshine?"

"Because you do have the power to destroy me," I confess.

He crawls up my body again, so his face is directly above mine. I feel embarrassed by my admission and look over his shoulder instead of into his eyes. "I need your eyes, Sunshine," he declares in a soft whisper as I take a deep breath before making direct eye contact with him. "I give you my promise I'll handle you with care," he declares right before he claims my mouth again.

Chapter 39

Connor
"Pussy Whipped"

Three weeks later.... As soon as I've gotten Willow fed and off to work, I head to the office. I never thought I could enjoy a domestic lifestyle and parenthood with a woman, but life has taken me by surprise. I can't imagine going back to a life that doesn't include Willow. She's told me a few times that I can break her, but the reality is losing her could destroy me.

I feel bad for keeping secrets from her. I would say I haven't found time to tell Willow I'm a werewolf, except I would be lying. Truth is, I'm chicken shit I'll lose her when I tell her. I know I can't keep this from her much longer and I need to man-up soon to tell her everything.

I'm the last one to arrive at the office again. The team gave me hell about it the first few times. It hasn't escaped my attention they're taking on more of tasks which allows me to spend more time with Willow. It's the new normal.

Normally, I'm the first to arrive and the last one to leave. Hell, sometimes when I was working on a case I didn't even go home, which is why I chose this office space in the first place. Like a lot of buildings located around New Orleans, this one has apartment space above the office.

I walk in the door to find the team hard at work on the Wendigo case. The Wendigos we're after seem to have fallen off the grid after shooting Drake. Apparently, they do have a sense of self-preservation, but I've discovered in my line of work that every creature out there's a creature of habit just like humans are. It won't be long before they go back to their flesh-eating habits.

I see Daniel and Drew deep in discussion, so I start there.

"What's up?" I ask as I approach them.

"Well, look who decided to join us today. Just come to work whenever you feel like it," Daniel says with a cocky grin. Like I said, they've been giving me hell about being late.

"Man, Willow's morning sickness has improved over the last couple of weeks, but she still has a rough time of it. There's no way in hell I'm leaving her alone to deal with that shit all by herself, so the team is gonna have to deal for a while," I explain again.

Drew chuckles. "Man, we're just given you shit. The action lately has been too damn slow anyway. When are you going to expose your girl to the team?"

"We have a doctor's appointment today, so she's coming here to pick me up on the way. Keep in mind she's human and clueless about our world, so until I figure how to explain it to her without freaking her the fuck out, keep tight lips on that subject. I would appreciate everyone being on their best behavior until she gets used to you all as I can't have a conflict between my woman and my team," I announce getting everyone's attention. I try not to sound so pussy whipped, but I know I'm failing miserably as I can hear Drake coughing the actual words pussy whipped. After I shoot him a go to hell look, I get back to business.

Drew and Daniel are looking at a drawing. I lean in to get a closer look. I realize it's the design carved into the amber medallion and shuriken that were found on the dead Wendigo the night Drake was shot. "Do we have any leads on the medallion or shuriken?"

"No leads, but after looking at the medallion I sensed some magical qualities about it. It's taken quite a bit of time to figure out. After researching the design, I've discovered its origin," Drew states. I raise my eyebrow to signal him to keep talking, knowing he gets off on this stuff. Drake and I take a seat in the nearest chairs preparing for the extended version of an explanation. Drew is a Druid, and if any magic is involved, he can sniff it out like a bloodhound.

With a gleam in his eye Drew begins, "Well, obviously, the basic shape of the symbol is that of a lazy curve that resembles the number eight lying sideways. The history of this symbol back to the seventh century with various meanings over the centuries. It's even used in math. It's a symbol of infinity or eternity, which is self-explanatory.

When you inspect the medallion up close under a magnifier, you can see the design is not just draw with a line in an infinity symbol, but appears to be a dagger," Drew pauses a minute to hand me a blown-up picture of the medallion and it does look like a dagger.

"OK, go on," I tell him as I hand the photo over to val.

"Well, daggers can also have a variety of meanings from negative to positive ones, such as sacrifice would be negative while protection would be positive. But the symbol itself doesn't hold the secret meaning or the use for the medallion. It's the amber crystal it is made from that holds the clue. Amber crystals have different uses such as healing and protection. If you look at this up-close picture of the amber of the medallion, you can see a streak of a ruby red color I believe is blood." This part grabs my attention.

Drake stands and interrupts Drew. "The blood on the amber could be from the Wendigo or from the owner which would be the assailant Daniel managed to lose." Daniel gives Drake the finger. "We need to find this woman to make it clear to stay out of our investigation and let the trained professionals handle this shit. We need to find her before she ends up hurting a bystander, not to mention the obvious need to interrogate her for any information that could help in this case."

Drew continues, "I didn't get to tell you everything I found out about the amber before Drake rudely interrupted me," Drake gives Drew the finger. "The blood is located inside the amber. After more digging, I found something interesting. Fae once used this symbol in various protection and cloaking spells.

With further research, I've uncovered documentation that a Fae and female alpha werewolf, a she-wolf, used this symbol along with the amber blood crystal to seal an agreement centuries ago. The Fae agreed to help the female alpha hide or disguise her identity to prevent male alphas from hunting her down and killing her. In return, the female alpha pledged loyalty to the Fae and to protected them from their enemies.

The dagger represents protection, and the infinity symbol means forever. It's like the old saying I will watch your back if you watch mine," Drew says as he concludes his educational lecture with a bright smile as always. I feel my temper rise with just the mention of Fae. It's just another fucking reminder of what they took from my people and me. I clamp that shit down so I can focus on the point Drew will eventually get to.

"You couldn't just say the last part and leave out the history lesson, could you?" Drake asks.

"Since the Fae no longer exist, this medallion is probably some old antique handed down through a family line," Daniel says adding to the discussion.

"That's the odd part. I may be wrong, but this medallion doesn't look that old. I know it doesn't make sense, seeing how the only creature capable of this kind of spell is a Fae, but I'll keep working on it," Drew says.

"Regardless of how old the thing is, are you suggesting our suspect is a female alpha? The shuriken has the same symbol as the medallion, and we know the shuriken belonged to our vigilante for sure," Val adds.

"That's the million-dollar question. I would assume both belong to the female I chased down since both have the same symbol. However, I didn't sense another werewolf, and since I had the medallion on me, wouldn't her protection be nullified?" Daniel asks Drew.

"One would think so, but maybe since the medallion was in close-proximity to her it still worked. If she is a she-wolf and we keep the medallion locked up here, away from her, we can find her. She-wolves are rare to come by," I tell the team. We all agree.

After a few hours pass, Willow arrives to pick me up. I get up from my desk and walk over to the door to greet her, so I can make introductions.

"Willow, this is my team I told you about. The man over there is Drew, that's Daniel next to him, that's Val the only female on the team, and of course, you know my brother Drake. Everyone this is Willow," I say as a good formal introduction. I can't believe how nervous I am, but I need my woman and my team to get along.

Everybody gives a welcoming hello or a nice to meet you, and Drake gives a 'what's up baby mama.'

"Give me a minute, Sunshine, and I'll be ready to go to our doctor's appointment," I tell Willow, then kiss her cheek. I can't help it, but I want to touch her all the time.

"Take your time. I'm excited about our visit today, so I came a little earlier than we'd planned anyway," my woman says as she follows me over to my desk. When I reach my desk, I gather up the files I want to take home with me. Much to my surprise, when I turn around, Willow's not behind me. She's standing by Drew's desk holding the picture of the medallion in her hand with all eyes of the team members staring at her.

"What is it Sunshine," I ask as I walk up to her.

"Is this a clue in one of your cases?"

Not wanting to or even being able to discuss the details with her, I give her a vague answer, "Something like that."

She catches onto my weak attempt to be vague and cuts her eyes at me. "Well if it is, I might be able to help."

"How?" Drew asks.

"I know this medallion or the owner of it," she continues.

"Who?" Daniel asks while coming closer to us.

"Are you sure? It could just look like a medallion you've seen before," I ask.

"No, it's this one. See the red streak in the stone cross in the middle, I would think that's not standard in all stones. I'm sure there are variations in each one."

"You're right," Drew says which makes Willow beam a huge smile. "Who is the owner of the medallion?" Drew asks.

"This belongs to my best friend, Ari. She was mugged a few weeks back, and they stole her necklace. She was heart-broken over losing it. Oh, since you have the necklace you can give it back to her. She'll be so excited! You see, it belonged to her mother, who died in a house fire years ago," Willow says with such excitement over her discovery. "Does that help any with your investigation?" she asks with pride beaming in her eyes like a child that brought home all A's on their report card; damn, she's so cute.

"That does baby," I tell her, making her smile beam even brighter. "We may have come across the thief that took it from her," is the only explanation I give her. "After our investigation, we can give it back to her, but right now it's evidence," I further explain.

"We need to talk with her first, of course, so she can iden-tify the necklace along with any details of the thief," Daniel interrupts.

"I have a great idea," Willow exclaims as she turns to face me. "I'm supposed to ask if you would like to meet my girls, meaning Ari and Nikki, tonight for drinks so they can interro-gate you. They've been feeling put off by me keeping you all to myself this long," she says with a smirk as she puts one of her hands to her mouth to stifle a following giggle.

Drake comes up behind me slaps me on the back then place a firm hand on my shoulder right before answering for me. "Why don't we all go out and meet the girls? That way, we can be Connor here's buffer and get to know you along with your girl posse all at once. We'll bring a photo of the medallion, so your friend can verify it belongs to her."

"That sounds perfect. Ari's going to be so excited when I tell her!" Willow says with a little clap of her hands.

"But it might be better if you don't tell her about the neck-lace until we show her the picture. That way she won't be too disappointed if by some chance it's not hers," Daniel adds playing the nice guy card. Everyone but Willow knows his ulterior motive is to catch Ari by surprise with the necklace to gauge her reaction. We should be able to tell right away if she is a werewolf.

If she's an unprotected female alpha, there's a good chance she won't come out due to fear. But she has nothing to fear from us on that part though. Killing female alphas is part of Old-World shit, but some tribes still follow the Old-World ways and have a genuine fear of female alphas. They kill she-wolves without any hesitation.

"You have a good point. I'll tell Ari I invited Connor and his friends over for a meet and greet." Willow replies in agreement.

After the doctor's appointment, Willow drops me off back at work. The team and I develop a plan of action since we've never come across a female alpha and need to be prepared for all possible outcomes. We need a break in our investigation, and hopefully, she is it and we can get a lead to locate the Wendigos.

We're all meeting at a bar located in the Marigny neighborhood just next to the French Quarter. Drake will arrive early and already be there when Ari arrives. The rest of us will come in at various times. Hopefully, Ari can help shed light on our case and in return we can make sure she keeps out of our way.

Chapter 40

Drake
"What the Hell"

At the bar.... I arrive early just as the team planned. I want to blend in, so I walk up to the bar and order a beer while scoping out the best location to have a full view of the whole inside of this place. The bar is one of the larger-sized ones in the Marigny. The bar counter is just inside the entrance against the wall and has bar stools lined across the front of it. It's early, so it's only half filled with tourist and locals.

The rest of the large room comprises about 20 tables with chairs. Nothing fancy, just a relaxed and inviting atmosphere. There's another room in the back that's smaller than the room where I'm standing which contains two pool tables along with more seating. After paying for my beer, I sit at an empty table against the far corner of the room. This table gives me the best view of the whole bar, including the back room and pool tables.

I don't have to wait long before the first member of our little party shows up. As I take the first sip of my beer, in walks Nikki. I haven't given her much thought since the night at The Club when Connor met Willow those many weeks ago. This is the first time I've seen her since then. I forgot just how hot she looks. Tonight, she's wearing cut-off shorts, sandals, and a tight black tank top. She has full lips, larger than average breasts, and a beautiful round ass. She has a short, brown hairstyle and is wearing loop style earrings.

Unfortunately, I can tell just by looking at her she's not my type of woman. I prefer meek and compliant; a woman down for nothing more than a one-night fuck fest, maybe two depending on how good the sex is. But my cock doesn't seem to care she is not our type. Nikki has a fiery attitude rolling off that tight little body of hers that unfortunately makes my cock twitch to life.

Unlike my mind, my cock doesn't have a specific type of female it's attracted to. It's happy with any hot woman that has a cunt to dive into. The first thing I notice about Nikki though, is she has a 'needs relationship before sex' vibe about her. My head on my shoulders needs to send the head of my cock another email stating the dangers of getting involved with that type of woman.

Nikki looks around, I'm guessing looking for Willow or Ari. When her eyes glance toward my direction, I look away, not wanting to be seen. A dick move I know, but I'd rather watch her from a distance. Besides, the lighting in this corner is just dim enough she might not recognize me.

If I were a gentleman, I would've gone over and directed her in this direction or some shit. I, however, have never claimed to be a gentleman. If I remember right from the night Connor and Willow first hooked up, Nikki is a spitfire I'd rather watch from a distance. When I look back in her direction, she's at the bar sitting on one of the empty stools. No surprise, the bartender notices Nikki right away and immediately heads straight to her, ignoring the already waiting customers.

I eavesdrop using my heighten sense of hearing. "What's your poison or pleasure beautiful?" the bartender asks, looking down at Nikki trying to display a sexy smile. I give him zero points for originality.

To my surprise, Nikki looks up and blushes a light pink at the compliment, then replies, "I'll have a glass of Sangria please."

As the bartender pours the glass of wine, he asks, "So, what's your name?"

"Nikki," she replies.

"Well, Nikki, my name is Mark, and I'll be your bartender tonight. So, let me know if I can get you anything else whether it be alcohol-related or not," he informs her as he exchanges the glass of wine for her money.

For some reason, this is pissing me off and I have a disturbing urge to go wipe that smile off his face. I don't want or need someone to be jealous over, especially someone I don't even know. I don't want a relationship, and I don't like commitments. Play but not stay is my motto, making sure everyone knows where I stand before the playing starts. I have little patience for the female drama, and the last thing I need is a clingy woman.

"Thank you," Nikki says with a sheepish smile.

"My pleasure," Mark says with a wink as he returns her change before walking off to wait on another customer.

"Crap," Nikki says to herself as she puts the change back into her small handbag. Nikki's phone rings and she answers it. I can hear her side of the conversation, but not the callers. There's too much background noise in this place blocking my heightened hearing.

"Hey Ari, where are you?" Nikki asks as she answers the phone. She listens for a moment then replies, "Just come in your work clothes, it'll be fine. I'll be at the bar waiting for you." Pause. "No, Willow isn't here yet. I need a favor. I switched handbags tonight and left my debit card at home. Could you spot me some money and I'll pay you back tomorrow when you come by the store?" More silence. "OK. See you soon. Don't take too long or I'll have to resort to batting my eyes and flirting for my drinks like the old days," Nikki replies then giggles as she ends the call then puts her phone back into her handbag.

I notice that the last little comment about flirting caught the attention of the douche bag sitting to her right. She glances up and sees the guy staring at her. She gives him her full attention by looking up at him under her batting lashes, then plasters a sweet smile on her beautiful face. The man perks up and smiles back at her. She looks back toward her wine glass, picks it up then takes a sip. I notice the douche bag licking his lips while adjusting his pants at the crotch as he watches her.

The douche bag clears his throat to get Nikki's attention again. She turns in his direction and slightly mumbles 'drink number two' low enough to herself under her breath that the douche bag can't hear her. With all my attention and heightened senses honed in on her, I have no difficulty hearing her. That's it. I decide if the woman doesn't have enough sense to be cautious, then I guess I'll have to step up and do the job.

Driven by a strange and unusual protective sense, I slip up behind her as they exchange names. She cuts another sweet smile at him, and he perks up even more. Just as he opens his mouth to speak again, he catches sight of my glare aimed at him. When his eyes meet mine, I shake my head slowly with a deadpan look. If he has any smarts at all, he'll get the fuck out of here. After a couple of more seconds of opening and closing his mouth, he grabs his drink, turns, and walks away. I know how intimidating I can be with my size and tattoos. I almost feel sorry for douche bag, almost.

"What the hell?" Nikki confusingly asks under her breath. I decide it's probably best Nikki doesn't notice that I was the cause of her drink number two disappointment, so I step back, slide over a couple of stools and have a seat at the bar. I order another beer along with a glass of Sangria.

A few minutes later douche bag number two wonders up to the vacant stool next to her, getting her attention to ask if the stool is taken. After she confirms no, he smiles at her and sits down. She returns his smile with one of her own. Motherfucker, does the woman not have any sense of self-preservation? Damn, when did this become my job?

Just like with the douche bag number one, when she turns towards his direction, I step up behind her with my beer and a glass of Sangria in my hands. Nikki turns her glass up and takes the last drink left in her wine glass. Douche bag number two takes this as an opportunity to do a quick scan over Nikki's body starting at her feet all the way up to her hair. That's the level where he sees my eyes peering down at him in a death glare.

I don't even have to shake my head at douche bag number two. He takes a swallowing gulp causing his Adam's apple to bob up and down in a tell-tale sign of fear as his face turns a shade pale. Nikki sits up straighter as douche bag number two now turns and walks as fast as he can away from her.

"What the fuck?" she asks this time out loud.

I decide I'm tired of playing guard dog for this woman and getting rid of the douche bags. Before she can turn back to face the bar, I lean in close to her ear without touching her body. At the same time, I bring my arm that's holding the glass of wine to the front of her still not touching her. The sudden movement startles her causing her to lean back, bringing her backside in contact with my front.

I tilt my head, so my mouth is closer to her ear so she is the only one who can hear what I have to say. "Here's a fresh glass of Sangria. We can't have you whoring that tight little body of yours out for drinks, now can we?" I immediately get a whiff of the sweet intoxicating smell of her perfume that's mixed with her scent. It's like an aphrodisiac to my cock, causing it to rise to the occasion. My comment causes her to twist her body to face me, so I stand up straight. Now it's her turn to sit there opening and closing her mouth like a stunned fish just like douche bag number one.

The priceless surprised look on her face disappears as the look of recognition, then anger overtakes it. "I'm not whoring myself for drinks," she replies hotly in a breathy whisper as she grabs the wine glass out of my hand. I lift my eyebrow at her remark. Her facial expression changes as I notice she tilts back and takes in my appearance from head to toe as if she's just seeing me for the first time.

"Hey, my eyes are up here," I say with a snarky tone to my voice.

Her eyes snap back to mine, and a light blush creeps up her neck to her cheeks. "I know that, stop flattering yourself."

I've about had enough of her attitude, even though the fire in her is a complete turn on for my cock. I reach for the wine glass and take it from her hand while pulling her ass off the stool she's sitting on. She doesn't have much choice other than to comply by following my lead or be dragged as we head back toward my table.

"What the hell are you doing?" she snaps in a rather loud, fierce tone.

I abruptly stop and turn back toward her while holding her wine glass out so as not to spill any wine. Not expecting such an abrupt stop, Nikki's front collides with my own. I lean down and whisper in her ear, "You're going to go sit at the table with me to stay out of trouble until the rest of our group arrives." I feel Nikki's body shiver. It's either from anger or desire from my breath on her neck. I'm not sure which, though I suspect the latter.

"I'm not some child who just got into trouble, and besides you're not the boss of me," Nikki says in response with a growl to her voice. Maybe the shiver was from anger.

"I may not be the boss of you, but I'm bigger and stronger than you are," I reply, adding a growl to my voice.

"You're not only a man-whore but a bully and stop growling at me. Did you even think about just asking if I would like to wait with you and not manhandling me?"

I take a deep breath to try to calm my nerves while dealing with this infuriating woman. With a calmer tone, I ask, "Would you like to come and join me at my table until the rest of our party arrives?" then adding a smile that feels more like a snarl.

"No!" she snaps back at me. That's it. I've had enough of dealing with this stubborn ass woman. With her hand still held in mine, I turn and proceed to the table pulling her with me. I hear her mumble a few choice words behind me, but she follows along compliantly. I'm trying not to think much into why I even care if she whores herself out for drinks or not.

After I deposit her ass in the chair beside me, I inform her, "Look, on the bright side I remembered to bring my money with me, so if you are a good little girl, I might buy you another drink."

"Fine... wait, how did you know I forgot to bring money with me?" Nikki asks while glaring at me with a confused look on her face, squinted eyes, and pursed lips. Damn, I would like to suck that plump bottom lip right out of that sour pucker.

Situations like this have taught me to be a quick thinker. After all, it's not like I can say I eavesdropped on your phone call from across the room. I casually reply, "I went to buy another beer at the bar and overheard you on the phone discussing your little plan," I say as I shrug at her and take a drink of my beer, waiting to see if I'm caught in my lie.

I notice a woman two tables over batting her eyes at me. I give her my panty-dropping smile with an added wink. Who knows, maybe she can be my late-night entertainment after I leave this place tonight. I hear Nikki scuff out a noise of disgust, so I glance back at her.

"Since your brother has knocked up one of the two women I cherish like a sister, I was hoping my first impression of you that night at the bar was wrong. Unfortunately, to my disappointment, I was right with my first judgment call of you," Nikki states still snappy in her tone and a deadpan expression on her face.

To be a dick, I egg her more by saying, "And do tell, what was your first impression? Please, don't keep me in suspense." I can tell by the look on her face I hit my mark enraging her up even more. I know the old expression says, 'don't poke the bear,' but I can't stop myself. Despite my instinct of self- preservation, poking this feisty bear is turning me the hell on.

"Man-whore; asshole," Nikki snarls in my direction with a raised brow, as if she's challenging me.

With her comments along with her facial expressions, I can no longer contain myself. I out-and-out laugh. This brings on what I like to call the slanted glare. I think I've added flames to the fire if that's even possible. My cock twitches again.

Before my brain can give my cock a mental confirmation that my mind agrees, the door to the bar swings open once again and in strolls Connor hand in hand with Willow. Nikki notices I'm looking past her and turns to check out what's caught my attention. Before I can get Connor's attention, Nikki is up and heading in their direction, letting them know the location of our table. The women come to a halt halfway to the table to chat for a minute while Connor heads my way.

"Hey Bro," I say as I greet Connor. He gives me a chin lift then sits down in a chair next to me facing the open room and door. This is an old work habit we've developed over the years. Always face the door and keep your back to the wall to eliminate people from sneaking up on you.

"Has the guest of honor shown her face yet?" Connor asks, wanting to know if Ari has arrived yet.

I give him an update, "Not yet. Based on Nikki's phone call I eavesdropped on she's running late but still plans to be here." We both sit quietly for a minute. Connor watches Willow like a wolf that's on edge, ready to pounce on any man that tries to approach her. This makes me burst out laughing again.

"What?" Connor asks, bringing his eyes back to me with a furrowed brow.

"What? Man, you're what. Why don't you get up and piss on her in front of everyone?" Connor looks down and shakes his head. "I can't get used to the fact you're so pussy whipped," I throw in for good measure.

I notice a shit-eating grin on his face as he looks back up at me. "Well, get used to it little brother because she owns me and my balls. I'm a ruined man." Damn. I smile at him as I shake my head in disbelief. I'm glad for my brother, and better him than me. Connor's eyes go back to guard duty, looking back at Willow.

"Nikki's glaring at you, and if the daggers her eyes are aiming at you are any indication, I would say you've been your usual charming self," Connor smirks. He knows me so well.

"What can I say, she wants me," I say with a chuckle.

"Yeah, I can totally see that's true," Connor says shaking his head. "Do me a solid and try to get along with her. She's like a

258

sister to Willow, and I want all the people that will be involved with my baby to get along," he explains. I give him a chin lift as a sign of understanding him.

That small movement triggered another muscle spasm in my chest where the silver bullet entered which is occurring more often lately than I am happy with. I rub the area trying to get the spasm to stop. "Did you talk to Kara about your chest?" Connor asks when he notices me rotating my shoulder. Being werewolves, we aren't used to any prolonged healing.

"Yeah, she said this is normal since the bullet contained silver. Anywhere the silver touched I can expect delayed healing, but it will eventually heal. She said not to overdo it with a lot of strenuous exercises."

With the authoritative look he always gets when he goes into the team leader mode Connor says, "Well, I think it's best if you limit your field work until you're completely healed." Damn, I didn't want to hear that shit, but I know he's right. I don't want to endanger any of my team members because of my pride, so I nod my head in agreement.

I guess Nikki's 15-minute bitching report is over, as the women finally walk over and sit at our table. Willow sits next to Connor and Nikki sits across from her, which happens to be the seat farthest away from me. I smirk and let out a little chuckle. She must have heard me because at the exact damn time I chuckle, her head jerks toward my direction with the damn dagger throwing glare back in her eyes.

Connor notices mine and Nikki's non-verbal conversation then elbows me while whispering 'behave' in my ear. At the same time, Willow nudges Nikki under the table and mouths the words 'stop it' to her. I'm guessing she must have received the same request of unity and peace I did just a minute ago from Connor.

"Willow, baby, are you hungry?" Connor asks as he takes her hand and rubs it gently before placing it in his lap.

Without thinking I blurt out, "I thought you two ate right before you came here." Nikki snaps her head around to glare at me at the same time pointing to her stomach to remind me that Willow is pregnant. From what Connor has told me, Willow's appetite has doubled, causing her to worry about losing weight after giving birth.

I try to cover my slip up by saying, "Oh, never mind. I forgot you're pregnant and need the extra calories. If the baby is anything like Connor, I'm sure it's hungry. Mom complained that Connor was her biggest baby, eleven pounds to be exact." With my announcement, Willow's eyes become the size of saucers as she glares in Connor's direction.

I glance back over at Nikki who is mouthing 'Not helping' at me. I shrug my shoulders and decide not to touch on the eating subject again anywhere near Willow.

Willow starts fussing at my brother, "Seriously, eleven pounds of baby to be pushed out of my…" she pauses and then continues "I'm definitely not hungry," Willow says to Connor. Now, Connor turns to glare at me.

Just then, I notice the rest of our team has arrived at the bar, and not a moment too soon. They spot us right away and head over. Val takes the empty seat next to Willow while Drew sits next to Nikki. Daniel takes the seat beside Drew leaving only one seat left for our guest of honor between Daniel and myself. They did this on purpose to try to isolate Ari from her girl posse, so we might get a better pick on any odd behavior. Everyone introduces themselves to Nikki, and she does the same in return. The increase in the size of our group has caught the attention of our waitress who immediately comes to take drink orders before we start any conversation.

When the waitress leaves Drew is the first to break the silence, "Been here long?" Drew asks as if he didn't already know our arrival plans.

"Just long enough to play referee to these two fighting kids," Willow says as she smiles at the same time pointing to Nikki and me.

"Foreplay," Val says as the waitress arrives with our drinks. I glance over at Nikki and watch in fascination as her face turns two shades of red. I'm now wondering if it's anger, embarrassment, or maybe a combination of both.

Before I can put much thought into it, Daniel asks, "Is your girl Ari still coming? I brought the photos of the medallion for her to look at." He places the envelope with photos on the table in front of him then pulls out one picture at a time from it glancing at each one.

"Yeah, she just called a little while ago to let me know she's running late due to some professors meeting. She'll be coming straight from work, so she should be here anytime," Nikki informs the group. She stares at the photos that Daniel now has in a pile in front of him.

"May I see them? Willow told me earlier today she believes you have found Ari's necklace." Daniel slides the pile of photos over in front of her. We watch as her reaction is an instant smile spreading across her lips. "This is it! This is Ari's necklace! She'll be so relieved to know you've found it. You know it was her mother's, and now Ari's after her mother's untimely death," she rambles as she continues flipping through each photo without looking up. The mention of the death of Ari's mother makes the smile on her lovely face evaporate.

"How did her mother die?" Val asks Nikki.

"Please, don't bring her mother's death up when she gets here," Willow and Nikki say in unison in a rush request, causing Val to snap back her head from the urgency of their appeal.

"OK?" Val responds as if questioning why.

"Sorry," Willow says.

Then Nikki explains as she stacks the photos back up in a stack and slides them over to Daniel who puts them back into the envelope. "Ari is really sensitive about the subject of her mother's death. She has spoken about her mom a lot over the years but rarely mentions the night of her untimely death. We only know the basic details. The house she and her mother lived in caught on fire late one night." Nikki pauses, frowns, and then takes a gulp of wine appearing to drown away unwanted sadness.

Willow finishes the story, "Ari made it out, but her mother didn't. She was only seven at the time. I or should I say Nikki and I," she says as she looks at Nikki then back at our group before continuing, "Think she has PTSD."

To finish the story of Ari's devastating past, Nikki adds, "She has this saying, Physical injuries are easily healed. It's….."

To my surprise, Daniel, not Willow, is the one to interrupt Nikki this time and says, "It's the broken pieces of the soul that do not mend." I look around the table, and everyone is staring at him just as surprised as I am. Val's mouth opens, then closes, then opens again. I can tell she wants to ask what the fuck just like I do, but we hold back because it's not just the team present at the moment. After this group meeting is over, I'll want an explanation of just how the hell he knows the ending of Ari's saying.

Willow gives Daniel a bewildered look and asks "You've heard that saying before? I thought it was some morbid saying she made up."

"I've heard it before," is the only thing he says with a glee in his eyes like he gets when he's able to put the pieces of a case we're working on together.

The door to enter the bar opens again catching my attention. Well speak of the devil, and he shall rise as the saying goes. Ari walks into the bar looking nothing like the sexpot I remember the night Connor met Willow for the first time.

Ari seems like a meek and mild school teacher. Her strawberry red hair is arranged into a sexy messy bun. She's wearing a white button up blouse that has the first three buttons undone, which would've revealed the cleavage of her full breast, except a pale-pink camisole with lace trim at the top is covering all the good parts.

My gaze falls to her hips and damn, a tight pencil skirt hugs her shapely hips, nicely outlining an exact hourglass figure. Her shoes are a dull tan color which would be boring except for the two-inch heels and the slit at the toes allowing her toes to peek out at the very tip. The two-inch heels give her legs the appearance of being a mile long.

I look back up at her face. To finish off the "I'm what every boy wants as his teacher" look, she's wearing glasses that do nothing to hide her gorgeous face and emerald eyes. She's every red-blooded American boy's version of a hot as hell librarian in a wet dream. She looks around the room until she spots us at our table in the back and heads our way. Nothing about this woman screams fear me I'm a She-wolf.

"There's our girl," Willow says noticing the guest of honor.

Chapter 41

Ari
"It's a Small World"

My day has been horribly long, and I finally make it to the bar where I'm supposed to meet my BFFs and Willow's man, Connor, along with his team. I suspect Willow is trying to merge Connor's friends with hers; which is fine with me, but I wish I had time to go home and change out of my Mary Poppins' clothes.

My outfit screams all work and no play, but with my meeting at work lasting longer than it should have I'm now forced to continue the evening in my work attire. You would think a bunch of professors could get together and agree over what textbook to use next semester with dignity and no bickering. Oh well, whatever.

As I walk further into the bar, I notice the place is starting to get pretty crowded. I pause after a few steps to see if I can spot Willow or Nikki. After a minute of looking around at everyone and feeling like an oddball because the way I'm dressed, I notice my party sitting in the back of the room.

Great, now I get the pleasure of wading deeper into the onlookers to make me that much more self-conscious. As I approach the table, I look around and take in everyone sitting at it. I recognize Connor and his brother Drake, or man-whore as Nikki likes to refer to him, from The Club. The thought of that memory gives me a little smile. There are three other people I don't know, and I assume they must be the team Willow spoke of.

Sitting beside Willow is a petite woman with medium

length black hair that's up in a ponytail. She has a single clump of white hair in the center of the front and appears to be around my age.

Beside Nikki sits an average-looking guy with sandy brown hair who's wearing glasses. He's smaller than the other men at the table and looks to be 30ish.

The last mystery team member is sitting with his back facing me. He has long, jet black hair that's curled at the ends and is shiny like the feathers of a raven. His black shirt is stretched tight across his broad shoulders, and his tan muscular arms have a hint of ink peeking out below the sleeves from tattoos.

I glance down his backside to check out his ass, but the back of the chair blocks the view damn it. He has nice size thighs and legs covered in faded denim jeans I'm sure he wears quite nicely. I hear Willow announce my arrival by saying, "There's our girl," but I am too fixated on this man to pull my eyes away.

I look up to the back of his head again, but instead of seeing curls, to my mortification my eyes meet a pair of piercing hazel eyes that have a knowing look. That look along with the smirk on his lips lets me know he caught me leering at his ass. I know my cheeks are glowing cherry red because I can feel them heating up like I'm standing in front of a fire. I need to break this magnetic eye contact we seem to have, but I can't bring myself to look away.

Right before I reach the table, I stumble as the recognition hits me, I've seen him before. As fast as the blood rushed into my cheeks, I now feel it drain just as quickly. Fuckity, fuck, fuck! It's him, but how? Shit! Does he know it was me that night? I glance around the table. Instead of feeling like a friendly gathering among friends and potential friends, it now feels like I've stepped up to the Knights of the Round Table and I'm awaiting judgment.

Breathe Ari, just breathe, I chant in my head to myself. More than likely they don't know who I am. I look over at Willow and Nikki who both have happy expressions on their faces.

No, he couldn't know. He never saw my face; I made sure of that. I'm so nervous I just want to get the hell out of here.

My mind is racing, trying to plan my escape from the bar as I realize the only seat available at the table is away from my girls between him and Drake. Well, damn. Upon seeing Drake, the details of that night fit together. The night we had our encounter is the same night Drake was shot! This must be the group at the warehouse that night. This gathering gives a whole new meaning to it's a small world right now. Why haven't I pieced this together before now?

Connor begins the introductions after I sit down, but the only name my mind takes in is his name, Daniel. I know from that night Daniel is a werewolf. Are they all werewolves? The fire that killed my mother also damaged me and impaired my ability to pick up on what individuals are, so it takes a lot of focus for me to do that now. I snap out of my mental state and smile. "It's nice to finally meet everyone," I say, hoping my voice sounds calm.

Damn, I've to get a handle on my emotions. I need to focus on the calm and in control Ari, not the freaked the fuck out Ari. I push my fears away with one small reassurance. The night my medallion was stolen, I went to Gran for help because without my medallion I'm a sitting target. The only relief she could offer is a temporary henna tattoo spelled with a protective cloak.

Nikki almost caught us that night, walking in on us just as Gran was finishing it. I wince as I look over at Nikki and Willow. I hate not having enough courage to tell them everything, but right now I have more significant problems. The tattoo will eventually fade away leaving me exposed, but for tonight I can take comfort in knowing I'm still protected.

I relax with the comfort that knowledge gives me. If I wasn't broken, I could have gotten a read on this group from a distance.

As everyone else continues engaging in conversation, I try to concentrate on getting a read on each at the table to know what kind of hornet's nest I'm currently sitting in. I know Daniel is a werewolf, so I move on around the table.

The next person is the woman, I think they called her Val. Right away I feel her trying to get a read on my emotions, which screams Empath. Well, good luck on that because not even she can break through my protection barrier. She turns her face in my direction, and I smile the sweetest smile I can muster.

Next, I concentrate on the man beside her, Andrew, or is it Drew? He's different from Val. I sense a Druid. I switch my focus to the next person, the Man-Whore. Immediately, I'm aware he's another werewolf. I feel my face going pale again.

I concentrate on Connor, but I already know what he has to be since the Man-Whore is his brother. Connor's another werewolf. How did I miss this the night Willow met him? I guess the alcohol and partying with the BFFs caused me to put my guard down. It takes my full focus to get a read-on people. The alcohol helped dull my already damaged senses and damn it, it was my birthday.

I wasn't concerned about anything that night other than fun with friends. Glancing at Willow, I now feel less worthy of her friendship, and hold back the sensation to vomit. I failed to protect her and keep this from happening to her. The baby, what does this mean for her baby?

The information is a lot to process and I haven't been paying attention to the conversation at the table. I snap out of my muse when I feel Daniel's fingertip brush my arm, sending a jolt of electricity through my body in a delicious way.

Damn, what was that about? Before I can give it much thought, I hear Nikki say my name, "Ari?" I glance up from my arm in her direction to find her staring at me, and everyone at the table has grown quiet. I must have missed something, a question maybe?

"Are you feeling okay Ari? You look a little pale," Willow says as I look over at her. She has such concern in her eyes. She's worried about me, but I'm the one who let her down as a BFF and she doesn't even know it yet.

I give her a small smile then reply, "I was thinking about my meeting tonight and the changes we're making in the History Department. Sorry, I guess I need a drink to help push work out of my head." I'm now the honorary shittiest friend, but I can't tell her the truth so what choice do I have?

"That's ok," Willow says as Connor lifts his hand and motions the waitress in our direction. When I get my drink, I feel the need to down it quickly and order another but refrain from that urge. I realize I won't be able to escape this situation without significant alarm bells going off, so I need to figure out how to get through this meet and greet.

Dom! Of course! He's always my backup, always my buffer. I've known him longer than I've been friends with Willow and Nikki. The story of mine and Dom's past is another thing I can add to my growing worst friend ever to Willow list.

I've never been completely honest about mine and Dom's history to my BFFs. Right after my mom died, they placed me in the care of an elderly woman. She is the same woman who rescued Dom from living on the streets of New Orleans a few years earlier. Every kid there called her grandma, including me as well, because that's what she felt like to us. She wanted every one of the throwaway children to always feel like they belonged to a family, albeit a family of misfits, but a family none the less.

Dom is a half-breed, the product of a werewolf father and an absent human mother. At the time I didn't know what I was, a purebred She-wolf, but I knew I differed from other children. My mom and I hid my indifference from others.

I became a scared, frightened child who was placed in a temporary home with a group of half-breed kids of all types not just werewolves, who by the way were only too happy to show off the unique things they could do to impress the new girl. It scared the shit out of me! I was clueless about the world I lived in.

Dom stepped up to be my friend, protector, and brother. I

call him my brother from another mother. He not only went out of his way to keep me safe but also educated me on a world I had no clue existed. When he learned how broken I was, he tried his best to help me by making sure I could protect myself when needed.

He hooked me up with some less than desirable friends that he trusted, with their help and to Dom's horror I excelled in my fighting ability. I became kick-ass Ari whose adventures give Dom regrets of having a hand in creating the kick-ass side of me. He's worried I'll eventually get over my head into shit I can't get out of. He's always complaining I'm like a beacon for trouble, which is probably right since I'm sitting at this table tonight.

The question now is how can I get Dom here without being obvious? I decide yet again to be the worst BFF ever and lie. I pull out my cell phone as I pretend to get a text message and look at my phone screen. Just as I expected one of them to do, Willow asks, "Who's texting you?"

I look up to find Daniel glaring at me with one eyebrow raised as if questioning why he didn't hear my phone vibrate, assuming I must be lying. I ignore his judgmental look. So, what if he is right? Whatever.

I tell Willow, "It's a co-worker. Give me a second to respond before the alcohol kicks in, and then I promise I'll put work issues away until tomorrow." I say while giving my 'I'm a sweet angel smile' which I've perfected over the years. I quickly text Dom.

Me: At Backspace Bar... need a buffer or a distraction QUICK.

Dom: What the hell have you gotten yourself into this time?

Me: Judge much? I just came to meet Willow's baby daddy and his coworkers who happen to be three werewolves, a Druid, and an Empath.

Dom: You're with Connor's team?

Me: Yeah, friends of yours?

Dom: They are Guardians. Sit tight and keep your mouth shut. Focus on being invisible and draw as little attention to yourself as possible. I'm already on the way.

Me: You're the best!

I put my cell phone away while giving everyone at the table my sweetest smile and say, "OK, done with work."

"Great! We wanted you here for more than a meet and greet today," Willow announces excitedly, as she bounces in her chair and stares at me. I glance around the table, and every set of eyes are on me. Well damn, there goes being invisible. Maybe Dom is right when he says I'm a magnet for trouble. Willow continues to explain, "When I was at Connor's office today, I saw some interesting photos I know you'll be interested in."

"Really?" I ask, trying my best to portray the sweet and innocent Ari.

"Yes. Daniel, can you show her the photos you have with you?" Willow asks. What photos? Shit, did I get caught on camera that night? Where's Dom? I feel like I'm about to get sick.

Chapter 42

Daniel
"Unleash the Python"

I hear Willow announce, "There's our girl," cluing me in that Ari's here. I turn my head toward the direction the rest of the people at my table are looking to get my first glimpse of our mystery woman and am surprised at what I see. I expected to see a fierce appearing possible She-wolf; but to my dismay, I find a meek and mild woman who's sexy looking in a Mary Poppins kind of way who is checking out my ass. It makes me chuckle. I want to tell her to look all she wants, but I keep that comment to myself. She's not at all what I was expecting. Nothing is radiating off her that remotely screams She-wolf, much less vigilante.

Ari is rocking the look of a sexy high school teacher in a teenage guy's wet dream. She's sexy as hell in her tan skirt, and the top she has on doesn't do an excellent job of hiding her well-endowed tits. With her pinned up red hair and glasses, she reminds me of a naughty wet dream where the teacher's about to do some schooling on a man's cock.

She finally looks up and sees I'm watching her check out my ass and damn if her face doesn't turn two shades red, accenting the little sprinkle of freckles across her nose.

As she reaches our table, she checks out her seating options. She turns pale when she realizes she has to sit next to me. Damn, this woman oozes innocence and nervousness. She can't be the fierce woman I encountered that night. As Willow starts the introductions, I focus on Ari and study her carefully. She seems a little too nervous and zoned out, almost as if lost in her own mind. I glance over at Val to see what she thinks, and as she looks at me, I raise one eyebrow. She knows exactly what my nonverbal cue is asking her. This isn't our first rodeo together.

Val shrugs her shoulders and shakes her head with a concerned look in her eyes as she silently mouths the word 'nothing.' That one word sends an alarm to both of us. Every living being has emotions that Val can detect. She can figure someone's mood and can pick up on thoughts too, often. To be a blank void to Val is suspicious.

Nikki must have caught on to her zoned-out appearance too as she calls her name, "Ari?" When Ari doesn't respond, I lightly run my fingertips across her forearm, barely touching her soft skin as I slide them across her arm. This touch sends an electric zap straight to my cock, and by the way she reacted to my touch, I suspect she felt the spark as well.

She glances up with a confused look on her pale face, reminding me of a skittish kitten, a hot kindergarten teacher-kitten. She gives some lame excuse about work. Wait, didn't Connor say she's a history professor? No one can be this unnerved about history, can they?

The thought of some asshole at her work giving her problems pisses me off. To my surprise, I feel protective over this kitten. What the hell? She announces she received a text from a co-worker, but I know damn well that phone didn't vibrate. She catches me watching her with suspicion but blows me off. I bet some dipshit at her work is upsetting her. It might be worth looking into later just to make sure no one is harassing her at work.

Willow brings up the subject of the photos and asks me to show them to Ari. Now we get to see her reaction to the medallion. I pull out the photos to hand her one, but stop momentarily before handing them over as she now has a look on her face that she's about to hurl at any moment. "Ari, are you ok?" I ask as one of her hands reaches out to take the photographs from me.

"Um… yeah," she replies as she looks down at the photos. A look of relief washes over her face as she flips through the pictures. For the first time tonight, her color begins to look normal.

"This…. this is my medallion. How? Where did you find it? Did you arrest the guy who stole it from me or something?" Ari rambles off questions as her excitement shows.

"Something like that," Drew says as he speaks up in offering some excuse, frowning on honesty since the fact we found it on a dead Wendigo might make her hurl not to mention having to explain what a Wendigo actually is. I seriously doubt this is the woman from that night. She looks up from the photos under her lashes at me with a bright shining smile instead of the frown she displayed before.

Her smile is like the sun breaking through the clouds. This smile lights up her eyes, making my cock twitch again. Damn, this woman is doing a number on my cock. What the hell is wrong with me? She's gorgeous, but she's like a sugar and spice and everything nice kitten type of woman, which has never been my type. I prefer a feisty, sassy, spicy pussy, not a kitten.

"Ari, are you positive it's your medallion?" Drew asks, speaking up again.

"I would know it anywhere as I wear it or used to wear it all the time that is until it was stolen from me," Ari replies while flashing that sweet smile at Drew which makes me want to hit the man. I prefer her smiles to be directed my way.

"It's a beautiful piece of jewelry. It looks like an antique," Val states.

Ari's smile fades as she turns her gaze to the center of the table, "It was my mother's. I don't know where she got it. My mother passed away when I was young, so I never got the history of it. She had the medallion as far back as I can remember. I don't think it's worth much in respect of money, but it's priceless to me because it's the only thing I have that was hers."

"We need to hang onto it for a little while longer because we found it at a crime scene we are currently investigating. I promise you though, we'll keep it safely locked up and give it back to you just as soon as we can," Connor tells her, which seems to bring her out of the memories and back to the present.

"Oh, of course. Thank you, I'm just relieved it's been found," Ari says.

"Hey man," I hear Drake say loudly, causing me to tear my eyes away from Ari to Drake. I follow his line of sight to see who he's talking to. It's Dom, a man I met a few years back. He's been a friend to Drake and Connor much longer though.

He gives a chin lift in response as he approaches our table. To my irritation, he walks right behind Ari and places his hands on her shoulders giving them a light squeeze. Why this irritates me, I don't have a clue, but it just fucking does.

The meek little kitten doesn't even bat one eyelash when he does this. Do they know each other? Are they a fucking couple? Ari reaches up to touch his hands and gives them a light squeeze back, leaving her hands resting on top of his much larger ones.

"Care to join us for a drink," Connor asks as his eyes drop to Dom's and Ari's joined hands. I can tell their connection is news to Connor too.

"I'm sorry guys, but the baby and I need a bathroom break. I'll be back in a minute," Willow announces.

"Do you need me to go with you Sunshine?" Connor asks, which earns him an eye roll from her.

"Dude, seriously? Your woman's going to take a piss, how much help do you think she needs?" Drake asks in an exasperated tone.

"Pussy whipped," Drew coughs out.

"I'll go with you. This is like my third glass of wine," Nikki tells Willow, and the two women get up from the table head toward the bathroom hallway in the opposite corner from us. Dom moves to sit in Nikki's now vacant seat, affording me the realization Dom isn't alone. He has a woman with him who walks to Willow's chair but doesn't sit down. She stands behind it.

I can sense instantly that she's part Wendigo and human, a half-breed. A half-breed of any kind usually carries a very faint scent of their non-human half compared to a full-breed. She looks a lot like Margot Robbie's character in the movie Suicide Squad except her makeup isn't smeared. It's done in bright colors with the blue eye makeup to go along with her blood red lipstick. She even has the two ponytails on each side, but her hair is brown instead of blonde. She's cute in an 'I'm a play-ground come and play with me' kind of way. Everything about her screams trouble in the making.

Ari gets a warm, soft glow to her face when she sees the other woman. "Zoey! Honey, I didn't see you standing with Dom. Dom, why didn't you introduce her?" Ari asks in a scold-ing kind of way.

"I'm sorry, seeing everyone caught me off my game. Everyone this is Zoey. Zoey this is Connor, Drake, Drew, Val, and Daniel, and of course, you know Ari. The two in the bath-room…" Dom says as an introduction but is cut off by Zoey.

"Are Willow and Nikki. I've met them a time or two with Ari," she says. She looks toward the back of the room where the pool tables are located, then back at Ari with a shit-eating grin. Ari gives a head nod to Zoey showing they are having a non-verbal conversation. Dom shakes his head. It seems he's in on the silent discussion too.

Ari stands up announcing, "We're going to go shoot some pool. Val, would you like to come? We can leave the gentleman here and have girl time."

"Sure," Val replies. I chuckle silently. Val, being an Em-path, picks up on my humor and socks a punch to my arm. She turns to follow the two women who are already headed to the pool tables in the backroom. I know Val will loathe every minute of girl-time.

Val has always just been one of the guys. She hates hanging out with other females as she complains they have too many emotions rolling off them, changing minute by minute from happy, to sad, to pissed off. She says it leaves her feeling exhausted and emotionally drained.

Before Zoey can get too far away, Dom reaches out and grabs her wrist to put her movement to a halt. "Do me a solid and no hustling tonight," Dom says.

"You better inform Ari of that not me," she replies pointing at Ari who is already in the room with the pool tables.

"You inform her for me," Dom says in a no bullshit tone.

"Whatever," Zoey says as she rolls her eyes.

"Zoey," Dom replies sternly.

"Ok, ok already," she agrees in a frustrated tone as she yanks her hand out of his grip and turns to catch up with the other two women already in the poolroom.

Shaking his head in disbelief, Dom turns back to face us. "I'll have to go back there in a little while to make sure they keep their shit out of trouble," he says, letting out a sigh indicating this isn't his first rodeo with those two.

"You know Ari?" Connor asks. Dom looks at him while nodding his head. Connor raises a brow at him to show he'd like more info besides a nod.

"Man, you got a woman already, you need to leave Ari alone. Stray from Willow and a man might snatch that sweet little bundle up away from you," Dom says.

"Don't even fucking go there again Dom," Connor barks. Again? I wonder what the hell that's about but fight down the desire to ask. Dom laughs as he watches Connor's face turn red while clenching his jaw tight.

"Relax, man," Drake snaps at Connor.

Dom explains how he knows Ari, "I work with her down at the center where I volunteer, but we've known each other since we were kids. Since Ari doesn't like to talk about her childhood, not many people know," Dom replies as he cuts his eyes at Connor indicating not to share that info with Willow unless Ari does first. Connor seems to get the message loud and clear because he nods his head in agreement.

"Do you know anything about her medallion?" Drew

asks.

An annoyed look crosses Dom's face. "Cut the shit. What exactly do you want to know about Ari and why?" Dom asks straightforwardly.

This time I speak up. "The night Drake was shot we had followed three Wendigos into a warehouse. While there, a Wendigo was killed by someone besides us. There was a woman outside in the distance that used a Shuriken to kill him. During my search of his body, I found the medallion that has the markings of protecting a She-wolf. The Shuriken has the same marking. We later found out the medallion belongs to Ari. If this mystery woman is Ari, we want any info she can give us, and then to tell her to stay the fuck out of our way so we can handle this."

"And you think Ari is your mystery woman? Have you spent any time with Ari? She's meek and shy around new people and thinks she's broken. Does that sound like a She-wolf or a woman on a killing spree?" Dom asks with sarcasm laced in his words. Well, the shyness could explain the different facial colors she exhibited.

"What is this shit about being broken?" I ask, wanting to know for my benefit, not the case.

"She was there the night her house caught on fire. She was only seven years old. Her mother was the only real family she had. Her mother's people were all gone before Ari's birth. She's never mentioned a father, so he's either dead or a deadbeat. Ari could hear her mother screams while she was burning up in the house. Ari tried to go back into the fire to get her, but a fireman held her back. I think she struggles with PTSD. That's about all I know," Dom says.

"Damn," I whisper, too disturbed by the tale to say more while imagining Ari witnessing her mother's death as a little girl and not being able to help.

Chatting with each other, Willow and Nikki make their way back to our table. They glance around and in unison they ask, "Where's Ari?"

"Pool room with Zoey and Val," Dom informs them. "Hopefully they're not hustling anyone, but you never know when Ari and Zoey are together."

"I thought I saw Ari's friend Zoey on the way to the bathroom," Willow replies.

"Oh… I remember Zoey. She's the one who told us about Hustler Ari, but I've never witnessed her in action," Nikki exclaims with delight.

"Hustler Ari?" I ask the women.

"Ari is a complex person with many layers," Willow says in explanation. "Let's go!" she says with bright eyes while pushing Nikki toward the pool tables.

Intrigued, I stand to go to the poolroom. "Daniel where are you going, man?" Drake asks.

"To check out Hustler Ari, where else?" I reply, unable to stop my smug smile.

"Fuckin hell!" I hear Connor say along with the unmistakable sound of a chair scraping across the floor. "I better go keep an eye on what's mine," he continues while not sounding too thrilled about it.

Connor and I walk into the poolroom to find Willow and Nikki sitting at a tall table near one of the pool tables with Val, so we head that way. Ari and Zoey are standing beside the pool table chalking the tips of their pool sticks. When I reach the table, I notice a small stack of cash in the center of the table. "Ladies," I say, getting the attention of Willow, Val, and Nikki. When they look at me, I raise my brow and nod my head toward the stack of money.

"We are the keepers of the winning money," Willow says proudly.

"I thought Dom told them not to hustle and here you with my baby are right smack in the middle of their shit. Should I even be surprised?" Connor asks as he makes his way to stand behind Willow. He snakes one of his arms around her shoulders and pulls her tight against him to stake his claim. He tenderly kisses her temple, which causes her to melt into him.

I need to look away because I'm feeling like a diabetic with all the sweetness radiating off of them. The man needs to just piss on her and get it over with. He has it bad for this woman. I hope she feels the same.

By the look on her face, I think she does. I'm shocked just how close the two of them have become in such a short period of time. Hell, maybe it's the baby causing them to throw caution to the wind and go warp speed with this relationship. I wouldn't know. I've never had a kid, much less gotten a woman pregnant.

"It's not like it's a ton of money, just a friendly bet they have against those two guys over there," Willow explains as she points out the women's opponents. Connor flips through the stack of bills counting with his free hand that's not on Willow. "Four hundred dollars, baby that's more than a friendly bet in my book," Connor tells Willow which brings me out of my thoughts.

I look over to see the two guys she's pointing to. They look like college students with their khaki pants and polo shirts, looking at each other talking while glancing at Ari and Zoey. They have cocky smiles like this will be taking candy from a baby. This should be interesting. I pull up a chair next to Nikki to wait for the show to begin, excited for the entertainment.

"I'm hungry. We need snacks, maybe popcorn," Willow says as she rubs her small baby bump. I'm thinking the 'we' in her statement is her and the baby not the rest of us. Immediately the protective baby daddy springs to action. Connor flags down a waitress and orders her snack, which turns out to be meal size, not snack size. In her defense, carrying a werewolf baby is stressful on a human, so her body needs the extra calories.

"Call it," I hear Zoey say and I turn back toward the pool table to watch the show.

"Heads of course," the taller of the two guys says while making a pointing reference towards his cock. He smiles, and the guys high five each other.

"Classy," Nikki says as she rolls her eyes.

"Heads it is. You break first," Ari announces after she flips the coin.

"We need some music, be right back," Zoey says to Ari as she walks to an old fashion jukebox sitting in the corner a few feet away. Damn, I thought it was just sitting there as decoration. It's so old that I didn't think it would still work, but apparently, it does because it didn't take any time at all for the music to start after Zoey put in money then picked a few songs. The quickness of her choices makes me suspicious that she already had a playlist in mind.

The first guy up breaks and knocks in a stripe. "Stripes," he calls unnecessarily, but it's part of the game. He lines up for his next shot when the real show begins. Paula Cole's song "Feelin' Love" plays through the speakers.

As he's about to strike the white ball, Ari unbuttons her blouse, turning her back toward the pool table as she slips it off her shoulders and lets it slide down her arms slowly as her ass sways seductively to the beat of the music. This reveals slender, tan shoulders covered with velvety soft looking skin and a small tattoo on one shoulder along with the spaghetti straps of a camisole and thin lacey straps of her bra also visible. Fuck me. My cock takes notice.

I hear Nikki ask Willow in a whisper, "Is that a tattoo on her shoulder? Did you know about that?"

"I don't know and no," Willow says through a mouth full of food that the waitress must have brought without me noticing. I can't seem to tear my eyes away from the show.

With her back still towards the pool table and her hips still swaying seductively to the beat of the music, Ari unpins her hair allowing lockets of red hair to cascade halfway down her back like a refreshing waterfall that would make a man dying of thirst want to grasp a handful of. She then runs her fingers through her hair at her scalp, massaging her head and letting out a barely audible moan.

"Damn," I hear one of the guys say. I couldn't agree more.

Damn, she looks hot as hell. My cock is twitching to life as the wet dream of a naughty teacher that every man has had as a teenager unfolds. I glance around the poolroom to discover she's captured every man in the room's attention.

The man waiting to take his shot seems to snap out of his trance as Ari turns around. He pulls back his pool stick to make his shot, but as Ari turns entirely around, we get our first glimpse of the front of her top that was concealed in her blouse.

The top on the camisole is all lacey and stretches across her luscious C-cup, no, definitely D-cup breast with a small bit of lace from her bra peeking out at the top corners around her cleavage. The tight-fitting top over the D-cup tits did its magic because the man scratched the shot and the white ball rolled around not hitting a damn thing but the sides of the table.

"Oh, is it my turn already?" Ari asks in a sugar-sweet voice while looking sheepishly sweet and innocent. Now I see why they said there are many layers to Ari just a bit ago. Gone is the shy, skittish little kitten and before me stands a very confident temptress, comfortable in her element. My sweet kitten has morphed into a tigress. Now, this Ari has fuck appeal. She's the type of woman I could grab up by the ass cheeks and slam up against the wall, then shove my cock in and out of her longing cunt making her cum until her throat is raw from screaming my name. My cock is paying attention now.

"Yes, I believe it's your turn," Zoey confirms to Ari.

The dudes they are playing against move back away from the pool table to give Ari free range and to allow them a better view. Ari morphs again into what I could only describe as 'Hustler Ari.' She leans over the pool table, calling shot after accurate shot while never missing.

With each shot, she leans over so the lace on the cups of the bra is visible and cleavage is revealed. She tilts her hips up just enough so that ass of hers is the perfect height and position to slide a cock right into her sweet pussy and fuck her from behind. The view we get varies based on what angle she needs to make the shot, but all of them are a sight to behold.

By the time she sinks the eight ball my cock is rock hard and straining against my zipper, wanting to burst out like an unleashed python to attack her pussy. By the way the guys are looking at each other and shaking their heads, I would say they realize they've been hustled, but they don't seem too pissed about it. Can you blame them? I would pay four hundred dollars myself to see that action again.

"Thanks for the game boys," Zoey says in their direction.

One of the dudes clears his throat as the other one finally finds his tongue to form words, "Anytime." He clears his throat again then continues, "Would you like to join…" but I interrupt him as I immediately jump to my feet and stroll over to stand by Ari. Fuck no, I know what the asshole is about to ask.

"Umm… never mind," he finishes when our eyes lock. Don't ask me why I now feel so territorial because I don't fucking know. All I do know is this woman has driven my cock crazy watching her for the last 15 minutes and I'm not ready to watch her walk away, not yet anyway.

She turns facing a rack on the wall to put up her pool stick. I come up behind her, closing the distance until I'm as close as can be without touching her. I take my hand and run my fingers through her silky hair I've been dying to get a hold of since she let it down. I swipe it off her shoulder and pause for a second as I get a good look at the tattoo I completely forgot about. It's an infinity mark identical to the one on her medallion, interesting. Thoughts of the case and of her being a She-wolf are quickly pushed out of my mind as I allow my cock to take over my thoughts for now.

I lean in close to her ear, so she's the only one who can hear me and whisper, "How about playing a game of one-on-one pool against me? But baby I must warn you, to distract me enough to lose, you would actually have to show me your tits." I hope tigress Ari hasn't morphed back into the kitten because I'm in the mood to play.

Without taking a step back, she turns completely around

to face me, and our faces are now so close our lips are but a breath apart. She smiles sweetly and replies, "I would have to step up my game, but I would still kick your ass."

"Is that right, baby? Are you not a little worried Karma might come around to bite that sassy ass of yours for being too cocky and cause you to lose?" I ask in a confident tone.

She smiles sweetly, lifts up her hand and pats my cheek while replying, "No, that's ok. I would be playing against you, so there's no risk of losing." She then winks at me as she takes a step back with a little more pep in her step than she had before.

As she turns to walk away, her hair flips in front of my face, and my nose picks up on a Vanilla perfume scent. Then I see the tattoo again on her back that's the same symbol as her medallion. Could Ari be the vigilante? What if the tattoo is what's protecting her? But how's this possible and who could do it for her if only a Fae, who are extinct, could perform the spell? I need to talk with Drew; maybe he can figure out what the fuck the mark means.

My mind is racing ninety to nothing. I glance over at the table where I left Connor and the other women to get a look at Ari again to study her for a few more minutes. Maybe I'm wrong, but my gut screams something isn't right here.

As I look around, I realize that Ari's not there, and neither is Nikki. Where the fuck did, they go? I look around the room and see she's not here. Maybe she went for a drink or to the bathroom with Nikki. Knowing how females like to go to bathrooms together, I bet that's where they are. I glance around the poolroom one more time and then head to search for her.

Entering the room where the bar is, I look around but don't see Ari anywhere. What I do see is Drew glaring at something across the room. I follow the direction of his eyes and see Drake all up in a dude's face over by the bathroom. He looks mad as hell, so I head over that way to see if I can be of help. As I approach the two, I hear Drake threatening the man, or should I say Wendigo, because the closer I get the stronger his scent radiates off him. His fancy blue suit may speak upper-class businessman, but the stench of a Wendigo is undeniable.

"I will rip your fucking throat out," Drake snarls at him.

As I get closer to them, I see Nikki and Ari come out of the bathroom, then stop to stare at the two men arguing. They make eye contact with me as I approach. "I got this," I mouth at them. They talk for a second, and then Nikki walks back toward the table while Ari heads back into the bathroom, strange.

"Hey man, what's going on?" I say to Drake as I place my hand on his shoulder, squeezing it and pulling him back out of the Wendigo's face before he does rip his throat out. Drake jerks from my grip and gets right back in his face again.

Since Drake was shot a few weeks ago, his tolerance of Wendigo's nasty attitudes has become shorter, which I can't blame him, but he can't lose his cool in a fucking bar filled with humans. "Not the place nor the time, man," I say to Drake hoping to bring him to his senses before he does something stupid. It seems to work because he backs away but keeps glaring at him. Movement in the corner of my eyes catches my attention. I glance over and see Drew standing by the bathroom door like he's waiting for a woman to come out, but I know he's watching to make sure this situation doesn't need an extra pair of hands.

"Listen to your friend's advice man," the Wendigo says while smiling. Dumb mother-fucker. I step in between them and grab the Wendigo by the neck bringing out my claws in that one hand sinking them deep in the base of his neck. He looks at me with wide eyes. I'm glad I finally have his attention.

I decided it would be best if I explain the gravity of the situation to him. "You stupid fuck, you need to shut your mouth and get the fuck out of here before I step away and let my friend here have his way with you, understand?" He gives a curt nod as I retract my claws, pat him on the cheek, and then wipe the blood off my fingertips onto his fancy blue jacket. "The back door is at the end of this hall past the bathrooms," I inform.

He turns and heads for the door with his hand covering the

spots where my claws went into him. I notice four small growing blood marks forming on his collar. He passes Drew who now has his back to us. As soon as the Wendigo walks past him, Drew turns and gives me a chin lift, he then follows the Wendigo out the door.

I turn back to Drake who's still fuming, "Man, please tell me you had a good reason to be all up in his shit."

"I was watching Ari and Nikki walk to the bathroom when he approached them and introduced himself. He looked at Nikki and wanted to know if she would like to have dinner with him sometime. The whole time he asked about dinner, he was staring at me, so I intervened. I know that is one of the mother-fuckers at the warehouse because he kept smiling and looking at my chest where I was shot," Drake explains while pacing back and forth and rubbing his neck trying to calm down.

"We can't take care of him here without starting a shit storm. That's why the stupid fuck was taunting you, but his big mistake was giving us a face to look for now. We'll get him along with the other one. Drew is tracking him now. You and I need to let everyone else know what's going on.". Drake seems calmer and nods his head at me. "First, I'll be back in a few," I say as I point toward the bathroom. Drake nods and walks away. I didn't want him to know, but I have another plan in mind instead of pissing. I step into the storage room by the women's bathroom to wait for Ari.

Chapter 43

Ari

"A Wolf in Sheep's Clothing"

Getting as far away from Daniel as fast as I can is the only thing on my mind as I walk away from him after our close encounter of the flirtatious kind in the pool table room. His intoxicating smell makes my head swim causing all my lady parts to wake up and take notice.

After putting the pool sticks up, I approach the table where Willow is sitting to see Zoey has already joined the group. I inform them I need a short bathroom break. I need walls along with doors to divide the space between Daniel and me but decide it's better to leave that part out of my announcement. Nikki decides she needs to come along with me because she wants to know when the hell, I got a tattoo.

I explain to her with my hundred and first, or so it feels like, lie of the night by stating it's a henna tattoo I got to cover up the ugly reddish-pink bruise from the injury I got when I was mugged. If I'm lucky, she will not want to get a closer look at it, and hopefully she's had enough alcohol to drink that she buys my story.

Just as we are walking down the hall to the bathroom, a weird guy in a flashy blue suit with a hand full of cash approaches us, stopping us to strike up a conversation. After a couple of seconds, I realize it's not a man, but a Wendigo with a menacing look in his eyes. He's not looking for conversation; he's looking for a meal.

"Ladies, you look rather delicious tonight. I'm Jay," he says as he extends his hand in a gesture of a handshake. Nikki extends hers in return, but I immediately grab her arm and yank it down before they make contact.

I recognize this asshole as one of the three I was chasing that night at the warehouse. I know he never got a good look at my face, so he doesn't have a clue I killed his friend. It seems he likes to dress nice in blue tailored suits and flash around money. He reminds me of the old saying 'A wolf in sheep's clothing' with his flashy clothes and display of wealth; he looks more like easy prey instead of the predator he is.

"Awe now, don't be like that, I'm just trying to see if you lovely ladies would like to leave here and go somewhere quiet to talk, maybe over some coffee and a snack," he says responding to my not so friendly glare. Yeah, I know exactly what he wants to eat for a snack, and it's not food or pussy. It's one or both of us as the main course.

"Ah, see we met before a few nights back," I inform him

"Really, did we?" Jay asks with a confused look.

Just as I'm about to inquire about how his friend with the hole in his chest is doing so this asshole would get the message to stay away from my friends before I kill his ass too, Drake appears. Drake wraps an arm around Nikki's waist, pulling her against him.

"Jay is it? I think the ladies are trying nicely to tell you to fuck off," Drake says with a growl. Why am I not surprised? Of course, he heard this Wendigo invite us out so we could become his entrée from across the room. He isn't broken, his ears were perked up and listening. Nikki opens her mouth to speak. Not sure what is about to come flowing out, I grab her arm and tug her away from Drake. He lets go of her quickly, which I imagine he is relieved to get us out of the way. I look back at him and mouth a silent thank you that earns me a chin lift. We leave Drake alone with Jay and head to the bathroom.

In the bathroom Nikki questions me, "That guy was creepy. Where the hell have you met him before?"

Here goes lie one hundred and two; damn, I'm on a roll tonight! "I saw him at a coffee shop hitting on the girl working the checkout counter. He was using the same stupid pickup lines." Had I known I would be telling so many lies tonight I would've bought several rounds of drinks for everyone to make my stories more palatable.

"Did his pickup lines work on her?" Nikki asks as we are finishing up with our bathroom business and washing our hands.

"Judging by the look she had on her face as he walked away, I would say not. I think she thought the same as we do tonight-CREEPY." She nods at me in the mirror as she mulls the information over in her head. We head back out into the hallway and find Daniel has joined Drake, who now seems ready to kill Jay.

Since Nikki is walking a step ahead of me, I grab her arm to stop her. As she turns around here comes lie number one-hundred and three flying out of my mouth, "I left my phone in the bathroom. Why don't you get us another drink and I will meet you and Willow at the table?" She looks at me for a second, then turns to look at Drake and Daniel, then back at me with a cocky grin. I'm going to BFF hell. I can see the wheels spinning in her head.

"What?" she asks, "You're trying to get rid of me, aren't you? Don't think I didn't see Daniel all up in your personal space in the pool room having an intimate discussion," she says with a sly look.

No, I'm going to eavesdrop on their conversation to see if I have to hunt Jay down and kill him to save your drunk ass from being next on his menu is what I want to say, but instead, I shrug and say, "Whatever." I hand her a twenty I pull out of my pocket. She gives me a little wave while heading to the bar.

I step back into the bathroom and turn around then lock the door before I press my ear against it. I concentrate hard to listen, but all I hear is the dumb ass Jay making a smart-ass comment, Daniel snapping this time at Jay, then Jay walking down the hall to the back exit and leaving.

But the door opens and closes twice. Twice? I think maybe Daniel or Drake went after him, but then I hear them discussing plans to go after him later after Drew tracks him, cluing me in that it was Drew who opened and closed the back door the second time. Daniel tells Drake they need to let everyone else know what's going on. I'm guessing that means the rest of the team which doesn't include any of us girls, except Val of course. I can tell when they walk away by how muffled their voices become. I decide to wait a couple of minutes before leaving the bathroom to allow them to make it back to the table.

When I feel it's safe to leave, I unlock the door and step out of the bathroom to head down the hallway. I make it about two steps before I'm grabbed by the waist from behind with a large hand pressed over my mouth before being yanked into a small room. It appears to be a supply closet based on what I can see of the room with the dim lighting.

I'm too stunned to react at first, but after a few seconds my mind snaps back into operation, and I stiffen my body. Just before I grab the arm holding my mouth, the intoxicating smell of Daniel engulfs around me and instantly my body relaxes into his all on its own accord.

"I think you and I should talk," he says almost like a whisper in my ear as his hot breath caresses the pulse point on my neck, causing shivers down my spine. He lets go of my mouth, spins me around and presses me against the wall, framing my body in with his.

"Talk," I croak out. I clear my throat and begin again, "talk about what?" Damn, what the fuck. Does he suspect I was the one from that night, or is he trying to get freaky in a closet? Please let it be freaky. I could go for freaky. His smell is driving me crazy!

This time when he speaks his mouth is so close to mine I feel the warm caress of his breath across my lips as it brushes by, "Yeah, talk baby. See the other night…." he begins but stops when the closet door opens, surprising both of us. Daniel turns his back to face the intruder.

Dom walks into the closet and shuts the door behind him. He looks at Daniel, then at me, and then back at Daniel. "Is there a problem, Ari?" he asks while keeping his eyes fixed on Daniel.

Just as I'm about to speak, the unthinkable happens. I feel something with teeny tiny little claws, fur, and a tail rush across my foot causing my stomach to drop in dread. I instantly know what a horrible, vicious creature is in the supply closet with us. I feel panic setting in, but I can't stop it. I try to make it to the closet door, but Daniel is in the way. I push on him to get him to move, but he won't budge.

Maybe he's scared stiff, but it's every man for himself, so I try to climb over him the whole-time chanting, "No, no, no, get it away, get it away." I feel his strong arms wrap around me, as I cling to him like a spider monkey with my arms and legs wrapped around him.

"Ari, what the hell?" Daniel asks. I can't seem to focus or stop chanting, so he grabs both sides of my face trying to get me to look at him.

As Daniel is looking into my eyes, it's Dom's voice that reaches my mind through all the panic. When Dom sees the little demon, he asks, "Seriously Ari, this again?" I look over at him and catch him rolling his eyes, which pisses me off enough to stop my panic attack.

I glare at Dom while yelling, "Don't you dare do this to me again, Dom."

"It's harmless," he informs me like he has a hundred times before. I'm speechless for a moment as I stare at him in disbelief with my mouth hung open. I can feel Daniel staring at Dom and me, moving his head back and forth in each of our directions like he's watching a tennis match.

"Would someone explain to me what the fuck is going on?" Daniel asks, breaking the silence.

"It's a mouse. See the tiny little creature over in the far corner?" Dom asks with irritation in his voice.

"All this panic over a harmless mouse?" Daniel asks me. I now realize I still have my body wrapped around his, so I put my feet back on the ground while staying close behind him in case the rodent across the small room charges at us.

"Harmless? Harmless?" I snap back at Daniel.

"Shit, here we go again," I hear Dom say. I glance over at him and see him shaking his head.

"Don't shake your head at me!" I yell at Dom as I turn to educate Daniel. "Haven't you ever heard of the bubonic plague that killed millions of people? It was caused in part by that creature," I state pointing an accusing finger toward the little beast.

He looks at the mouse and then back over at me, then jokingly mutters, "Kitten; it's over there shaking and scared to death."

I huff at him in disbelief, "Look at the black beady eyes scoping us out. Haven't you ever seen a cat do that ass shaking thing before it attacks? How do you know that's not what it's planning?" I retort.

He does that tennis watching thing again, looking from Dom to me. Finally, he speaks again, "I tell you what we're going to do. Dom, you walk Ari out of here nice and slow. Then when you're gone, I'll trap it and take care of the fierce creature." I can see the threat of a smile trying to break out across his face.

Narrowing my eyes at him, I say, "Whatever." and slowly head out the door not turning my back on the rodent until I make it out of the supply closet safely with Dom at my heels.

I glance over at Dom who's looking at me and shaking his head. When we are halfway to our table, he stops me and asks, "Why exactly were the two of you in the supply closet to begin with?"

"He dragged me in there wanting to talk to me, but you came in before he had the chance too. Do you think he suspects anything about that night?" I ask in the quietest voice I can muster.

"By the way you were climbing his body like it was a tree just because of a tiny mouse, not a chance," Dom says with a smirk.

"I was not climbing his body like a tree!" I blurt out.

Chapter 44

Nikki

"Curiosity Killed the Cat"

I can't believe I let Willow talk me into running this errand for her. Why did I agree again? Oh, because I'm a sucker for Willow's whiny pleads, and she knows it. I need to calm down and not let Drake's arrogant attitude get the best of me. I'll make this quick and painless as possible, at least as painless as possible for me. A quick in and out visit, then I'll be on my way back home. My little mini pep talk is already making me feel better.

It's been several weeks since I saw Drake at the little meet and greet at the bar. He's still having trouble with muscle spasms in his chest, and his team members don't want him in the field with them until he's one hundred percent. Who could blame them? If I was in a hostile situation, I would want to know my back-up could watch my back.

Their private physician examined him, then prescribed total rest for those muscles. The fool is delaying his healing by trying to do too much too soon. The organization that employs Connor's team put Drake on strict house rest for the week. If he doesn't comply, he's off the case.

So, with Willow being Willow and wanting to help the world, she asked me to mix up an herbal mixture that will help him. I had no problem with that and was glad to be of assistance, but when she sweetly volunteered my ass to hand-deliver it to him I drew the line. It's not my fault or problem she's scheduled to work and can't go. I have no desire to visit the man-whore who's crawled under my skin and festered.

When she broke out into one of her pregnancy hormone rants, I caved. So, with the help of my GPS, I'm now on my way to hand-deliver it to him at his house.

Drake's house is located on the bayou about an hour from New Orleans. I love the bayou country. With my occupation, I've spent a lot of time in the area, allowing me to make many good friends here.

The people here have their own pace and culture that is rich from the many Native Americans who lived in this area, such as the Choctaw and Chitimacha Indians, along with the Acadians that settled here in the 1700s.

Many of the homes can only be reached by boat. People not from this area refer to the bayou as a swamp, but that's incorrect. Swamp refers to an area of land while bayou refers to a body of water.

You can find plants here that you can't find anywhere else in the world. I've spent countless hours searching the bayou for plants and herbs to stock my store, and in the process spent time with the people while learning home remedies made from the plants in this area that have been used for generations.

The only negative aspect about the bayou I don't care for is the creepiness. There are legends of monsters, half human and half whatever, that prey on the innocent along with tales of people getting lost and never seen again. The animal sounds and other unique sounds of the bayou can make your imagination run wild after dark.

My GPS finally informs me I've arrived at my destination, which appears to be a dirt road in the middle of nowhere. There are no houses anywhere in sight, so I turn onto the dirt road hoping it's the driveway to his house.

As I head down the road, I pay close attention to my surroundings in case this road doesn't lead to his house. I refuse to end up as one of those missing people the legends talk about. So far, the only thing I see is trees on both sides of the road. After a few minutes of driving slowly down the road, a house appears in the distance. It's hard to believe how isolated one has to feel by living out this far.

As I pull close to the house, a shiver creeps up my spine. It's not a good shiver, as this place is a little too creepy for my taste. I feel like I've driven into Deliverance and the surrounding hills have eyes watching me.

Drake lives in an old one-story house that looks like it's from the 1800s era. The outside is painted light green with forest green Bahama shutters. The front porch spans the length of the house and has six colossal fern plants hanging from it.

I pull up and park my car close to his home, then grab the bag I put the herbal oil treatment in along with my cell phone and car keys. I'm still not able to shake off the creepy feeling that's crawling up and down my spine. I feel like someone is watching me, so I look around one last time before opening my car door.

"What the.....," I say as I see something moving. "Is that a wolf? Do we even have wolves in this area?" I whisper to myself. I close my eyes for a few seconds and then open them again in the same direction. I now see nothing but trees. I immediately mutter, "I'm going crazy. I'm sitting in my car talking to myself while my eyes play tricks on me."

Willow told me that Drake was expecting me, so I get out of the car before the ass in the house sees me sitting here talking to myself. I quickly rush up onto the porch to the door. I pause for a moment to assess my appearance. I lean over to straighten my green loose chiffon top with a V-neck zipper which I have left unzipped just below were my breast begin, low enough for sexy but not appearing trashy.

I'm wearing my favorite jeans that hug my bottom just right, topped off with my comfortable chucky heel short boots that match the color of green of my top. I shake my head and berate myself for caring about my appearance. I shouldn't care what this man-whore thinks of my appearance, but I do. After a few seconds of pressing the doorbell, I hear Drake yell, "It's open, come in."

I walk into the house, and the first thing I see is Drake sitting on a sofa in the middle of a large, open room I'm guessing is his living room. He's fumbling with a stack of papers in front of him on his coffee table. He seems transfixed on his paperwork, so I take a minute to take in my view while I have the chance.

When I look at him, I notice his hair is a mess, like he has run his fingers through it several times. He's wearing a plain white t-shirt that's just snug enough to show off the outline of a muscular back. It's paired with midnight blue sweatpants and bare feet. Damn, who would have thought bare feet could be sexy. He looks like yummy eye candy, the bastard. I'm waiting for him to open his mouth and say something to piss me off that will ruin my hot guy observation.

"You just going to stand by the door gawking at me?" he asks in a grumpy voice. There, he's ruined it. The vision of hotness is melted away by attitude.

I know he hasn't seen me ogling him because he hasn't looked my way yet, so I respond, "You wish." The comment earns me a snort from him. Whatever, I walk further into the house then stop when I'm halfway between him and the door.

"I hate the paperwork part of our job, but I told Connor I would get this shit caught up while I'm banished to the house. Just give me a minute to stack these papers up. If I walk away from this mess without organizing it, I'll lose the progress I've made," Drake explains in an exasperated tone, while his eyes never drift from the papers.

I absent-mindedly turn to my left and walk a few more steps to explore the room to pass the time while waiting for him to finish when I hear a low growl escape from Drake. Startled, I turn back to face him and find Drake's body has gone completely ridged. He's standing straight up, no longer hovering over the papers he was gathering up, with an odd expression across his face as he inhales deeply. I stand still for a minute watching him stare into space. Concerned that he might be in pain from the odd angle he had held his body over the papers I inquire, "Drake are you ok?"

"Oh yeah, fine. Your perfume is just distracting," he says with a deadpan look directed straight at me.

"My perfume?" I snap. There's no way he can smell it from this far away. "Yeah, like you can smell it from there. Can you not be an ass for five minutes?"

Drake looks at me with a smirk on his lips then replies, "Light Blue." He then raises an eyebrow at me as if challenging me to prove him wrong. He looks even sexier with his confident expression. This ignites a whirling sensation in my stomach that settles between my thighs, damn him. Of course, I can't rise to the challenge, because that's exactly the name of the perfume I have on.

"Must have put way too much on for you to be able to smell me all the way over where you're standing," is the only reply I give him before looking away.

I hear papers rustling again as he continues his paperwork task. "Nah, probably the fragrance got caught in the draft the front door caused when you shut it. It smells deliciously edible, not too much at all." I look back and catch him scanning my body from head to toe. I feel a warm sensation sliding up my body with the movement of his eyes that causes my nipples to harden.

When his eyes drift back to my breast, I remind him, "Hey, my eyes are up here," just like he said to me that night at the bar. This causes him to snap his eyes back up to mine where he keeps them fixed. I can practically feel the heat radiating from his hooded eyes. I lick my lips like a natural reflex, and his eyes drop to my lips with a deep look of hunger that causes wetness in my panties. I force my eyes away from his before the sexual tension between us causes a full out war between my mind saying no and my body begging yes.

I turn away from him and mumble, "Man-whore," under my breath to try to lighten the sexual charge in the room. It seems to work as I hear the chuckle that escapes his throat.

Surprise overtakes me as I take in the surroundings of the living room. It's not what I expected the house of a man-whore to look like, not that I'm an expert on man-whore dwellings or anything. I guess I expected to find empty condom wrappers, porno magazines, a tube of lube, or any variety of women's undergarments thrown around. I'm taken back by all the antiques that are located throughout the room.

There's a standing bookcase on one wall with antiques on display on most of the shelves. I take a few steps closer to get a better look at them, not daring to touch anything from the fear of breaking something. I turn to look at the next wall as I slowly walk, finding various artifacts mounted on the wall.

After a quick one-eighty, I take in the other side of the room and see what appears to be antique vases and small statues spread throughout the sitting area of the room I hadn't noticed when I first walked in. The walls are painted in a light gray accented with white detail trim at the ceiling and around the base of the wall which looks elegant against the dark hardwood floors. The furniture pieces are all modern, dark gray leather and primarily designed so a man could fit comfortably in them. Accent pillows of red and black are on the sofa. The end tables and coffee table have marble tops with a swirl of gray, black, and red. There is a 60-inch wide-screen TV in the room, the only thing that doesn't surprise me.

"What can I say, I love history," Drake says causing me to jerk around to face him. In all my wonder, I had forgotten he's still in the room.

"You have a lot of antiques. Are they real or copies?"

"They're real. Nothing fake here, babe," Drake comments, which makes me roll my eyes at him again. I berate myself mentally for allowing Willow to con me into coming out here to spend time with an arrogant pig.

He's sexy as hell, but still a pig of a man. I'm going to be mentally and physically exhausted when I leave here. My mind wants to scream at him as my body wants to jump him to experience the sex-feast I'm sure he's perfected with as many women as he's probably had rotated in and out of here.

I feel I've overstayed my 10-minute visit and now I'm ready to get the hell away from him. "Whatever, I brought the oil for your muscle spasms. I will show you how to apply it, and then I'll leave so you can get back to work," I tell him, hoping to prod him into speeding up so I can leave.

"Do you like antiques? I noticed the necklace you're wearing. It's the same one you had on the night Connor and Willow met, and you wore it again the night we went to the bar. It looks like it was made from antique gems," Drake replies while completely ignoring my hurry-up I want to leave hint. I'm still a fair distance away from him, so how the hell can he see my necklace good enough to tell it's made from antique gems? Maybe he got a good look at it at the bar.

"It's an antique. It was made from an antique ring that my father wore. He inherited it from my grandfather, who inherited it from his father, and so on. I had no brothers to pass the ring down to. When my father passed away, my mother had this necklace made for me. She gave it to me right after we moved into my grandmother's home. I still live with my grandmother today, but it's to help her out now. She has a quite a few antique books." I shut my mouth when my brain catches up to it.

What on earth made me want to share all that with him? I turn away from him to get a hold of myself. Being alone with him is nerve-racking. Unfortunately, my nerves are causing me to ramble on. I glance back at him to gauge his response, and he's staring at my ass. When he notices I'm looking back, he gives his head a shake as in trying to clear his mind. Well good, apparently, I'm not the only one feeling this way. Looking straight ahead again, I take a deep breath and try to get a handle on my body's response to Drake.

Unable to clear my mind of all thoughts of Drake, I walk over to the antiques hanging on the wall and concentrate on them instead of him. As I approach the wall, the first thing that draws my attention is a rope with a medallion hanging from it.

The closer I get the faster the realization of what it is hits me. Shit! Is that what I think it is? Not wanting an audience, I look back at Drake and see he's now placing papers on a desk located on the other side of the room. I turn back to the medallion, and with a shaky hand, I extend my pointer finger out to touch the medallion lightly with the tip of my finger. I instantly feel a burning sensation and quickly yank back my hand. It's just what I thought, cold iron.

"Done with the paperwork," Drake announces.

I quickly turn around to face him. "You need," I start to say, but my voice comes out more like a squeak. I clear my throat and begin again, "You need to take off your shirt and lie down so I can show you how to apply the oil." I head in his direction, getting as far away from that damn medallion as I can.

Before I reach him, I hear a little voice in the back of my mind screaming, 'dumbass, write the instructions down and leave,' but the curiosity of how his body will feel under my fingertips wins out. I guess I should remind myself that curiosity killed the cat. As I approach him, he turns and heads down the hallway. "Where are you going?"

"To do what you asked," he mutters looking back at me with a devilish grin as he's walking away. "You don't expect me to be comfortable lying on the sofa, do you?" he replies with a chuckle as he walks down the hallway.

"Unbelievable! Just like a sexy, arrogant, man pig," I say under my breath as I retrieve the oil out of my bag. I place my bag on the corner table by the sofa and head down the same hallway he just disappeared into. He's no longer in the hallway when I reach it. My mind keeps telling me I should walk away and leave, but my body takes the lead, and I saunter down the hallway, looking into every room I pass to see if he's there.

I locate him at the end of the hall in what I assume is the master bedroom based on its much larger size in comparison to the other rooms I've passed. There are large windows on the right-side wall with wooden Bahama shutters allowing filtered sunlight to illuminate the room, lighting up a large bed

300

centered against the far wall.

As I walk into the bedroom, Drake is standing beside the bed, already taking off his shirt. He reaches with one hand to grab the back of the t-shirt just below the neckline pulling it swiftly up and over his head in one smooth move, exposing all the sexy muscularity in his back the t-shirt concealed.

I get a better view of his ass as he bends to sit on the bed. "So, you think I'm sexy?" How the hell did he hear me make that comment from all the way down the hall when I didn't say it loud; it was more like a whisper under my breath. I decide denial is the route to go but before I can open my mouth to do just that he speaks again, "Don't deny it; I heard you."

So partial truth then, "No, I called you an arrogant, man pig," I say correcting him.

"But first you said I was sexy," Drake responds with a knowing smile as he corrects me. I can feel the blush rising from my neck up to my cheeks.

"You shouldn't eavesdrop on someone else's private conversation," I educate him.

"It's only a conversation if you're talking to someone other than yourself."

"Still counts, now lay back and behave so I can show you how this is supposed to be applied," I say, deciding a change of subject is needed. He fully complies as I make my way over to the bed to sit next to him.

I don't dare look at his chest yet, knowing I'll have a good reason to be able to stare and touch it in a few moments. I can't help but feel like I'm going to medical ethics hell, but I'm not feeling guilty enough to stop. Besides, I'm not his physician and at this point there's little chance I could make Drake feel sexually assaulted.

"You need to squeeze out about a quarter size drop of oil into the palm of your hand," I instruct as I demonstrate what I'm telling him. "Next, you need to massage the oil in a circular motion over your chest around the area where you were shot while applying pressure like a deep tissue massage, rubbing it all in completely," I continue with my instructions feeling proud of how professional I'm sounding.

As I'm about to apply the oil to his muscular chest, I notice a paw print tattoo. A paw print tattoo? No, after closer inspection I realize it's a paw print birthmark, causing me to freeze for a moment as a cold sensation races down my spine. I've seen that birthmark before, but I can't remember where. I don't have a good feeling about it and should have listened to my intuition.

As I stare at the birthmark, my mind races through my memory trying to figure out where I've seen it before. It's as if a bucket of ice water was dumped over my head when I realize where I've seen it. It's the same mark I've viewed many times in one of Gran's old journals. But this can't be possible, can it? It can't be; none of them survived.

As my mind races to grasp the situation, the tiny burn on the tip of my finger caused by the medallion hanging on his living room wall pops into my mind. Suddenly, I feel like the girl in Little Red Riding Hood. I feel like I'm living the last scene of the story; the part where Little Red Riding Hood was confronting the wolf. Grandma, what big ears you have- the better to hear you with my dear.

Drake heard me all the way down the hall when I called him sexy. Grandma, what big eyes you have- the better to see you with my dear. Drake noticed my gem necklace in detail from across the room, even noticing it looked old. Grandma, what big teeth you have- the better to eat you with my dear. "Shit" I absentmindedly mumble out loud.

"What's wrong? Why do you suddenly look so pale?" Drake asks pulling out of my muse. I look up and see concern in his eyes. I've got to get the hell out of here. There's no way in hell I'm going to hang out here to be eaten by the big bad wolf.

"I... I... I just remembered I'm supposed to pick up something for my grandma, I mean grandmother. Lie back, I'll quickly show you how to rub the oil in and then I need to go," I tell him, wincing at how nervous my voice sounds coming out of my mouth. I can't keep my hands from shaking when I touch his skin as my eyes keep darting back and forth from my hands to the birthmark. "Done," I announce after a few minutes. I start to move my hands away when Drake places one of his large hands over my much smaller one.

I barely hear him say my name over the pounding sound of my heart in my ears. "Nikki," he says again. I slowly lift my eyes to meet his. His eyes are darting from one of my eyes to the next, studying me. Then, I see his eyes drop to the pulse located in my neck. Damn, he must notice my rapid heartbeat. What the hell am I thinking? He can probably hear my heart beating!

I try to pull my hand out from under his as I explain, "I really have to go." He releases my hand, and I rush to the bath- room connected to his room under the pretense of needing to wash my hands, but in reality, I've got to get a handle on myself and tone it down, so I can get the hell out of here.

As I wash my hands, I keep reminding myself to stay calm and get out fast, but I can't shake the sickening feeling that the big bad wolf is going to be the one who survives this real-life fairy tale I'm currently living if I don't get the hell out of here. After drying my hands, I head back into the bedroom and feel relief when I see Drake isn't in here anymore. I pause for one last calming breath before walking down the hall back into the living room to find Drake standing in the middle of the room with his white t-shirt back on.

"I hope you get to feeling better. I need to leave now," I say as I grab my bag then hurry to the front door. As my hand reaches the doorknob, two large hands appear on each side of my head, reaching past me to hold the door closed tight. I feel Drake's body lean into mine.

The heat from his body sends shivers down my spine as I notice how good he smells. The smell of spice, woods, and alpha male cocoons my body causing tingling sensations in my female parts. What the hell is wrong with me? I'm about to be eaten by the big bad wolf, and my traitorous body is getting turned on wanting to be eaten by the big bad wolf. I realize how close Drake's head is to mine when I feel his lips brush against my ear.

"You're not going anywhere," he says with a slow growl that sends a whole new type of shiver down my spine- true fear that is. I manage to twist my body around to face him while still caged in by his arms and body.

"What are you doing?" I ask as I try to turn my body to escape under his arm. Drake slides one of his knees up between my legs and presses against the apex of my thighs, pinning me exactly where he wants me.

"I know you know my secret from the way you kept staring at my birthmark. The same way I can hear your heart race and the same way I can smell fear radiating off you. Now, what I want to know from you is how do you know? We don't tell outsiders about the birthmark, so exactly how do you have this knowledge?" Drake demands in a low deep voice.

"I don't know what you're talking about," is the only response that rushes out of my mouth, but it doesn't even sound believable.

"Liar," Drake growls. I let out a surprised squeal when he surprises me by reaching an arm under my legs and another around my back, then lifting me up into his arms. "You're not going anywhere!" he roars at me causing me to flinch.

I 'm too nervous and frightened to think. My heart is pounding in my chest and my lungs feel as if they are being squeezed, allowing me to only take in small gulps of air. My mind is in self-preservation mode trying to think fast of what to say to salvage the situation, but all thoughts jumble together in my panicked state. Unfortunately, my mouth doesn't have the same problem and blurts out, "Don't eat me!"

My outburst causes Drake to stop in his tracks. With his arms still holding me tightly, he looks straight ahead for a moment then a wicked grin spreads across his face as he turns his head slowly and looks into my eyes. I would typically think the mischievous smile on his lips had some measure of sex appeal, but the freakish way he turned his head toward me reminds me of a Chuckie doll in a horror movie that sends a cold chill through my body.

"I promise if I was planning on eating you, your plump sexy little lips couldn't beg your way out of it sweetheart. Actually, once I got started you would beg me not to stop." Well, leave it to the man-whore side of Drake to quench the fear and morph it into anger. I narrow my eyes at him then open my mouth to respond, but before a word escapes my lips, a squeal comes out as he releases me to drop me into a chair in the living room.

Self-preservation kicks in again. I'm not prepared for an encounter with a werewolf from the Rougarou tribe. Why would I be? The tribe's members are supposed to all be dead. I can't think of even one magic spell to get me out of this situation, so why did I spend so much time sneaking behind Gran's back studying the damn things?

I watch Drake walk over to the desk across from me, pull something out of a drawer, then step back. He grabs my left wrist, slaps something cold and hard around it that makes a click sound. As I try to yank my arm away, he leans over, and I hear another click. When I look down, I see he has handcuffed my wrist to the leg of one of the end tables with the heavy marble top.

Drake pulls the coffee table closer taking a seat on the edge of it facing me while invading my personal space to the point his knees are between mine and his face inches from my face. Oh shit, what now? As if reading my thoughts, he begins, "Now, you will tell me how you know and who else knows."

I sit still staring into his eyes, knowing he's trying to intimidate me. His sensual smell is intoxicating and now enveloping me, triggering an unwanted tingling in my core. Does my body have no damn self-preservation? I must admit the eating comment not only pissed me off but also awakened my curiosity. I can't remember the last time I had an orgasm induced by someone other than me. Maybe that's the problem.

Note to self- make sure I'm well sated before getting into another dangerous encounter with a hot guy.

Drake lets out a long deep anxious breath. The tickle of the air blowing across my lips causes me to lick them and brings me out of my muse. Drake's eyes immediately dart to my lips. That's when I realize he's waiting on an answer to a question, but I can't seem to remember the question.

Drake lets out a low, frustrated growl sound as he gets up and paces back and forth. He keeps running his hands through his hair and rubbing the back of his neck. Every few seconds, he stops to glares at me. The cold iron medallion hanging on the wall behind him catches my attention, and a dreadful feeling runs through my body as I think about the torture that simple little object is capable of causing to a Fae.

I quickly snap my eyes back on him before he notices the fear that has washed over me, but I'm too damn late. I watch in horror as I see him looking from me to the direction I was looking and then back at me with a suspicious glare. As his eyes widen, I know he has pieced everything together.

"Not fucking possible," are the words I hear spoken under his breath as he stares at me. I give a small shrug with my shoulders and forge an innocent look in my eyes, hoping to look confused. When he strides over to the wall and removes the medallion, I realize I've failed miserably, and real panic ensues. I forget about the handcuffs and try to stand so I can run, but I'm quickly reminded of them when my quick movement causes the damn things to bite into my wrist. I have no other choice but to sit my ass back down to wait for the face off with a werewolf who, by history, hates my kind. Hopefully, as the old saying goes, time heals old wounds.

I watch as Drake has his mental meltdown. "Fuck!" He glares then paces. "Not possible!" he blurts out. He pauses then glares some more. "You are... Fuck!" he mumbles, as he steps closer. "You're a fucking Fae," he roars. I guess time doesn't heal old wounds in this situation. I feel the blood rush out of my face and take a gulp of much needed air as he approaches closer.

He takes a seat on the coffee table in front of me again but this time with the medallion swinging on its rope held by the grasp of his hand. Wanting more distance away from that torturous thing that is swinging from his grip, I gather my legs up under me as best I can and bury my body as far back into the chair as I can go until the cuff unbearably digs into my wrist.

His brows frown as he squints his eyes at me with a confused look; then the realization that the medallion is causing my fear sets in and he puts it down beside him on the coffee table. We sit in complete silence staring at each other as he takes deep breaths, which I assume is to calm himself. I wince as the pain from my wrists registers in my head and try to reposition my arm to ease the pain from the handcuffs. Concern flashes across his face. He looks to my wrist, rolls his eyes, then grabs my ankles and pulls them out from under me to force me back into a more comfortable position.

He places his hands on my knees to keep me in place before he speaks with more calmness and control than before, "I thought the Fae went extinct centuries ago. No one has seen or heard about your kind in years."

That comment doesn't sit well with me. The way he said it was as if he said how dare I exist. Before I can think I snap, "You're the one who's supposed to be extinct. Your tribe was supposed to be dead centuries ago."

Yeah, I should learn to keep my mouth shut as I can see my comment just added another spark to his already fiery temper. "No! A few of us survived no thanks to your kind. If one chant or spell starts to come out of those plump lips of yours, I'll stop you so don't even try. Damn Pixie!" he says as the glare in his eyes returns.

"I'm not a Pixie! I am a Fae you... you... Dog!" Does the man not have any sense? Pixies only exist in fairy tales. The dog comment seems to have the same effect on him as the pixie one did on me. If I could chant my ass out of here, I would; threat be damned. He keeps opening and closing his mouth while shooting daggers at me with his eyes.

"I need proof," he finally announces.

"What?"

"I have to figure out the magnitude of the situation and what this could mean for my tribe, but before I do, I want proof of your claim to being a Fae. You may only know the myths and legends behind my people and the Fae, or you could be making this up to distract me from the truth. I sense nothing mystical from you, but I do know Fae can easily use cloaking spells. I want to see your butterfly shaped birthmark as proof," he demands.

"No way in hell," I say between my teeth as I clench my jaw.

"We'll just see about that," Drake responds. It's as if my comment is some sort of challenge. He stands up then takes long purposefully strides over to the same desk he retrieved the handcuffs from earlier. He grabs something and then returns. My eyes go wide as I see a knife in his hand.

"What the hell Drake? Are you planning on killing me?" I screech at the sight of the knife.

Rolling his damn eyes again, "No sweetheart, I'm not going to kill you. My people aren't the cold-blooded killers in this little equation of ours. If you are a Fae, then you should know your history. Your Pixie ancestors did the killing spree," he says with distaste laced in his words.

"Stop calling me a Pixie. I'm not a Pixie! As a matter of fact, I do know my history. It was your tribe who shed first blood you Dog!"

He seems to consider this before responding. "Maybe so, but it was one woman from your clan that was killed and not all of my people agreed with it. Your people put in motion a killing spree like serial killers! Now, are you going to show me the birthmark or am I going to go on a little scavenger hunt and find it my damn self? The choice is all yours Pixie," Drake says with a devilish grin as he holds up the knife and twists it in the air while examining the blade.

"You wouldn't dare."

"Try me. You have no idea how dangerous I can be trying to get what I want; so try me," he challenges. For some reason, I believe him. I sit here thinking of my options, which I come to realize is only one. Before I can move, he leans forward with the knife in one hand, and grabs the hem of my shirt with the other.

"Ok! Ok!" I say as I slap at his hands with my only free hand while being careful not to slap the blade of the knife. "Fine, I'll show you, but first put the knife away. Then, you'll have to undo the handcuffs so I can stand."

"Why do I need to undo the handcuffs?" he questions as he slides the knife behind him onto the coffee table.

"I need to stand," I explain again. He gives me a suspicious look, so I continue, "I'm sitting on my birthmark."

A full grin spreads across his face making him even more attractive, but I'm too mad for my traitorous body to even respond. He pulls a key out from his pocket then leans over to undo the cuffs while warning me, "No tricks. I promise I can outrun you."

That information wasn't necessary. I already know he can overpower me. As I rub my wrist where bright red marks have now appeared, Drake gives me a hand signal indicating to hurry up I'm taking too long. I roll my eyes as a response then sigh while getting up on my feet. I turn around slowly as I'm overcome with the mortification that my waist is the same height as his head, which will put my bare ass right in his face in just seconds. Wanting to get this over as quickly as possible, I unbutton and slide down my pants. My mortification is instantly increased as I remember I'm wearing my red thong panties which match the bra I am wearing. Well, at least I'm not in my granny panties which would be way worse.

After about a minute of silence, I deem that should be long enough for him to have examined my birthmark. I start to slide my pants back up, but I'm abruptly stopped by a large hand. I open my mouth to snap at him, but the words get lost in my throat as I feel a tingling sensation from the tip of one of his fingers as it begins to trace my birthmark.

The feather light touch causes goosebumps to break out across my skin. I gasp as I feel a hot, moist breath caress my skin signaling how close his face must be to my bottom. Then more fingertips join the first one until I feel a full hand gripping the right side of my buttocks. My mind screams to slap his arrogant hand away, but my body is overcome by the sexual tension pulsing through the room. It races through my body, and my mouth goes dry as wetness pools between my legs.

I say a silent prayer that he can't and doesn't notice. I realize Drake is no longer sitting when I feel his hot moist breath on my ear. The heat radiating off his body starts to consume me while his hand is still caressing my bottom.

"You're so fucking wet," Drake says in a deep gravelly voice that only makes me wetter. His warm breath is now flowing across my neck. I feel his breathing increase in rate indicating he's as affected by our contact as I am. His large warm hand slides from my ass slowly up around to my side, stopping on my stomach under my shirt leaving a hot fiery path in its wake. The feel of his hand on my bare skin is tantalizing.

Now his front is completely plastered to my back, and I feel the undeniable hard appendage pressing against my bottom. We stand completely still for what seems like hours, but I know it's just minutes. Drake breaks the silence, "Damn, a fucking Fae." This time when he says it there's no malice lacing his voice. It's meant more as a fact than an insult, but the torturous nature of it breaks through my desire like a cold bucket of water poured over my head and snaps me back to reality.

Again, I reach for my pants to pull them up. This time he doesn't stop me, he steps away. After I snap the button on my jeans, I turn and sink back down into the chair before I fall. My legs are shaking so that without his arm around me holding me up I'm afraid I'll collapse onto the floor.

"You do have the mark of the Fae," I hear Drake mutter more to himself than to me. I glance over to see him take a deep breath as he runs his hands back through his hair. I come to realize he does this often when he seems frustrated. As I sit here, exhaustion seeps into my body from the roller coaster of emotions I'm experiencing. I've never been around a man who had such an effect on me.

This man can annoy me, scare me, piss me off, and completely turn me on all in a matter of minutes. I need to put distance between us and get the hell out of here before I either kill him, fuck him, or maybe both. As good as his hard body felt pressed against mine, perhaps I should just try to fuck him to death.

For the first time since I've been held captive in this chair, I realize I still have my bag which is lying right beside me. After formulating a plan, I slowly ease my hand into my bag then feel around for my keys while Drake continues pacing lost in his own thoughts. After I locate them, I cup my keys tight in the palm of my hand to keep them from rattling before gently slipping my hand back out of the bag. I clear my throat, which draws his attention back to me as I hoped it would. "I need to use the bathroom," I announce.

"Fine, let's go, it's the first door on the right down the hall," Drake instructs. When I don't move, he stops and looks at me with a raised brow.

"You're not seriously going into the bathroom with me, are you?"

He studies me for a minute then on an exacerbated exhale replies, "Fine, go by yourself but leave your bag here." I jump up to head to the bathroom. "And Nikki," I hear him call. I glance over my shoulder to look at him before he continues, "Don't try anything stupid or you'll live to regret it."

After I enter the bathroom, I lock the door and survey the room for a possible escape route. The bathroom has a window located beside the toilet. It's on the smaller size for a window, but I think I can fit through it. I must be quick.

Afraid he'll hear the window opening with his supersonic hearing, I flush the toilet with one hand while unlocking and raising the window with the other. Then, I turn on the sink to help disguise any noise and buy more time to escape. I have to shimmy my hips through the tight opening of the window before sliding out and landing not so gracefully on my ass. Free at last!

I stand while dusting off the grass from my hands. After a quick survey of my surroundings, I take off in a mad dash toward my car. When I reach the corner of the house, I take a sharp left heading for my car. I abruptly stop when I come face to face with a wolf.

After the initial shock, I give the wolf my best glare, "Really Drake? Wolf form to scare me?" The wolf growls low and deep with his ears flat against his head. A second later, the realization hits me. He can't shift because of the curse. Damn, this must be the wolf I saw when I thought my mind was playing tricks on me when I arrived earlier.

I immediately walk backward, tracing the same path I just ran saying, "Nice wolfie," to calm the beast when a second wolf appears. For every step I take backward, the wolves take one forward towards me. When I am parallel with the bathroom window, I chance a quick glance and instantly know there is no way I will be able to climb back in it.

I continue to walk backwards until I come to the corner of the back of the house. I debate my options to either stay on my current path heading into the woods or turn the corner to stay close to the house. I choose the house. I continue with my backward walking as I turn the corner, not wanting to turn my back on the two wolves.

In an effort to come up with a plan, I glance behind me and notice the back door standing open. My only two options are staying out here to get attacked by angry wolves or going back inside to deal with a human wolf. I choose the human one. When I'm a few feet away from the door, I turn then take off running as fast as I can without stopping until I'm back inside the house.

Before I shut the door, I see the wolves sitting on their asses about a foot away from the door. I swear I think one of them has a smile on his face. This pisses me off. I slam the door shut. As I press my forehead to the door taking deep breaths to calm my racing heart, I hear laughter behind me. I turn around, barely noticing I'm now standing in Drake's kitchen and spot the bastard laughing at me.

"I told you not to try anything stupid, or you would regret it," Drake says, struggling to get the words out of his mouth through all the laughter.

"Relatives of yours?" I ask as I stomp past him, pushing him out of my way as I enter the living room again. I walk back over and sit on the couch.

"Not quite, my kind and regular animal wolves have always had respect for one another. They're not my relatives and never my pets, more like my neighbors," he explains as he follows me.

"You put a whole new meaning to neighborhood watchdog!" I exclaim, causing him to burst out into a fit of laughter again. "I swear one of those bags of fleas out there was smiling and laughing at me!"

"No sweetheart they don't smile, that's more of a snarl," Drake says as he heads into the hallway.

"Where are you going?"

"To unlock the bathroom door and turn off the water you left running. Don't go anywhere," I hear him say with a chuckle from a distance.

"Like I have a fucking choice," I mumble to myself as I sit down on the couch.

"No, you don't," Drake says as he comes back into the room.

"Your supersonic hearing is really annoying," I state while emphasizing the word really.

"Then stop talking out loud to yourself."

"Whatever," I say, ensuring to give him a prim and proper glare with that statement.

Drake walks over to the sofa. Before sitting, he reaches out and moves the coffee table into the original position it was in when I arrived. With a sigh, he sits down on the couch beside me, stretches out his long muscular legs and rests his bare feet on the coffee table. We sit quietly for a few moments, the silence almost peaceful, both lost in thought and staring straight ahead.

When he finally speaks, the loud tone of his voice mixed with concern startles a jerk reflex from my body causing my head to twist in his direction. "Willow's your cousin?" he asks for clarification.

"Right…" I respond while nodding my head like a mother trying to coax a child to continue, wondering where he's going with this.

"Which means she is a Fae…" he continues as the realization of the direction of his questioning hits me full frontal.

"The baby!" I gasp with widened eyes while looking at Drake as the shock of what today's revelation could mean for Willow's precious baby suddenly enters my mind. Drake jumps into action, stands and swiftly pulls his cell phone from his pocket. "What are you doing?" I ask, already knowing in my gut but afraid to hear the answer I know is coming.

"I've got to call Connor," he says swiftly.

"No!" I scream, which startles him. He twists to face me with a look of surprise.

"What do you mean no?" he roars. I don't respond with words, but with action instead. I spring from the couch jumping up on the coffee table and quickly snatch his cell phone out of his hand.

The surprised expression on Drake's face is priceless. He stands there glaring at me with his mouth open and arms still in the same position they were in when he had possession of his phone just seconds ago.

"Woman, have you lost your damn mind?" he asks while squinting his eyes at me like I'm some mysterious equation that needs solving.

"No, I'm not out of my mind!" I snap as I take a step up onto the edge of the coffee table directly across from him. I then step off the coffee table back onto the floor while never stopping the backward motion. This seemed to be the quickest way to get farthest away from him. I need to gain as much space as quickly as possible and earn as much time as I can to try to explain to him why he can't just call Connor without hearing me out first.

"Why the bloody hell did you just take my cell phone?" he asks as he slowly rounds the edge of the coffee table like he's the predator and I'm the prey.

I hold the cell phone behind my back with one hand, while my other hand is stretched out before me, trying to keep him from getting the cell phone as I continue to make the backward pass. I know I have very little time before we make contact, so I speed talk out my reasoning.

I take a deep breath, knowing I will need it to get out as many words as I can as fast as possible and begin, "Because Willow has no idea that she's a Fae or any idea what a Fae is for that matter. I mean if you tell Connor he will more than likely tell Willow and she doesn't know her kind and sure as hell doesn't know about your kind and I need to tell her first to break the shock before all hell breaks loose," there I said it. I take a couple of deep breaths. He stops for a moment to process what I blurted out, so I pause in my retreat hoping he sees reason.

"How is that even possible to not know your true nature?" he asks with a bewildering look.

"It just is, so leave things as they are for right now," I say with a pleading tone. He raises an eyebrow up as if requesting further explanation.

I continue on, "To keep the events such as what happened between your people and my people from ever happening again, the elders at the time decided it was best if only one family line knew everything while the rest stayed ignorant," I explain in a much shorter version of a history lesson hoping it will appease him.

He seems to be giving more thought to my request, but as a wicked grin spreads across his lips a second before he moves to pounce like the true predator he is, I realize how wrong I am. He crashes into me then pulls the front of my body tightly to his while reaching a long arm around me and grabbing the wrist of my hand holding the phone as his other arm cradles my waist in a firm hold.

I lean back to create more distance between us, which puts me in a semi backbend causing me to lose my footing. Right before the inevitable impact with the floor that I know is coming and ending with this huge man crushing me, Drake twists his body which in turn twists mine since he still has a tight hold on me. This allows us to land with me on top and him on the bottom, with our bodies utterly horizontal with the floor. After the impact, I hear a hissing noise coming from Drake. I raise my head off his chest and see a look on his face that can only be described as twisted in pain.

"Are you ok?" I ask in an almost whisper.

"Hunky dory," he hisses as he takes the hand of the arm that's not holding my wrist with the phone and places it on his chest over the area where he was shot. I wince because as much as this man pisses me off, I hate that I'm half responsible for his pain. Stupid, I know. A look of amusement crosses his face.

I narrow my eyes at him, "What?" I ask, not trusting the bastard.

"Actually, with as much manhandling as you've done to me today my chest surprisingly feels better. Before, an impact like this one would have been a harsh blow. I guess your witchy potion is working," he smirks.

"I'm not a pixie, and I'm not a witch. If you want to compare anything to what I do, I would say Voodoo," I inform him, knowing with how rich in Voodoo Culture New Orleans is, most people can grasp the comparison.

He raises his head to peer into my eyes and speaking with a moan while still rubbing his chest. "It's time Willow knows the truth. Connor also needs to know the truth. You have no fucking idea of the ramifications this is going to cause. He needs to know the truth about the shit storm he's sitting in. This is going to rock his world. He's been sleeping with our number one archenemy." Drake lowers his head back down onto the floor with the last word that's spoken. I wiggle to try to loosen his grip, but the more I wiggle, the tighter his hold becomes. "Stop wiggling," he growls.

"Seriously? Back to the growling again?" my voice trails off when I feel his response to my wiggling. His cock hardens and grows against my pelvis with impressive size. "Seriously?" I ask as I become completely still and stare at him in disbelief. He chuckles without even asking what I'm talking about because he knows I can feel him.

"What can I say? My cock doesn't have a preference of friend or foe," he says with an almost apologetic expression. He then jerks his upper body up in lightning speed and slightly rotates our bodies so that now he's on top and I'm on the bottom. His legs are on the outside of my legs, and the arm I kept behind me is now pinned under me.

It takes me a few seconds to realize what just happened, and not only am I now flat on my back with Drake on top of me, but also have lost my grip on the cell phone and no longer know where it is. He gives me a cocky grin with a wink as he holds the damn cell phone away from us and dials Connor.

"Damn it!" I screech as I realize he got possession of the phone during his maneuvers. I stretch out the only free hand I have to get the phone back or at least knock it out of his hand, but it's of no use. He grabs my free arm with his other hand and pins it onto my chest. The only thing I can do now is lie here and listen to the ringing I hear coming through the phone.

Chapter 45

Connor
"Nervous as a Whore in Church"

As I'm on the way to pick up my baby mama and take her to dinner, I think back on how my life has changed so much in so little time. I want to change Willow's baby mama status to wife, but I'm not sure if I've given her or us enough time to take that next step. Am I ready? A better question is can I see myself without her? I guess I can answer the last question as I can't even fathom a life without her. She's like my addiction, a drug that no amount of rehab could rehabilitate me from. I want her and only her.

My phone breaks through my thoughts. Seeing its Drake, I answer, "Hey Bro, how's the chest feeling? Willow said Nikki was heading out to your place earlier today to give you something to help you heal."

"Actually, yeah it helped," Drake admits.

"Good."

"Connor, there's something urgent I need to discuss with you. Do you think you can drop by?" Drake asks with a worried edge to his voice.

"What's this about?"

"It appears the Fae are no longer extinct," he says with a sigh. Could this be true? I pull off onto the side of the road to give Drake my full attention.

"Drake, what are you talking about man? The Fae clan no longer exists. What's in that ointment Nikki made for you?" I ask, trying to wrap my mind around what he's trying to tell me. Could it be possible after all these years? If true, this could have profound effects for our tribe. We may be able to reverse this forsaken curse on our people.

"Listen to me; I'm not hallucinating. Just come over and I'll prove it," Drake says in a serious tone.

"Okay, but first I need to call Willow to cancel our dinner plans..." I state, but he interrupts.

"Bring her. Nikki's still here. She's the one who helped me discover their existence."

"Nikki? Please tell me she doesn't know what we are...." I reply, but I'm interrupted yet again.

"Just trust me," Drake says with irritation.

"All right, man. We'll both be there. You need to have food ready when we get there though, Willow will be hungry..." I state as I'm cut off with interruption number three. If this discovery weren't groundbreaking, I'd be pissed.

"Okay, Okay. See you in a while," Drake says, then immediately disconnects.

An hour and a half later, we pull up to Drake's house and park beside Nikki's car. Willow says, "I'm shocked Nikki is still here. I figured she would bolt as soon as she could to get away from the Man-whore" (she states man-whore with air quotations) because that is how Nikki likes refer to Drake. "Hopefully, they're cooking something good and lots of it; I'm starving." I hear her stomach growling.

I turn and smile at my beautiful woman. Now that her nausea episodes are under control, she has that pregnant glow going on. She was already beautiful. The pregnant glow is like icing on the cake. She turns and catches me smiling staring like a lovesick schoolboy. She smiles back before I reach out to touch her cheek with my palm.

Instinctively, she turns into the touch of my hand on her cheek and leans in closer towards me. I gently kiss her soft lips with my own. Light kisses at first until I feel the tip of her moist pink tongue barely graze my bottom lip. Such an innocent gesture is enough to ignite the overwhelming desire I have to claim her. I deepen the kiss, sliding my tongue to meet hers. Her warm moist tongue instantly makes my cock hard. I pull away before I end up taking her in my car.

"Ready?" She nods, and we exit the car.

I knock on the front door to announce our arrival, then open it without waiting for a response. I allow Willow to enter before me. As we enter the living room, the first thing I notice is the tension in the air. Nikki is sitting on the sofa biting her bottom lip while bouncing one of her legs and looking as nervous as a whore in church. She looks up and sees my eyes are on her; I raise a brow as if questioning what's going on. The only response she gives is sitting up straighter while stilling her bouncing leg.

I look over to see Drake pacing the length of the room. He stops when we make eye contact, seemingly to have just realized my presence, which I find unsettling. He should have heard my car drive up with his enhanced hearing. Something is heavy on his mind, which I assume it's about the Fae he mentioned on the phone. Who can blame him? The very thought of those demon creatures makes my stomach turn. I look over to Willow to find she is oblivious to the pulsing tension in the atmosphere as she makes her way around the room taking in the many artifacts my brother has collected over the years.

"Willow," I say holding out my arm in her direction. She immediately turns my way giving me an odd look when she sees my arm reaching for her. Willow notices Nikki squirming on the sofa out of the corner of her eye causing her to turn her head in that direction.

I know the exact time she sensed the thick tension by the frown of her sweet mouth, drawn brow and the concerned look on her face. Willow comes to tuck her body into my side, allowing me to wrap my extended arm around her and place my hand over her baby bump. I feel the tension leave her body as she melts into me. I take pleasure in knowing Willow feels safe in my arms because I know deep in my soul, I will always protect her and our child or die trying, especially from the Fae if they actually still exist.

"What's going on?" Willow asks the group in the room in an almost whisper. My natural response to her worried tone is to pull her even closer.

"Drake and I need to talk about business for a minute alone. You mind sitting here with Nikki?" I ask, then lightly kiss the top of her head which is tucked nicely under my chin.

"She needs to be a part of this conversation too," Drake announces. I glare at Drake for his proclamation. What the hell? What could he be thinking? Any talk of Fae will lead to the discussion of our true nature, which I have not disclosed to Willow.

I open my mouth to disagree with Drake. He knows what I'm about to say and immediately holds up his hand to stop any protest from escaping my mouth. "Trust me bro, this is something she needs to hear because she's right in the middle of this situation," Drake says. Now he has my guarded attention and concern. I lead Willow over to the sofa to sit by Nikki then take my place on the other side of her.

"You ok?" I hear Willow ask Nikki.

"Don't ask," Nikki says, then turns a glacier glare with her eyes toward Drake.

"Oh," Willow says as she watches Nikki try to kill Drake with her glare. "Are you and Drake still not getting along?" Willow asks, nodding her head as if she's deciphered the situation. She gives a sigh, then faces me and announces in a soft voice, "This will require food." That's when I realize Drake has prepared nothing for Willow to eat as I told him to. Damn it!

I nod my head, then start to get up to fix her and my baby something to eat, but I hear Drake request, "Wait," bringing my exit plan to a halt. I slide my ass to the edge of the sofa and give him my full attention. The faster we get on with this, the quicker I can feed my woman and baby.

"Nikki has the mark of the Fae," he blurts out as he stands still and stares at me. It takes a minute for me to even comprehend his accusation.

"Are you sure?" I ask in disbelief.

"What mark?" Willow inquires, joining in the conversation.

Drake ignores her and addresses me instead, "Yeah, I'm sure. I not only saw it, but touched it. It's there."

"I want to see it for myself," I say as I stand and turn to Nikki. Nikki looks mortified.

"Hell no! No one lays their eyes on that birthmark but me," Drake roars. I swing my head back to face him as the surprise of Drake's possessiveness hits me. I watch in fascination as Drake tells Nikki, "No one but me, do you understand?" Nikki, looking somewhat mollified, nods her head as a look of relief washes over her face.

Willow brings everyone's attention to her when she says, "Wait a minute! The birthmarks we have that are identical, the one that's on your ass? You showed Drake your ass? You let him touch your ass?" She then turns her attention to me and with an irritated look asks, "And why do you want to look at her birthmark on her ass?"

The only words I heard in Willow's rant are the birthmarks we have that are identical. Fuck, it can't be! I feel as someone has knocked the breath out of me and the ground is crumbling under my feet. Shock and fury wash over me like flowing waters of a waterfall. It can't be true.

"You have identical birthmarks?" I ask. The realization I've kissed or licked every inch of her body and never seen a butterfly mark on her delicate skin pops into my mind. "I've never seen it, where is it?" I ask, hanging on the hope that Drake is wrong but feeling the dread in my heart he's right.

"Yes, it's on the back of my neck on my hairline. It's hard to see it because it's covered up by my hair. People rarely notice it and mistake it for a tattoo when they do because it looks so much like a butterfly," Willow says nonchalantly as if she hasn't rocked my world to its core.

She lifts her hair up as she turns her torso to show me the mark. I reach up to touch the mark of the enemy. It's true. It's there. I must get away from her. The feeling of betrayal is creeping up in my throat and choking me. I back away from her then start my pacing this time, trying to get a handle on the many emotions coursing through my body.

I glance at Willow who now looks even more confused. She asks, "Why do both of you look so shocked about our birthmarks? You two have similar ones that look like paw prints." I pause and glare. She either doesn't notice or doesn't care because she continues, "Where's the food? I'm starving." She knows about our birthmarks, so she must know who we are. What the hell? Was this some fucked up plan of hers all along? I feel rage boiling up inside me. Drake puts his hand on my shoulder, bringing me out of my thoughts.

As if reading my mind, he says, "She doesn't know Connor. Unlike her counterpart sitting next to her she's clueless," he whispers. Unbelievable. I turn my head slowly to come face to face with him. He winces at the look on my face, which I'm sure is riddled with all the confusion and betrayal I feel. He pulls me into the far corner of the room then quietly gives me a quick account of how Willow could be so clueless of her own true nature.

I glance at Nikki who looks guilty as she stares at Drake and me, she mumbles, "Meddling dogs," under her breath.

Willow whispers to Nikki, "What the hell is going on?" Nikki shakes her head at Willow. Unfucking believable, I think as I rub my hands over my face and through my hair, trying to get a handle on my emotions while I wrap my head around this fucked up situation. I walk over and take a seat in front of Willow on the coffee table, so we're face to face. I've got to know for sure what she knows.

"What's wrong?" Willow asks.

"Have you ever heard of the Fae clan?" I ask her. I can see Nikki out of the corner of my eye shaking her head and whispering don't under her breath towards me.

Willow glances at her in confusion, then turns to face me to answer, "No, I haven't. Can we get some food now?" I focus in on her facial features for any indication she's lying and can't find one. Well damn, this is fucked up. I let out a heavy sigh.

Drake interrupts saying, "I'll go fix Willow a snack. I'll be right back." Willow looks at him, giving him a smile of gratitude.

"Willow, look at me," I say to get her attention focused back on me. "I need you to focus on what I'm saying. I'm trying to explain something significant to you Sunshine. Have you ever heard of fairies?" I ask trying again, to explain.

"You mean the little pixies in fairy tales like Tinkerbell?" Willow asks with a curious look.

Drake enters the living room from the kitchen carrying a tray of snack food and a drink for Willow. He hears Willow's comment and chuckles, "Yep, just like the pixies," he tells her as he hands the tray over to her. I noticed his eyes were on Nikki when he made his comment. Nikki rolls her eyes in response while she shakes her head.

Through clenched teeth, Nikki interrupts, "There's no such thing as pixies."

"Of course, there's no such thing as pixies. That's not what I said," Willow says looking at Nikki with a bewildering look.

"Okay, Okay, we're getting off track here," I tell her, trying to bring her attention back to me. "The Fae were a clan of human-like creatures that were fairies," I begin. I continue a brief history lesson of the Fae of the Willows and the werewolf clan called Rougarou.

At the end of the short lesson, I explain that Fae carry the birthmark of a butterfly and the Rougarou carry the birthmark of a paw print. When I'm finished, I lean back on the coffee table and sit still to take in her reaction to what I've explained to her, allowing her time to soak in the information. I glance around the room because everyone has gone completely silent and all eyes are on Willow. I face Willow again, and she's looking at everyone in the room with a skeptical expression.

Finally, she breaks the silence as she sits the plate of food beside her, "Soooo, you are telling me you think, no wait, you all think," she says as she moves her fingers in a circle to indicate all of us, then continues, "I'm a descendant of some Fairy clan. And that Fairy clan has somehow cursed a tribe of were- wolves that you supposedly belong to?"

"Exactly," Drake chimes in with a relieved look on his face.

Willow continues to look from one of us to the next before her next rant begins, "I Don't believe in Fairies! Are you all out of your damn minds? Is this a joke? Am I on a reality show with hidden cameras?" She turns and glares at Nikki accusingly as she asks, "Are you in on this?"

"She needs proof," I tell Drake hoping for some assistance here.

"I got it," Drake says as he reaches down and lifts a medal- lion off the coffee table. "Here this might convince you," he says to Willow, and continues to explain as he holds the medallion by the rope. "Fae cannot touch cold iron. It's like their version of Kryptonite."

"Fuck no! Keep that away from her!" I growl. "What the fuck are you thinking?" I ask as he shrugs his shoulders in response.

"Why don't you take a piece of silver and shove it up your ass as proof," Nikki snaps.

"Oh, for goodness sakes, toss it here. Let's get this nonsense over with, so I can finish eating," Willow insists.

As Drake tosses the medallion toward Willow, rage over- takes me. Willow is pregnant with our baby, my baby. If the medallion is poisonous to her, then it must be toxic to our baby as well. What the hell is Drake thinking! I lean over just before the medallion reaches her hand and block her from grabbing it, catching it in my hand. I feel engulfed with anger.

Needing to put distance between me, Willow, and my brother, I step a couple of feet away from the group. All I can do for the moment is close my eyes tight while tilting my head toward the floor and taking slow deep breaths to gain control over my emotions before I lose my shit. I want to beat the shit out of my brother at the same time while throttling Willow's throat for endangering what's mine. I'm on the verge of taking

Willow across my knee and spanking her ass for her lack of judgment in protecting our child.

I look up to see Drake walking over to sit on the arm of the sofa next to Nikki. He says to her, "Tell her the truth Nikki. Don't you think you've kept her in the dark long enough? Give her the proof she needs to understand."

"I don't believe this! Nikki if it's true, then prove it. Cast a spell or whatever it is we can do," Willow challenges.

"No!" Drake and I both yell. Drake reaches over and puts a hand over Nikki's mouth. "Your spells do nothing but cause problems for my kind. No fucking spells!" Drake growls as Nikki pushes his hand away from her mouth.

"I don't know any spells by heart. If I did, I would have gotten the hell out of here earlier today before you handcuffed me!" Nikki snaps at Drake.

Nikki takes a deep breath as she appears to be mauling over the suggestion in her head. Finally, Nikki seems to come to some a kind of agreement in her mind. Clearing her throat while turning to face Willow she begins, "Do you recall the old journal that was lying on my bed the night I gave you that black dress?"

"You mean the one that had that rather weird poem with the crazy directions on how to move while saying it?" Willow asks.

Nikki nods her head when a startled look crosses her face. "Wait! What! I thought you said you didn't read any of it? Did... Did you do what it said?" Nikki asks looking shocked.

"You were acting strange about the book, so I told you I didn't read it. I thought it was silly, but I did what it said. What's the big deal?" Willow replies as her voice gets pitchy as she squirms and looks defensive.

"Oh my, oh my..." Nikki replies as she bounces and holds her hands in front of her like she's made the best discovery since ice cream. "Now it makes sense!" she exclaims.

"Well, I'm glad something makes sense because you sure as hell aren't," Drake says as he makes air quotes with his fingers when he says sense. Nikki rolls her eyes at Drake.

"Haven't you wondered why a Fae and a werewolf came together after a century of not knowing the other still exists? It's a book of spells. It makes sense of why Willow and Connor crossed paths the first night at the bar and again at the hospital," she explains to us then focuses her attention on Willow. "Gran warned me of the dangers of using magic. I thought if I cast the spell, I would cause the dead to rise or at least zombies. Now, this is a whole other mess. We have two wolves back; you're pregnant by one of them and the other keeps wanting to look at my ass."

"You can create zombies?" Willow asks Nikki with a frightened look.

Again, with an eye roll, Nikki responds, "No, you're missing the point here. You cast a spell for true love, and now you not only have a baby but Connor." All at once everything that Nikki explained hits me like a Mack truck.

"What the fuck?" I roar causing everyone to jump and glare at me as I start to pace. "You're saying Willow cast a spell, correction; she cast a fucking spell on me. An enemy from the Fae clan has fucked with my life and cast a mother fucking spell on me! So, this so-called love and devotion I feel isn't real; it's just some kind of fucking spell!"

"Brother," Drake starts to say, but I don't give him a chance. My anger is almost out of control. I stop pacing and set my glare on the two Fae.

"Is this some fucked up joke between the two of you? Is the baby really mine?" I ask with an angry look. Willow gasps with a stunned look as if she'd been slapped, which quickly turns to a look of hurt. She sits quietly and says nothing. I can't think straight. All I see is red. Rage consumes me, and my inner wolf is ready to attack.

I hold my head back down and take deep breaths, trying to calm the beast. If I don't, I'll end up physically hurting someone. I have no idea how much time has passed before I realize the whole room has gone quiet.

When I look up everyone gasps, but all I can focus on is the large crocodile tears racing down Willow's cheeks. The way those tears cut through to my soul pisses me off more. When we make eye contact, she looks terrified and presses her back against the back of the sofa, trying to get as far away from me as she can. Does she actually think I would physically put my hands on her? Now, that pisses me off even more.

"Oh my," Nikki says in a whisper which catches my attention. I look over at her and notice she has pressed herself back against the sofa too.

Drake positions himself between the two women and me, looking at me with bewilderment. I scowl at him.

"Connor your eyes, man you need to turn around and look in the mirror at your eyes," he says as he points to an antique mirror on his wall. Annoyed as hell, I walk over and look, and take a minute to comprehend what I'm seeing. My eyes are no longer the same brown eyes I've seen my whole life looking back at me. Instead, for the first-time glowing fluorescent yellow eyes have taken their place- werewolf eyes.

Chapter 46

Willow
"Don't Give a Flying Fuck"

I listen to Connor's ranting and accusations but can't believe what I'm hearing. This must be some bizarre dream induced by some bad food I've eaten. There's no way the man I love, and the father of my baby is accusing me of something as horrible as lying about our baby. I put my hand on my arm and give it a pinch which I feel so this can't be a dream. Connor looks so hurt and betrayed, but I don't understand why. He's the one doing the betraying, to not only me but our baby as well.

Finally, he gives up spewing shit from his mouth and stops ranting. He looks down at the floor and starts deep breathing. After a few minutes I think he's calmed down, but when he looks up at me, I don't see regret in his eyes. As a matter of fact, I don't even see his eyes! The eyes glaring at me are a strange fluorescent yellow, not the chocolate brown I've been staring into for months!

I don't understand what the hell is going on. I'm incapable of forming words. All I can do is stare at those eyes as my body kicks into self-preservation mode and presses as far against the sofa as it can go, getting further away from those eyes. I hear Drake telling Connor to look at his eyes.

Drake walks over to his brother, and they are both mesmerized by his eyes. "What the hell just happened? Is the curse finally lifting?" I hear them say. Maybe they were telling the truth.

I need a break from this situation to get a mental control

over my racing thoughts, so I mumble, "I need the bathroom," and without looking at me, Drake points down the hallway. I stand and quickly head down the hall into the bathroom.

After closing the door, I lock it, hoping to have a moment alone. I turn on the water to wash my face when I realize my nerves can't take anymore. My stomach riles and I barely make it over to the toilet before the food I've just consumed finds its way back up again. After a few minutes of dry heaving, my stomach catches on that it's empty then settles down. I stay seated next to the toilet just in case this episode isn't over.

I think it's a good time to recap and choose to run the last half-hour back through my mind to make sense of everything. If it weren't for Connor's eyes changing, I would think they were all full of shit. I decide to examine this from a medical stand point; Chimeras actually do exist in the world with organ transplants and being pregnant with a baby.

Just last year a man discovered that he fathered a baby with his unborn twin's sperm. I guess it's not far-fetched to have Chimeras of other types. Legends come from partial truths with a lot of fiction mixed in. This is a well-known fact. Maybe there's more fact than fiction after all. I think about the possibility of being the creature they described called a Fae. How could I be a Fae and not know it?

With my mind trying to wrap around my new reality, I maul over the hurt words that erupted from Connor's mouth. They rained down on me like hot burning lava rushing out of a volcano. I feel a stream of fresh warm tears flowing down my cheeks and wipe them away with the back of my hand.

I refuse to think he could have meant what he said about our baby and me. He was just shocked about Fae existing and said hurtful shit without meaning it. People do that all the time. He'll eventually feel bad and apologize, which I will accept but only after I put him through a week of hell.

With all of this situated in my mind and my stomach settling down, I decide to leave the safety of the bathroom and merge back into the living room. I only wish I could do more right now about brushing my teeth instead of having to settle on rinsing out my mouth. I hate the after-taste of vomit.

I amble back down the hall, trying to straighten out my clothes as I walk when I hear Nikki say, "Shhh... damn it she'll hear you; you'll upset her, and you'll regret it." This causes me to pause to eavesdrop on their conversation.

"Regret? Regret? I'll tell you what I'm regretting; it's the fact that the enemy of my tribe has invaded my life. I'll regret that every time I look down upon my own child, I'll hope I don't see a demon spawn, half wolf, and half Fae, staring back at me. I'm having a child with someone that's been a sworn enemy of mine my entire life, so you'll just have to forgive me right now, Nikki, if I don't give a flying fuck," Connor says in a low growling voice. Those words have the power to steal the air out of my lungs and slash through my soul, shattering my heart into tiny pieces.

It's one thing to say hurtful things about me, but it's unforgivable to direct this misplaced hatred toward my innocent unborn baby, OUR baby. I feel like I can't breathe and I'm becoming light-headed from the lack of oxygen. The hallway feels like it's spinning.

I find my way back to the bathroom, not being able to breathe until I latch the lock. Then the waterfall of tears pours out in an unstoppable downpour. The fight-or-flight response kicks in as I feel a sense of panic set in over how my life has gone from wonderful to shit all in one late afternoon. Connor isn't the man I fell in love with.

After hearing those words come out of his mouth, I wonder why the hell I never saw his true colors. The man I fell in love with would have never turned his back on his own child. Hell, he hunted me down and demanded to be part of our baby's life. I feel betrayed, by not only Connor but by Gran and Nikki also for concealing the truth of what I am from me for all these years. I feel genetically tainted.

With the only thought of escape, I pull out my phone to call Ari. As I start to push the numbers, I realize I need to feel safe for my baby's sake, so I end up calling Dom. His home isn't that far from here.

He answers after the third ring. I'm no longer able to take a deep enough breath to form words, which come out chopped up between sobs. "D... D... Dom," I mutter.

"Willow, what's wrong? What's happened?" he asks in a panicked rush.

"C..C... Connor... He, he isn't the... the... the man I thought he was," I try to explain, but fail terribly.

"Wait, where are you?" Dom asks. "He came clean?" I think I hear him mumble, but I'm not sure since I can barely hear over my wailing.

"What?" I ask to clarify.

"Where are you?" he says slower.

"I'm at Drake's."

"I'm about ten minutes out. I'm on my way. Hang tight," Dom instructs and then hangs up.

I stay rooted in a daze for several minutes, trying to figure out how my world crumbled again. I decide enough time has passed that Dom should arrive any minute, so I emerge from the bathroom to come face to face with the people that have destroyed the world I once knew and replaced it with science fiction. I feel as they have thrust me into a new world where legends are facts, and they have left me to stumble around like a newly born deer all on my own.

As I enter the living room on my way to the door, the three of them freeze, and the place becomes quiet. Anguish and a trail of guilt wash across Connor's face when his eyes meet mine. Apparently, the pain of their betrayal is obvious on my face.

"Willow," Nikki says as she takes a step in my direction. Connor also steps towards me. Nikki halts when I raise my hand in the air and shake my head. Connor doesn't.

Apparently, Connor either doesn't know the universal sign for stop, or he's just arrogant enough to think he can do whatever the fuck he wants regardless of what I want. Those days have come to an end. I'm flying through the seven stages of grief at warp speed. First shock and denial hit me causing the pain which is still lingering.

By the time he takes his third step towards me the third stage of anger is consuming me and an unearthly growl I've never heard nor created before works its way up through my body. My hand shakes, and my body trembles with rage. The chair off to the side of his path shakes. With a startled look on his face, Connor halts in his steps and stares at the chair. The sight of the chair shaking causes Nikki to gasp and put her hand over her mouth. She appears as shocked as Connor does.

Connor looks back at me with a surprised look that morphs into a look of worry. Before my mind can catch up with my body, I move the hand I'm holding up sideways. To my shock and horror, the chair moves by itself across the floor to block the path of Connor, almost knocking him down as it hits the side of his knee.

Just then, the front door slams open causing a colliding noise as the doorknob forms a dent in the sheetrock from the force used to open it. In walks Dom, my rescuer, to take me away from my current hell. I ignore the chair incident for now because there's just so much my brain can handle at one time, and I push that unexpected event to the back of my mind to analyze later.

I address the three, so they know exactly how I feel before I make my exit. Pointing toward Drake and Connor while never taking my eyes off Nikki I start to speak, "Don't…. Just don't…" I tell Nikki as her mouth opens to speak to me.

My words cause her to keep her words to herself immediately, so I trench onward with mine, "Their betrayal cuts deep. They didn't know, but you… you and Gran knew all this time about our family's secret. It affects me, and now my baby but you both chose not to tell me."

Out of the corner of my eye, I see movement toward the front door and look that way to see Dom walking towards me. There's a pity in his eyes. Damn, I've always hated that look when it's directed at me. I'd rather see anything but sympathy. I must look and sound pathetic. It's time to end this and leave because there's no way to stay and repair any of this. What's done is done. I take the final steps to reach Dom and grab his afforded hand then squeeze it to absorb the silent support he's offering.

I hear Connor growl out in a low, sinister voice demanding, "Don't you fucking dare leave with Dom!"

Still in stage three of grief, another wave of anger surges through my body. I swing back around in time to see Connor advancing toward me again. I throw my hand back up for the second time in a gesture to stop. This time Connor has the good sense to stop dead in his tracks, probably afraid of more flying furniture. Little does he know I have no idea how I did it to begin with, much less how to do a repeat performance.

In a deep voice equal to the tone Connor just used I speak, "How dare you! How fucking dare you try telling me what I can and can't do! You lost any fucking say so the moment you denounced my baby. You managed to do the one thing you promised not to. You didn't just shatter my heart you broke me."

Dom moves to put his body between the three betrayers and me, while at the same time instructing me to wait for him in his car, which I gladly accept his exit invitation.

As I'm walking out the front door, Connor gives Dom a warning, "Don't take this as your invitation to move in on what's mine."

The only reply Dom gives as he makes his way to the door is, "You were warned," then shuts the door as he leaves.

After Willow and Dom leave the house……. Connor leaps to go after Dom, but Drake grabs his arm giving it a jerk and pulling him backward as he says, "You need to get a fucking grip. Get control over your feelings and your damn mouth. Its obvious Willow heard every fucking word that came out of your mouth during your angry rant. If you think you might want to repair the damage you've single handily caused today, let her go for now. By the way, for the record, by the look on your woman's face just now, she was clueless to all of this. I share your resentment toward the Fae, but she's carrying one of ours, so this changes everything. She isn't responsible for the past, and if you want her as your future, you need to wise up really quick, really fast."

"Don't you think I realized that the moment I saw the hurt in her eyes when she walked in here? But here's the thing, how can I trust something I don't understand? How will I know if what I feel is real or just some damn spell cast upon me?" Connor asks Drake as he turns around to confront his brother head on.

Nikki clears her throat to get the attention of both brothers. "Let me clear up something for you by educating you a little. To cast a love spell on you and make it work, Willow would've had to have something personal of yours in her possession when she spoke the words. The more personal the object is, the more effective the spell is. For example, pieces of your hair would have a stronger effect than say, your business card. Since she didn't even know you at the time, this would have been impossible. The only one she could have cast a spell on would've been herself. I'm not an expert in casting, but my best guess would be the spell caused your paths to cross then they would continue to cross until the two of you wised up to realize your soul mates. The spell didn't cause you to fall in love. It gave you the opportunity to find your true love. That's all."

"Since your kind denied each other a proper education of magic, how powerful can a Fae be?" Drake asks with a disdained tone to his voice when saying denied, still disagreeing with the choices her ancestors had made.

"You mean the chair?" Nikki asks to clarify.

"Exactly," Connor answers before Drake can.

"I have no fucking clue about the chair trick, along with that bizarre growl she made. I'm not an expert on hybrid pregnancy, being this is the first one I know of, but my best guess is this has something to do with the baby. I don't know what because I've never read about that kind of power in any of the Fae history journals," Nikki replies.

Chapter 47

Dom
"Demon Spawns"

In the car driving away from Drake's house I look over to find a Weeping Willow, no pun intended. Her head is hanging down as streams of tears glide down her cheeks, dripping down towards her hands that are lying in her lap. She looks lost in her sorrow.

I'm pretty sure Connor told Willow about being a were-wolf, and she isn't taking the news well. I need to tread lightly to find out exactly what she knows to try to help her come to terms with this and realize this is still the same baby she loved before the big announcement. Otherwise, I might have another half-breed to add to my ever-growing home.

After a few minutes her tears slow. I grab her hand from her lap with one of my own hands as I continue to drive and squeeze it lightly until she looks at me. "What happened back there?" I ask in a soft voice while trying to calm her.

"I don't want to go home. Take me to a hotel or bed-and-breakfast. Take me anywhere but not home," Willow replies. Okay, not the answer I was shooting for. My place is close, so I head in that direction. There's no way in hell I'm letting her deal with this alone in some hotel room.

"Okay, I won't take you home. Willow, what happened?" I try again.

"I don't know how to explain without sounding crazy," Willow says as her bottom lip trembles again.

"Try honey," I encourage her.

"Connor.... Connor said I'm pregnant with a demon

spawn," she says, and then bursts into tears again. This comment sets my blood on fire. I hold my tongue until I get a hold of my anger. Willow isn't the type of woman I thought she was. I thought she would be more open-minded and could handle the truth about the baby being half werewolf and love her child all the same.

We pull into my driveway and up to my house. I drive further into the yard towards the back where I can hear the children playing, then stop and put the car in park.

"Look at the kids Willow," I say, not meaning to put anger in my tone but unable to keep it out.

"What?" she asks looking up at me confused with tear-stained cheeks and red puffy eyes.

"I know about the unsettling news Connor told you today."

"What? How would you know?" Willow asks as her tears stop with the shock of my revelation.

"I want you to look at the kids over there playing in the yard and tell me what you see," I say as I take her chin between my forefinger and thumb pushing her face into the direction of the kids.

"I don't understand," Willow says, voicing her confusion.

"Do these kids look like demon spawns to you?" I ask.

"No," she whispers while still looking confused.

"All of these kids are just like your baby, Willow, except their mothers chose not to love them and threw them away like they were trash instead of seeing past what they are," I explain to her. It takes her a moment to comprehend precisely what I'm trying to explain to her, but I can tell by her eyes the second she understands.

"Are you telling me that these children are all Fae?" Willow asks with a gasp.

"Yes... wait, what?" now I'm the one that's confused.

"No, Willow, Fae don't exist. You've somehow gotten something confused. Connor is a werewolf. The kids you see are half-breeds, the same as I am and the same as your baby," I explain. Damn, how the hell did Connor fuck up that conversation?

"You're a half werewolf?" Willow asks. I nod my head, half expecting to chase her down as she bolts from the car at any moment. But to my surprise, she sits there appearing to maul over this new information in her mind.

"Uhmmm…. I need to tell you something, but first I need to know how you feel about the Fae people. Do you hate them as much as Connor does?"

"Nope, I don't have Fae issues; mine are more like daddy issues since he was the one that knew exactly what he was when he fucked my mother," I explain.

"Ok, I'm a Fae," she says somewhat as a matter of fact.

"You're a Fae as in one of the fairies from long ago?" I ask with a wince. Damn, I didn't see that coming. Knowing how much Connor's tribe hates all things Fae, I wonder how that happened.

"I just found out today along with the announcement that Connor is a werewolf. Connor hates Fae and referred to my baby as being a demon spawn because of me," Willow says then the damn lip trembling starts up again, which is getting to me. I hate seeing a woman cry.

"How do you feel about the baby?" I ask, not really wanting to know but needing too.

"I love my baby no matter what. This is still my baby," she says. I exhale as relief rushes over me knowing that Willow is the type woman I thought she was, except for the added detail of being a Fae. "Dom, is there more than werewolves, Fae, and humans?" Willow inquires.

"Let's go inside the house to the library. This may take a while to explain. Books will help." I say as I open my car door.

"I was afraid you would say that," Willow replies as she opens her car door.

Chapter 48

Willow
"Falling Down the Rabbit Hole"

After a group dinner with Dom, Flame and all the kids, I spent what seemed like hours looking through books and listening to Dom, who with the help of Flame explained all the various types of non-humans to me. My mind feels like it's about to explode. It's like being in an episode of Grimm where they research all those old books and try to identify a Wesson, except without the crime part that seems to be in every show.

One positive thing came out of my history lesson- I discovered a lot more about my ancestors and what it means to be a Fae. I realize now I'm not as genetically corrupt as Connor made me feel about myself. Flame made me feel uniquely special with his excitement of knowing a 'legendary creature' as he called it, thought to be extinct. Now I feel like one of those rediscovered lost species I've seen on TV.

I head up the stairs with a book that categorizes non-humans, so I can review back over it to become more knowledgeable about my new world. I'm assigned to a bedroom next to Baily's bedroom. Dom says I can stay here as long as I need to. It's late, so I try to be quiet as I walk down the hallway trying not to wake any of the children living here. I hear movement coming from Bailey's room as I pass the door, so I peek in to see if she's ok.

"Bailey, are you ok honey?" I ask as I peak into her room. Her room has a white dresser and a toy box inside the door to the left. There is a single canopy bed against the far wall that's covered in a pink comforter and many big fluffy pillows with pink pillowcases. The cover is turned down, and Bailey is climbing back into bed.

"I had a bad dream. I wanted to sleep with my penguin that was on the dresser," Bailey informs me as she crawls back into her bed holding on tight to a stuffed penguin. I enter the room to tuck her back in bed, thinking I'll be doing this with my child soon, so I might as well get some practice in. I see a reflection of light flicker off a gold chain that's barely visible around her small neck.

Reaching to take it off her I explain, "Bailey, honey, you shouldn't sleep with a chain around your neck. I feel like it will choke you. Let's take it off and put up for the night. Ok?"

"No! I can't!" she says with panic laced in her voice. I managed to pull the necklace out from under her gown but froze at the clasp when I saw the fear in her eyes.

Feeling like shit for scaring her, I sit down on the floor by her bed, so my eyes are eye level with hers. "It's ok. We will leave it on. Shhh,… it's ok," I whisper as I stroke her hair with my free hand trying to calm her. "This must be a special necklace to you," I say. She nods her head while taking a deep breath. "Would you like for me to stay with you until you fall back asleep?" I ask, trying to make her feel safe.

She moves over and holds the covers up with her small hand, so I leave the book on the floor and climb into bed with her. My talking seems to relax her and surprisingly acts like a balm to my frail nerves. We lay there in the dim glow of the room's night light sharing the same pillow and staring at each other eye to eye, feeling as though the light has cocooned us into our own little world.

"Do you want to talk about your bad dream?" I ask in a whisper of a voice.

"No," she whispers back. I glance at her necklace that now lies outside of her gown instead of inside. The gold chain has a medallion hanging from it. I pick it up to get a better look at it. Stunned by its appearance, not for the unusual shape or that the stone is an amber crystal, but for the intricate design inside of it. If it wasn't for the variation in the shape of the crystal, I would have sworn I was looking at Ari's medallion. I know Ari has spent a lot of time out here with these kids as well as with the kids at the shelter. Maybe she had it made for Bailey.

Thinking of the shelter makes me wonder if Dom volunteers there to locate half-breeds as they call the half werewolf/half human children. Maybe I should volunteer there. I plan to stay here at Dom's house for a while and plan to help here as well. I need to learn as much as I can of any special needs that my baby might have so I can be prepared for anything. I might as well start now by calming Bailey's fear of her nightmares and coaxing her back to sleep. Otherwise, if I get up to go to my room, I know all I must look forward to is a night full of tears and dwelling on heartbreak. I'd rather stay here with Bailey to live in denial just a little longer.

The medallion brings Ari to mind. "You remember we share a friend, Ari?" I start to ask. Bailey nods again, this time bringing her thumb up to her mouth and sucking on it while rubbing her nose. I smile and continue, "Well, she used to have nightmares too when we were little. I would climb in her bed too at night, so we could talk until she fell asleep. She has a medallion almost like yours that she said helped her feel safe because her mommy gave it to her. It helped with keeping her nightmares away."

At the mention of the medallion, Bailey's sleepy eyes become open wide like large buttons. Slowly she pulls her thumb out of her mouth and begins to talk in a low, soft whisper. "Ari told you about her necklace keeping her safe?" she asks me. This time it's my turn to give a nod with a reassuring smile. "Are you special friends with Ari like me," she continues.

"Yeah, right now I guess you could say she's the closest friend that I have," I tell her, leaving out the part that she's the only old friend I have that hasn't betrayed me like Nikki has. Pushing my hurt and betrayal out of my mind, for now, I continue, "Did she give you your medallion to help you with nightmares too?" Bailey nods again.

"You know Ari used to talk to me about her nightmares, which seemed to help her feel better. I will be glad to listen if you want to talk to me," I tell her, hoping she will open up to me and let me help her fight the demons from her sleep.

"She told you about the bad people in our dreams that want to hurt us?" Bailey asks with surprise lacing her voice. What the hell? Bad people wanting to hurt them both? I feel like Alice, and I've fallen down the rabbit hole. The more I think the bizarre has finally ended so I can analyze and process my new reality, the more I'm hit with other surprises.

To keep her from clamming up on me, I keep a straight face to look neutral like Bailey hasn't introduced me to another shocking discovery I feel is about to be revealed. I answer her with a nod. Bailey looks down at her medallion like she's processing what I told her.

"Is that why Ari gave you your medallion, to keep you safe?" I question, trying to encourage her to keep talking.

"Kinda, she took me to see my fairy godmother and she made it for me," she says while keeping her eyes on the medallion never looking up. This one statement sends chills down my spine. Any other time before today if any child had said anything about a fairy I wouldn't over-think into it, but today is a whole different story.

I pull my phone out of my back pocket with a feeling of dread while explaining to Bailey, "I think I know your fairy godmother." I swipe through my pictures until I find one I took with Nikki and Gran a couple of months ago, and then turn it, so Bailey can see it. "Is that her?" I ask.

"Yes," Bailey says while at the same time taking her tiny finger and placing it over Gran's face. "She was nice even though she poked my finger," Bailey says. She looks up at me with hope in her eyes right before she speaks words that shove me deeper into Alice's rabbit hole. With a concern almost like desperation, Bailey says, "I tried to give Ari my necklace to keep her safe because someone took hers, but she wouldn't take it."

"That's because Ari cares about you more than herself and

wants to keep you safe," I try to explain, even though I have no idea at this point of how to respond.

"But Ari is broken, I'm not. Do you think you could ask the godmother to make Ari another necklace? I know we're only allowed to get one, but Ari lost hers and now the bad people can find her," Bailey says with fear in her voice. What the hell? Broken? Who are these bad people or bad things she is talking about?

"Don't worry honey; we found Ari's necklace. She should get it back real soon. If not, I will get her another one made, okay?" I say, trying to comfort her fears away. I get the now familiar nod, but with a smile added to it. "It's late. Try to go back to sleep now," I say in a soothing voice.

With my request, Bailey closes her eyes and snuggles up closer to me. After a few minutes, I hear Bailey's breath even out in the all too familiar sounds of sleep. I'm grateful for the peace and quiet the nighttime brings so I can finally go over all my new knowledge. I focus on Ari for now, pushing thoughts of Connor away while wanting to swim in denial just a little longer.

I have a few more questions for my tutors of all things non-human concerning Ari that I fully intend on getting answers. Why did Bailey say she could have only one medallion? To hell with that! I'm a Fae too; if she can't get hers back in the next day or two, I will find the book of spells and make her another one myself. I cast a spell for Connor without meaning to so how hard could it be to cast a spell on purpose.

After being unable to fall asleep for what seems like hours, I ease out of Bailey's bed to go to the kitchen in search of milk to heat up, hoping it will help induce the sleep my body desperately needs. I pass by a closed door just before I get to the kitchen that has a glowing light springing out from the bottom crack of the door. I knock gently hoping it's Dom that's up late, so I can get answers to my questions.

I hear someone say, "Come in," so I grab the doorknob and let myself into the room. It's a medium-sized study that's mint green in color. Dom is seated behind what appears to be an antique wooden desk that's illuminated by a desk lamp on each front corner.

The desk sits on the opposite wall and faces the door. There is a large built-in bookcase against the wall behind the desk that has a large floor to ceiling window on each side of it covered in thick dark green drapes. Facing the front of the desk are two old appearing high back leather chairs. I head straight toward the desk Dom is sitting behind and sit down in one of the two chairs facing him.

"You're up late. Can't sleep?" Dom asks.

"I could say the same about you," I retort.

"Can't sleep so I thought I would come down here to get some work done. And you?" Dom responds, looking at me awaiting my answer.

"I found Bailey was still up when I headed to bed earlier," I pause trying to think of a way to bring it up but decide it's better to get it out into the open. "Bailey told me some things about her and Ari. What exactly are they? Why is Ari 'broken' (yes, I used air quotes with fingers)? And who the hell are the bad people after them?" I interrogate.

"Bailey just came out and said all of those things to you?" Dom inquires with a pissed off look on his face. I've overstepped some boundary of information, but I still want to know.

"Well, I think I tricked her into saying most of it. I told her some things about Ari, and she assumed I knew the rest," I respond trying to smooth the situation over but from the look on Dom's face it didn't help, especially when he mumbles something about a sterner talk with that child.

After a few moments of silence and him staring at me, he finally gives a nod as he concluded that I'm trustworthy of this top secret. I sit back in the chair relaxing and absentmindedly rubbing my stomach.

Dom shakes his head, lets out a deep breath, and then begins, "Remember in the old books, the section of werewolves when I explained the difference of the alpha and that they can be male or female?"

"Yes, I remember and recall you were saying that alpha males feel threatened by the female alphas, called She-Wolves, so they tend to destroy them after they're born," I say nodding my head.

"Well, Bailey isn't a half-breed. She is a true-blooded She-Wolf, and so is Ari," Dom says trying to educate me as I'm falling down Alice's rabbit hole again.

"Why is Ari broken?" I ask, wanting to know more.

"The fire that killed her mother damaged some of Ari's heightened senses and they no longer work," he says shaking his head with a grief-stricken look on his face.

"And the bad people…." I say prompting him to continue.

"The bad people are the alpha males still stuck on the practice of getting rid of them. For example, the fire that killed Ari's mother wasn't an accident," Dom says revealing more shocking news. He continues, "This goes without saying, you can never reveal their identity to anyone. I would normally tell you it's none of your concern, but Bailey has already overstepped the boundaries of too much information. I need you to understand the true danger they live in and the importance of secrecy, even from Connor." Then he tells me the rest of the history between the Fae and the She-Wolves, along with the history of the medallion that he left off earlier in the evening.

When he's done with his history lesson I respond, "I won't tell anyone," to reassure him.

"When is the last time you seen Kara?" Dom asks while watching closely the hand that's rubbing my baby bump.

"The baby and I are fine. I like to rub the baby bump. Wait, how did you know who my doctor is?" I quiz.

Rolling his eyes Dom replies, "We only have one doctor in this area that specializes in Chimeras and knowing Connor, let's say it's not that big of a leap to figure out. I will call her to come out in the morning just to make sure you and the baby are fine. You had an emotionally stressful day today. It will make me feel better if she checks you."

"Ok," I agree because there is no reason to argue when the concern is for the baby.

"I was on my way to the kitchen for some warm milk before I saw your light on. I think I'll go do that now and let you get back to whatever you're doing," I respond smiling as I get up to head for the door. I hear Dom say goodnight as I leave the room.

True to his word, shortly after I wake up the next morning, Kara is waiting downstairs for me.

"Good morning," I say in greeting her.

"Good morning to you too," she responds as we make our way to Dom's study so she can do an examination on the baby and me with no on-lookers. After a full exam and a confirmation that indeed all is well with my pregnancy, we sit and chat for a while.

I ask her about my concern about her being the only physician that the non-humans must turn to in this area and inquire about her patient load. I tell her about the idea came to me this morning as I was getting ready. I'm going to turn in my notice at the hospital and would like to join her practice where there's a much higher need. We discuss the details of the extra training I would have to endure to become knowledgeable in the differences in how to treat each non-human because of each unique makeup.

After a lengthy discussion, Kara agrees to be my preceptor with enthusiasm for finally getting some much-needed help. For the first time in the last twenty-four hours, I feel like I'm finally finding my place in the reality of my new world with goals that could make a positive difference.

Afterwards, we discuss the big elephant in the room, meaning the reason why Dom called her out here. Through tears, I give her a play-by-play of yesterday's events, which surprisingly feels good to have another woman to talk to about this especially since I think I've lost most of my support system that I had depended on all my life.

I know in my heart I'll have to forgive Nikki and Gran, but today is not that day. When I get to the part of the shaking and the sliding chair, she looks concerned and states that's not usually in the realm of the Fae power, but contributes the added strength to being pregnant with a werewolf which is known for its strength. We both conclude that my blood mix with the baby's blood must be why my abilities have also expanded.

I wonder if this ability will disappear after I give birth. I hope not. I like having something uniquely mine. She too wondered if the curse is lifting once I told her about Connor's eyes changing colors. Kara explains to me in detail that I'm not having a half-breed, but a hybrid baby which is not common.

Chapter 49

Kara
"The Cat is Out of the Bag"

I leave Willow with her promise of seeking me out when her notice at the hospital is completed, and she is free to begin working with me. This should give me time to get a handle of the 'cat is out of the bag' so to say information of Fae's existence and stop any negative outlash this information might stir, mainly with a certain werewolf tribe I know who will be in an uproar. They must learn to deal with their new reality because I'm in desperate need of help in this community and I'll be damned if their stupidity of blaming the present for the past will get in my way.

I decide the first step is to deal with Connor first and straighten the boy out. I call his cell phone, but it goes straight to voicemail. Next, I call his office, but his coworkers explain that Connor and Drake had some family emergency meeting they had to attend so they would not be in until later that day. Well, it appears I'm going to their father's home, the alpha, and dealing with them all in one gathering. This will save me time from trying to track them all down individually. I pray that I'm successful for Willow's sake.

When I pull up to the large family estate 30 minutes later, there are quite a few more cars in the drive than I expected. The house is an off-white two-story antebellum home with six massive white columns stretching from the floor of the porch up to the roofline of the second story. The porch is large and spans the width of the house. There are multiple outbuildings located to the rear of the house. It's a massive estate that would be mistaken for a former plantation by the average onlooker. The house was designed and used for more than a century as a werewolf compound.

I ring the doorbell and wait patiently until James, their butler, opens the large door. James has been working for the family for as long as I can remember. He has been the one that usually greets me first with each visit I have made here.

James is a very meek and mild manner older gentleman. He politely explains that the hierarchy of the family is in a closed meeting. I can either make an appointment and come back or wait in the parlor room to be seen. I give him my sweetest smile, then ignore his instructions and walk right past him.

I march across the foyer toward a room where I hear a loud discussion taking place, with James on my heels protesting the whole time. The voices get louder as I approach the closed French doors of the dining room signaling a heated discussion is taking place.

With one last deep breath for courage, I turn the doorknob then walk straight into a heated argument that appears to have been going on for a while. I glance around the room to see who all is present, so I know who I will have to take on.

At the head of the table is Jessiah, father to Connor and Drake and better known as the alpha of the pack. They usually call themselves a tribe, but I call them a pack since that's how they operate. Jessiah's face is blood red with rage over whatever they're all arguing about.

Jessiah is a rugged-looking man with dark, almost black looking hair with several strands of gray mixed in. The graying hair is the only feature on the man that gives any indication of his actual age. He's one of the tallest men of his tribe, built like a stone wall with pure muscle and the strength to match. He has scars all over his body from the many battles he's been involved in over the years. I have seen him after many of those occasions and treated a lot of his battle wounds.

Werewolves are known for the ability to heal quickly, but if the injury is large and deep, they scar just like everyone else.

The only scar visible right now is the jagged one cutting across his forehead through his right eyebrow just missing his piercing brown eye and ending just below his right temple. That scar adds to his fierce, unrefined rugged look. I have always thought he looked like what I imagine a Viking warrior would have looked.

I've known Jessiah for years and have been the primary Doctor for his pack. When you deal with any issues with a pack member, you direct your questions and concerns to the alpha. Not only out of respect but also because he's like the pack's king who not only has the command and control over the pack but the strength and power to back him as well.

The only tribal members I've ever seen go head to head with this man are the ones who are currently seated at this table. I've never cared to learn the details of the inner workings of the hierarchy of any werewolf pack. That's much deeper than necessary to get my job done, but I would assume if any lower ranking werewolves get out of line they are dealt with quickly. What I do know about this pack is that although Jessiah is stern and may rule with an iron fist, he's known to be a just and fair man. I hope I can still think that after this meeting.

As I approach the table, I feel a familiar prickly sensation running up my neck, and I immediately know Jared is in the room. I slowly glance around the table and lock eyes with him. Jared is Jessiah's brother and is his beta. Every time I look into his eyes my breath catches in my lungs. He always seems to have a primal sexual charge to him that calls out to every cell in my body every time I'm in the same room as him.

He's six-foot-four with dark brown, thick wavy hair that I would love to run my fingers through to see if it's as silky soft as I've imagined. We make eye contact, and there's a hunger in his eyes just like every other time our eyes meet. The desire in his eyes causes me to lick my lips which have suddenly become dry as all the moisture in my body seems to pool in the apex of my thighs, another effect that happens every time he looks at me.

His eyes immediately move to my lips, and he stares for a second, watching my tongue as it glides over my bottom lip, then looks back into my eyes. I see a faint twitch of the outer edge of his lip which gives me an indication he knows how he affects me.

We've always had a powerful attraction toward each other over the years, with me being the one to always pull away because of the very news I'm here to announce today. I wonder if the hunger will still be there after I've said what I come to say? The fear of the unknown must have shown on my face because the hungry look that was direct towards me, now has transfigured into one of concern with a questioning look in his eyes.

I notice his body has gone stiff. He places both of his hands on the table like he's ready to stand up and come to my aid. I give him a barely there shake of my head, and without lifting my arm, I hold up my palm facing him to provide him with a silent communication of please stay seated. He does what I ask, but I can tell with his body language he's not happy about it. That's how it has always been between us; we're able to communicate a conversation by just reading each other's body language like we're the only two people in the room and no one else exists.

I give myself a mental shake and continue to survey the rest of the people in the room, trying to get my head on straight again by focusing on the mission that's brought me here. Four more pack council members are sitting two on each side of the table. I've treated all four medically in the past, but that's where my relationship ends with them.

Next, I see Connor's younger brother Jonas and his sister Katarina sitting across from each other. I haven't seen them in a while, and I'm a little surprised to see them here at the meeting. But since this meeting probably concerns their future niece or nephew, I have a feeling their mother must have demanded their presence. Jonas is a younger version of both his older brothers. He's like the perfect combination with an appearance that resembles Drake's playboy appeal and a mind like his more serious older brother Connor. Katarina is her mother's mini-me, with all the grace and beauty of a princess.

I continue to look around the table. I notice Connor and Drake are sitting together. Connor looks rougher than I've ever seen and that's saying a lot. His eyes are looking off in the distance like he's somewhere else instead of in this room. His appearance looks like shit, with dark circles under his eyes appearing as if he hasn't slept in days. I would feel sorry for him if I didn't know he brought this onto himself with his own stupidity.

Drake, on the other hand, looks much more like his father with a red face that's ready to explode and his eyes glaring straight in the direction of their father. I suspect Drake has been pro Willow since he's staring daggers towards the alpha. Last, I see Sasha, Connor's mother, sitting at the opposite end of the long table across from Jessiah in her rightful place as his wife. She is as beautiful as ever with as much poise, and grace as a real queen would have.

This woman has earned my full respect over the years. Once while suturing up a deep wound on Jessiah, I had the very rare opportunity to witness this woman verbally chew him up and spit him out, turning the alpha into a baffled blubbering idiot for putting himself in danger by risking his life while scaring the hell out of her in the process. Her love for this man runs deep as does his for her, with each other very aware of that fact.

It takes a powerful woman to be married to an alpha. She has the mental strength to stand up to her husband, consequences be damned. She has the ability to convey her thoughts to her husband without letting on to anyone around them of her disappointment in their alpha.

I guess I notice the signs because Jared and I do the same kind of communication. Like now she seems to be the doting wife that's quietly supporting her husband, but with the stiffness of her back and the indifferent look on her face raising one eyebrow slightly with eyes focused solely on him, I know as well as he does, she's pissed off big time.

I'm brought out of my thoughts and back to reality when everyone in the room stops speaking, signaling all have noticed my presence. James immediately apologizes for my intrusion, reassuring his alpha he did indeed instruct me to wait, but I defied his instruction. I roll my eyes as James is dismissed.

"I will have to ask you to please wait in the parlor Kara, we are in the middle of discussing tribal business," Jessiah says with all the authority in his voice you can imagine.

"I come on behalf of Willow Black so if this meeting concerns her, then I'm exactly where I need to be," I explain with all the authority I can muster up in my own voice.

With the mention of Willow's name, Connor's head pops up, bringing him out of his trance. He now has a look of concern written on his face. "What do you mean you're here on behalf of Willow? Is she ok? The baby?" he says with urgency and concern in his voice.

I hold up my hand to stop his questioning rant. "She and the baby are fine. They called me out this morning due to the extreme emotional distress she endured yesterday," I say as I cut my eyes at him. His face morphs into a look full of regret and guilt. Good, he needs to beg for forgiveness for all the shit he said to the mother of his child.

Connor stands and announces, "I need to go to Willow's house and talk with her."

"She isn't staying there," I inform him.

"Where is she?.... Dom's," he says as his face drops with the answer of his question. I nod to confirm his suspicion.

"This meeting is not over with, and you'll not go anywhere until it is. You are the one who invited that Fae into our lives!" Jessiah roars.

At the other end of the table, Sasha clears her throat as she stands, and all eyes turn to her. "I have heard enough. Jessiah, you may rule this tribe, but I rule this family. That Fae, as you like to call her, is a lovely woman who saved one of our son's life, not to mention the fact that Fae is also carrying my grandchild by another son. The baby is not my half grandchild. He or she is my whole grandchild. You can stay here and spew your views of the past all you want, but Willow isn't responsible for a fight that happened centuries ago. I'm leaving," Sasha says in a steadfast and controlled voice. I'm guessing on dealing with the subject of her grandchild she couldn't give a shit if other members of their tribe see her lashing out at her husband. Good to know.

"What do you mean you are leaving?" Jessiah spews.

"I mean exactly what I said. I'm leaving to go stay with that Fae, as you call her until you can get your head out of your ass!" Sasha spews back. With that announcement, Connor's younger siblings jump up out of their seats, stand and turn to walk out with their mother.

"Where do you two think you are going?" Jessiah asks his younger children as in a dare to walk out.

"I like to eat, and Mom's the one who cooks, so I'm going to where the food is," his younger son Jonas explains.

"Sit!" Jessiah commands, and his son sits back down, obeying his alpha. His daughter, on the other hand, gives an "Uh" sound, shakes her head then walks over to stand behind her mother. Both turn and walk across the room to leave out the door behind me but as they approach, I ask them to wait to hear me out for a moment. They stand beside me as I face off with the room. With the women at my side, I feel somewhat empowered to give the speech I never thought I could give.

As I open my mouth to speak Jessiah speaks first, "With all due respect Kara, you do not know anything about this. Fae are evil, and they wreak havoc on others," he declares.

"Allow me to speak without interruptions, and I'll leave," I say. Jessiah pauses, stares at me, then after a few seconds, gives a chin lift for me to continue. I trench onward, "You all have known me for years," I say which gives me nods from around the table in agreement. "I have not only earned your trust and respect, but I deserve it. I have taken care of your sick and helped deliver your young. Essentially, I've done every-thing for your tribe from the womb to the tomb, and I've done it all with strict confidentiality. I've never given you any reason to distrust me. You all know I'm part of the non-human race, but I've never confirmed or denied anyone's guesses of what I truly am until today," I explain as I look around the table.

With all eyes on me, I unbutton the top few buttons of my blouse, just enough to pull my arm out of the sleeve but not enough to expose my breast. I raise my arm and reveal my hid-den birthmark of a butterfly, the mark of the Fae. I hear a round of gasps and mumbles as I button my blouse back up then turn to my girl posse next to me to avoid looking into Jared's eyes. I don't want to see that disappointment has replaced his hungry look.

Glancing back at the table I continue, "Just so everyone is aware, Willow will join my practice as soon as she works out a notice at the hospital where she works, so if you want to be seen by a physician that's not a Fae then I suggest one of you start going to medical school right away."

I cautiously glance at Sasha, worried about her reaction to my announcement, but to my relief, she smiles sweetly. "Shall we?" she says as she stretches out her arm into the direc-tion of the door. I nod. The three of us leave the house together and head for my car. I open my car door, and as I'm about to lean down to get in, I feel a strong-arm wrap around my waist pulling me back tight against someone's front.

Immediately my body knows it's Jared and I automatically melt into him. Shivers run through my body as I feel his warm breath caress my ear as he speaks. I know he felt my shiver be-cause his arm immediately tightens around me.

"So, I take it this is the reason you pull away from me every time," he quietly whispers, sending chills to my core. Not able to form words, I nod once. "You will learn I don't share the same views as my brother on this subject, and baby you better plan on being a fast learner," he finishes saying.

He then gives me a light kiss on my neck below my ear,

stealing my breath for a second, and he's gone just as fast as he appeared. I immediately miss the warmth of his body, and as I get into my car, I feel a wave of excitement as I wonder when his lessons will begin.

Chapter 50

Connor
"Cluster fuck"

The dining room has gone completely silent after the women stormed out. Uncle Jared stormed out right after like a man on a mission, which I have a good suspicion his mission is Kara. Without a word I get up and leave, noticing Drake hot on my heels. I should have been the one who stood up to the tribe for Willow, not Drake, but I was still having a time wrapping my mind around this cluster fuck.

The bottom line is I'm still in love with Willow. Curse or not I know deep down she's my soul mate and I want, no I need to be part of my child's life whether Willow can forgive me or not. I will get her back though. Willow moving on with another man is not an option. I'll kill any asshole who tries to put his hands on what's mine. It's a good thing Willow knows exactly who and what I am, so she can understand the extent I'm willing to go to claim what's mine. She'll soon learn that she's most definitely mine.

"With all that growling and huffing you're doing, I assume you've pulled your sorry head out of your ass and will finally get your woman and child back without doing more damage by saying some fucked up shit," Drake says as we drive back to the office. I give him a chin lift to agree. "About fucking time," he mumbles in response.

After we arrive at the office, my cell phone rings. I pull it out of my pocket hoping it's Willow, but it's Dom instead.

"Willow ok?" I ask.

"Yup. To my surprise, I now have two new members of

the women who Connor pissed off club, not that I'm complaining or anything. Your mother is already in the kitchen cooking up a feast, explaining cooking helps calm her nerves. Your sister has already become our official homework tutor for the kids. Plus, we have our own physician that arrived last night. Just wanted to make sure we need not to expect any other additional members because we're getting low on spare bedrooms," Dom cackles as he tries not to laugh while saying it.

I shake my head. Just fucking great. I can hear in his voice how much he loves my misery. "Thanks for letting me know they're staying with you. Hopefully, this will blow over soon. Keep your hands and cock away from what's mine if you plan on living. No playing doctor with the personal physician," I emphasize.

"So, it's like that again, no more demon spawn and evil Fae?" he asks, and damn I hate he has the right to even ask.

"Yeah, it's like that. I pulled my head out of my ass. I'll make this right, just give me time to figure out how," I let him know.

"Will do, but if you add another member to the women Connor has pissed off club just be sure she's hot and fuckable because my bed will be where the next one ends up," Dom exclaims, and with that comment he disconnects the phone line before I can make any more threats.

When we walk into the office, I discover we've gotten some leads about the Wendigos that need my full attention. I make the decision I'll focus on work while giving Willow some space to forgive me, but at the same time, I plan to text and send gifts to her so she doesn't forget about me. With that thought, I continue working.

Chapter 51

Willow
"Actions Speak Louder than Words"

Three weeks have passed since Dom's hotel for wayward women took in Connor's mother, Connor's sister, and me. I've enjoyed getting to know them, and I'm thrilled to know they're not as closed-minded as the men in their tribe. Connor sends text messages and leaves voice mails every day, but I haven't responded.

He even had a few deliveries made to the house of my favorite foods and various stuff for the baby including a teddy bear. It must be his way of not only saying he's sorry but showing it too with the "actions speak louder than words" motto. I've received a daily text from Nikki and a few from Gran asking if we could get together to talk, but I don't feel ready to just yet.

I answer Ari's calls when she phones to check up on how I'm doing though. She respects me enough to give me the time I need to heal from my fresh wounds. I talked to her about being a Fae. A fact I know she already knew, but I avoid letting her know I know because I'm not sure how to say it without bringing up what she is in the process.

I haven't told her I know what she is, a She-Wolf. That's her secret to tell. I understand her dilemma of knowing what I am and not telling me. Her situation is very different compared to Nikki's and Gran's. She kept the secret because she's bound by a protective spell that she needs to keep safe from the "bad people" as Bailey calls them. Gran and Nikki had no reason not to tell me.

Connor's team hasn't returned Ari's necklace yet. I need to get my hands-on Gran's books to find a way to give her another protection medallion. I might have to let her know I know her secret if it comes down to me needing to poke her finger like Bailey said Gran did to hers. If the spell calls for blood, I don't know how I'll get it otherwise.

Dom left on a field trip with the kids this morning. Those of us that stayed behind had a late lunch, and now Flame has decided it's a good time for him to brush up on his cocktail making skills. He rings an old-fashioned dinner bell in the kitchen to call an impromptu girl meeting of the POW club, short for the pissed off women's club, which he has joined.

Since the first week of our arrival, Flame has been calling weekly meetings he officially calls pow-wows in which Sasha, Kat, Flame, and I get together to do various things. The first pow-wow meeting consisted of marathon movie watching while eating as many sweets as our stomachs could hold. On the second week, our pow-wow included shopping, which I enjoyed because we shopped for my baby.

For this week's pow-wow, Flame planned to make cocktails and have a stay at home spa day comprising sitting around doing Mani Pedi's while drinking cocktails. Unfortunately, after the third round, with me not drinking I'm the only one sober, so I'm in charge of the nail polish as I'm the only one who can paint a nail with a steady hand. I still get to sample the cocktails, but it's before Flame adds the alcohol. If they don't slow down, I may become the club's official hair holder while they puke person.

Sasha jumps into the therapist role and starts openly asking questions about mine and Connor's fight that I've been trying to avoid thinking about. Sometimes ignorance is bliss. They have been kind enough to not ask too many questions until this point, but now they have the liquid courage from the alcohol pulsing through their system.

"Honey, what exactly did that son of mine say to you that day?" Sasha asks, causing Flame and Kat to come in closer to hear.

"Well, to sum it up he said he regretted the fact the enemy of his tribe has invaded his life. He then said every time he looks down upon his child he hopes he doesn't see a demon spawn half-wolf/half-fae staring back at him, topped off with I'm having a child with someone that's been a sworn enemy my entire life," I finish saying as I look around to find everyone just staring at me in shock, disbelief, and my least favorite- pity.

"What did you say to him?" Kat asks curiously.

"I don't remember exactly, because I was a blubbering mess, but something strange did happen that made me think for a second, he might be right. Maybe I have something evil in me lurking below the surface," I confess to them.

"Don't leave us hanging here, tell us!" Sasha orders.

"After I told Connor and Nikki how hurt I was by their betrayal, Connor walked towards me, but I wanted nothing to do with him at the time. A strange growling noise bubbled up from down inside me, and as Connor was walking towards me, I held up my hand, then a chair beside him shook violently and moved over to block his path," I tell them as I anxiously wait to see their reaction.

"Wait, you growled and then shook a chair causing it to move, and that's what made you think he might be right about you being evil?" Flame quizzes me. I nod my head yes. "Did the chair fly through the air and hit anyone?" he asks with sarcasm laced in his voice. I shake my head no. "Girl you haven't seen evil. Shaking a chair is nothing compared to some horrors I've witnessed through the years," he responds as Sasha and Kat both verbalize their agreement with his statement.

After a moment Sasha responds, "I'm curious if that deep growl you did wasn't something to do with the baby. In all the legends and myths I've heard, I've never heard of a Fae growling. That's more of a werewolf trait. You're having a hybrid baby, so there's really no telling what this little boo-ger is capable of having werewolf strength combined with Fae magic."

"That's exactly what Kara thought when I talked to her about it. She thought that maybe the baby's blood has mixed with mine and has somehow increased my magic, explaining what happened with the chair," I tell them. Bringing up Kara reminds me of the shock and surprise I felt when I found out that Kara is a Fae. Apparently, her family line of Fae didn't agree with the whole secrecy decree. She said she hadn't met another Fae with the knowledge of their heritage. That knowledge has me wondering how many people in the medical field could be Fae and not know it since the few I'm now aware of are involved one way or another in healing the sick.

"Well hell, in that case, let me mix us all another drink so we can get to investigating this newfound ability. Let's test it girl!" Flame exclaims as they all excitedly agree.

I'm not sure this is such a good idea, but I know better than to argue with the force of the pow-wow women and man, especially when alcohol is mixed in, so I go with it. Half an hour and another drink later I'm still unsuccessful at making anything move.

We moved our powwow into the dining room mid-investigation because, according to Flame, the chairs are lighter and should be easier to move. I didn't think it would matter how easy they were to move by hand since I'm using my mind, but I kept my mouth shut and just went with it.

"Put some anger into it! Think of something that pisses you off, like my dumb ass brother," Kat utters with a slurring voice.

I don't want to relive the painful memory of that day afraid I'll burst into tears. So, I concentrate hard, focusing first on Ari and the men who wanted to hurt her, then how my own family has denied helping her by not providing unlimited protection without expecting something in return. Anger must be the missing ingredient because, after a few minutes of focusing on the injustice surrounding Ari, the growl rumbles up then the dining room chair I've been focusing on shakes. The women all squeal with excitement while Flame jumps up and down, clapping his hands. I can't help but join in on the excitement, causing me to lose focus and the growl goes quiet, then the chair stops shaking.

"That growl is a wolf's growl. I would recognize that warning growl anywhere," Sasha says with pride in her eyes and the others all agree.

"I agree. That growl is all wolf. Wow, have any of you ever heard of a wolf in the womb growling?" Kat asks. The other two shake their heads. For me, I stay quiet because hell I just found out werewolves are real less than a month ago and I can't say I've ever taken care of one of them much less one that was pregnant.

"That's one pissed off baby. But isn't that sweet, the little fellow wants to protect whatever has gotten his mommy all upset," responds Flame as he joins in with his opinion.

"Hell, with the strength of a werewolf and the magic of a Fae, this little babe is going to be a force of nature to be reckoned with," Sasha remarks with the sound of awe in her voice.

Now I feel like a bad mommy for already getting my baby upset. After a few minutes of shame, I pushed the negative thoughts about being a lousy mom out of my head. I'm finding that living in a state of denial as a coping mechanism is getting easier and easier. As I try to focus on a solution to what made me mad, I realize I've put helping Ari off for a lot longer than I intended and I need to suck it up, put my big girl panties on and face off with Gran and Nikki. Then, if Gran won't help, I'll demand the books so I can try to help Ari myself. With a renewal of motivation, I tell the group I feel its time I confront Gran and Nikki, and I plan to do it now instead of waiting and talking myself out of it. After wishes of good luck from the other pow-wow members, I set off to do just that.

Chapter 52

Connor
"A Force To Be Reckoned With"

We've made a lot of progress this week at work and only have one more Wendigo to round up. One is dead, and the other is off the streets after we tracked him down and cornered him. He is severely wounded but locked up. We figured out that the last one is Jay, also known as Blue Jay because he wears flashy blue suits.

Unfortunately, the last time we laid eyes on the asshole was the night we met Ari at the bar when he was just a person of interest. He must have known we were getting close because ever since that night it's like he crawled under a rock and disappeared. We're leaving no stone in New Orleans unturned trying to find him.

He seems smarter than the rest, which makes him the most dangerous one. Maybe he left town, but I doubt it. New Orleans is a city he knows well, and if you need to hide from the supernatural law, you need the home turf advantage.

I take a break from focusing so hard on the case, hoping new ideas on how to trap the last Wendigo will pop into mind if I'm not so focused on the goal. The only problem with this is when I calm my mind my entire thoughts float back to Willow and my need to see her. I've been breaking down and calling Dom to check in to make sure she's doing ok since she refuses to talk with me.

After about an hour of not being able to clear my mind of Willow, I decide enough is enough. Fuck it, I'm going to claim my woman and child even if I must go caveman. I will drag her home with her kicking and screaming all the way if I have to.

I'm tired of cold showers and sleepless nights in a lonely bed. I had a moment of stupidity, and I regret everything I said on that shitty day. I made a mistake which I consider just one of the many mistakes I'm sure to create where Willow is concerned, but I want what's mine. Willow can sit at my house and not speak to me just as easily as she can at Dom's. The only difference is I'll be the man taking care of her and our baby.

I decide to treat this as like any other retrieve and rescue mission by picking the team members I need to complete the task. Drake is always my wingman so I know I can count on him. Although still not thrilled about the baby being half Fae, the revelation Kara hit us with went a long way towards softening my father up.

Once Uncle Jared realized the truth of why Kara has kept him at arm's length, he said to hell with the consequences; he wasn't living without his woman any longer and he went to stake his claim to her. That was five days ago. No one has seen or heard from either of them since, so we assume it went well.

News of Fae still existing has now circulated through our tribe. With half of our tribe accepting that coexisting with Fae is tolerable, I'm hopeful that my father will come around and be accepting of them too. Jonas called me a few days ago and was complaining of being tired of dealing with my father's grumpy attitude. He said my father misses my mother and is ready to put his foot down, so I'll add my father to the team member list and hope it won't blow up in my face. I plan to recruit my youngest brother Jonas as well.

Since Kat left, he has not only done his chores, but has been stuck doing hers as well. No matter how old you are, if you live at home with our parents, one of the house rules is doing chores. I make the calls to rally my father, Drake, and Jonas to help bring the women home.

We all arrive at Dom's house at about the same time. Like a force to be reckoned with, we stormed the porch together to claim our women. Whether lover, mother, wife, or sister they're all coming home today. Dom answers the door after we pound on it.

"Welcome to my home of your wayward women," is the greeting he delivers as he extends his arm to welcome us in and moves out of our way so we can enter. He then swings his arm back across his chest and bows a little to make a theatrical display. I'm so glad this asshole finds entertainment in our misery.

"Keep in mind, the condition you'll find your women in is not my doing. I just arrived home a few minutes ago," he says cryptically. We follow the laughing and howling down the hall until we locate them. My mouth falls open, and I glance at my team to see their reactions. My father looks speechless while Drake and Jonas stand rock still with eyes wide open as we take in the women and Flame. It's like the midnight margarita scene in the movie Practical Magic, the part where the four women are dancing around the dining room drunk off their asses on tequila. Our women are laughing and dancing around the table, but instead of the Put a Lime in the Coconut song, they're dancing to Black Horse and a Cherry Tree.

Dom moves to where they have placed a radio on the table; I presume to turn it off. To my shock, my little sister dances up behind him and grabs the waistband on his pants, pulling on him while demanding him to dance with her. Dom responds with a shit-eating grin as he hits the off button of the radio.

My mother is the first to see us, "Did my baby come to apologize to his woman?" she asks with a slur while cooing at me like I'm five years old.

"Yes mother," I say, not knowing what else to say because I can't remember ever seeing this woman who is usually so full of grace this drunk before. She heads straight for me with open arms to give me, her favorite son, a hug of approval. My father reaches out to catch her when she stumbles as she is coming towards us.

Slapping my father's hands away she tells him, "Don't you dare man-handle me, you big bully."

"Baby, why does Connor get the benefit of the doubt when you see him, but you hit me as soon as you're close enough?" my father asks while looking all put out with an actual pouting expression. My mother is the only person I know that can turn my father into a groveling man. She walks away from him rolling her eyes. I look over at my sister to find she's staring at Dom like she's a starving woman that's just discovered her last meal. I turn to Dom and raise my brow to question him. He catches my eyes and shrugs his shoulders like he's totally the innocent party, so I let it go for now. At twenty-two years of age, Kat isn't a baby, but she'll always be my baby sister.

"Why have these hot males interrupted the pow-wow meeting?" Flame asks while acting like he's the Queen of Sheba and fluttering his fingertips as he waves his hand through the air.

"Pow-wow?" I inquire.

"Don't ask," Dom says as he shakes his head. "I'll go make coffee," he adds as he heads into the other room, which I assume is where the kitchen is.

"I'll help you!" Kat blurts out then heads in the same direction, but before I can even move Jonas has her by her elbow, shakes his head and forces her to sit down in a chair at the table. Apparently, I'm not the only one displeased with her hungry eyes focused on Dom.

"Where's Willow?" I question the powwow members.

"She went to...." Kat starts to speak but is interrupted by Flame. I could strangle that man right now, but I have a feeling I would never get the answers I need because the pow-wow women would strangle me.

"First, state your business... your business with member Willow," Flame demands as he pops his hand down on the table. Apparently, alcohol makes this werewolf eight foot tall and bulletproof.

"I want to apologize to her and beg her for forgiveness," I say through clenched teeth.

My mother may be three sheets in the wind but must

have noticed by my anger that Flame is treading dangerously on my last nerve. He's the next obstacle preventing me from claiming what's already mine, Willow. "About time Dear, but she's not here. She went to make amends with her cousin and grandmother," my mother says slurring.

"Great, then I'll wait here for her return," I say as Dom brings in a pot of coffee and enough cups for everyone to drink. Hopefully, the coffee will help in getting the pow-wow to sober up a little instead of trying to drag them out drunk. I look down at my watch and take note it's five p.m. I'll give her two hours to get everything settled before going after her.

It's now 7 p.m., and Willow still hasn't come back, so instead of calling and demanding her to return like the caveman I'm feeling like, I decide to do something productive. "Kat, show me which bedroom is Willow's," I instruct my sister.

"Why?" she questions as Dom grins and shakes his head. He probably has a good idea of what I'm up too.

"I will pack all her stuff up for her. When she gets here, I'll apologize and try to convince her to come home with me. If she agrees, then I've saved her time by packing. If she tells me to go to hell, then I'll plant her little ass in my car and take her anyway. Whether she agrees to spend the night at my place or I handcuff her to my bed, she'll be sleeping with me tonight," I declare.

"Such an overbearing ass, but kinda caveman hot at the same time," Kat says as she gets up. "Come on, I'll help you," she says as she leads the way. We go upstairs to the bedroom then find Willow's suitcase in the closet. Kat begins to pack everything out of the drawers and from the closet. As I head into the bathroom with her smaller bag to pack her toiletries, Kat stops me to ask a question.

She points to three flower arrangements that are sitting on various pieces of furniture throughout the room. "What if we leave the flower arrangements you sent her here, and I'll bring them to you tomorrow? That way I can pack them carefully and not damage them," she adds.

As I start to agree, an uneasy realization hits me. I only sent two flower arrangements this week. I recognize the two I picked out and had delivered, then head straight for the third arrangement. My gut tells me something is wrong, and I'm good at my job because my gut is usually right.

"Are you sure all three were sent for Willow?" I ask Kat to verify.

"Yes, I'm the one who answered the door all three times. Each time the delivery man said they were for Willow. Why, what's wrong Connor?" she asks in confusion.

I don't answer, but instead, push the flowers around until I find the card attached to them. They came from the same florist I used. I pull the card out to see its blank except for a picture of a blue jay in the middle of the card. The bird makes my stomach churn.

"Mother Fucker!" I yell out at the top of my lungs, causing Kat to jump back. Without thinking I sling the vase of flowers across the room, causing the glass to shatter everywhere.

"What the fuck?" I hear my brother Jonas ask from the doorway. I hear voices of children gathering in the hallway, along with Flame and my mother's voices trying to sooth them as they try to herd them back to their rooms. I feel like I can't breathe and time around me has slowed down as true fear edges up my spine.

"Son?" my father asks as he approaches me with Dom and Drake close behind. He looks at my sister who still looks confused. "Kat, honey, go help your mother with the children," he tells her. She does what he asks and snags Jonas by the arm, pulling him out the door with her. The two of them are close, just like Drake and me.

"Brother?" Drake asks as he approaches me on my other side. I slowly hand him the card from the flowers.

"I only sent Willow two of the three flower arrangements. The shattered ones on the floor I didn't send, but the women assumed they were from me. They're from Jay. He must have been watching me, following me and trying to get to Willow. I'm sure it's meant to make a statement, which I can hear loud and clear," I say through clenched teeth. I grab my phone out of my pocket to call Willow. Fear is consuming me knowing that Willow and my baby are out somewhere unprotected. The call goes straight to voicemail. "Willow, Sunshine, it's imperative I get in touch with you. I need to know where you are. If you don't want to see me, that's fine. I'll send Drake or Dom to get you. Baby, please call me back."

I hear Dom calling her too, but no answer. I hear Drake on his phone talking to Nikki, who confirms Willow never arrived at her house and her grandmother has been with her all day. My stomach continues to churn. I just know that sick fuck has somehow gotten his vile hands on her. I pray he hasn't done anything to her.

Drake is back on his phone with Daniel, notifying our team of the situation. They automatically load up and head our way. Just hours ago, I remember how I was thinking about treating this as a retrieve and rescue to get Willow back. Now it's indeed turned into one.

"Let's go downstairs and wait for everyone to show so we can form a plan," my father suggests. He's right. I've got to focus on this like I would any other case we've worked on, but I don't know if I can separate from my emotions this time. As we head out of the room, I hear the door to the bedroom beside Willow's open, and a small little girl comes out and heads straight for Dom.

"Willow is in trouble and Ari is coming," she whispers to him. She must have heard our conversation through the adjoining wall. I wasn't too concerned about keeping quiet earlier. This must be the little girl Bailey; the one Willow brought the dress to when she told me the story of how she met Dom.

I feel bad for worrying such a small child. "You didn't have to call Ari. I promise you I'll find Willow," I tell the little girl.

"I didn't call her," the little girl informs me then wraps

her small arms around Dom's neck. I look at Dom for an answer to how she knows Ari is coming, but instead of answering he walks past me, heading back downstairs with the child still in his arms.

My team members arrive here at Dom's house with our equipment, and we set it all up. Even though I have no proof the bastard has her, my gut knows he does. So, until I have confirmation otherwise, we're treating this like we would a kidnapping.

I have my cell, along with Dom's cell and house phone all lying in the middle of the dining room table. We know Jay will make a call with his demands if he has her, but aren't sure which phone he will call. Nikki has come over but left her grandmother home in case Willow isn't missing and shows up there.

Ari arrived shortly after Bailey announced she was on her way. I notice Daniel has kept one eye trained on her since she arrived. Something seems to be going on between them since the night we all met at the bar. I'll have to remember to ask him about that after this nightmare is over. Ari has Bailey perched in her lap, rocking her. I glance down at my watch. It's 11 p.m., and I can't help but wonder why someone hasn't taken the kid back to bed. I continue scanning the room and see Dom on the other side with my father, mother, Jonas, and Kat. It appears no one is leaving until we find Willow. I see Flame walking around refilling coffee cups for everyone who needs a refill. With the stress of the situation getting to me, I pace back and forth. What am I going to do if I lose the love of my life tonight along with our baby?

I rake my hands across my face and up through my hair. I feel a soft hand touch my forearm as I put my arms back down to my sides. It's Nikki. "They're going to be ok," she says in a soft voice that only I can hear. "In case you want to know, it's a boy," she says.

"What?" I ask.

"The baby is a boy. You're having a son, Connor," she

explains.

"How do you know? Did Willow change her mind and find out?" I ask, a little in awe of the knowledge I have a son.

"No, Raven told me in a dream," she responds.

"What? Who?" I start to ask, but the ring of a phone breaks into her story. I turn to find everyone staring at me, and I immediately recognize the special ringtone. It's my cell phone ringing, and hopefully it's Willow calling, but I fear it will be Jay's voice I hear. Drew gives me the go-ahead to answer, letting me know he and his computer are ready to trace the phone. We have my phone connected to a blue tooth speaker, so everyone in the room becomes silent with anticipation. I answer, "Willow, baby?" Not wanting to disappoint me, I hear the voice I didn't want to hear on the other end; it's Jay's voice.

"Well, well, well, it seems me and my new boys have something you want," Jay says smugly. Boys, what boys are Jay talking about? Has he recruited more Wendigo's to replace the ones we killed?

"What do you want Jay?" I ask, getting straight to the point. I can hear the familiar soft muffle of a growl in the background but can't remember where I've heard it before. My mother lets out a soft gasp, so I turn to look at her. She seems shocked with her hand resting on her open mouth and her eyes open wide.

"The baby is growling," Kat who is standing beside her mouths quietly to me. Then I remember that's the same growl I heard the day I said all that stupid shit to Willow. I thought it was Willow, not the baby. I don't ever recall hearing a growl from an unborn baby before. I don't think that's normal.

At that moment I notice everyone has taken a step back from where they were standing and are all looking at my father who is standing on the other side of my mother. I look over at him too and find his eyes are a bright fiery red and are glaring down at my phone still resting on the table. Because of the curse I've never seen my father's eyes turn red, the color which shows his alpha status. Somehow, the curse must be lifting.

I take in all the details of his face. His mouth is in a quiet snarl position, and the only noise he is making is the panting of breaths. He looks like he's barely holding onto his temper. The growl of his unborn grandson is enough to melt the ogre's heart and put him right into protector mode.

"I want what everyone wants Connor," Jay says.

"What would that be Jay?" I counter. I see movement out of the corner of my eye and notice Bailey has walked up to the blue tooth speaker with her ear turned towards the speaker listening intently. Ari is at her side listening too.

"Freedom. I want you and your team to back off and leave my boys and me alone. I want my brother you have locked up freed in exchange for your bitch, and the bastard she's pregnant with that I assume is yours. Otherwise, we'll have ourselves a meal with a plum for dessert," Jay threatens.

"You better not have harmed her or the baby mother fucker!" I growl.

"Calm yourself. To give a show of good faith, I'll let her speak to you," Jay replies. I hear footsteps like he's walking into another room. The soft muffle of the growl I heard gets louder.

"C... C... Connor?" I hear Willow say through the speaker as the breath I didn't realize I was holding escapes my lungs. It's a small relief to hear her voice.

"Willow, baby I'm coming to get you. Hang in there. I...." I speak trying to reassure her, but she cuts my words off.

"I love you. I've missed you. Missed seeing the blue iris of your eyes the most," she says. What the fuck my eyes are brown, and she knows it. What the hell is she trying to tell me?

"Willow, its Flame. Try to stay comfortable, even if you have to move some chairs around to do it," Flame cuts in as I shoot him a what the fuck look, waving my hand for him to shut up.

"That's enough." I hear Jay say in the background, and then he muffles the phone. Damn it; I didn't get the chance to tell her how much I love her and our baby. The next voice I hear on the phone is Jay, "Get my brother ready; I'll be in touch later to make arrangements. And Connor, don't fuck with me." The line goes dead.

I look at Drew, but before I can ask if the trace on the phone worked, Nikki speaks up, "She's in the bayou, and I can narrow it down to three different locations." Everyone turns and looks at her. "The blue iris is a plant I pick in the bayou from three different locations. One is close to the water, one is not, and the last is near an old abandon cabin, which is very close to the water," she explains.

"The cabin," Ari says as all eyes turn to her to find Bailey whispering into her ear. "It's the cabin. There was water nearby and the floor he's walking on is wooden." I narrow my eyes and raise an eyebrow in questioning. I didn't hear any water.

"Are you sure about the water?" Daniel asks.

"Bailey heard the water nearby, and we all could hear the wooden floor," she clarifies. Now, how the hell could Baily hear the water when all the werewolves in the room didn't pick up on it.

"You need to trust her," Dom says like he knows something about the kid that we all don't, which I'm sure is true.

"What the hell was that about the chairs?" I ask Flame while trying to get all the details of the phone call squared away before we make a plan. Flame fills in the details of how Willow made the dining room chair move and how they could hear the baby growling.

"For us to hear the baby growl, it must have something to do with Willow being a Fae. For the first time, I'm thankful Willow is a Fae. That might be a big advantage for us," my father adds. "I'm calling a state of emergency on this and will have every tribal member ready to be at your service son. No one fucks with my grandchild," my father declares.

My mother beams a bright smile at him. I take this as a sign he's ventured to the dark side and is now at peace with the Fae. He still has glowing red eyes piercing at me.

"Dad, your eyes," I say to him. I don't know if anyone has made him aware of the change. Apparently, they have, because he gives me a wink and a sinister smile as he turns then pulls out his cell phone to make his calls.

"Connor," I hear Val say. I turn to look at her. I watch as she moves her cell phone away from her ear and places it back in her pocket. She continues, "I was checking on how the wounded Wendigo we captured is doing; he's dead."

"Damn! We've got to locate Willow and get her back before Jay finds out," Drake says.

Chapter 53

Willow
"The Domino Effect"

Jay hangs up from the phone call with Connor, then turns to walk out of the room. "Watch the bitch closely; I'm going back into town to check on a few things. I need to get away from that damn growling before I rip her throat out," Jay informs the other two men as they all leave the room. He thinks the growls are coming from my throat. I don't dare correct him because I don't want to bring any more attention to the baby.

The door slams shut, and I hear the all too familiar locking sound coming from the other side of the door. They have had me locked in this room since we arrived here. At least I know where I am since I've been in this cabin before. I explored it when Nikki dragged me out here to the bayou to find the Blue Iris plant she uses.

I search around the room with the small battery-operated lantern they left me, trying to find a way out. The old unpainted boards are tightly secured, and there are no windows in this room. I rub over my baby bump as I pace, which seems to soothe the baby because the growling has stopped.

I would have thought with this cabin being so old it would be easy to escape from, but it appears they replaced the rotten boards I saw the last time I explored this place. I guess this must be their new hideout. I hope Connor can figure out why I said I miss the blue iris of his eyes. That was the best clue I could think of to help him find us. Hopefully, Nikki was around when I told him. He must be at Dom's because I could hear Flame talk about moving the chair. I need to figure out how to use my new abilities to help myself out of this situation, but how?

After what seems like hours, the movement and talking in the next room has quieted. I haven't devised a plan of action yet and decide the best thing to do is to get the door unlocked with my newfound powers then see what happens.

I try concentrating on the door lock hoping to get it opened, but I have no idea what I'm doing. After a few minutes of deep concentration, I break out into a sweat. I try to open the door with my hand in case the lock is now open and turn the knob only to find the door is still locked as tight as ever.

I need anger to get this to work, so I apologize to my baby and think about all the ugly things Connor said that shitty night at Drake's house. Then, I focus on the three bastards that have taken me and my baby hostage and about how they are threatening us.

As my anger builds, I remind myself how they tricked me earlier when I spotted their car on the side of the road. One of them was faking an injury. They must have known I'm a doctor somehow and knew I would pull over to help.

When I got out and walked over to the one that appeared injured, that sleazy Jay popped up behind me, wrapped his arm around me and covered my mouth with his stinky hand. The other two creeps grabbed my legs, and they all carried me back to my car then tossed me in the trunk. Luckily, I landed on my back instead of my stomach when they tossed me in.

As the memories come flooding back, I feel the anger course through my body, and the baby is now growling the loudest I've ever heard. I hear a sudden loud pounding on the door as one of the assholes yells at me to be quiet. It startles the shit out of me, and before I realize what I'm doing, I too let out a loud growl and fling my hands toward the locked door.

The next few seconds seem like a horror movie that's running in slow motion. I feel as though I'm stuck in cement and can't move as the domino effect plays out. It's like watching the dominos I used to play with as a child. I would line them up close enough to watch them all fall one at a time, barely hitting the next and causing it to collapse and so on.

The locked door shakes, then the door frame around it cracks in all directions. The cracks grow until they cover the walls and then spread up to the ceiling. I barely have enough time to come to my senses and move my ass before the roof crumples down around me.

As I dive under the only table in the room, I hear the two assholes in the next room yelling. I hear cracking noises close to my ears and glance up, realizing the table I'm under is now breaking from the weight of the debris on top of it. I roll into a fetal position cradling my stomach right before the table falls. I feel a sharp pain on my forehead as a piece of the table hits my head causing my world to turn black.

Chapter 54

Connor
"The Unicorn"

I'm grateful for my father's support but decide to only use my team for the retrieve and rescue because this is what we're trained to do. We move like a well-oiled machine and can depend on each other to get the job done. I don't want to fuck up by having too many people for Jay to spot and end up getting Willow killed. Drake, Daniel, and Drew are with me in the bayou while Val stays behind in case we need any technical support.

It's now in the early morning hours, the time of morning when the moon isn't high enough in the sky to aid in lighting our way, but still too early for the sun's help. Even with having a heightened sense of sight we're having difficulty locating the cabin Nikki described. We fan out with about 20 feet between us and walk while looking for any tracks or signs of the cabin. The only thing I hear is the bugs around us humming. There's never a shortage of mosquitoes or insects in the bayou.

In the distance, I hear something approaching, quickly closing in on Daniel. "Daniel," I say into the earpiece we're all wearing.

"Already on it," he whispers back. The team encloses Daniels location. As we get near, I see Daniel staring at what appears to be a wolf. As I get closer, I see it's a giant red wolf. It's larger than most other wolves. This tells me it must be a werewolf.

"What the…?" I whisper as I see the glowing emerald green eyes staring back at us. I've only seen yellow or red eyes on a werewolf, never green.

"An alpha," Daniel clarifies without me having to finish my sentence.

"I'll be damned," Drake whispers in response. We've all seen alphas before that have shifted, even though we've lost the ability to change ourselves; but none of us have ever seen an alpha like this. The emerald green eyes can only mean one thing- a She-Wolf or female alpha. It's the equivalence of walking up on royalty because of the rarity of ever being in the presence of a She-Wolf, definitely the unicorn of werewolves.

Within seconds she gracefully sprints off. "We need to follow her," Daniel orders. We head toward the She-Wolf, who stays a good ten feet ahead of us always regardless of how fast we're running to catch up. She suddenly stops dead in her tracks, causing us to do the same. I take another step forward when I feel it. The ground shakes.

"What the fuck?" Drake whispers.

"Earthquake?" Daniel asks.

Suddenly we hear a horrible crashing sound ahead of us and see debris along with dust rising into the air above the trees just ahead of us. I can't see what's causing it because the underbrush is too damn thick to see through. "The cabin," I hear Daniel say through the earpiece.

I take off running at full speed toward the debris cloud. As we approach what appears to be where the cabin was, the dust is still floating around in the air and debris is everywhere. I stop dead in my tracks for the second time with my mouth open, taking in the horrible sight before me.

The pile of rubble looks like a cabin that imploded and collapsed into itself. I keep telling myself there's no way this is the cabin where Willow is being held captive, but in my gut, I know it is. For the first time, I pray with all my heart that my gut feeling is wrong.

I hear the whine of a wolf and look in that direction to find the She-Wolf on top of the back of the debris pile digging. Daniel reaches her before I do and lifts wood pieces, throwing them off to the side. We all join in, and it's not long before I can see what looks like a table that is half collapsed with the other half still standing.

Under the standing part is an unconscious Willow curled into a protective ball around her belly. I can see her chest rise and fall with each breath she takes. It's the most beautiful sight I could ever have hoped for at this moment. I crawl under the table next to her to check for injuries before we move her.

"Willow, baby," I say to her as I take my hand to brush her hair away from her face. She opens her beautiful eyes wide, and I see recognition in them.

She tries to speak, "Connor," but her voice comes out more like a hoarse whisper that dissolves into coughing. I move my hand from her hair to finish my assessment of her body. That's when I notice the blood on the palm of my hand. I immediately lean forward to get a closer look and see she has a head wound. I quickly continue running my hands down her body and find no other issues.

When I reach her stomach, I stop my hand over the baby bump. It has grown so much since the last time I saw her. That's when I feel the most amazing thing. It's a kick, but not just any kick. It's a strong kick from my baby. My son feels like he's doing kickboxing with the amount of movement he's doing. I need to get Willow out of here and get her to Kara to make sure the little guy is ok.

"Willow, I'm going to put my arms around you to pick you up. If you feel any severe pain, you need to let me know. I didn't feel any broken bones, but that doesn't mean you don't have any," I say as she stares up at me.

"Wait," she says as she clears her throat. I pause to give her a minute and she continues, "I need you to promise me, Connor, if for some reason I have injuries that put you in a position to choose the baby or me, you pick our baby." I stare at her for a minute before I speak.

"You listen Willow, losing either one of you is not an option," I growl out through clenched teeth while feeling my throat close with the fear that maybe she knows of an injury she has that I can't see.

"Promise me," she rasps out. I say nothing as I lift her. "Promise me," she says, this time with a plea in her tone.

"We promise," I hear Drake say from above me. I look at him with a glare. "But we plan on saving the both of you," he continues while staring back at me. "Lift her up to me brother, and I'll hold her until you can climb out of the rubble and take her back," he says. I nod, then carefully lift her to Drake. As I pull myself from under the table, I hear Drake speak with an urgent tone, "Willow honey, I need you to stay with me. Keep those gorgeous eyes on me now."

When I make it out of the hole, I glance back down to see where she had been lying and see a large puddle of blood where her head had been just moments ago. I feel as though someone has punched me in the gut. I look back at Drake who's cradling Willow. "We need to hurry, her pulse is getting weak, and I can't wake her," Drake replies with urgency.

I look around at our surroundings. We're in the middle of the fucking bayou, we don't know where Jay or the other men that were with him are, and Willow is slipping away. In the distance, I see the wolf that led us to the cabin disappear into the thick underbrush.

I reach out and take Willow's body from Drake. She's like a rag doll, lying limp in my arms. "Sunshine, don't leave me. Please hang on for me, please!" I plead into her ear as I cradle her body to mine with her head tucked under my neck. "Let's move," I say to the others.

With as much speed as I can muster, which I know is a hell of a lot faster than a human, I run carrying her body through the woods. I hear Drake in the distance telling Val to get in contact with Kara. If it comes down to it, we might have to save both Willow and the baby by supernatural means that a human hospital can't provide. Kara instructs us to bring Willow to her.

Once we make it back to our vehicle, I cradle Willow in my

arms in the back seat. With her head tucked under my chin, I support her back with one arm while my hand rests on my son making sure I feel his reassuring kicks. All the way to the hospital I continue talking to Willow, reminding her of the happy times we had together and all the future plans I have for us.

Willow never opens her beautiful eyes. I feel as though she is slipping away right before my eyes and I am powerless to stop her. For the first time in my adult life, I feel tears running down my cheeks as the helplessness of the situation sinks into my bones.

Chapter 55

Willow
"Straight from the Heart"

I try to look around, but all I see is darkness. At least the pounding in my head has dulled. I feel cradled in warmth with a big hand lying on my stomach gently rubbing my baby bump. I feel alarmed with concern for my baby, but then I feel the strong kicks and calm back down.

My baby is moving and not growling anymore, which must be a good sign. I hear Connor's voice in the distance talking about how much he loves me. I try to look for him in the darkness but can't see anything. I try to open my mouth to call out for him, but for some reason, I can't seem to form words. I panic, and then darkness consumes me again as I fall asleep.

I wake in total darkness again unable to force my eyes open, but this time the warmth I felt is gone. I listen to see if I can hear Connor's voice again, but only hear a fast heartbeat like a fetal heartbeat would sound. I listen for a few minutes and determine it is a fetal heartbeat which must mean it's my baby's heartbeat. I listen to the rhythmic beats as they lure me back into the stillness of sleep.

I wake again, still in the darkness, but I hear voices around me. I try to open my eyes again, but they feel too heavy. I hear a man's voice I don't recognize telling someone to go home and get some rest. I hear Connor's voice growling out that he isn't going home until he takes me home with him. I try to open my eyes again and can't. I try to move my body, but it feels heavy, so I decide to concentrate on one body part. I choose my hand. I can feel something tighten around my hand like someone is holding it. I focus on that hand, and a few minutes later I'm able to squeeze it.

I hear Connor in my ear calling to me, begging me to open my eyes. Darkness still surrounds me, but I try to follow his voice. After a couple of minutes, I'm able to pry my eyes open. The light in the room is so bright it makes me squint. When I'm able to focus the first thing I see is Connor's face. As my vision clears up, I look at the details of his face. His eyes are staring into mine and he has the darkest circles under his eyes. His five o'clock shadow on his face looks more like it's from five o'clock last week.

"Baby, you're awake," he states softly and then gets a pained look that engulfs his whole face. "Are you hurting Sunshine?" he asks as he takes his hand and gently rubs my furrowed brows. "What's wrong baby?" he asks again.

"You," I try to speak, but my throat feels as dry as sandpaper.

"Wait a minute," Connor says, then reaches over for something. I feel a straw touch my lips and realize he's giving me the water I desperately need. After a few sips, he pulls the cup away and tries again. "Are you in pain baby?" he asks.

"No, you," I say causing him to furrow his brows.

"What about me, baby? And please don't ask me to leave..." he says in a pleading voice.

I shake my head, which makes me feel dizzy, but continue to try to speak. "No, don't leave. I want you here, but you look terrible," I inform him. Connor's face morphs into a huge smile, and he bellows out a loud laugh like I'm the funniest comedian in the world then bends down, placing kisses on my forehead.

I hear movement to my left and turn my head to see Kara entering and smiling a huge smile at me. That's when I realize I'm in a hospital room. "What happened...?" I ask but visions of the man, Jay, then the other two men pop into my head, and the memories flood my mind. I remember the cabin falling in on top of me. I reach out with the hand Connor isn't holding to touch my stomach. Connor places his hand over mine as I rub my belly.

"Our son is fine," Connor says as he smiles at me. I smile back as his words soak into my brain.

"Son," I whisper. I didn't think I wanted to know the sex of the baby, but I take comfort in knowing I'm having a son and that my little man is doing fine. "What happened to the men?" I ask.

"Dead, killed when the cabin fell in," Connor informs me. The realization hits that I caused the death of two men. Connor must read my expression because he tries to comfort me. I stop him. Parts of that night I can't remember. I tell him and Kara the details of that horrible night. When I'm done, Kara and Connor fill in the blanks of my story with the details of why they kidnapped me and that the three men were Wendigos who had gone rogue killing people and eating them. That strangely gives me some comfort. At least the men I killed were horrible creatures. Their leader Jay is still at large, but Connor assures me his team is hot on his trail and that the vile man will never get close to me again. The firm conviction in his voice causes me to believe him.

Kara does an assessment, and other than a nasty bump on the head, along with some scrapes and bruises, assures me I should fully recover with no permanent damage. She also assures me the baby is excellent, and the pregnancy is progressing nicely. She wants to keep me one more night for observation, but I should be able to go home in the morning.

After she leaves the room, I get a swarm of visitors. Nikki and Gran stop by, which I'm glad to see. We come to an understanding of no more secrets and a promise from them I can read all the journals. Next, Connor's family stops by to visit. This is the first time I get to meet his father, who reaches down and hugs me.

For the first time, I realize I must look worse than Connor does. That mortifies me, but there's nothing I can do about it, so I decide to not worry about it. The whole family seems warm and welcoming. I'm glad, especially for my baby's sake.

After everyone but Connor leaves, I realize how exhausted I genuinely am. Connor must have read my mind because the next thing I know he's climbing into the hospital bed with me and positioning me so I'm cuddled up close to his side with my big belly lying against him. We lie like this for a while, not speaking, just enjoying each other. I almost drift off to sleep before I hear Connor's words, "Willow, I love you more than I ever thought possible. There's no way I can live a minute without you in my life. I want you to marry me as soon as you're feeling better. Sunshine, I'm a desperate man for you, so I'll be honest and tell you if you don't agree to marry me, I'll be kidnapping you myself and chaining you to my bed until you agree we're perfect for each other."

As I laugh, I say, "That's a terrible marriage proposal."

"But it's straight from my heart," he replies.

"Well, since I've had my fair share of being kidnapped, I guess I'll just marry you," I respond, trying to sound put out and not laugh, but failing. "I love you too," I say and as if on cue, the baby kicks Connor in the side as to say he agrees with the decision too. Connor and I both laugh.

Chapter 56

Willow
"Cold Feet"

Two months later...... I awake in my bed wrapped in Connor's strong arms. I sigh because this is pure bliss for me. I glance up at the clock to see it's 7:30 am. Elijah, our son, should wake soon for his feeding. I wiggle my bottom closer to Connor, and his impressive, hard cock meets my ass. I realize he's awake when he firmly grabs my hips and flips me over, causing me to squeal.

He hovers over my body and leans in to kiss me. That's when we hear it. Not the soft meow sounding cry of our son, but his mother's voice echoing through the house. Damn, there goes the mood. His parents declared they were staying with us for a few days after we got home to help with the baby, but it's been a month and they're still here.

"You got to give them credit they are dedicated grandparents," I say.

"No, their dedicated cock-blockers!" Connor growls.

"That's it; I've had it with you. Not only do you not share giving me time with the baby, but now you think you can pull that you're the Alpha of this tribe and you don't have to share crap with me. I'll inform Connor of how ridiculous you're being. He'll put a stop to this," Sasha says as her voice seems to be getting closer to our door with every word.

"Woman, if you'll keep your ass away from their bedroom door and give them some time alone maybe they'll make another grandbaby so you can have one to hold too," his father suggests.

"Maybe you're right. That's not a bad idea," I hear Sasha say as her voice gets softer indicating she's turned around and walking away from our door.

"Who would have thought a few months ago, that my parents would squabble over holding their grandson? You lie here and relax. Daddy will rescue and retrieve the baby because that's what this daddy does for a living," Connor says, then kisses me before leaving the room to bring me our son.

I do as I'm instructed rest and wait, but I think back over the last three months of how my life has taken such a change for the better. I convinced Connor to compromise on the getting married as soon as I left the hospital post-kidnapping idea. I wanted time to plan a small wedding. He agreed, as long as we got married before the baby was born.

Just thinking about it now makes me laugh a little. I almost didn't pull that off. On our wedding day, I had everything perfectly planned with the help of the pow-wow members, including our newest members Nikki and Ari. I had just the right number of flowers, the perfect dress, and the pow-wow as my bridesmaids. Even Flame was a bridesmaid, but instead of a dress, he wore a flashy suit. Bailey was my flower girl, and all this fit nicely at Connor's family estate in the garden area behind the house. We even had tents set up for the food and a small dance floor for the reception.

Everything was perfect until two hours before the wedding when my contractions began. I was so determined to make sure Connor and I were married before our son's birth that I kept that little information to myself. I got through the ceremony with minimal discomfort.

I saw the concern in Connor's eyes when halfway through our vows a sweat broke out across my forehead. Connor said later that he was afraid I was having cold feet and second guessing marrying him. We made it through the ceremony and even back down the aisle before my water broke, and thank heavens we were outside so I didn't make a mess.

I turned to Connor and said, "I'm having the baby?"

"I know that Sunshine. Remember, I've known you are pregnant for months now," Connor says with a confused look on his face.

"No, my water just broke all over the ground," I try to explain.

"That's ok, I'll just go get you a new bottle of water," he said as he turned, but before he took a step, he finally understood what I was trying to tell him. Jerking back around with eyes as big as saucers he yelled, "Now? Like you are in labor right now?" His panic startled me and I tried to get him to be quiet. In the end, I was glad he yelled because my big, strong, confident husband who organizes hunts and kills terrible creatures turned into a babbling fool. Drake ended up driving us to the hospital and Kara met us there still in the dress she wore to the wedding.

Labor took a while. Connor ended up getting a handle on his emotions and calming down enough to be the best birthing coach I could ever want. Everyone close to us came and waited it out while our other wedding guests stayed to enjoy the food at the reception.

After one and a half hours of pushing, just a few minutes past the witching hour, 3:07am to be exact, Elijah Jessiah graced this world weighing in at ten and a half pounds and screaming his beautiful head off. The pow-wow members were the first visitors to rush in and demand to know what we had.

"Boy," was my response confused because they already knew but that wasn't the answer they were looking for. They wanted to know if he was a full werewolf, or does he have the traits of a Fae since he is the first hybrid baby between a Fae and a werewolf.

Since the baby didn't get delivered with an owner's manual, everyone will have to wait and see as he grows. I don't really care because with Connor at my side, I know I can deal with any obstacle that comes our way, and I know my life has turned out better than I could ever have planned.

Epilogue

Daniel
"Game On"

Two weeks later..... I'm following a lead the team received two hours ago on Jay, the sleazy Wendigo. As far as we know, he hasn't recruited anymore Wendigos to help his lost cause. Either they're smart enough to realize working with him will get them killed, or he thinks his chances of getting caught increases by having more people he needs to keep up with. Whatever the reason, I don't care. He needs to be eliminated.

I volunteered to check out this lead. I could've waited until later for Connor and Drake to join me, but it only takes one of us to take down a lone Wendigo. The real reason I want to check this lead out is that my gut tells me she'll be there too, and I will not let her handle this alone, no matter if I know she's over qualified. The urge to protect her is becoming as innate as breathing.

I arrive to a club Jay has visited several times in the past week. It's a little hole in the ground close to a neighborhood you wouldn't want to raise kids in. This is a step down for him. He likes to wear nice suits, and a suit is overdressed for this place. I take a chance and glance through the club's only window on the front door, and spot that ridiculous blue suit right away.

I walk around to the back of the building to hide in the shadows until Jay leaves. The team discovered he's a creature of habit that always enters the bar using the front door, and leaves using the back, especially if he has a victim with him. Most places around here have more security cameras in the front than they do in the back, since customers come and go through the front, while few come and go through the back. They have found no other victims since before the dumbass kidnapped Willow, so I know his appetite for human meat must be gnawing at his gut.

I find the perfect spot to hang out, so I can keep a close watch on the back door without being seen. As I wait, I try to listen and pick up on every faint noise I hear to see if it could be her. My gut tells me she wants this guy taken care of just as much as I do and she'll show.

After a few hours, Jay doesn't disappoint. He prances out the back door and enters the alley as predictable with what looks like his next meal, a young woman known around this part of town as a prostitute.

"Well, well, look who I've found. It's my old friend Jay," I announce as I casually stroll up behind them.

They quickly turn around. The woman looks up at me, and even with the heavy makeup on her face, she can't hide her surprise as she looks back to Jay. Jay looks irritated. "Look, it's going to cost you double if your friend joins in, two cocks are two times the payment," the woman announces to Jay.

I reach in my pocket, get a twenty-dollar bill and hand it to the woman. She grabs it eagerly. "That, my dear, is for you to turn around, go back into the bar, and forget you ever saw either of us," I tell her. She looks at Jay then back to me, gives a quick nod of understanding before doing as I instructed.

Jay looks nervous as he shifts his weight from foot to foot while holding his hands out in front of him like that will keep my hands off him. "Look, taking Connor's bitch was a total misunderstanding. It wasn't any of my doings. I was just following along, really... it was those other two men that made me do it..." Jay rambles on, taking one step backward for every step I take forward.

I plan on taking my time with him and make him suffer for daring to touch one of our loved ones. This shit can't go on without retribution, so I plan to go against the rules of the

Guardians and dump his brutalized dead body where I know other Wendigos hang out, just to make sure the word gets spread that no one fucks with one of ours. His back hits the brick wall behind him. I watch his Adam's apple bob up and down as he tries to swallow his fear.

I pull back my fist, and just as I'm about to deliver the first blow to his face, I hear it. It's a little tale-tale sign of what I've been listening for, the quiet whistle of something moving with precision and speed through the air. Before I can even look around to identify the familiar sound, Jay gasps for air while grabbing onto his neck as blood pours out and the horrible smell of sulfur fills the air.

I watch as Jay hits the wall behind him and slides at an angle down to the ground, deader than shit. His hands fall away, and I see her shuriken sticking out of the side of his neck. The shuriken tells me my gut feeling was right, she's here.

I speak out loud without ever turning around to look, "I had this covered, didn't need any help."

"Really, because from where I'm standing it looked like you were taking your sweet ass time. For a minute there, I even thought you might be trying to ask him out on a date or some-thing with all that chit-chat going on," she responds with her snarky smart mouth which makes my cock twitch.

I turn around slowly, trying not to spook her because I know she'll bolt like a flash of lightning. I enjoy a chase like the next man, but right now I want to try to get this woman to trust me. I even go as far as holding my hands up in front of my body like she's pointing a weapon at me, in a gesture of peace. When I've completely turned around, it takes only a second to locate her standing off in the shadows in the same spot I was standing in while I was waiting on Jay to show his face. "You going to run?" I ask.

"You going to chase?" she snaps back.

"No, I just want to talk," I say as I put my hands down be-side me.

"Then, no I will not run," she responds with less of a smart mouth attitude. "What is it you want to know?" she asks.

"Well for starters, a few weeks ago I had a sweet little kitten tied up in my apartment. I received an emergency call and had to leave her there tied to my bed. Imagine my surprise when that same little kitten wonders up beside me later that day. When I question her, she gives me this bizarre tale of how some woman broke in and set her free then stole a necklace I was keeping safe at my apartment for the little kitten. You know anything about that sugar puss?" I ask, as I suspect they are one and the same. I watch her hand reach up and grab something hanging on her chest. I assume it's the necklace, but I don't want to turn my eyes into my wolf's eyes. I would love to see the details of the necklace and her face, but I know she'll bolt.

"How would I know anything about that, and don't call me sugar puss," she says as the smart mouth attitude comes back.

"If you would tell me your name, I wouldn't have to find a nickname for you. I could call you sweet kitten, but a sweet kitten wouldn't have just taken down a Wendigo," I tell her.

"Whatever," she says as her smart-ass attitude snaps again, which makes my cock twitch for a second time. I let out a low growl hoping for some relief, but of course, there is none.

"That smart mouth might be a defense against most men, but baby I've got to tell you it's a complete turn on for me. Now my last question for you, are you going to let me get near you to ask you out on a date? I want to get to know you a hell of a lot better, or do you prefer to do this as they did in the olden days where I chase you down and claim what's going to be mine?" I ask, giving her the option.

I hear her laughter right before I see two piercing emerald green eyes glowing at me. "A chase it is," I say as I change my eyes too.

"Game on," I hear her say as she turns to run. She is exactly right; the game is on. She bolts and I give chase.

TO BE CONTINUED...

Printed in Great Britain
by Amazon

81738736R10231